Sanctuary

Arliss Ryan

ISBN-10: 0989367932
ISBN-13: 978-0-9893679-3-6

www.arlissryan.com

Cover painting "Direct Assent" by Adam S Doyle Copyright 2013 www.adamsdoyle.com
Used with permission.

Praise for the novels of Arliss Ryan

The Kingsley House

"Good historical fiction brings the past to life. In *The Kingsley House*, Arliss Ryan gives us wars, the Ford assembly line, the Depression, the spread of the auto industry through southeastern Michigan and modern commercial development, but most importantly, she makes us see the past through the lives of good people we can't help but care about."
-Linnea Lannon, *Detroit Free Press*

"[Ryan] has created in *The Kingsley House* an unforgettable portrait of her own family...All family members are true-to-life individuals, with plenty of flaws and foibles, and as with every family, there's the occasional black sheep. It's remarkable that in a tale of over 400 pages, the story never drags: the action-filled storyline and the personalities of the characters keep it alive. I enjoyed every minute."
-Sarah Johnson, *Historical Novels Review*

How (Not) to Have a Perfect Wedding

"The skillful use of multiple narratives elevates this novel above the usual women's wedding fiction...Ryan uses distinctive viewpoints to great advantage, building tension and developing characters from the very first page, including everyone from the bridal party to the bartender, mansion staff, and caterer. She blends humor and poignancy with a light hand, taking a serious look at weddings and marriage, friendship and family, without taking it all too seriously. A worthy addition to the genre."
-Amy Brozio-Andrews, *Library Journal*

"OMG! This book just blew my socks off!...Written from the various points of view of key characters in a society wedding, the author transcended the genre by NOT reducing any of them

to a one-note stereotype…the prose was witty, precise, and dead on with some of the most original and entertaining descriptive phrases that it has been my pleasure to read in quite some time."
-Deana W., *Enchanting Reviews*

The Secret Confessions of Anne Shakespeare

"This story is a fantastic view of life in the theatre, and one woman's struggle to maintain her family; her attempt to keep the love for her selfish husband; and, understand the remarkable stories that are piling up inside her own head… This author brings her abundance of research and well-written verse to her own audience, and literally transports readers back to the world of William Shakespeare, and the secrets that he left behind…After reading this, you'll not only applaud Anne Shakespeare, but you'll also give Arliss Ryan a standing ovation for a job well done."
-Amy Lignor, *Feathered Quill Book Reviews*

"Arliss Ryan knows her Tudor London and the theater of that era. *The Secret Confessions* brings Anne Hathaway out of the shadows into real life, not as the neglected shrew William happily left behind in Stratford, but as a sensual, humorous, talented, and daring woman. This is a compelling novel with unexpected turns in every satisfying chapter."
-Jeane Westin, author of *The Virgin's Daughters*

Author's Note and Acknowledgments

When I lived in Newport, Rhode Island, I was out birding with my friends one morning when one of them teased, "Arliss, you should write a novel about birders."

"As a matter of fact," I confessed, "I already am."

That was back in 2001-03, and the novel was *Sanctuary*. It was born of my love of nature, birding and flying, and my fascination with the concept of a sanctuary as both a sacred place and a haven for those in need of refuge. As the story began to take shape, I relied on a number of people for feedback and advice, and it is my pleasure to offer them my sincere thanks.

Birders Jay Manning, John Fenton, William Saslow and Nikki LaMonica not only taught me almost everything I know about birds, they were wonderful company on our many hikes. We stood in the rain, tramped through mud, and scrambled through thickets together in pursuit of the next great sighting.

Writers Clint Hull, Jim Huston, Judith Porter, Jan Shapin, Jack Galvin, Bill Goetzinger, Sylvia Smith and Andrew Wilner, MD, listened to my novel chapter by chapter at our twice monthly meetings and kept me on track with encouragement and constructive criticism. Every writer should be so fortunate to have such a talented support group.

As always, my husband Eric and our children Kira and Dane read and critiqued my manuscript. In addition, their combined artistic expertise is responsible for the beautiful and compelling book cover design, which features original art by Adam S. Doyle.

Since it has been more than ten years between the writing of *Sanctuary* and its actual publication, I ask the reader to picture the story taking place in its original 2003 time frame. The ages of the characters in relation to World War II will then make sense as will the state of the art of technology at that time.

Arliss Ryan, 2013

Sanctuary

Prologue

Think of them as planes.

A ruby-throated hummingbird beats its tiny wings into an accelerated blur, a miniature helicopter hovering over the exposed throat of a trumpet flower.

Wrens, finches, sparrows, warblers—the little birds that flit from tree to tree—are the single-engine Cessnas and Pipers that flock around the local airports in easy camaraderie.

Owls have flight feathers designed with an extra-soft leading edge that muffles the wing beats. Virtually soundless, they swoop in like stealth bombers to pluck a squeaking mouse off a field.

Then watch a mallard descend to land on a pond, wing flaps down, pitch up to enter the flare, webbed feet skimming the water, a controlled splash. No seaplane could do better.

Eagles are screaming F-15s, lethal weapons defending their airspace.

Canada geese are lumbering, honking 747s.

Finally, the hawks, the fearless warbirds. They careen through the clouds, outrace the wind, sharp-eyed to every movement above and below. They soar in circles, dark specks in the sun, precision flight for the wild joy of it, because they can. They lock talons and free fall in a screeching spiral, each claiming the air, refusing to yield.

Wings spread, earth abandoned, no touch but the sky.

Chapter 1

The house is gray stone, meant to have the grandeur of an English castle, and the local residents were indeed impressed when Deerfield was built in that last quarter of the nineteenth century when rich Americans vied to show off their untaxed wealth. In earlier years, many in this seacoast town halfway between Boston and New York had owed their livelihood to the Deerfield family, enterprising New England ship owners and merchants who knew when to take a risk. They stitched the canvas sails, tarred the wood hulls, forged nails and metal rims for the cooper's barrels, wound hemp in the ropewalk, and lost their lives to bring glazed blue-and-white dishes from a faraway land where slant-eyed men wore pigtails and ladies and concubines tottered, smiling, on brutally deformed feet. So yes, the locals were impressed by the Deerfield mansion, as well as jealous, scornful, envious, wishful and delighted to accept any meager crumb of invitation to enter the gates. Hypocrites. It's always that way toward the rich, and if the Deerfields were not in the class of the Astors or Vanderbilts, they were at least minor kings in their corner of the world.

Come to the present, when Jane Avery arrives at Deerfield in her pickup, and the house speaks quite differently to passersby than it did to the long-dead townspeople who watched its stones rise. Jane glances at the locked, wrought iron gate, then following the directions given on the phone, continues along the shore drive to the service road by the gatekeeper's cottage. There is no one to stop or greet her, and she parks her truck and walks up a side path to the front door under the portico. The location is still magnificent, the house set well back from the road on a slight elevation facing eastward to the sea. Even on this cold March afternoon, the slaty ocean dull beneath scudding clouds, anyone can see it's prime real estate. Yet the mansion lacks its former impact, and Jane wonders as well at its odd positioning. Instead of presenting a broad façade to the road as might have been expected, it puts its narrow end to the front, like a shoebox on a store shelf, and much of that is hidden from view by the massive beech trees on the lawn and an excess of shrubbery that conceals the first floor halfway up the windows. The castle-like architecture seems, like most monarchies, diminished in the twenty-first century, its spare, towered design out of place in a modern world. A palpable sense hangs over Deerfield that there was money here once, and now it is gone.

Jane chooses the heavy, old-fashioned knocker over the insignificant doorbell recessed in the wall and knocks twice. For a minute, no one answers, nor is there any sound of footsteps approaching, yet she almost imagines someone lurking silently on the other side. She is about to knock again when the door suddenly opens, and there stands a short, twisted creature who seems to relish the startled look Jane gives her. She has a pointed, fox-like face, black hair drawn into a stiff topknot and a burst of red bloodshot in her right eye. Her height is perhaps four foot four or five, and it's her spine, crooked from birth, that has misshaped her. She smiles, almost sneers, as if to say, *You see, you think you are fair-minded, you would never judge anyone by their appearance, oh no, but already I have caught you. Go on, try to pretend you weren't repulsed.*

"I'm Jane Avery," says Jane firmly. "I've come about the caretaker's position."

"I know that," the woman scoffs, then she turns abruptly, as if she's had enough of the way people look at her. "Follow me. She's upstairs, in one of her painting moods."

"I...thank you."

Ahead is a hall leading to a great room with a grand piano and crystal chandelier, but Jane gets only a glimpse as her guide turns right and begins to mount a narrow staircase. The short woman wears a dark-colored dress, nylons and high heels, and the twist in her spine makes her clump a little as she ascends the stairs. Her topknot is a trussed-up little bundle, a blot of ink that bobs defiantly atop her skull. Dyed black, surely, because the woman is seventy, seventy-five? She keeps her back to Jane, disinviting conversation. Half-way up, the staircase switchbacks at a landing to reach the second floor, and Jane is led into a large open room at the front of the house, an artist's studio.

"Tell her you admire Jackson Pollock," the woman hisses over her shoulder. Then, to the other woman in the room, she announces, "This is Miss Jane Avery, applying for the position of caretaker."

The painter at the easel turns and frowns, whether at what she sees or at the interruption, Jane can't tell. This woman was pretty once, a lingering hint of a cameo face, but the chin-length wave of dyed red hair is somehow desperate, for she, too, must be past seventy. And how can an artist do such a poor job of applying lipstick, an uneven smudge that bleeds into the withering lines above her upper lip? She is dressed theatrically in a long green paisley tunic over gold harem-style pants, a matching green scarf around her hair. The room, which extends the full width of the house, is high-ceilinged but poorly lighted by its diamond-paned windows, and an assortment of chairs, small tables, and one or two loveseats is pushed out to the perimeter. On one table is a silver tray bearing the remnants of afternoon tea, an indication of servants somewhere in the house. Spattered drop cloths cover the floor, and encircling the room, on the walls, in the window seats, propped on other easels and stacked against the furniture is a multitude of framed and unframed paintings in varying sizes. Jane recognizes a confusion of styles: classical, impressionistic, cubist, Grandma Moses, Andy Warhol. The canvas now on the easel appears to be a self-portrait, an emerging face haloed in a fiery nimbus of hair.

"I'm on to something good today, Bella. I *feel* it," says the artist, pleading toward her picture.

"If you say so." The little female shrugs and gives Jane a sideways look and a roll of her eyes that says, *Humor her.*

"I'm here about the caretaker position," says Jane, since no one appears terribly concerned about the subject or about making an official introduction. Back at the coffee shop she had spoken on the phone to someone who identified herself only, curtly, as Miss Deerfield's secretary, apparently this woman named Bella. That leaves the artist as Miss Deerfield. She dabs her brush on her palette, not bothering to face Jane as she speaks.

"Why do you want the job?"

"I've recently left an engineering position on the West Coast, and I'm contemplating a career change."

"And you consider becoming a caretaker a step up?"

"I consider it an interim step while I reassess my priorities."

"So there's no guarantee you'll be staying."

"Your ad said the position was temporary."

Miss Deerfield turns now, one eyebrow raised inquisitively. Bella also is watching. Jane returns them both a level gaze. She knows the story doesn't quite fit her—or does it?—but she's sticking to her answers. The artist and her secretary exchange glances.

"We were hoping for someone bigger, burlier," Miss Deerfield continues, assessing Jane's slender five-foot-two frame, her delicate face framed by tendrils of blond hair. The equation of size with capabilities is a misconception Jane has dealt with most of her adult life and has learned to counterattack.

"I can do whatever lifting is required," she says, "clearing, pruning—"

"No!" The word, almost a shout, comes from both women together. "No, that's not the caretaker's job," Miss Deerfield says, ruffled. "Bella, didn't you explain?"

"Not on the phone," Bella retorts.

Miss Deerfield gives a last frustrated glance over her shoulder at the interrupted painting and sets aside her palette.

"We don't need any pruning or gardening done," she says to Jane. "It's a security position. The job is to keep trespassers off my land, as long as it is *my* land," she adds, tight lipped. "Do you know anything about birds, botany, wildflower identification?"

Jane shakes her head, the swing in topic beyond her.

"Well, they all want it, you see. Can't wait for me to die to get their hands on it." She utters a dry laugh.

"Who?" asks Jane. The question is pure curiosity. She's already thinking this is probably not the place for her, and in a minute she will excuse herself, keep going, drive on. Yet she can't help but be fascinated by this setting, by these two women who appear, putting it nicely, to be slightly cracked. Jane pauses, emitting a dry inner laugh of her own. Isn't she, too, cracked, damaged, broken?

"The land trust people, the tree huggers, bird watchers, environmentalists." Miss Deerfield spits the words. "Also, the art association, historical society and town council, to name a few more." She sweeps her hand as if knocking pieces off a chessboard, then eyes Jane critically, although not measuring her size this time. "You drove through the town on your way here?"

"Yes."

"Not very big, is it?"

"No. It seems to have quite a number of antique shops." Jane recalls the clustered stores on the cobbled main street, a typical old New England village that has reinvented itself as a quaint, upscale shopping mecca. "Art galleries, an art museum," she adds, remembering a gray stone structure that dominated one corner, similar in style to this house but on a smaller, friendlier scale. Similar in style to this house…

"Yes." Miss Deerfield nods at the connection dawning on Jane's face. "My grandmother founded our art association and donated that building. Art runs in my family." Pride enters her voice, and Jane's gaze goes again to the pictures ringing the room. She doesn't pretend to any artistic judgment, and perhaps it's the clutter that makes it difficult to appreciate any one painting in particular, yet nothing extraordinary stands out. Nonetheless, as Miss Deerfield continues her story—her grandmother and mother both esteemed artists and generous patrons—Jane begins to comprehend. Talented or not, these are the sort of people a nonprofit art organization can't afford to turn down or offend. Put a bust or a bronze plaque in the lobby, admit a canvas or two into every show, bestow—surprise!—an award here and there, and the donations will keep coming.

"Now they think that when I die, having no heirs, I'll leave them my mansion and estate as a haven for artists, a summer camp for talented young people." Miss Deerfield's lip curls. "Then there are the land conservation people who want to protect me and my three hundred acres of woods and fields from rapacious development. If I'll just sign everything over to them, they'll guarantee to permanently preserve it as an invaluable buffer adjoining the state forest." Her hand flicks toward the rear of the house, indicating an extensive property.

"Don't forget the birders," Bella eggs her on. "They're the worst trespassers." She picks up the recital herself, usurping the narration. "Five years ago we had a rare seagull from China land down on the shore, and for weeks we were overrun by people peering through binoculars. They camped on the road so we could barely get out our own gate, and when the gull wasn't around to amuse them, they tried to sneak onto the estate, snooping around the house and poking into the bushes for more birds."

"So your job is to patrol my land and keep everyone

off my property," Miss Deerfield concludes, "except for once a week when I am now obliged to open my estate to the public for a Sunday morning stroll in return for certain tax considerations. You will lead these nature outings." She ends on a resentful tone at this violation of her realm.

Jane takes a deep breath. She's still standing, no one having offered her a seat, although except for a computer desk and chair tucked into one corner, there's no furniture free to sit on. The ad in the local paper had read: *Caretaker wanted. No experience necessary. Temporary position. Cottage and small remuneration.* It did not read: *Security guard/naturalist/tour guide.* Yet she can't keep running, and this place, quiet and isolated, may be what she needs. Miss Deerfield seems far less interested in asking about her than in airing her own grievances.

"I don't have any experience or training as a nature guide," Jane says, ensuring this point is made clear.

"It's not necessary," Miss Deerfield replies blithely. "I doubt many people will actually show up. If visitors do materialize, all you need do is lead them in circles and keep them from straying while they *ooh* and *ahh* at whatever exciting flora and fauna I'm told inhabit my private property. You like hiking, the outdoors." She glances at Jane's blue jeans and work boots. "That will suffice."

"And the cottage mentioned in your ad is the gatekeeper's cottage where I drove in?" Jane asks. "Is it furnished?"

"Charmingly! You'll be entirely self-sufficient there. Bella will give you the key."

"Remuneration?"

"Two hundred dollars a week."

Jane pauses. It was only idle chance that she opened the discarded newspaper on the coffee shop counter as she passed through town. The job isn't quite what she expected, these two women certainly aren't, but their needs are apparently met by the household staff, and she'll be left alone in plenty of privacy. She can always stay a week or a month and move on. With any luck, she'll be able to turn around and go back. Her eye travels once more around the ring of art, building itself inward toward the center of the room, and it strikes her that of all the varied styles and imitations she sees there, one is missing.

"What do you think of Jackson Pollock?" she asks.

"Spatters! He paints spatters!" The words spew from Miss Deerfield's mouth in indignation and wrath. Her hands fly apart into the air. "How can anyone call that art? That joke, that mockery! He—" She stops, veers her glance from Jane to Bella, her eyes narrowing. Jane, too, watches Bella, who looks back in lamb-like innocence.

"Well." The word elongates itself as Miss Deerfield resumes an unaffected pose. "Never mind about him. We're settled then. You will lead the walks and otherwise keep people off my land. Either of us may terminate this employment at any time."

"Agreed," says Jane.

Bella goes to the desk with the computer, opens a drawer and returns to disdainfully hand her a key.

"You'll find it's dusty inside," she says with satisfaction.

"I'm sure it will do," Jane replies.

Bella escorts her downstairs and out the door, then resets the buttons on the alarm system panel. When she returns to the studio, Charlotte Deerfield is adjusting the focus on a pair of binoculars as she follows Jane's progress across the lawn.

"She's too smart for you, Bella. Jackson Pollock. You really meant to antagonize me today, didn't you?"

"I don't like her," snaps Bella, watching at Charlotte's side.

"You don't like anyone."

"She doesn't know plants or birds."

"All the better. People will get bored and not come."

"The town and the land trust will say you didn't fulfill the provisions of the agreement, and I'll be the one who has to deal with them."

"That's your job. Besides, I advertised. She's the only one who answered."

"She's the *first* one who answered. The ad only appeared today."

"Lucky us. We're spared the effort of any more interviews."

"You didn't even ask for a resume," Bella accuses. "How do we know who she is, really?"

Charlotte hands her the binoculars. "Get her license plate number. Check her out on your computer or whatever else it is you do."

"She's hiding something," Bella warns, but Charlotte makes no response. She picks up her palette and brush, but the painting on the easel looks stiff and dry already, a depiction of artificial youthfulness. Not an hour ago, she thought the portrait was trying to tell her something; now it doesn't please her, it isn't right. Her expression slips from confusion to rejection to grief. *What do you want from me?* she begs.

"It's no good, is it?" she asks.

"Too much yellow in the flesh tones," say Bella and shrugs.

Chapter 2

When the first nature walk is due on Sunday morning, Jane isn't prepared. She meant to be, to make some preliminary excursions over the property, but anyone harboring the notion that living in a nineteenth-century stone gatekeeper's cottage is cozy and romantic is likely to have that expectation dashed in short order. In Jane's case, all it took was opening the front door. To Bella's smug prediction of dust, she instantly added a sweeping vision of grimy windows, tatty furnishings, and of far more immediate concern, a burst pipe under the kitchen sink spewing a fountain of water, a small lake pooling on the floor. It took several soaking minutes on hands and knees to locate the rusted shutoff valve in an outdated configuration of piping and gingerly twist it closed. Then wet as a half-drowned cat, she ran back to the main house where her news threw Charlotte into angry contortions, yelling at Bella for allowing this to happen, Bella vociferously reiterating the perils of deferred maintenance. It was ten p.m. by the time a grunting, soggy and exorbitantly compensated plumber emerged from under the sink; at midnight, Jane was still mopping water from the floor. Fortunately, the loft bedroom was spared the flood, and by then she was too tired to inquire as to the last time the sheets had been laundered. It took the next two days to dry out the cottage and salvage the furniture. The sodden, threadbare carpet was beyond repair, and she had to rip it up and haul it out the door.

Luckily, there aren't many participants for this inauguratory hike, two to be exact, as Charlotte and Bella observe through the shared binoculars kept by the studio window. The visitors are waiting uncertainly by the locked front gate when Jane emerges from the cottage at five minutes to eight and walks over to meet them. The man is tall, skinny and quite elderly. The woman, although gray-haired, appears more robust. Both are properly attired for the weather in parkas, boots and wool hats, binoculars strung around their necks.

"Hello!" the woman tootles and waves as Jane approaches. "Are you our fearless leader?"

"I'm Jane, the caretaker," says Jane, unsure how warmly she should respond to the woman's cheerfulness.

"I'm Hortense." The woman holds out her hand. She's tall, six feet, Dutch-boy haircut with bangs, glasses, a squarish face. "This is Roy. We're birding buddies, and we've come for the walk."

"Pleased to meet you," says Roy in a reedy voice, extending his mittened hand. He talks a little loudly to be sure everyone can hear. People don't do that enough nowadays, have consideration for others, speak up.

"We're really looking forward to this," says Hortense. "Cardinal!" She swings up her binoculars, and Roy instantly follows. "You know, everyone takes cardinals and robins and such for granted most of the year, but to see them after a barren winter is so uplifting, that beautiful flash of red zipping through the trees like a flame on the wing. Wasn't it Thoreau who said something about that, Roy?"

"The scarlet tanager," says Roy, as they both lower their binoculars. "He said it flies through the green foliage as if it would ignite the leaves."

"Ah yes," says Hortense. "I stand corrected." She smiles at Jane. "Will the naturalist be arriving shortly?"

Jane hesitates before answering. She never saw the cardinal, doesn't possess binoculars, and although this pair strikes her as a bit quirky, they're hardly the rowdy mob of trespassing birdwatchers Bella's tale of the Chinese seagull had led her to expect.

"You know," she says carefully, "I'm not really sure what the scope of these Sunday morning walks is meant to be. I was hired only three days ago, and I have no experience as either a nature guide or a birdwatcher."

Hortense and Roy exchange puzzled glances, trying not to appear impolite.

"You're not a naturalist?" Hortense asks.

Jane shakes her head.

"An ornithologist? Biologist? Botanist?"

Jane shakes her head again. "The ad I answered was for a caretaker."

"Well," says Hortense, her tone now equally careful not to presume or give offense, "we only want to look at the birds, and we're very grateful to Miss Deerfield for opening her property to the public. It is open to the public?"

"Yes, although…" Jane lets out a breath. "Perhaps you could fill me in on the specific arrangements? Miss Deerfield wasn't very communicative."

"Hmpf!" snorts Roy. "I'll bet."

The three of them regard each other, sensing the ice break.

"Let's walk," suggests Hortense. "You all right, Roy? Not too cold?" She pats his arm.

"I'm fine," says Roy, though his nose is a little blue, his eyes watering behind his glasses in the windless cold.

"What about the others?" Jane asks, checking her watch. "Is there likely to be anyone else coming?"

"Oh, it's probably just Roy and me today," says Hortense, "although the land trust people will be anxious to meet you. And next week we'll bring Melanie—she's a dear child, you'll love her—but she's in New York this weekend with her father. Let's get away from the house."

She beckons, and Jane and Roy follow. Deerfield indeed has a stony look this morning. South of the gate-keeper's cottage is a large field of straw-colored grass, briars and milkweed, tangled waist high and bisected by a long, crumbling stone wall. They skirt along the edge where the field meets a stand of bare trees.

"We're not really into spring migration yet but keep your eyes open," says Hortense. "We understand you have some diverse habitat here, and that's the great thing about birding, you never know what will turn up."

"Do you know what I had in my backyard this week?" Roy demands of Jane. "A yellow-breasted chat! It's not even supposed to be here yet, but I saw that brilliant yellow breast and white eye ring, and I knew it in an instant."

"Roy's backyard is a legend among the local birders," Hortense confirms, regarding him affectionately. "Whenever a rare bird comes to town, it always seems to alight at his feeder first."

"Mallards!" Roy's binoculars shoot up, Hortense's follow in a flash. Jane can't tell at first what they're looking at, then she catches two indistinct dark shapes winging away. To her eyes they might have been crows, seagulls, geese.

"Bet they came from the pond," says Roy.

"Won't it be a thrill to get down there!" says Hortense. "If they put up boxes, they might get wood ducks in the spring. Are you from around here, Jane?"

"I'm from California, between jobs," Jane answers, wondering what boxes have to do with ducks. "About Miss Deerfield..." She pauses. Roy's and Hortense's eyes are darting everywhere as they walk, scanning the field, the stone wall, clumps of bushes, and she wants to give them a moment to adjust to the shift in conversation. "What exactly is her arrangement with the town for these Sunday walks?"

Hortense snugs down her red wool cap and shrugs. "Well, the negotiating—or should I say the wrangling?—has been going on for about two years, but despite some public hearings I suspect the real deals were made behind closed doors. Basically, Miss Deerfield agreed to give the town and the land trust first refusal should she ever decide to sell and meanwhile she opens the estate once a week in exchange for a reduced tax rate. Personally, I don't think it's right to grant tax exemptions to favor the rich." She casts a dubious glance back toward the main house, only its rooftop now visible above the trees. "On the other hand, this is a critical piece of land between the state forest on the west and the beach to the south, and it would benefit us all to preserve it as open space. The land trust offered to provide a naturalist to lead the walks, but Miss Deerfield insisted it was her prerogative to hire her own expert."

"Which would be me," Jane guesses, and Hortense nods.

They've reached the far end of the field, and Roy wipes his sniffling nose with his mitten. He's tuned out most of the conversation between Hortense and Jane, or rather his ears have tuned it out for him. It's not always bad going a bit deaf, as he discovered a few Christmases ago at his daughter's house in Florida. They had all gathered to watch *It's a Wonderful Life* on television, and Roy was basking in the final redemptive scene, a joyful George Bailey hugging to him his loving wife and child, when his sixteen-year-old granddaughter jumped up from the couch.

"That wasn't a wonderful life, it was a terrible life!" she cried, scornful and appalled. "George Bailey gave up every dream he ever had, he let people walk all over him, and then in the end he's supposed to be grateful for their charity? What a waste!"

A waste? How could anyone say that about a noble, classic story and especially about a role played by Jimmy Stewart, who was not only a great actor but a patriotic American who left Hollywood in World War II to serve his country as a valiant bomber pilot flying missions over Germany. Worse, this blasphemy came not from some lazy, disrespectful child but a bright, talented girl already on track to become class valedictorian. If this was how the best of the younger generation regarded hard work and self-sacrifice, Roy didn't want to hear more.

Since then he has tuned out many an unimportant

matter, including Hortense's rendition of the town's negotiations with Charlotte Deerfield. He knows that story already, and it's far more important to save his hearing and eyesight for the birds. Do you know he has four hundred and ninety-seven species on his life list? Four hundred ninety-seven! And he only started birding ten years ago, after Myrna died. Now if you're diligent your first year and go out, say, once a week, you might get a hundred species, if you go with a pro who can get you started on those identifications. Then the second year, you pick up another seventy-five—you have to be quick those weeks in May when the warblers migrate through. The third year, you add fifty or sixty more, honing your skills, getting the familiar birds down pat, so when a different silhouette flies overhead or an unknown chirp sounds in the leaves, you know—aha!—got something new here, better stick around and flush it out. You try to take trips, too, because after about two hundred fifty birds, you're running out of the usual population. So Roy budgeted to visit Maine, Florida, Arizona, imposed on his son in Oregon, and there you go, he was over four hundred. He even went to France, first time since the war, and after laying a wreath for his fallen comrades at Normandy, he did a week of birding and got forty-five. Now it's getting hard to travel, Roy is eighty-two, and though he told Hortense he's fine, in truth his joints ache with the cold. But he has to keep going, eke out rare species closer to home. He wants five hundred birds.

"You know," Jane is saying to Hortense, "I only took this job on a temporary basis, and maybe that was Miss Deerfield's intention, just to have an interim person until she can hire an expert full-time. Meanwhile, I'm here, so why don't you tell me where you'd like to go. You said there's a pond?"

"The pond." Roy nods, his hearing miraculously restored on the word. "We used to go there as boys, me and my brothers, go fishing, skinny-dipping. Don't recollect we ever caught much."

"Then the estate was open to the public in the past?"

"Clarisse Deerfield, the present Miss Deerfield's mother, used to open it sometimes to us kids and to picnickers and her artist friends." Roy savors the memory. "That was a long time ago, before the war. A real gracious lady, she was."

"From the maps we saw at the public hearings, the pond is about in the center of the property," Hortense adds, pointing westward through the trees.

"Thataway," agrees Roy. He lifts his feet, eager to be moving, needing to keep warm. "There's no real trail but what the deer make, but I'm game if you ladies are. Onward!"

No compass, Jane thinks too late as they set off. No water bottle, flashlight, matches. She does know the basic rules of survival. But the property is only three hundred acres, you can't get far lost, and both Hortense and Roy seem themselves like deer, adeptly picking their way through the woods. It occurs to Jane that she knows the names of almost none of the trees. Devoid of leaves, their trunks range in texture from a smooth pale gray to wrinkled brown, deeply grooved as ancient skin. She does, however, recognize the slender, white-barked trees as birches, and the acorns crunching underfoot clue her that still others are oaks. Suddenly, a narrow trail presents itself, and after ten minutes' walking in single file, the trees thin, and they step out onto the bank of a pond.

Stillness.

It enters the lenses of their eyes like a photograph, echoes in soundless vibrations in the chambers of the ear. The March sun casts a low, pale gleam onto the waveless water, fringed by tall reeds and brown-velvet cattails, a circle of silent trees. Perhaps a hundred yards across, the pond is nowhere very deep, and a few lichen-spotted rocks hump out of the water like the scaly backs of slumbering sea monsters. Snags of dead trees, stripped of their bark, stand like jagged sentinels in the shallows. Here on the south side a raised bank leads to a wooden footbridge, dense forest beyond. Before them, a weathered bench constructed of a half log on two stumps sits at the water's edge. It's as if the pond has been waiting for someone to come, yet for the longest minute neither Jane nor Hortense nor Roy stirs. There's a sense of breathing suspended, an encompassing hush. It feels as if they have stepped into the heart of something, and they're waiting for it to beat.

Slowly, from under the bridge, comes a steady trickle of traveling water. Then a squirrel rustles a branch to their right, a faint *plop!* disturbs the pond's surface, and the three of them exhale in unison.

"Is it as you remember, Roy?" Hortense asks, and he nods and beckons them along the bank to the footbridge. Jane follows cautiously. Something about the pond still seems secretive and enigmatic, and she glances around as if someone might be watching them. But a slow smile cracks Roy's face, and as he steps onto the wooden planks, he's grinning. The bridge is about three feet wide and thirty feet long, railings on both sides. Underneath, water lips over a small concrete dam.

"Mrs. Deerfield used to keep a rowboat here so we kids could paddle around, and this is where we used to jump off into the water," says Roy, patting the railing, as Jane and Hortense step up to join him.

"Goodness, Roy, you might have broken your neck," Hortense counters. "It's nowhere near deep enough to dive into."

"I said 'jump,'" says Roy, "feet first, we did, trying to see how big a splash we could make."

"Then you're lucky you didn't break your ankles," Hortense admonishes.

They stand a minute, listening to the shallow trickle of water running away to the south, watching for any winged shape that might emerge from the trees.

"Scan the treetops and the water's edge," Roy advises Jane. "Look with your eyes first for a shape or movement or color, then home in with your binoculars."

"Here," says Hortense, removing her binoculars from around her neck and offering them. "This knob is the focus."

Jane scans as Roy directed. A dark shape partially hidden in a fretwork of branches seems promising, and she lifts the binoculars and twiddles the knob. The far side of the pond leaps into clarity, the whitened, pointing finger of a bare branch, a broken limb dangling. The dark shape is gone, but no, when she lowers the binoculars, there it is again. She gets a better fix on its position, notes the width of the trunk and the angle of the branch where it's perched. Luckily, the bird hasn't moved. Again she raises the binoculars, adjusts the focus…It's a clump of dead leaves. Meanwhile, Roy and Hortense are naming off species: robin, chickadee, song sparrow, tufted titmouse, blue jay. A pair of mallards swims out from the reeds, and Jane trains the binoculars on them, nice big targets that are hard to miss. They're the everyday ducks you take for granted, so it's a revelation to really look at them, to see the glossy green head of the male, his chestnut front and bright yellow bill. Even the mottled brown female has an unexpected mark of color, a small violet-blue patch near the end of her wing. Hortense and Roy are still naming: towhee, catbird, Carolina wren. Jane hasn't seen any of these.

Then a telltale odor wafts her way, and Jane sniffs, her nose wrinkling. It's Roy. He doesn't realize he does this. At his age, intestinal gas is a fact of life. Besides, it's always soundless, and he doesn't smell it either because he's losing that sense, too. But Jane and Hortense do, and Hortense shoots her a quick, appealing look. *Don't say anything, he'll be mortified.*

"Well, where to now?" Jane gestures nonchalantly ahead. Across the bridge they face another stand of trees, no visible pathway or trail. Roy and Hortense confer. Not too far into the forest there should be a long ledge of rock that runs north to south, then a narrow valley and another ledge beyond. Who knows what they may spot if they keep on? However, as Hortense points out, it's been a quiet morning thus far, it is cold, and they don't want to wear out their welcome. Maybe they'll pick up a flicker or a downy on their return.

"I'm sorry," says Jane, feeling unaccountably responsible for the lack of bird life as they retrace their steps past the pond, through the woods and along the field. Not even a downy or a flicker, whatever those are. She casts a last glance upward and sees, quite high, a small circling plane. For an instant she freezes at the soaring shape, her heart clawing up her throat. Then her brain corrects, reassesses the distance, not a plane but a large bird.

"There…something," she says faintly, pointing.

"Red-tail," Roy responds in a flash.

"Red-tail," confirms Hortense, binoculars up.

The bird is scribing a slow circle, soloing, wings outspread on an unseen current of air. Roy and Hortense stare intently, and through the tightness in her chest, Jane forces herself to focus on the masterful form, gliding effortlessly in an ascending spiral. A cheery voice pierces the air beside her—"Here, have a better look!"—and she clutches not to drop the binoculars Hortense thrusts into her hands, to lift them to her eyes. For half a minute she can't relocate the bird, can't gauge where to look, and all she sees is a blank expanse of sky. Then the bird finds her, it sweeps into view, out again, and Jane swings the binoculars, no, yes, don't let it go, fighting to hold the binoculars steady when her legs are trembling, wobbling like rickety spindles. Hortense is explaining something about a belly band and Roy is zestfully recounting the time a red-tail swooped right into the maple tree in his backyard. Then the bird disappears, spiraling into the sun, and Jane can't find it with either the binoculars or her blurring eyes.

"Here we are." Hortense pulls a worn paperback from her jacket pocket and thumbs the pages. "Broad wings, fan-shaped tail, couldn't positively see the belly band but given the size and the fact that it's our most common buteo…" She points to an illustration labeled "Red-Tailed Hawk."

"I don't think I've ever seen one before," says Jane, which of course isn't true. She must have seen hawks; she just never *felt* one.

"Then that's your first sighting," says Roy. "You can put it on your list, plus the cardinal and the mallards and the other birds we saw at the pond."

"Good eyes!" Hortense rewards her with a hearty thump on the back. "Just wait till May when the warblers come in."

She and Roy chatter enthusiastically about warblers all the way to the front gate, where they thank Jane, pump her hand, and assure her they'll return next week with Melanie. As Roy gets into his car, Hortense catches her aside.

"As the weather warms up and more people start coming, you'll want to keep Roy downwind," she confides.

Jane waves as they drive away. Her legs are steady, her heart calmer, and she's determined to keep it that way. The reaction to the hawk was unpredictable, but she won't let it engulf her. She has survived the first nature walk, and she recalls the tug of sensation she felt when they stepped out of the trees and into the circle of the pond. That lonely bench, the footbridge leading on…Not today, but tomorrow she will go back again. In fact, she'll have to go over the entire property, scout out the deer trails, trace the flow of the stream, establish landmarks in the woods. By next Sunday she will at least be better prepared.

"They're gone," says Bella, monitoring from the studio window. "Nine-thirty. They didn't even stay the full two hours."

"I told you," says Charlotte, painting a new self-portrait. "There's nothing to worry about."

Chapter 3

"How many this week?" asks Charlotte.

"Four," replies Bella, squinting. "The same two as last Sunday, a fat child, a man…He might be leaving."

"All that fuss and clamor about experiencing nature on my property and three people show up," Charlotte scoffs, pleased.

"It is still March, still cold," Bella observes. She lowers the binoculars and grimaces at the latest painting on the easel. Charlotte has been in a self-portrait mode for several weeks now, another egocentric crisis of identity, and the only thing Bella can say for the likenesses so far is that they exhibit a disturbing tendency to grow younger and younger. Prior to this, they endured a six-month Georgia O'Keeffe phase in which Charlotte painted big flowers in dense, vibrant colors, convinced that what one woman did, she could do better. She couldn't. Frankly, Bella thinks little more of O'Keeffe than she and Charlotte do of Jackson Pollock. For all her gaunt black striding through the New Mexico desert, O'Keeffe was just another still-life painter, clever enough to do latch onto something different.

"You're using too much pink," she informs Charlotte.

"Last time you said too much yellow."

"Yes, so you overcorrect, you exaggerate."

"I don't! I've barely begun this one, and already you're criticizing."

"It's too much pink, look at it!" Bella flourishes her

hand at the painting.

"Maybe it's your bloodshot eye," Charlotte retorts.

"At least I'm not color blind, as you seem to be today."

They snap and bicker, each relishing the moment when they can inflict a tiny wound on the other. They are careful to keep the wounds tiny.

"Well, you can't paint at all," Charlotte concludes peevishly.

"I don't much care for cooking or cleaning either," Bella snorts, changing the subject. "We need to hire another couple."

"To steal from us again?"

"Perhaps you should pay them better."

They exchange disgruntled looks. Since their last domestic couple quit without notice a week before Christmas, they have made do with a weekly housekeeping service and caterers as necessary for entertaining. For the most part, it suffices; the two of them hardly get the place dirty. In fact, Bella suspects it is the servants who by their mere presence disarrange and disorder the premises, creating the very mess it is their job to clean. Nevertheless, a live-in staff is desirable, both to maintain their status and to counteract any perception that Miss Deerfield and her secretary are two cracked old women holed up in a decrepit mansion. The arrival of Jane Avery as caretaker is a step in the right direction; it implies there is something at Deerfield worth taking care of. Now as spring begins and the town gears up for art shows and tourists and summer residents from New York, Charlotte must uphold her position by hosting luncheons, fundraisers and formal dinner parties.

Bella reiterates these points aloud, but Charlotte is no longer listening, staring again at her painting.

"There's something here, Bella, I feel it, as if I'm aiming at a moving target that wants me to find it and hit it." She reaches into the air, snatches the invisible in her grasp.

Behind her back, Bella makes an exasperated face.

Charlotte is dressed today in tights—black tights on a woman her age!—topped by a fringed, peacock blue serape. Beneath that, for warmth, she wears a black turtleneck. Bella wears black, too. It is her color. Black, dark gray, dark brown, once in a while dark blue velvet. She sews the dresses herself, and her sewing machine is a top-of-the-line German model that can execute every stitch from fancy to plain, a gift from Charlotte during one of those infrequent spells when they have decided to make the best of it. But all those fancy stitch settings are no use really, because Bella has long ago found the one dress style that is the most concealing of her deformity and the one color that is the most flattering, black. If she wore yellow, red, lime green, she would resemble a circus freak.

"Keep trying," she says to Charlotte, offering a truce about the painting. "You may get it yet."

Focused on her canvas, Charlotte fails to acknowledge the encouragement, and Bella turns back to the window and raises the binoculars. The man has indeed left, driving off in a silver BMW, and Jane and the three visitors are moving toward the field beyond the gatekeeper's cottage, the same route they took last week. Bella has typed the name "Jane Avery" into the Internet and produced a flood of results, including an African-American poet, a city councilwoman in Dubuque, Iowa, an MIT graduate student who coauthored a paper on astrophysics and a British woman who runs a Princess Diana website. She has searched various records using the California license plate on Jane's pickup and zeroed in on a San Diego area phone listing and street address. The phone, however, has been disconnected, the pickup is not stolen, and there is no FBI record of a Jane Avery being an escaped convict, an on-the-lam axe murderer, bank robber, counterfeiter or scam artist.

Investigating Jane would be a step easier if Charlotte let Bella issue their employees legal paychecks, for then she would have Jane's Social Security number. But that would involve official accountability, the payment of taxes and disability insurance, all of which Charlotte particularly resents in her artistic phases when she feels compelled to be a free spirit rebelling against the establishment. At such times, she leaves everything to Bella; she doesn't want to know when the bills are due or how much her investment portfolio has shrunk. She wants to plead ignorance of the mundane and commercial, and in company she lavishly praises her secretary's financial acumen. "Bella handles everything for me! How fortunate I am!" Naturally it will be Bella who lands in the clink if there is ever an audit.

Never mind. Bella purses her lips. She is sharp. She doesn't need a Social Security number, a resume or references. She prefers the challenge of ferreting out Jane's personal story on her own, and there must be one, for what could have driven an intelligent young woman to a menial job like this? All this week Bella has observed their new caretaker's diligence. The lights in the cottage come on at six-thirty. By seven-thirty, Jane is setting out to patrol the property. When she returns mid-morning, she goes to work on the cottage, continuing to repair the damage from the burst pipe, cleaning, painting, washing windows inside and out. Bella has instructed Jane she may charge any supplies she needs to Miss Deerfield's account at the hardware store, and when she stops by the cottage to observe the progress, the labor is unexpectedly skillful, Jane's reports brief but articulate. Could it be her story that she's between careers is true and she is simply blessed with the youth, good health and freedom to go wherever and do whatever she wants? Bella sighs enviously and looks at Charlotte. It hasn't turned out as either of them expected so long ago, and there is no way to change it now.

"I'm going to mass," she says, clumping off in her high heels. "I'll bring back three-bean salad from the deli for lunch."

She descends the stairs, dons her wool coat, covers her topknot with a maroon silk scarf, and exits via the rear door to the garage, formerly the stables for the estate. You might think her physical shape would hinder her venturing very far, but Bella is deformed, not weak. She can stand and walk as long as any woman her age; she can drive a car by tilting the steering wheel and adjusting the seat. It is people's expectations that are her greatest handicap. It is their perceptions that limit her, and limit her they have done. But it is also hard to be bitter all the time, so on days when she is relenting Bella goes to mass at St. Joseph's to renew her love/hate relationship with God. Without him, who could she plead to? Without him, who could she blame?

She gets in her car and heads north on the shore drive. Deerfield is the last residential property on the road, which dead ends further south at a small public beach. Once, a decade ago, a bunch of brazen nudists claimed that territory—horrors! It wasn't the nudity that infuriated Charlotte and Bella, however, but the crowds who flocked to see the nudists, as if bare-naked humans were a new species of rare bird. Then, as with the Chinese gull incident, Deerfield's boundaries had been threatened, this time by an overflow of voyeurs. Fortunately, the town council quickly went into a Puritan fluster and banned nude sunbathing, although for weeks afterward rogue skinny dippers were arrested as they emerged dripping from the water. Bella smirks to recall the solution she had ready, namely to march down to the beach herself and disrobe. That would have cleared the shore in a hurry. She must remember to enlighten Jane about possible trespassers from the beach as the weather gets warmer, for they still get some locals and meandering tourists who don't realize they're supposed to patronize the much bigger, kiosk-lined beach on the opposite side of town. Perhaps, Bella thinks, as her car passes the art association, the shops and galleries, and nears the church, they ought to invite Jane to tea to review this matter, and in the meantime she can see no harm in two old people and a fat child wandering about the property.

The fat child is Melanie, and at this moment Melanie is pishing. Melanie loves to pish. She puts her lips together as if to pucker for a kiss, but instead of a smack, she shapes her mouth to create a faint "p" sound followed by a sustained, blown-out "sssh." You mustn't do it too loudly, soft and gentle is best. "Psssh, psssh, psssh." She's doing this to draw out a Carolina wren hidden in a large bush at the edge of the field. They know the bird is there, Roy, Hortense and Melanie do, because it has uttered its rolling three-syllable call, *tea-kettle, tea-kettle, tea-kettle,* in a characteristically loud volume out of all proportion to its five-and-three-quarter-inch length. Now Roy and Hortense watch intently for any sign of movement in the branches as Melanie pishes to coax out the bird. No one knows quite why some birds respond to this peculiar sound, although the theory is that it rallies them to a feathered comrade in possible distress.

"There," breathes Hortense, giving the slightest nod of her head. "Right side of the bush, about halfway up and a foot in. It's moving behind the leaves. Keep pishing, Melanie."

"Psssh, psssh, psssh," Melanie coaxes.

Tea-kettle, tea-kettle, tea-kettle! chirps the bird.

"Psssh, psssh."

Tea-kettle, tea-kettle! A hopping motion.

"Psssh, psssh."

Tea-kettle! A tiny brown bird pops onto an exposed branch and sits with its tail cocked, eyeing them.

Jane's mouth falls open. It's as if the child and the bird have been talking to each other. "That's amazing!" she says, and Melanie beams. Each time she does this and a bird comes out, Melanie feels very special.

"Look at the white eye stripe," says Hortense, thumbing through her bird book. "That's the quickest way to distinguish a Carolina from a house wren. The Carolina is also slightly larger and more reddish-brown on its back and breast. And of course, the call is a giveaway."

She points to the wren illustrations, and Jane studies the seven species of little brown birds, almost identical in size and coloring, wondering how anyone can keep them straight. When she looks up again from the book to the bush, the wren has turned its tail to them. How are you supposed to tell which species is which when all you can see is its butt? The next instant the bird darts deeper into the bush and is lost from sight.

Roy pats Melanie's shoulder and says "Attagirl!" as they move on. Already Melanie likes this new place, likes Jane, is glad her father didn't have too much work this weekend so he could come home instead of Mrs. Egan, the housekeeper, delivering her to New York where her father says they'll have something called quality time in spite of his meetings and telephone calls. Melanie only wishes he wouldn't bundle her in this heavy jacket, scarf, mittens, hat. It turned spring four days ago, and besides, Melanie doesn't get cold, she's fat. She wishes, too, that her father hadn't insisted on bringing her this morning; usually he lets Hortense or Roy pick her up. In fact, her house is less than a mile up the shore road from Deerfield, and she's eleven, she could walk.

Yet this is a new place, a new person, and when they arrived, her father immediately took Jane aside to lecture her. Melanie pretended to drift away, focusing her binoculars on a pine tree empty of birds, but the words reached her over Jane's shoulder nonetheless. "...serious car accident...brain damage...imperative that she be treated like everyone else." Melanie is ashamed she has brain damage, although she understands it's not her fault. She also understands that despite it being over a year since the accident, she isn't getting any better, and her father seems angry about that. Now, as they walk along, Roy regales them with an account of a red-breasted nuthatch at his feeder this week, and Melanie takes his hand. She and Roy often walk together like this, and she doesn't mind that Roy is old and partly deaf and that he often repeats himself because Melanie, with her disability, often needs to have information repeated. Also, she has an important job to fulfill, to keep Roy a little away from the rest of the group when he has gas.

They aren't seeing many birds yet, so a few steps ahead Hortense begins telling Jane about when she used to be a gym teacher. Hortense has four children, six grandchildren, and she wishes at least a few of them lived closer, but they don't. She makes up for it by volunteering as a playground monitor at Melanie's school, organizing games and making sure the rude, selfish children, of whom there seem to be more and more these days, don't hog the swings or the soccer balls. Later in the day she is a volunteer coach at the high school for girls' basketball. Being six feet tall and agile in her youth, Hortense was no slouch on the court, and her slam-dunk still earns high-fives from her girls. She enjoys hiking, too, and would come for the Sunday walks even if there were few birds to spot. It's a bit sunnier this week, and with Melanie so well bundled, perhaps they can go past the pond today and onto the first ridge.

"Have you had a chance to do much trekking around the property since last week?" she asks Jane.

"Quite a bit. I also stopped by town hall to verify the estate boundaries on the plats." Jane slips a khaki knapsack off her shoulders and pulls out a folded map. She has come prepared this time, water bottle, a basic first aid kit, flash-light, matches, her cell phone. She thought about purchasing binoculars and a bird book but decided to skip the expense; she won't be here that long. The map shows a close-up of the downtown streets on one side, an overview of the surrounding area on the reverse. "I sketched in Deerfield's boundaries for reference," she explains, and Hortense points around the map to some of their other birding sites, a park in town, an area of marshland, a stretch of woods to the north.

"We could take you sometime," Roy offers. "Last year we got a winter wren in those woods, quite a sighting since they're pretty secretive."

"That might be nice," says Jane, then lets the invitation drop. They're threading their way through the trees toward the pond, with interruptions for a catbird, which does indeed mew like a lost feline, and a downy, which Jane learns is a black-and-white woodpecker, red patch on the back of the head if it's a male. In her patrols around the property so far, she has ranged south to the beach at the end of the shore road, where a sign posted to a weathered shack advises a ten-dollar entrance fee between June and September, and west across the ridges into what she calculates is the state forest. There are no fences around Deerfield marking either boundary, yet she has encountered no trespassers or any litter that might testify to intruders. She's beginning to wonder if Charlotte Deerfield's trepidations about invaders aren't more paranoid than real.

"We're almost at the pond," says Hortense in a quiet voice. "Let's move slowly so we don't startle off any birds that might be there."

They step carefully out from the trees, and Jane pauses to see if once again the pond will affect her. It does. It affects all of them. Hortense and Roy take a long breath, Melanie's mouth opens, Jane feels a pull in her chest. It's as if the pond has a presence that allows you to enter yet holds onto secrets, a place you can step into but can't easily step out of. Enclosed and guarded by the woods, it's an inner space, a breathing space. If you stay, you might learn something about yourself. To Jane it feels once again as if they have stepped into a heart, suspended between beats.

"Can I walk out there?" Melanie whispers, pointing along the bank toward the footbridge, and Hortense gives her a little pat on the back to send her forward. She's been excited ever since Hortense told her they had permission to come here, and when she drove up with her father, the sight of the mansion made her eyes go wide. She pictured beautiful ladies in gossamer ball gowns and gentlemen in velvet frock coats and horse-drawn carriages arriving for a ball. This still, green pond ringed by tall trees is even better, a magical place like in a fairy tale. Before the accident, when Melanie was smart, she was getting too old to believe in fairy stories. Now she adores them and spends hours lying on her bed on her stomach, reading and eating puffy marshmallows.

Melanie can still read; it's only after she's reached the end that the words melt together in her head, leaving a vague sense that the story was happy or scary or sad but without any details. Her father has made sure that at home all her books are happy ones.

"Can I make a wish? Please?" Melanie turns on the bridge, imploring.

"You mean like a wishing well?" Hortense asks. "You want to toss in a penny?" She hesitates as Melanie nods. "Is that all right, Jane?"

"I can't think why not."

"Here, cup your hands together." Roy curves Melanie's mittens into place and digs into his pocket for a worn leather coin purse. He spills a miniature treasure into her palms, skinny dimes and fat nickels, round brown pennies and three rich quarters.

"Okay, make a wish and throw," says Hortense, gripping the back of Melanie's jacket as she leans over the railing as far as she can go.

Fling! Up fly Melanie's arms, up twirl the coins spangling high into the air. They peak like a range of little mountains, then madly spill down, tumbling over and over, and Melanie forgets to make a wish, her brain suddenly blurred by a memory of herself in a car, tumbling over and over and over. The coins splatter into the water, *plop-plop, plink, plunk!* and sink out of sight in the opaque pond.

"Attagirl!" says Roy. "You'll bring us good luck! Now, ladies, shall we press on?"

He points to the next stretch of forest that leads to the ridge, but for a moment Jane hesitates. Back at the front gate, Melanie's father, Peter Babcock, had made it quite clear that if any harm befell his daughter he would hold her personally accountable. Offended by his directives, she had been about to suggest that if Melanie wasn't up to the walk, she shouldn't be there, when Hortense intervened. "You know Melanie is perfectly safe with us, Peter," she said. Now it's Melanie who pipes up with a vigorous "Onward!" They cross the footbridge, enter the woods, and after ten minutes reach a long rock shelf running north to south.

"Up we go," tootles Hortense, and it's not steep, not difficult if they hold onto trees and pull each other up. The cobbled texture of the ridge, like many smaller rocks tumbled and set in concrete, affords them footholds. "Puddingstone rock," Hortense explains to Jane. "It's a conglomerate formed by strong pressures deep in the earth that stretched and elongated the boulders and cemented them together." So here is another facet Jane knows nothing about, birds, trees, plants, now rocks. Atop the ridge the growth consists of a few low bushes and small, scraggly evergreens, and they make their way to the end where the ledge drops off steeply to a salt marsh below. In a panoramic view they take in the coastline from east to west, the sandy main beach, the inlet to the town harbor, the shore road on which Deerfield sits, the smaller beach and forested acres curving away to their right. Pale blue light suffuses the air.

"I love this place!" cries Melanie, throwing her arms wide.

"We're like explorers coming on a new land, a new ocean, stout Cortez silent on a peak in Darien!" Hortense proclaims, then adds, "Of course, everyone knows Keats got it wrong in his poem and it wasn't Cortez but Balboa."

She tugs her scarf closer to her chin, and Roy removes his glasses and wipes his watering eyes. Despite the rising sun, the wind is also picking up, and on this exposed ledge they will soon feel its brunt; in a minute it will be prudent to start back. Yet they stand a moment longer, reluctant to leave this compelling sweep of earth and return to the world below. Does Charlotte Deerfield ever come here, did she ever used to come here, Jane wonders, and a sudden intuition tells her no, not for ages.

Why not? Why not?

Chapter 4

"We have to invite her to tea," says Bella.

"No," says Charlotte.

"Yes," says Bella. "There are six people this week."

"Six? Who are they?" Charlotte looks up in consternation from her easel.

"How should I know?" Bella turns from the window, binoculars in hand. "You think I should know everything?"

"You act like you do."

They glare at each other.

"I'm going to invite her for tea." Bella clumps to her desk and pulls stationery from a drawer. "Word is getting around that Deerfield is open, the land trust has posted it on their website, and we still haven't answered their letter about holding an official opening day and announcing it in the newspaper. At the least, they want to send a delegation."

"No, no! We'll be overrun! I don't want those pushy people on my property."

"Neither do I, but we made a deal."

"Can't you just poison them or something?" Charlotte fumes.

"You know I gave that up a long time ago," Bella sneers.

They stop. The wounds are slicing a little too deeply.

Charlotte presses her lips. "All right, talk to her, but not tea. That's too friendly. You can't be friendly with servants."

"I'm inviting her to tea, and you can't stop me," says Bella, writing. "We need her as an ally. Four o'clock. Be ready." She tucks the note into an envelope and clumps away.

Charlotte slumps onto a chair that already holds two paintings. She would like to mutter to herself, but she has always detested muttering old people and she refuses to become one of them. She also refuses to stoop or sag, and it infuriates her that she has nevertheless shrunk two inches from her original five-foot-eight and that her once-slender body has softened and thickened in the middle like a pudding. The very thought makes her sit straighter in the chair. She wants to be young and beautiful forever, and she dyes her hair coppery red, or rather she has Bella dye it for her, and she tries every wrinkle cream and ointment on the market, sends Bella into the stores to buy them, makes her call the numbers for the miracle rejuvenation products advertised on late-night infomercials. If only she could per-suade Bella to concoct her cosmetics and potions, the way she used to, the little Borgia. But then again, suppose Bella decides to poison her?

"What is the point of being rich, if you can't make people do what you want?" Charlotte mutters.

She reaches for the two-week-old letter on Bella's desk. It's on the land trust's stationery, but they're in tempo-rary league with the art association and the town council, and the three entities are eager to pay her a joint visit, meet the naturalist she hired, and continue their discussions on developing a comprehensive preservation plan for this unique property. Isn't it obvious that the best way to preserve her estate is to stay off it? And still give her the tax reduction, of course. Charlotte grunts. She and Bella have been playing these organizations off against each other for years. They were supposed to have a naturalist hired by the first of January but stalled by combining the perfectly reasonable objection that few people would visit during the winter anyway with valid concerns that if anyone slipped on ice and injured themselves they might all be held liable. Their next line of defense was that it made more sense to hire someone on a full-time rather than a once-a-week basis to ensure the property was protected continuously—how could anyone disagree with that? Now they must disguise the fact that Jane Avery hasn't a clue about trees or birds or wildlife, that she has been hired expressly for her lack of knowledge in a ploy to discourage visitors. Perhaps Bella is right. They do need Jane as an ally. Tea might be appropriate after all.

Charlotte returns to the easel and picks up her palette. Her recent attempt to be the second Georgia O'Keeffe bloomed garishly before wilting into a series of lifeless bouquets. Before that she tried to be Seurat, all those miniscule dots, maddening! Nor in the past has she had any success at being Mary Cassatt, Picasso in his Blue Period, or the entire Hudson River Valley School. Even when she tries to be completely fresh and original, it always turns out someone else has done it before and done it better. Then about six weeks ago in sheer frustration she began painting these self-portraits that keep getting younger and younger and younger…What if she painted her whole life backwards?

The brush stops an inch from the canvas, tipped in a rosy flesh-tone, and for a minute Charlotte hardly breathes, blinded by the dazzling white light of revelation. *Paint her life backwards.* Has any artist done that? Could this be the concept of genius she's been seeking? She dims the intensity of the revelation to a glimmer so she can examine the self-portraits already completed. Put aside Bella's carping about too much yellow or pink and her own earlier doubts, and the work when viewed in this new light becomes suddenly pleasing. So this is what the portraits were trying to tell her. This is what they want to be, not isolated likenesses but an unreeling emotional testament to her state of being. This is how I *felt* at seventy, at sixty-seven, at sixty-three, she thinks, observing the progressively youthful paintings, and there will be years when, much younger, she felt so broken she will paint herself cracked, flayed, botched, as misshapen as Bella.

There will be years she doesn't want to paint at all...
Charlotte's chest tightens. Perhaps this is not a good idea.
Bella won't like it. But then, she doesn't have to tell anyone.
She could start, see how it goes, let everyone think she's only
dilly-dallying again. She could call it "A Retrospective in
Retrospective." The brush moves toward the canvas, begins
to paint.

Outside, the Sunday walk is underway. Roy is sick
today, but in addition to Hortense and Melanie, Jane is
leading a late-twenties couple who introduce themselves as
graduate students in an environmental studies program,
another young man named Burt who works at the town
library, and a dislikable middle-aged woman.

"Can we go in the mansion? Is it open for tours?" she
demands when Jane first meets the group at the front gate.

"No, sorry," Jane replies firmly, smiling. As she leads
the visitors toward the field, she discovers the woman has
sneaked away to peer into the windows of the caretaker's
cottage. Jane halts the group and strides back to collect her.
"Excuse me," she says, politely enunciating each word and
resisting the urge to grab the culprit and haul her away by the
collar. "That's a private residence."

"Well, who lives there? Who lives in the main house
these days?" the woman counters, unfazed. "I own an
antiques store in town, and I could offer them some decent
prices to help clear out the clutter that's probably crowding
up the place."

"I'm sure if Miss Deerfield wants to sell anything,
she'll make the necessary arrangements. Now, we're going
this way."

Jane gestures for the woman to precede her, and she
huffily joins the others, annoying them throughout the walk
with derogatory comments about rich people who think they
own everything, don't keep up their property, don't pay their
fair share of taxes. It's too bad, because otherwise today's
hike would be the most enjoyable yet. The graduate students
are a lively newlywed pair, who give mini-lessons on iden-

tifying pine versus fir trees and how photosynthesis affects the spread of pond scum. Hortense has brought along her spotting scope, providing them with stunning close-ups of perching birds. Burt from the library chips in bits of local history. The weather has warmed considerably over the past few days as March has slipped into April, and in the course of her morning patrols Jane has traced a circuitous route around the pond. It involves thickets, mud puddles and jumping a stream, and the grad students would no doubt love it. Hortense, Melanie and Burt might also be game.

But the antiques dealer is harping again as they cross the footbridge into the woods. How can anyone call this a nature reserve when there aren't any proper trails to walk on? Why don't they lop these overhanging branches that keep slapping her in the face? It's clear from their expressions that the others are growing irked by her as well, and Jane reluctantly shelves the pond circumnavigation for another day. When they double back and the cottage comes in sight, the woman hustles off to her car, still complaining. Jane finds herself apologizing to the rest of the group as they leave. It's as if the peace and quiet of the place has been affronted; even the pond seemed to retreat, appearing flat and neutral today.

"Don't worry about her," says Burt, the last to linger. "I know her from times she's come into the library, and she's always a pain."

"Thanks," says Jane. "I hope you'll come again."

"Oh, I will except..." He hesitates, then confesses. "See, I'm not really a birder or a hiker and working at the library is just my day job. What I'm really doing is writing the Great American Novel. It's about this family of tremendous power and prestige and how greed and corruption bring it down. But don't worry, I'm not trying to steal any Deerfield family history, although I am researching it to get a feel for how it might have been." His blond face blushes as he pours out his ambitions, simultaneously waving his hands and shaking his head in disclaimer.

"That's okay." Jane smiles. If he's come out of curiosity, he's decent enough to admit it. "I don't know anything about the Deerfields myself, and I'm only here temporarily. Excuse me a minute…" Her glance catches on a small white envelope taped to the cottage door and, puzzled, she goes to retrieve it. Inside is a notepaper bearing, in handwritten script, an invitation to tea. Both the envelope and paper are monogrammed with an elaborate gold "D." Jane chews her lip. Why invite her for tea? She's fine with the terms of her employment so far, working on the cottage, reporting to Bella, collecting her weekly pay. She doesn't require any social contact, and until now neither Bella nor Miss Deerfield have offered any. She returns to Burt, who is craning looks toward the cottage.

"Do you know a lot about the family?" she asks.

"Oh yes, I've researched them at the library and the historical society, books, maps, documents and journals from the period, everything I could find."

"Would you like to see the gatekeeper's cottage, and in exchange maybe you could fill me in on a little history?"

She gestures toward the door, and Burt eagerly blurts an affirmative. No one has said she can't have guests inside, and while she makes coffee, Burt roams over the cottage. It's almost exactly as he pictured it, an open first floor with secondhand chintz sofa and two armchairs, a maple dining table with four seats, and kitchen fixtures which, except for a more modern stove and refrigerator, appear to date from the 1930s. Above the kitchen is a loft bedroom and bath replete with pedestal sink and claw-footed tub. Add a gabled ceiling so low you'll hit your head if you don't duck in the corners, and downstairs, a cushioned window seat for curling up to read, and Burt is in near ecstasy. You know you're on the right track when you imagine something you're going to write about and then it turns out your vision is reality. He runs his fingers through his hair, visualizing the book jacket as his opus hits the number one spot on the *New York Times* bestseller list.

"Tell me about the Deerfields," says Jane, bringing him a mug as they settle on the couch.

"Sure. Well, the fortune started with Samuel Deerfield and the China trade after the Revolutionary War when British rule ended and the Americans were finally free to trade on their own. The town was a bustling seaport—you've probably seen the harbor front where the docks and old warehouses are?" He pauses to sip his coffee, and Jane nods. She passes through town regularly on trips to the hardware and grocery stores, and the waterfront area has been admirably restored to house upscale shops and restaurants and a marina of sleek yachts. "Anyway," Burt continues, "Samuel Deerfield shipped out as a cabin boy at age twelve, became a captain at twenty-one, and by thirty he was financing his own voyages with other investors. Fast forward a couple generations and you get to John Rufus Deerfield, that would be Charlotte Deerfield's great-grandfather. He's the one who built the house."

"When was that?"

"In 1871. The old China trade ended with the Opium War in the 1840s, so the Deerfield investments shifted to banking and real estate, and the family had residences here and in New York. They weren't the real upper crust, but they weren't slumming it either. From about 1900 on they also had a villa in Capri where they used to go every winter."

"What's left?"

"This house. The money dwindled away somehow, although the crash of 1929 didn't help."

Jane sets her mug on the coffee table, thinking what she wants to ask next.

"Miss Deerfield said it was her grandmother who founded the art association. Do you know anything about her?"

Burt nods. "Louisa Deerfield, she was a talented amateur painter. So was her daughter-in-law, Clarisse, who married Vincent Deerfield, Charlotte's father. He was the ne'er-do-well, always having affairs."

Jane mulls the information. Clarisse—that was the gracious lady Roy remembered who let the children come swim in the pond. It also seems that the artistic talent supposedly running in the family came, in the two previous generations, from women who married into it.

"Okay," she says, her thoughts caught up, "what about Miss Deerfield? She has no children? She never married?"

"Oh yes, three times, only she went back to her maiden name after each marriage ended. But you're right, no children, and she herself was an only child, so unless there are distant cousins waiting to crawl out of the woodwork..." Burt spreads his palms and shrugs. Everyone knows Deerfield is up for grabs.

"And you're going to write a novel about all this?" Jane concludes.

"No, not that I haven't uncovered some pretty serious scandals in my research." He shoots her a knowing look, unable to resist a little bragging. If people only knew what he has discovered in the historical society's musty files! Then he vehemently shakes his head. "My story's going to be totally different, pure fiction. I don't mess up people's lives by telling tales."

Jane smiles at this declaration of integrity, and they finish their coffee, talking of books and general news.

"See you soon, Burt," she says when he leaves.

At five to four, freshly showered, tendrils of hair air-drying on her neck, Jane heads to the main house. She wears neat black jeans and a sky-blue sweater that can pass for dressy, and the information supplied by Burt will provide sufficient background for social chitchat. Yet there has to be more to the invitation, a change to her job status...an announcement that the temporary assignment is at an end? Halfway across the lawn, Jane balks at the thought. It's quiet here, a self-imposed haven, and between the physical exertion of repairing the cottage and tramping daily over the property, she can keep herself productively occupied, keep her mind off what's past, focus on her goal. She just needs a little more time.

"Good afternoon," says Bella, opening the door to Jane's knock and smiling as best she can. A smile isn't an expression in congruity with Bella's face or her fortunes in the world. "Thank you for coming. This way, please."

She leads Jane into the great room in the center of the first floor. Outside, an overcast has moved in, and despite the artificial log Bella has lighted in the fireplace, a mildly gloomy atmosphere persists. That's the curse of an old stone house on a gray day, and as for the décor, what else can you do with this style of architecture? It's doomed to Oriental rugs and heavy antique furniture, a grand piano, a crystal chandelier. A wide, curving staircase leads to the second floor, and Jane wonders if Charlotte Deerfield descended it as a debutante many years ago.

"Good afternoon, Miss Avery," says Charlotte, indicating the chair opposite hers. Her smile, unlike Bella's, works fine. "I trust you're comfortable in the cottage? The repairs are progressing to your satisfaction?"

"Yes, thank you," says Jane, accepting the gold-rimmed teacup Bella hands her. Charlotte is wearing a silky, peach-colored caftan, Bella a chocolate brown dress of some nubby fabric, her inkblot topknot stiff with hairspray. It's Bella who presides over the tea service, offering lemon slices and sugar cubes, and this confirms what Jane has already surmised, that contrary to her first assumption Deerfield has no live-in staff, only the weekly appearance of the house-keeping van. From the rundown state of the gatekeeper's cottage, it's also fairly certain no one has held that position in years. How long have these two women been here alone? she wonders, suddenly disturbed at the idea. What if one of them got sick or fell down the stairs? What if there was a fire?

"Have you had many visitors on the Sunday morning walks?" Charlotte inquires, as Bella passes around a tray of petit fours, miniature cheesecakes, powdered sugar cookies.

"Six today," Jane replies.

"And who are they? Local people? Birdwatchers?"

"Two birders who have come before, two graduate students in environmental studies, and two local people who just wanted to see the property." She lumps Burt and the antiques dealer into the latter category and decides against upsetting Charlotte by recounting the behavior of the nosy woman since she's unlikely to return. "We're sticking to the easy trails, what there are of them, down to the pond and south on the ridge."

"Yes, yes," say Bella emphatically, "by all means, take the easy routes and keep to this side of the pond. Our agreement stipulates we aren't liable for any injuries or accidents sustained on the property, but you know how quick people are to sue."

She takes her teacup to a side table and seats herself in one of the smaller chairs; even so, her short legs dangle an inch above the floor. She has started a log of the number of visitors each week and will add to it this latest demographic information. If attendance remains low, what is the point in keeping Deerfield open to the public? If it jumps too high, they can argue the situation is out of hand. If no one is truly interested in nature, if the majority are mere curiosity seekers, the idea that Deerfield could or should become a nature preserve is a delusion. Documentation, Bella tells herself, it's all a matter of documentation.

"And we trust the visitors have enjoyed themselves?" Charlotte pursues. "They're happy with the arrangement of you guiding them around the property?"

Jane pauses, an uneaten sugar cookie resting in her hand. "I think some of them were expecting an expert," she says, putting careful emphasis on the word. "However, once the hike gets underway, anyone who has a special knowledge tends to share it with the others." She pauses again, the statement gaining more truth on reflection. Hortense, Roy and Melanie may have hoped for an ornithologist, but they seem to be getting as much of a kick out of teaching her to pish. The grad students didn't wait but jumped right in to give their mini-lectures. "It could be taking on the aspect of an outdoor classroom," Jane concedes, "and I'm probably learning more than anyone. The only problem would be if, on a given Sunday, everyone who showed up was a complete amateur. Then my lack of qualifications would be glaring."

"Oh, they won't, they won't," Charlotte and Bella protest, exchanging gratified glances. They hadn't anticipated this outdoor classroom angle; it virtually solves the problem. Let the land trust, the art association and the town council representatives come in a joint delegation. They'll each be so puffed up trying to demonstrate their own expertise, they'll hardly notice Jane's absence thereof. If they do, she can revert to this democratic vision of cooperative learning, adding any tidbits of information she may pick up meanwhile. She has only to pass the test, not ace it.

"That's settled then," says Charlotte jovially. "Now we can talk about more pleasant subjects. Is there anything else you need for the cottage, Miss Avery?"

"Well, I'd like to rent a sander and redo the wood floor," Jane offers, not quite sure what's "settled" but willing to move on. "Since I had to rip out the carpet when the pipe burst, the wood is exposed anyway, and with a new finish it could actually look quite good."

"Of course. Arrange credit for her, Bella. Anything else?"

"I'd recommend cleaning the eaves. I can do that, if you have a ladder, and some gardening, if you have tools?"

"Wonderful! There are tools and a workshop in the garage. Bella, give Miss Avery a key."

"I will." Bella takes a slow sip of her tea. When Charlotte is feeling gratified, she can become overgenerous, forgetful of the balance in the checkbook. She also gets a little too expansive with her commands. *Arrange it, Bella. See to it, Bella.* And Jane Avery wasn't slow to take advantage, harmless as she may appear. "We're fortunate to have your skills, Miss Avery. I believe you said you were an engineer?"

Jane stops with her teacup halfway to her lips, lowers it again. "Yes, with a small firm on the West Coast, but it didn't turn out to be as interesting as I hoped."

"What a shame, and after you earned a degree in it, I presume." Bella purses her lips in sympathy.

"Mechanical engineering, University of Southern California. I forgot to mention," Jane smiles at Charlotte, "one of the visitors on the walk today was complimenting your family's support of the art association."

"Oh yes," says Charlotte. "Bella, pour Miss Avery more tea and I'll tell her about that."

Afternoon tea is so civilized, thinks Charlotte, as she spends the next hour discoursing on her artistic lineage. She and Bella have secured Jane as an ally against those who would usurp her property; what's more, Jane has volunteered to do additional work at no increase in pay. She won't have Bella badgering her with suspicions—anyone can see the young woman's not dangerous, and there's nothing in the cottage worth stealing anyway—although it won't hurt to check out that degree in engineering, as she's sure Bella intends to do. Best of all, her painting went well today, it went gloriously. The inspiration for "A Retrospective in Retrospective" has renewed her faith in herself. She is an artist and she has years, decades, ahead in which to fulfill her talent. Afternoon tea is so civilized. Charlotte adds a fresh slice of lemon to her cup.

Afternoon tea is so civilized, thinks Bella, as she listens to Charlotte declaim. How else could anyone get two perfectly intelligent women, namely Bella and Jane, to sit politely pretending interest in such drivel? Never mind. She and Charlotte have found the angle they need to appease those who covet the estate, and under cover of sociability, Bella has gathered her own valuable bit of news. A degree in mechanical engineering from the University of Southern California—now she can narrow her investigation with just enough of a clue not to spoil the challenge. And did you see how adroitly Jane turned the conversation after that? Perhaps it's a faked degree, leading to exposure and disgrace? Bella munches on a pink petit-four. Afternoon tea is so civilized.

If afternoon tea is so civilized, thinks Jane, as she struggles to keep the smile on her face from wavering, why does this hurt so much? She gave her story, no one questioned it. With that hurdle surmounted, they shouldn't need to ask any more about her past. If they do, there's much of which she could be proud. But when you can't tell the full story, even the truths you can tell make you ache. Just give it a little more time, she promises herself. Her position hasn't been terminated, she has more assignments to keep her busy, and she is beginning to look forward to next Sunday's walk. She doesn't care what games Miss Deerfield and her secretary want to play with their antagonists meanwhile. Charlotte is describing her grandmother's bust in the lobby of the art association, and Jane stretches the smile on her face. One more try, in a week or two. She'll be strong, she'll be ready. She's going to get her old life back.

Chapter 5

Jane's degree is bona fide. More, she earned it with honors. Bella puzzles over this as she observes the activities at the cottage from her window vantage in the studio. Lights on at six-thirty. Out the door at seven-thirty to patrol the property. Back mid-morning to clean the eaves, rake last autumn's dead leaves from beneath the hedges, trim overgrown shrubbery. If they're not careful, the cottage will soon look far more presentable than the main house. Perhaps they should negotiate with Jane to take on gardening projects? They used to hire a landscaping service, but the charges grew exorbitant and over the winter they have let the grounds go. Not good. Not a good impression to create at all, especially with spring sending out rampant new growth. If Jane enjoys the work, she might be the answer.

Why is she here? Deeply, cautiously, Bella ponders the question. Jane is obviously intelligent, self-disciplined, not in obvious need of money, quick to assess and execute a job, no wasted time or slacking off. Who is she? Bella has made more searches on her computer. Military records—no. Law enforcement—no. Deadbeat parent—no. Does Jane Avery really exist? For a moment, Bella startles herself, then reframes the question. What if this young woman's real name isn't Jane Avery? What if it's an alias, an assumed identity? Bella's curiosity piques and glides into a pleased *ahh*. Further investigation will be required.

She turns from the window, contemplates Charlotte's

latest canvas.

"Too much red," she says in passing and is rewarded by a frustrated shriek. Actually, Charlotte finally has the red just about right, but Bella is in an antagonistic mood. Somebody has to be. They've been sniping at each other so long, the relationship feels off-kilter without it, and Charlotte has been entirely too smug about these self-portraits lately.

Outside, dressed in sweatshirt, jeans and work gloves, Jane is on her hands and knees groping to dislodge piles of matted brown leaves from around the shrubbery. The April sun and the exertion raise the beginning of a sweat on her back. It feels good. Work, don't think. She has been at Deerfield almost four weeks now, and each mile hiked, each stroke of paint applied to the cottage, each wheelbarrow load of twigs and debris hauled to the brush pile is a solid accomplishment. She is starting once again to trust her body, to let muscle and bone move without anticipating disaster, and she exaggerates her movements, testing their limits, reach, pull, stretch, lift. Her head feels clearer, too, despite what the goat-faced psychologist predicted.

"You're not sticking it out," he admonished in a smooth, superior tone when she informed him she was curtailing the sessions, the hypnosis, the childhood regressions, none of which had done anything more than make her feel probed and violated. "You can't run away. You have to stay and work it through. We need to further explore your sexual relationships."

"I've tried! I've done everything you suggested. It hasn't worked."

"You're not giving it enough time. Look, I'm busy, but I can increase your sessions from two to three a week."

She walked out. She packed clothes in a duffel bag, threw them in her truck. To her face, her friends remained encouraging. "Sure, put some distance between it and yourself. A change of scene, that'll do the trick." Privately, they were writing her off. They have to, in self-defense. It's dangerous, everyone knows that. You train constantly, prepare meticulously, but you take risks. Accidents happen, and this wasn't her fault. Yet it's been since October, and the longer she lets it go on…

Distance. She left California in February and in a determined odyssey she put behind her the Southwest, the Rocky Mountains, Great Plains, Mississippi River, the Appalachians, the Chesapeake, now she's onto the northeast seaboard. That's three thousand miles. Time. It has been, to the day, six months. This last month especially has put her body back in motion here at Deerfield, cleared her head and her soul.

"Don't worry." Her friends clapped her shoulder when she left. "You'll get it back."

She is ready, this afternoon, to find out.

She quits her yard work at four o'clock. Neither Bella nor Charlotte has ever said what her exact hours are to be; she's well aware they're getting far more labor out of her than they pay for and doesn't care if they're gloating in private. She wipes off the garden tools with a rag, replaces them in the garage, goes into the cottage and consults her laptop. Then she gets into her truck and checks the road map, driving through town to reach the highway. Don't think. Occupy yourself with the extraneous. She calls up Burt's description of the harbor in its nineteenth-century heyday, clipper ships moored to the pilings, the waterfront cluster of sail makers, chandlers, dry goods stores, the stately homes where prosperous merchants dwelt. She pays closer attention to the red brick library, wondering if Burt is there at the circulation desk or holed up somewhere laboring over his Great American Novel. On the north side of town, she passes a playhouse, or maybe it's a dinner theater. Although the weather isn't yet warm enough to dine outside, the wide verandah looks designed to accommodate tables and chairs, and posters announce a production of *Cat on a Hot Tin Roof* to open in May.

Outside town, the landscape shifts to strip malls and chain stores, and Jane takes the highway north for half an hour. Don't think. That was the problem in the beginning, too much thinking, trying to analyze what went wrong. Too much ruthless self-questioning, even after the official investigation delivered its verdict. *It wasn't your fault.* She brings down a deliberate blank in her head, focuses on the rush-hour traffic. This time it will be all right. The only near lapse she's had lately was that morning of the first Sunday walk when she was caught off guard by the hawk. Since then, she has kept her eyes lower to the ground. She pulls off the highway, follows the map, then slows her truck at the entrance to an access road. A rectangular metal sign on the fence shows the silhouette of a white plane on a green background and the message LEARN TO FLY HERE!

Jane parks beside the nondescript office. The small, non-towered airport has a hangar large enough to accommodate a half dozen Cessnas or Pipers and one paved 2,200-foot runway aligned to the prevailing winds. On the grass is a grand total of twelve planes, including an old Aeronca Champ and a snazzily painted, orange Grumman Tiger. It's a quarter past five and the office looks empty, but the gate to the field is still open. All Jane has to do is get out of her truck and walk toward the planes.

The nearest aircraft, a Cessna 172, is a hundred feet distant, and Jane concentrates on the details as she takes the first steps forward. Wear and tear mark the blue-and-white paint job, yet someone takes good care of it. A wraparound canvas cover protects the windshield, wooden chocks are firmly positioned on either side of each wheel, and a stack of three rubber tires at the tail tie-down will prevent the tail from bucking and hitting the ground in the event of a strong wind. She's eighty, seventy-five feet away. Pitot tube cover, aileron locks, foam inserts for the engine cowling to prevent birds from building their nests inside. Seventy feet, sixty-five. It's a good plane, your basic vanilla Cessna, the trustworthy trainer favored by flight schools, a plane that practically flies itself. Though the air seems to be thickening around her, she resists the urge to make a dash toward the aircraft. Fifty feet, forty-five.

Walk! she tells herself. Breathe! You can do this. She inhales, exhales, but her breath has the ragged quality of a ghost. Her head is starting to spin, to rebel. Move, Jane, please! Get to the plane! There's nothing to stop you! It wasn't your fault! Thirty-five. Needles pierce her knees and run down her calves, as if her legs are shaking and falling asleep at the same time. She tries to break for it, but her ankles wade in cement. Round and round inside her skull whirls a terror that brings tears to her eyes, blurring the out-of-reach plane before her. She manages two more steps before her body locks, buzzing from head to toe as if she's been shot through with an overpowering dose of Novocain. No, please, no. Her eyes rivet on the disappearing plane in longing and despair. She stands rooted to the spot, a complete paralysis of body and will, lips parted, no cry emerging. If her heart is still beating, she can't feel it. Her ribcage has become just that, a cage, and as her trapped breath fails, the blue-and-white Cessna dissolves, the little airport swirls away, and she's back in California about to strap in and take off on a beautiful October day...

Her solo act comes first, a crowd-dazzling performance that catapults her candy-red Pitts biplane across the sky. Air show crowds want to *ooh* and *ahh*. They want daring aerobatics, artistic flair. They want hammerhead stalls that make them suck in their breath in disbelief as the tiny plane claws straight up, up, up into the blue, until it runs out of airspeed and seems to fall out of the sky. They want eight-point hesitation rolls so precise they can pinpoint each degree of turn. They want end-over-end tumbles, knife edge flight, reverse Cuban eights, they want the plane to hang from its propeller, tail slide down the sky through its own smoke trail. They want it to happen at eye level, because the more skillful the pilot, the lower minimum altitude you're allowed. When Jane started flying air shows, she was a speck in the blue. Now the spectators see her in the cockpit as the Pitts flashes over the runway in inverted flight. When she finishes her routine and taxis back past the cheering crowd, she smiles and waves. It's her best performance yet, and Jane, a per-fectionist, is satisfied at last. If she keeps up the relentless practice, the mental focus, she can aim for the nationals, the competition that pits the best against the best to represent the U.S. at the world aerobatic championship.

Air show crowds don't want to see pilots die.

When Jane straps into her plane for the second act, she double-checks the sequence of maneuvers she and her partner Jill have choreographed. No, not that kind of partner, although Jill will mischievously prolong the uncertainty after making the introduction by waiting several seconds to gauge the expressions on people's faces. "*Flying* partners," Jane will stress, when it's clear Jill isn't about to relinquish the joke. The air show announcers have a field day with the pair of them. "Watch these dueling damsels as they engage in thrilling head-to-head maneuvers!" "Witness the fabulous formation flying of our airborne Amazons!" "Now they'll follow one another in copycat maneuvers...Ladies and gentlemen, do I dare call this a catfight? Mrrrow!" Jane shrugs off the commentary. It's the flying that matters, and outside the cockpit it's Jill who is the showman, who relishes the applause and works the crowd. They take off, entering from opposite ends of the aerial stage, climb to begin their first maneuver, and everything is fine. They have practiced this duet hundreds of times, performed it flawlessly at air shows across the country all season long. At ten thousand feet, Jane spirals straight down while Jill flies descending circles around her. The ground rushes up in blurring speed, the engine roars, the landscape twirls into a corkscrew of colors, as if it's the earth, not the plane, that is spinning. Then something happens, and she feels the merest *thunk* on her wing...

"Hi there, you lookin' for Joe?" grumbles a slightly suspicious voice. "He left already."

"No, uh no." Jane is standing again in a small New England airfield on an April afternoon, staring at a blue-and-white Cessna an impassable thirty feet away. Her jaw unhinges painfully to make the reply, but the need to appear normal, to act normal, forces out some acknowledgment. "No, I just stopped to look." She lifts her right hand in a casual gesture toward the Cessna, and a bolt of pain shoots up her arm. If she can just step back, move away.

"Yeah, always a pretty sight, aren't they?" The man's tone relents. He wears grease-stained gray coveralls, and he's short, wiry, a tuft of sandy crewcut poking through his backwards VFW baseball cap. "Well, the 172 belongs to Joe Reynolds, and that's the only plane we got on the field for instruction. George and Dotty own the Piper, Skip Clark's got the Tiger, that Aeronca belongs to Mel, but he doesn't fly it much anymore." He's decided she's all right, and he rattles off the names and brief histories of the aircraft. "You lookin' to get your ticket, rent, buy?"

"Rent," lies Jane, "but I'm not current." She has to say something because she needs to hear his voice, scratchy and garrulous, to pull her out of herself. She focuses on his stubbled face, a smear of engine oil on one cheek. He's telling her more about Joe's Cessna, uses it for flight lessons, rents it out for eighty-five an hour wet. Jane smiles, her face fracturing as it breaks out of its freeze, listening as the mechanic rambles on about his glory days as a chopper pilot in 'Nam. The goddamn government took away his medical because of his high blood pressure, even though he's on medication to control it. She nods in agreement at the unfairness of it—"Is that any way to treat a guy who fought for his country, I ask you?"—using the reality of his voice to take one step back. Her knees seem to splinter, as if the bones have to break to move. Through the buzzing in her legs she feels the ground beneath her retreating heel. She manages another step back, as though it's the normal shifting of your body as you stand talking to someone on a late Friday afternoon on a clear April day when you're rooted to the ground and your heart aches to be flying, dancing, soaring through the sky.

"You come back here tomorrow, talk to Joe, and he'll set you up," the mechanic assures her. "You'll be current again in no time. I know how it is. Once you got it in your blood, you can't stay away."

He slaps her back, and Jane gratefully accepts the whack to break the frozen column of her spine, gather the pieces of her body into a functioning whole. She offers him a thank-you and turns away. She walks to her pickup, not too fast, be steady, be calm, gets in, drives off. All the way back along the highway, through town, out the shore road to Deerfield she concentrates on details like the texture of the road, the song on the radio, as if these things matter. When she pulls up to the cottage, she gets out of the truck but doesn't go inside. Now that she's moving, she can't seem to stop, and she crosses the field and turns into the woods. She picks up speed, running, careening along the deer trail, veering between trees. Her thigh muscles begin quivering, her heart pounds, not in fear this time but in choking despair, her mind flooding with images she hoped would never return…

Jill grins. Up there at ten thousand feet, Jill grins and waves to her, and Jane signals back as the maneuver begins. Everything is fine. And when she feels that merest *thunk* on her wing, her plane trembles, as if the plane itself is asking, "What was that?" Instant reflexes kick in and Jane recovers, no problem, but that was close, way too close, and she shouldn't have broken her concentration even long enough to wave. Then she hears the announcer's voice in her headset asking everyone to please stay back, and his tone is eerie, panic suppressed under the authoritative calm. They told her afterward that the crowd went utterly silent, which Jane can't believe because as she jerks her Pitts around and sees Jill's plane plummeting to earth, all she hears inside her cockpit is screaming. *No! No! No! Pull up! Pull up! Pull up!*

"No!" Jane stumbles into the clearing on the bank of the pond and crashes to her knees. "No!" The shriek rises into the sky, and on the water, on the rocks in the pond, on the dead tree snags where the wrens like to perch, and in the treetops all around, winged shapes start up and wheel away in panicked flight. She pounds her fists on the ground, tears streaming. The pond is horrifyingly quiet, every creature fled.

What use is a pilot who has lost her nerve? What good is a bird without wings?

Chapter 6

The day after her breakdown at the airport, Jane purchases a pair of binoculars and a bird identification book. By that Sunday, when Hortense, Roy and Melanie arrive along with four others, she has read and re-read the introductory section and scanned page after page of color illustrations. She has memorized the terminology for the parts of a bird: crown, eye stripe, lore, mandible, breast, belly, rump; primary, secondary and scapular feathers; upper and undertail coverts. She has studied the ways to identify species. Is it as large as a robin or small like a sparrow? Is its breast plain, spotted or streaked? Does it have the needle bill of an insect-eating warbler or the stout seed-cracking bill of a finch? Is its tail long or short, square tipped or forked? Confidently, she meets the visitors at the front gate. Then they start the walk, a bird flashes by and an instant cry goes up, "Eastern kingbird!" All Jane sees, turning too late in the direction of the shout, is a disappearing flutter of wings. She returns to the book that night and makes it her regular bedtime reading, drilling each picture and accompanying description into her head.

The binoculars and book also go along on the morning patrols, although her main purpose on these outings is still to scout for trespassers. She picks up some beer cans and fast food litter at the south end of the estate where it abuts the beach and learns during her progress report to Bella that although there is no fence, there are supposed to be posted signs that read PRIVATE PROPERTY–NO TRESPASSING. The signs have apparently fallen down or been stolen years ago with no one at Deerfield the wiser. Bella orders new ones for Jane to erect as near the property line as she can gauge. The patrols double as an opportunity to search out safe paths for the Sunday visitors, and one morning Jane retraces her circumnavigation of the pond. The spring rains have made it even muddier than in March, but on the far side is a rock outcropping where a few intrepid birders might huddle to watch any feathered activity from a concealed vantage point. Jane is crouched there when a loud crashing startles the brush behind her, and whirling, she loses her balance and plunks one foot in the water. For a half second her heart pounds in suspense at the swish and sway of branches as the unseen animal bounds deeper into the woods. It's most likely a deer; they have been following deer trails, after all, and Hortense had mentioned that white-tailed deer occasionally wander into the neighborhoods near town. Jane nods to confirm the identification, not admitting that for an instant she imagined it might be a bear.

Along the shore road, she encounters joggers and dog walkers. Charlotte doesn't like either category of passersby, but it's a public road and as long as the joggers keep moving and the mutts are properly leashed there is nothing she can do about it. She does, however, issue a decree that no pets, leashed or otherwise, may be brought on the Sunday walks. Most of the dog walkers offer Jane a wave or a hello, casting an inquisitive glance toward the house as they do so. A few pause to ask if she lives at Deerfield. "I'm the caretaker, recently hired," she answers, to deflect any impression she's a family member or confidant of Miss Deerfield and Bella, in a position to divulge gossip. As it is, half the Sunday visitors so far are neither birders nor nature lovers but locals who have come to satisfy what appears to be a long-standing curiosity in town about the estate. Once they've tramped around the property, they don't return. Meanwhile, if spring is going to bring increased foot traffic on the road and eventually car traffic to the beach, it can't hurt to let word spread there is now a caretaker in residence to discourage unauthorized entries.

In the afternoons, Jane continues improvements to the cottage. Some days she glimpses Charlotte or Bella driving out, each in her own car. No limousine, no chauffeur. It seems a comedown from the mansion's glory days but reassuring to discover the two women aren't the recluses she feared. One afternoon Bella approaches with a proposition from Charlotte. Jane seems to enjoy outdoor work; would she care to take on gardening chores around the main house as well? They could pay her an extra fifty dollars a week, and she may charge any additional tools or supplies she requires to Miss Deerfield's account at the hardware store. Jane pauses to survey the expanse of unkempt lawns, hedges, shrubbery and flowerbeds. The money is a joke, and they both know it. Jane accepts.

In the evenings, she studies the bird book and on her laptop researches ornithology, open space preservation, pond ecology and landscaping. On the cottage's small TV she watches nature and gardening programs. She doesn't love this job, birds or nature. She doesn't care about the decrees of Charlotte Deerfield to keep people and dogs out, or the clamors of the land trust, art association and townspeople to be let in. It isn't even, any longer, a question of distraction, of trying to lull the past to sleep so she can tiptoe by it and escape back into the sky. After that afternoon at the airport, she knows she can never dodge or forget the accident. She couldn't shake it there in California with her fellow pilots' support, or in hour after hour in the psychologist's office. She couldn't put it behind her when, fleeing east, she stopped at those homey little airports in Arizona, Texas, Arkansas, Virginia, and tried to walk out on the field, telling herself each time that if she could just break the spell, the paralysis, she could turn her pickup around and reclaim her life. From Deerfield, she could still press on northeastward; there are more airports between here and Maine and into Canada, if need be. But there's no point. It doesn't matter where or how far she goes. She herself is the disaster, the wreck. To be caretaker at Deerfield is her life now, and whatever she does, Jane will master it and do it well.

And now she must pass a test. Bella informs her that this coming Sunday a delegation from the conservation do-gooders will join the walk.

"A few representatives from the art association and town council as well," Bella concedes. She and Charlotte have agreed the best tactic is to play down the event. Of course, the officials are welcome to come for a short stroll. "Let them chat among themselves," Bella advises Jane. "You probably won't have to say much, and if a specific question about birds or plants does arise, refer it to one of the experts in that open classroom format you mentioned. Also, we feel it would be more appropriate if, instead of calling yourself the caretaker, you used the term 'property manager.'"

"Fine," says Jane, keeping to herself the wry obser-vation that in the past week she has earned both a stunning pay raise and an impressive promotion. Let Charlotte and Bella play their games. When Jane goes down early to the front gate on Sunday morning, she can tell you that wrens cock their tails up, flycatchers hold theirs down, the white pine has five needles in a cluster, the red pine has two. The only guests at the gate so far, however, are Melanie and her father, waiting in their silver BMW.

"Melanie insisted on coming," says Peter Babcock, clearly not pleased. "I normally don't allow her anywhere without strict supervision."

"Where are Hortense and Roy?" asks Jane, surprised not to find her two regulars.

"Palm Sunday services," Babcock replies curtly.

"Oh." Jane, never raised in any religion or feeling the need of one, barely noticed the date on the calendar. Babcock's tone seems simultaneously annoyed at Hortense and Roy for remembering and at Jane for forgetting, although he's not at any service either. A square-jawed man with a stocky, boxer's build and thick salt-and-pepper hair, he gets out of the car and begins repeating the lecture he delivered the day of Melanie's first visit, describing in detail her disabilities and his stringent requirements that she be treated like any other child. Yet let his daughter so much as scrape her knee…Jane glances at Melanie's hopeful face. She is indeed a sweet girl, but her father's overprotectiveness is irritating, and perhaps today with the officials coming is not the best time to be babysitting.

"Well, it's understandable if you're not comfortable leaving Melanie here without Hortense or Roy," Jane agrees. "There will be other walks on future Sundays."

"No!" Melanie pops out of the car. No, this isn't fair! She wants to go birdwatching. She waits all week for this at school where her teacher Ms. Shaw is nice, but some of the kids are so mean, and she sits at her desk not remembering where yesterday's story about George Washington left off in her reader or why Canada is orange on the globe but the United States is green or why it matters how many thirds of an apple equals how many sixths of an apple. Can't you just buy enough apples for everybody? What matters is that Melanie lives for her Sunday morning excursions, and now with this wonderful new place to explore, she can't bear to miss it. She will throw a tantrum, if she has to.

"Daddy, please!"

She runs to Jane and clasps her hand, imploring both of them. She knows why her father is worried. Once upon a time, Melanie used to be a different girl. That girl was slender, dark-haired and very smart. During the week she lived in Manhattan with her father, an important lawyer, and she attended a private school. On weekends and vacations she came here to her mother's house for fun. There are pictures of her in the photograph album, riding horses and swimming at the country club pool where her mother waved to her from a chaise lounge while sipping iced tea. That girl had certificates on her bedroom wall for winning essay contests and horse show blue ribbons. Also, that girl had friends. There are pictures of them laughing, hugging. They had sleepovers.

Then Melanie remembers tumbling over and over, and when the tumbling ends, the photographs and the friends stop and her mother is gone. Melanie has to leave her private school—her father argues about it with the principal—and go to special education. After special ed, a tutor teaches her at their apartment in the city until her father gets home. One cold February day the tutor doesn't come. She's been hit by a cab that ran a red light and taken unconscious to the emergency room. But nobody knows this, and Melanie, bored, puts some cookies in her jacket pocket and goes out for a walk in the big park across the street. Several hours and several wandering miles later, a policeman on horseback finds her sitting alone in the winter dark on a bench beneath a streetlamp. She can tell him her name but not her phone number or address. She knew them yesterday, but they've slipped out of her head again. It's almost eleven o'clock when her father storms into the police station and sweeps her into his arms. If he's glad to see her, why does he hug her too hard, sound so mad?

He won't even listen when she tries to tell him about the bird that kept her company, although she can describe it perfectly. It was small and plump and comical. It had a black cap, gray back, a white chest with cinnamon color under its wings, and a black bib on its throat. It hopped and danced on the metal armrest of the park bench, cocking its head to peer at her with bright black eyes. It talked to her. It said *chick-a-dee-dee-dee* and sometimes just *dee-dee-dee*, and when Melanie sprinkled the cookie crumbs from her pocket into her hand, the bird jumped right onto her palm! Melanie wasn't wearing mittens, and the bird's feet tickled the way a sneeze does before you sneeze it. She wanted to take the bird home, but it flew away when the policeman came. After that, her father said the city was too dangerous because he couldn't watch her all the time, and now she lives here with

Mrs. Egan, the housekeeper, and her father commutes to see her on weekends. Even so, he doesn't let her go anywhere without her cell phone and ID necklace...that's it! Eagerly, Melanie pulls the necklace out from beneath her tee shirt to show him she'll be safe at Deerfield today, but her father and Jane have stopped talking because another car is approaching. A man and two women get out, and the man hails her father. They talk heartily, and to Melanie's joy, her father is letting her stay.

"I'm Jane Avery, the property manager," says Jane, invoking her new title as she shakes hands with the mayor and councilwomen. Two more cars pull up in quick succession, three representatives from the art association, four from the land trust, including a biologist and a pair of ornithologists. Perhaps because it is Palm Sunday, no other visitors appear...Jane draws a slow breath. Uh-oh, no friendly birders or science grad students, not even Burt, the history buff. She's going to be on her own. Or is she? She squeezes Melanie's hand and murmurs low in her ear. "We have some important visitors today, Melanie, so stay close and be my birding expert, okay?"

Melanie nods, awed by the seriousness of the charge, and Jane starts them off as usual across the field, then through the woods toward the pond. Day by day, spring has been creeping up on Deerfield; today, it's an explosion. Birds dart in and out of trees, songs compete from budding branches, squirrels chase each other in mad spirals up and down the trunks, and tiny white wildflowers unfold beside the path. It's spring. It's seduction. It's sex. This is what nature is all about, an orgy of blossoming, pollinating, courtship, mating. A Roman bacchanalia, spring break in Fort Lauderdale are nothing in comparison to this primal outburst of lust. The human visitors, too, are animated by it, although their reaction is not a conscious manifestation of sexual urges. The artists rhapsodize over the way the sunlight strikes the pond; the ornithologists, in subtle competition to claim the most sightings, practically preen each time they call off another species to be added to the day's list. The mayor and two councilwomen, after exchanging the necessary pleasantries with the rest of the group, confer aside in greedy territoriality as to the future of the estate. Jane presses her lips to conceal a smile. This is going to be easy after all, except perhaps for the biologist.

His name is Dr. Tim Hennessey, he's employed by the state Division of Fish and Wildlife, and he volunteers as a consultant with the land trust. He's the only member of the delegation who seems to recall that one of their main objectives in visiting today is to assess the qualifications of Miss Deerfield's new resident expert.

"Exactly what field is your degree in?" he asks Jane as they cross the footbridge into the second stretch of forest.

"Mechanical engineering."

"Do you have any experience in environmental management?"

"It's a hands-on position. I'm learning." Jane's tone is unapologetic. At first glance, she found him attractive, but Dr. Hennessey is a redhead, and there's a stubborn set to his mouth. Jane can be stubborn, too, and she's not about to back down with the excuse that this is a temporary position. It's not any longer, and the more she overhears the council representatives whispering about Deerfield's tourist potential, the more she begins to sympathize with Charlotte. They would happily bury her alive and have almost picked out the headstone for her grave.

"The spring migration is already underway," Hennessey persists. "You're going to be getting some advanced level birders here."

Jane lifts her eyebrows in the direction of the two ornithologists, arguing not so subtly now over possible variations in coloring of hybridized warblers. "They don't seem to require my assistance."

"Yes, but—"

"Towhee!" cries Melanie, pointing left. She's not sure what Jane and the redheaded man are arguing about, but sometimes at school when kids start to pick a fight you can stop them by changing the subject. Also, Jane did ask her to be an expert birder. "Towhee!" she repeats brightly, nudging Jane.

"Good eyes, Melanie!" says Jane, smiling, though she hasn't a clue what Melanie saw or heard.

"Geologists, too," Hennessey continues, not impressed. They've reached the first ridge, and he gives the stone a pat. "I imagine they'll find this formation fascinating."

"Puddingstone," says Jane. Let him quiz her. Hortense had mentioned the name of the rock the first time they explored the ridge, and since it's one of the main geographical features of the estate, she has already researched the geology. "Conglomerate rock formed by rock fragments or pebbles cemented together in a matrix of clay or silica," she recites to let him know she's on to his tactics. "Everyone please watch your footing." She smiles to the others, lending a hand up where needed. When she joins them at the top, a sound catches her ear. "Oh, Carolina wren," she says nonchalantly at the loud *tea-kettle, tea-kettle* call. That's the little bird Melanie pished out of the bush on her first visit, and Jane has heard it almost daily on her walks. She turns to the art association contingent. "Are any of your members wildlife painters in the style of Audubon or Alexander Wilson?" she asks, shamelessly name dropping. And that does it. The artists draw her into their conversation, and Dr. Hennessey is forced to back off.

They make their way to the end of the ridge, and for once everyone stops talking. The view is superb, the second ridge and state forest unrolling to the west, the beach and glittering ocean due south, to the east the inlet to the harbor and the sandy shoreline stretching beyond. The sun, growing warmer by the minute, spills out of the robin's-egg blue sky.

"What a vista!" sighs one of the artists.

"It would make a beautiful painting," Jane agrees, "especially with those seagulls flying by."

She gestures, and Melanie freezes. So do the two ornithologists, the president of the land trust and Dr. Hennessey. Jane said *seagulls*. There is no such bird as a seagull, not to a real birder. There are many species of gulls—greater black-backed gulls, herring gulls, ring-billed gulls, laughing gulls—but no single bird called a seagull. The word is like chalk screeching on a blackboard. The artists and the town councilors don't notice, they don't realize the enormity of Jane's mistake. But Melanie does. Worse, Jane has just said "seagull" to the artist again, and Melanie cringes as the ornithologists roll their eyes. Oh no, oh no! She was supposed to help Jane today, and now her friend is in trouble.

"Gulls! I love seagulls!" she cries. Sometimes when Melanie makes a mistake at school, Ms. Shaw, her nice teacher, makes it better by sharing the mistake, talking it away. If everyone joins in, it's not so bad. She turns and pulls the artist's hand. "I love gulls!"

"Oh, me, too," the woman agrees.

"It's not a seascape without seagulls," another of the artists laughs.

Then the mayor, her father's friend, chimes in with a story of how an aggressive seagull stole his son's lunch last summer at the beach, which diverts the ornithologists to pressing a case for more beaches to be preserved for the endangered piping plover. It's getting better, but Dr. Hennessey isn't convinced yet. Melanie has to get Jane to say it right.

"I love *gulls*," she says to Jane, as clearly as she can, and Jane pats her shoulder.

"Then of course we'll go see the gulls sometime, Melanie," she promises.

There. Dr. Hennessey's face grudgingly relents, and Melanie sighs in relief. Jane has used the right word and enough other people have used the wrong word to make it blend into the conversation. Plus, Melanie now has two important jobs on Sunday morning, to teach Jane about birds and, her original responsibility, to keep Roy away from other people when he's farting. She skips all the way back to the front gate.

"They look happy," Bella reports, lowering the binoculars.

"Good," says Charlotte. "Now maybe they'll go away and stay off my land."

Chapter 7

In May a blizzard of birds descends on the estate. So does a blizzard of birders. Jane, a little stunned, finds fifteen people at the front gate the first Sunday in May, twenty the next.

"It's warbler heaven!" rejoices Hortense. "The spring migration is at its peak."

Jane quickly consults her bird book. Wood warblers, it informs her, are brightly colored, active birds, usually smaller than sparrows. After wintering in warmer climes, they migrate north to breed. Their names alone evoke the rich variety of their plumage: cerulean warbler, black-throated green, chestnut-sided, bay-breasted, blue-winged. When you see them, poised for an instant amidst the new green leaves, their colors are so vibrant it seems as if they have been dipped in fresh paint. Warblers typically seek the sheltering cover of full-leafed trees, and they love old-growth forests. Deerfield is perfect for them. Birders know this, and come.

"Who are all these people?" Charlotte rages at Jane when, summoned by Bella, she comes to the studio to report.

"A mix," she replies, flipping open a pocket note-book. She has begun keeping her own notes on attendance, as well as a list of questions visitors have asked to which she doesn't yet have an answer. Hortense, Roy and Melanie are faithful, and some of the new birders are from their circle of acquaintances. Others have heard of Deerfield through the land trust or Internet links to birding websites. Usually, one or more will bring a spotting scope, which they're happy to share. Burt the librarian and Great American Novelist has come again, and when anyone asks a question about the history of the estate, he gives mini-lectures on the Native Americans who used the area as a summer fishing camp or the early colonists who cleared and farmed the land. The science grad students have never returned, but one week an amateur botanist comes wearing a miniature magnifying lens on a cord around her neck. Through it, they peer into the soul of wood anemones and buttercups, viewing details so exquisite, the petals seem to pulse with life. A few more of the visitors are local artists who, alerted by the delegates from the art association, are anxious to see the views at the pond and from the ridge. Finally, there continues to be a steady trickle of curiosity seekers.

"Snoops," Charlotte seethes, turning on Bella. "I told you we should never have agreed to open the property. I told you we'd be overrun."

"We needed the tax break," Bella retorts. "You think you can do nothing but paint all day, and you leave me, me alone, to figure out how the taxes and upkeep and utilities are to be paid."

"You've lived a fine life on my money, under my roof. Why shouldn't you earn your keep?"

Their voices grow vitriolic, little splashes of acid, Bella's bloodshot right eye growing redder in defiance. Jane stands back, wanting no part of this. She hasn't pried into the history of Charlotte and Bella, only surmised that it is long-term and braided of many fibers, twisting strands of servitude, friendship and contemptuous familiarity into a mutually binding rope. Watching them try to fray it is disturbing, like intruding on a marriage on a bad day.

"I'll be going," Jane says firmly.

"Find out who these people are and keep them off my land!" Charlotte yells after her.

That week Jane begins encountering trespassers on the property, and it doesn't take long to discover the breach.

The culprits drive down the shore road and park at the beach, which is still unattended by anyone in the entrance booth, and come onto Deerfield land from the south. Four of the six birdwatchers she confronts feign innocence—why, they must have walked right past those new PRIVATE PROPERTY signs without seeing them!—and acquiesce good-humoredly like children caught in a prank when Jane points the way out. The other two are obstinate.

"You don't understand," says the short, bald man, accompanied by a tall blond woman, both of them rather ludicrously garbed in camouflage. Jane has sighted them from the ridge and intercepted them before they can penetrate to the pond. "We've had reports of an orange-crowned warbler in this vicinity. Do you have any idea how rare that is?"

"No, *you* don't understand," she replies. "This is private property, and you are trespassing. You're welcome to come back on Sunday morning, eight o'clock, when the estate is open for two hours for guided," she stresses the word, "nature walks."

"This is science. We've come all the way from Hartford," the blond woman blusters. "You're interfering with a scientific pursuit."

"By what organization?" Jane demands, and when they hesitate in answering, she pulls her phone out of her knapsack. "This is private property, you are trespassing, and I'm phoning the police."

They splutter and mutter but turn and trudge off. Jane escorts them to the edge of the estate, watches them get into their car in the beach parking lot and drive away. On a quick thought, she uses her binoculars to get their license plate number and jots it down in her notebook along with the make and color of the car. The encounter leaves her angry, a little shaken and determined to be more vigilant. She had thought Charlotte Deerfield's rantings against trespassers to be at least greatly magnified, if not completely imaginary. The blatant attitude of the two invaders shifts her sympathy in

Charlotte's direction. She reports the incursions to the main house, and when Charlotte has calmed down after excoriating the violators, Jane embarks on what she hopes will be a productive talk.

"Miss Deerfield, I do agree with you there are real security concerns. If it had been necessary for me to phone the police, would they have responded? Have you discussed the problem of trespassing with them in the past?"

"Loudly and frequently," Charlotte declares.

"They'd come," says Bella. "Who do you think is the largest private contributor to their drug education programs? Nevertheless, I'll call to advise them of this latest incident and inform them we now have you as our resident property manager. That way they'll recognize your name should you need to summon them."

"Good," says Jane. "I've already added the police station number to my phone. What about security at the house?" She gestures around the studio, sunny and far more inviting today than it appeared during her interview in March, and notices a new row of self-portraits along one wall. There's no time, however, for more than a passing glance. "Do you have an alarm system? Are you sure it's in good working order?"

"You don't need to know how our alarm works," says Bella coolly.

"I didn't ask how it works, only if it's been tested lately to ensure it's reliable," Jane replies. "And do you have smoke detectors in the house? Fire extinguishers? If not, we should get some immediately for both the house and the cottage. I can install them."

Charlotte nods vigorously. "Excellent points, Miss Avery. See to it, Bella."

Bella bites back the urge to mimic. *See to it, Bella.* So that's where this discussion is heading. Charlotte and Jane, in cahoots, planning expensive refurbishments to the estate and Bella expected to juggle the books to pay for it. Do you notice how quickly Jane has inserted herself? Do you notice how, when speaking of fire extinguishers, she said *we* should get some, not you, but *we*, as if she is an equal in this establishment? Now Charlotte is dramatizing to Jane how they have indeed had thefts in the past, but always an inside job, nefarious servants, bungling by the local constabulary. As if Jane isn't also a servant...Wasn't it Charlotte who didn't want her invited to tea on those very grounds?

Inwardly, Bella huffs and puffs. If anyone were to tell her she's exhibiting signs of jealousy, she would hotly deny it. She is only safeguarding their interests, hers and Charlotte's, and now here is this young woman out of nowhere always one step ahead of her. Bella pauses and chides herself. She hasn't been feeling well lately, a physical unease she can't quite pinpoint, and it's distracting because despite her deformed and seemingly painfully twisted body, she has in fact enjoyed a lifetime of almost perfect health. She must get back to her investigations, uncover the fatal flaw in Jane's past.

"Another matter," says Jane. "With more visitors each Sunday and only a few narrow paths to follow, I am worried about people tripping over straggling roots and getting poked in the face or eyes by low-hanging branches. Also, the botanist who came last week said that a lot of the undergrowth on the property is invasive honeysuckle and Asiatic bittersweet that choke out the native plants. Should I do any clearing to eliminate them or widen the trails for easier access?"

"No!" Charlotte and Bella reply instantly, together. "It wouldn't be a wild, pristine landscape if we did that," adds Bella, smoothing the skirt of her dark gray dress. "The land trust doesn't want us to touch anything."

"Then I assume that rules out people wanting to pick the wildflowers or collect leaves or rocks?"

"No flower picking! No collecting!"

"Photographs? I'm only trying to clarify the rules," Jane adds, holding up her palms before Bella and Charlotte can shout at her again. They huddle a moment.

"Discourage it," say Bella more calmly now that she and Charlotte have a reunited front. "Especially no photographs of the house."

"Fine. You should also know that a couple of the artists who've come have hinted they'd like to spend an afternoon painting at the pond."

"What?" Charlotte shakes her head in disbelief. "My grandmother gives this town an art association, pays for a museum, we sponsor scholarships, lectures by visiting artists, but it's not enough, oh no, it's never enough. They want this house when I'm dead to use for classes, retreats, studio space. Now they can't even wait. They want to camp out by my pond and paint. Bella, stop them!"

Aha, who does Charlotte need now? Bella rubs her hands, then a gleam flashes in her clear eye. "We should let them come."

"What?"

"Let them come. You want some pictures in the summer exhibition? You want another one-woman show?"

Charlotte glances to the self-portraits along the wall, and her expression shifts to a crafty smile. She has finished five canvases, working backward from the present to age sixty-three, and in each one you can read the anguish of a once-lovely woman forced to grow old. Today's enlightened women can claim all they want that youth and physical beauty don't matter, but have you ever noticed that the more enlightenment a woman professes, the uglier she is as well? Tell the truth: If you could stay young and lithe and desirable forever, wouldn't you? Charlotte nods to herself in the paintings. She's ready to begin the next series in her "Retrospective in Retrospective" depicting the years of her third marriage to Morton Fischer. When the retrospective is complete, she will definitely want a show.

"Go on," she says to Bella. "What are you thinking? What do you have up your sleeve?"

"We invite the art association members to an afternoon of painting by the pond, a formal invitation—not engraved, too expensive—but fancy looking." Bella shapes the size of the card in the air. "Except we limit the acceptances to twenty spaces. We pick the oldest, feeblest members and set the date for late June or early July. The weather will be very, very *hot*."

Charlotte breaks into laughter and claps her hands. It's not a dry, cackling laugh but the pretty, lilting sound of a girl being entertained as she and Bella continue plotting the demise of elderly painters by sunstroke and dehydration. Fascinated, repelled, Jane can almost see the fraying rope that binds them repairing itself into a sturdy cord. Yet she won't leap to conclusions about their relationship, as that goat-faced psychologist in California did when he tried to twist her friendship with Jill, her flying partner, into a sexual liaison that wasn't there.

"Two pretty, single women, both in your early thirties, competing in what I assume is still a man's field," he mused. "You must have felt a special bond. You even look like sisters," he offered their own publicity photograph for her inspection, "and ponder the similarity of your names, Jane, Jill."

"Yes, we felt a special bond," Jane could only repeat in growing frustration, "but our names were coincidence, our looks were, too, and we *weren't* that kind of partners." She wonders what that psychologist would make of Charlotte and Bella. If she could put him alone in a room with these two women, they would eat him alive.

"About the birdwatchers," she interrupts to get the conversation back on topic. "May is a big month for them, all these migrating warblers flying through, and since I'm not the expert some of them may be expecting, I'd like to get a little extra instruction. There's a woman who comes regularly, a retired gym teacher named Hortense—"

"The tall woman with gray bangs," says Bella.

"Yes." Jane pauses. Hortense has never mentioned meeting Bella. "With your permission I'll ask her over one weekday to help me plan a route that will give people the best chance to see birds without letting them wander too far. If I have twenty or more walkers to keep track of, I don't want them straying off any more than you do."

Charlotte raises her eyebrows appreciatively. "Be nice to them on Sundays so they don't feel they have the right to come sneaking in the rest of the week," she says to Bella.

"Then the warblers leave, the birders go," Bella flicks them off with a wave of her hand, "and by late June, as we were saying, the weather can get very hot."

"Mosquitos," adds Charlotte. "Don't you imagine they'll be a problem this summer, especially down by the pond?"

"Swarms of them." Bella nods, her topknot bobbing.

"So with luck," Charlotte gloats, "we'll be rid of everyone by July!"

They chortle together, ignoring Jane. She has begun to look forward to the weekly walk and suspects that neither pesky insects nor sweltering heat will deter her small band of regulars from their ornithological pursuits. Nor does she necessarily want to deny the curiosity seekers a pleasant visit. Deerfield is a beautiful place, and it strikes her once again that neither Charlotte nor Bella ever stroll about the estate, although in Bella's case the physical challenge is probably a factor. Meanwhile, Jane's job will be to maintain a fair balance between the machinations of her employer and public access to the property.

"Right then," she says, preparing to leave. "No pets, no flower picking, minimum photography, and I'll keep a sharp watch for any more trespassers."

"You should carry a gun," says Charlotte suddenly. "Do you have one?"

"No, she doesn't," states Bella, a known fact because she has already researched for any gun registrations in Jane's name, although that doesn't mean she couldn't possess one illegally.

"No," says Jane emphatically, both to second Bella's statement and in perplexity at the secretary's positive tone. What is going on here? She was just leaving...

"You need a gun." Charlotte strides briskly to a small table pushed against the studio wall and opens its single drawer. She turns around, pistol in hand.

Jane's jaw drops. Her voice squeaks. "Is that real? Is it loaded?"

"Of course, it's loaded. What good is an empty gun?" Charlotte waves the pistol, walks back to Jane and holds it out. "You take it. I have several around the house."

"No!" Jane backs a step, palms up in protest. Charlotte is offering her the weapon as blandly as if it were a candy bar. In the space of a minute, what had almost been the conclusion of a fairly sane, fairly productive discussion has dived into the realm of the bizarre. "Miss Deerfield, put the gun down."

"Don't worry. I'm an excellent shot, and I have permits for all my weapons. We'll arrange target practice for you, if you like." She aims at a lamp and squints.

"No!" Jane practically jumps. "Please, Miss Deerfield! Put it down!"

She motions with her hands, and Charlotte reluctantly lowers the weapon, disappointed but tolerant of Jane's apprehensions. Some people just don't understand the value of guns. She hands the pistol to Bella, who returns it to the drawer. Jane takes a deep breath to slow her hammering heart and considers what to say next. Charlotte, dressed today in a salmon-colored kimono, is looking at her as if nothing is wrong. Bella's expression is unfathomable. Sadness, amusement, embarrassment, resignation? The one emotion Jane doesn't read on the secretary's face is fear.

"Miss Deerfield," Jane says, "I won't be needing a gun. It's unlikely any of the trespassers I meet will be armed. Let's stick to our plan that I'll simply phone the police if I need them."

"Very well, suit yourself. We are pleased with your work here, Miss Avery. Bella will show you out."

Bella beckons and with a final "Thank you" to Charlotte, Jane follows as the secretary clump-clumps down the staircase in her high heels. At the bottom of the stairs, Bella heaves open the front door and looks up at Jane, whose skin is still pale from the episode.

"Don't worry about the gun," says Bella. "She only uses it when she's come to hate her paintings. Then she lines up the canvases in the rose garden and shoots them full of holes." She studies Jane's face, a pretty face, elfin, blue eyes, blond hair. Smart, young, erect. Bella has spent a lifetime teaching herself not to envy. "Why are you still here?" she asks. "You should have left by now. Everyone else does."

"I have nowhere else to go," says Jane, at a loss to do anything but tell the truth.

Bella's hand reaches up, her twisted little body attempting to straighten, and awkwardly pats Jane's shoulder.

"Neither do I," she says.

Chapter 8

The walk with Hortense takes place that Thursday, and Jane finds herself enjoying every minute of it. In the past few weeks, the estate has unfurled its greenery, millions of leaves uncurling in simultaneous rapture to drink in rain and sun, and delicate wildflowers sprinkle pink, purple and blue underfoot. She gets a crash course on warblers, and between the cottage and the pond they locate several hot spots where the birds are most active and visible. Hortense devises a strategy for crowd control, enlisting the help of her birding friends. She and Jane will take the lead. Halfway along, they'll position Russ and Charlie, who own a café in town and yes, they are that kind of partners, or Jim and Lois, retired attorneys who sail up to New England from their Florida home each summer and live aboard their sailboat in the harbor. If Roy and Melanie bring up the rear, that will create a string of reliable people Jane can count on to keep the group well-informed and herded together. On their walk, Hortense helps her identify a Canada warbler—blue-gray back and a "necklace" of short black stripes on its bright yellow breast—a vividly striped black-and-white warbler, and a flame-throated blackburnian.

"Good sightings!" she says, as they head back. "You can add them to your list, Jane."

"Which raises another question," Jane replies. "What exactly is this 'list' the birders keep talking about?"

Hortense laughs. "Well, most birders keep a list of

some type, the most common being a life list of all the species they've seen. Some also keep a separate North American list for species seen here as opposed to those seen on trips to, say, Europe or South America."

"Does it matter where you see a bird?"

"To some people. They think it's more impressive to have five hundred birds on your North American list alone because it's so easy to pick up new species when you go abroad. You can also keep a state and county list, and the true fanatics keep annual lists for each location, trying to outdo themselves each year." She chuckles. "Once, I met a fellow who even kept a list of every bird he saw on TV."

"What kind of list do you keep?"

"Just a life list. I write mine down in a notebook at home, rather like a journal. I record the species, the date, where I saw it, who I was with, and notes about the bird's behavior or what made it a special sighting. Other people use a checklist from Audubon or one of the other birding organizations." Hortense slips a leaflet out of her book, a list of species arranged by their scientific order and family, each with a space awaiting a check mark. "It's handy for reference, but for me it doesn't capture the spirit of the sighting."

Jane pulls her notebook out of her knapsack. "Could I jot my list in this?"

"Of course, but I warn you, once you start listing, you're hooked."

They emerge from the woods into the field, and after a minute Jane asks, "What got you into birding, Hortense?"

"Love of nature, I guess, exercise, fresh air." Hortense pauses a moment, then confesses. "Companionship. That's really why I started, companionship. My children are grown and moved away, and about four years ago my husband was diagnosed with Alzheimer's. He's in a home now, doesn't recognize me."

"I'm so sorry." Jane lays a hand on the older woman's arm, but Hortense, as always, bucks herself up.

"Well, that's life, isn't it? I'm grateful for the good years we had together. Now my birding friends are my family. Do you know Roy is up to four hundred and ninety-seven birds on his life list? We're hoping this is the year he cracks five hundred, and when he does, we'll have a big celebration."

"Could we help him find three new warblers?"

"He probably has all of those that usually migrate through New England, but you never know what might pop in." Hortense lifts a hand and an admiring glance toward the canopy of trees behind them. "If I were a migrating bird, I'd certainly rank Deerfield high on my stopover itinerary."

"Tell me about Melanie," says Jane, as the cottage comes in sight. "I don't mean to pry, but sometimes she seems perfectly sharp, about birds especially, then other times she almost drifts away from us."

Hortense nods, pulling a burr off her sleeve. "I don't know much about the accident she was in, but Julie Shaw, the special ed teacher, is a friend of mine, and from what she's told me, Melanie suffered some kind of traumatic brain injury. In school, she's able to grasp facts and stories when she first hears them, but she has trouble retaining them. It's as if they evaporate from her memory, and she has to relearn them over and over again."

"How sad! That must be so hard for her. Is there any chance she'll get better?"

"Probably not. It's a miracle she came out of the wreckage alive."

"Yet she remembers birds, their plumage, their songs."

"The common ones, yes. I always write down the day's list for her on our way home, and seeing the same birds here every Sunday and during the week in her backyard seems to help it stick. It was Julie who noticed that Melanie liked to watch the birds outside the schoolroom window and asked me to take her into our group—under our wing, if you'll forgive the pun."

They reach the cottage, and Jane invites Hortense in, her second guest after Burt. Hortense accepts with pleasure and takes the short tour of the ground floor and loft bedroom. Would-be novelists aren't the only ones who nurture romantic visions of living in a gatekeeper's cottage. If Hortense lived here, she would bird, garden, read books, look forward to her grandchildren visiting and cavorting on the grass. Then she reminds herself that's what she does now; it just seems more idyllic here. Jane pours two glasses of orange juice and fills a plate with cookies, and they sit outside on a pair of sagging lawn chairs retrieved from the garage.

"I meant to tell you," she says, "it seems Miss Deerfield's secretary knows you."

"Knows me?" Hortense's eyebrows rise. "No, we've never met, although I did attend some of the town council meetings when the proposals about Deerfield becoming a nature preserve in exchange for tax relief were discussed. I raised some questions, too, come to think of it. But Miss Deerfield and her secretary never attended. They sent a lawyer to represent them. Do you suppose he reported back to them the identities of anyone who spoke up? It would be rather amusing at my age to be considered a subversive influence." She chuckles, then ventures a question. "So you're definitely staying, Jane? You said that first Sunday you were only temporary until Miss Deerfield hired a real expert, but I, we all, think you're doing a fine job."

"Thank you." Jane raises her glass to her lips, delaying an answer. Since that final paralysis at the airport, she has stopped believing *I'm only here a short while, till I'm flying again, till I'm myself.* She is never going to be herself again. Yet she hasn't fled to the other extreme either, she doesn't despair *This is it, I'm here forever, I can never leave.* She just thinks, every morning, *I am here today.* And it works, this jettisoning of past and future, blocking out everything but what is present and immediate. Hortense has confirmed she's doing a fine job. Jane lowers her glass. "Well, Miss Deerfield seems satisfied, and to my knowledge she isn't looking for a replacement. She even gave me a slight raise and a new title. I'm no longer merely the caretaker, I'm the property manager."

"Bravo!" Hortense laughs and hoists her orange juice in a toast, and Jane smiles in reply. So far, she has volunteered little personal information even to her regulars, and perhaps it's Yankee reticence that they haven't asked her more. But it wasn't just politeness that compelled her to invite Hortense to stay for refreshments, was it? Jane looks at the plate of cookies, acknowledges that in addition to juice, she bought several varieties of soda and a sampler of herbal teas to be sure to have on hand something Hortense would care to drink.

I like them, I want friends here, she confesses, and this is how you start to become friends with people. Bit by bit, you tell them about yourself, your history, your aspirations, your private thoughts. Didn't Burt share with her his hopes for his novel? Hasn't Hortense, despite her seemingly active life, just confided her loneliness at losing her husband to Alzheimer's? Jane would like to reimburse them, to talk easily and not hold back. Not hide, as she did that afternoon she had tea with Charlotte and Bella, because there's one painful sentence that keeps constricting her throat. *I was a pilot and I killed my best friend.* How is she ever going to say that? But there are safe things she can tell about herself. The college degree and engineering work she spoke of to Charlotte and Bella. Her father, retired Air Force, lives in Washington, DC. Her mother resides in Sarasota with her second husband. Her sister Susan, eight years older, married an Australian businessman, and they have two kids in Adelaide. Maybe that's the way to do it, stick to the good news, let it eke out in normal conversations like this. Because it wasn't just politeness, was it, that made Hortense accept her invitation in return. Jane begins to tell about her family, and before you know it, a pocket album of grandchildren photos comes out of Hortense's purse.

"I forgot to ask," says Jane, as their morning ends and

they stroll to the gate, "how many birds do you have on your life list?"

"Only two fifty but I'm in no hurry." Hortense shrugs amiably. "If I don't see a new species today, it just means I have something to look forward to tomorrow."

The next Sunday goes brilliantly.

"Hello, I'm Jane Avery, the property manager," Jane greets the twenty-two people at the front gate. "Welcome to Deerfield. We're pleased you could join us for this morning's stroll. Since this is a nature preserve, we do ask that you not pick any flowers or leaves or do any rock collecting and that you respect the property by not smoking or littering. For those of you interested in birding, we have some experts on hand today. Let me introduce Hortense, Roy, Melanie, Russ, Charlie, Jim and Lois."

The birders each raise their hand as Jane calls out their name, then she invites the first-time visitors to introduce themselves and say where they're from, data she will later enter into her log. Then she and Hortense lead the group on the timed route, taking a long look at each hot spot and notching up a double bonus at the pond: a great blue heron wading unconcernedly at the far edge and a sudden loud *skyow!* as a green heron flies in for a landing. Promptly at ten Jane has them back at the gate, Roy and Melanie, holding hands, bringing up the rear. She closes with a tip garnered from a PBS nature program, advising everyone to check over their clothes to ensure they haven't picked up any ticks that can carry Lyme disease. They thank her for the tour, and some promise enthusiastically they'll return. The next two Sundays go equally well, even when Dr. Tim Hennessey shows up unannounced on one of them.

"It seems quite well managed," he admits. "I may have been wrong that Deerfield required a scientific expert."

"Thank you," says Jane, since that seems the closest to a compliment she's going to get. The welcoming atmosphere on Sundays has also apparently obviated any need for people to sneak in mid-week; she has encountered no more trespassers on her patrols.

Most unlikely of all, she's actually enjoying her role and her growing knowledge. She adds a wildflower identification guide to her knapsack, bug spray to ward off the mosquitos that true to Charlotte's prediction are beginning to pester them. As May glides into June and the temperature heats up, the number of visitors does decline slightly to a steady twelve to fifteen. After the walks, her regulars linger to chat. Hortense announces that two of her grandchildren are coming to visit, Russ and Charlie have perfected a new carob-banana muffin for their café, Jane offers that her sister in Australia emailed to say she's expecting again. The news gets folded into the conversation, but it's as if a small weight has lifted and not only from Jane. It becomes okay for the others to ask her personal questions. How did she like living in California? What kind of engineering projects did she do there? She gives brief, friendly answers, recognizing with a tiny stab of pleasure that they now look forward not only to seeing the birds but to seeing her.

Then Raven comes.

Raven—what a name! Yet it suits her completely. She's an inch or two above Jane's height, but where Jane is slender, blond, boyish, Raven is lusty, busty, flashing dark eyes, a tumble of brunette hair. Her face is vivacious rather than beautiful, she flings out her hands and arms in exaggerated motions, and she has a bold laugh and an audacious smile. Somehow it comes as no surprise when Raven announces to the group, as they make their introductions at the front gate, that she is an actress.

"In fact," she purrs, "I'm Maggie the Cat on a Hot Tin Roof at the playhouse. Come see it. I'm magnificent!" She strikes a feline pose, drawing a laugh from everyone except Jane.

"Great," says Jane, smiling. Great, now she has a drama queen on her hands. "What brings you to our walk?"

"My therapist thought it would be a good idea,"

Raven replies blithely. "Get in touch with nature, stop hanging around with neurotic actors, you know." She laughs.

"Great," repeats Jane, pointedly refraining from commenting on Raven's attire, a tight red tank top revealing ample cleavage, a flowery, tiered skirt that swishes around her calves, flimsy white sandals. Who wears clothes like that on a nature hike? Even the first-timers they've had the past few weeks had the common sense to wear jeans and sturdy athletic shoes. Fortunately, it's a small group today, only five newcomers total, so Jane imagines controlling them should be easy enough with the help of her regulars.

She's wrong. No one controls Raven. Oh, Raven stays in line, keeps her voice seductively low, gasps admiringly when Jim and Lois point out to her a catbird giving its mewing call. Anyone can identify a catbird, for heaven's sake. Moreover, she hasn't thought to bring binoculars, and before you know it, two of the outsiders, both young men, are falling all over each other to loan her theirs. She laughs as they show her how to focus, gets dizzy as she tries to zoom in on a darting bird. Even Roy leaves off his determined search for his four hundred ninety-eighth species to assist her with a wise word.

"Look for the bird with your eyes first," he advises, motioning her to lower the binoculars. "Then when it settles—see on that branch there?—use the binoculars to study it."

Raven follows his advice, and in a few seconds comes a squeal of delight. "I found it! What a cute little thing! It's gray with orange sides and a peak on its head. What is it?"

"Tufted titmouse," says Melanie, opening her book so that when the bird flies away and Raven looks down, there is the picture to confirm it.

"You're smart!" says Raven, and Melanie beams. As they head on to the pond, one of the young men asks about the playhouse and how Raven came to act there, and she tells them breathlessly about the audition, the tough competition, then getting the thrilling call. "Of course, it meant I had to leave New York, but I've always wanted to play Maggie. What a character! She's to die for!"

"You should be in Hollywood," the young man insists.

"I have been. I was this close," Raven squeezes her thumb and forefinger until they're a hair's width apart, "to getting a movie with Julia Roberts. Do you have any idea how depressing that is? That's when my therapist said I should get out of California for a while." Raven sounds anything but depressed. She tells the tale as if it were an action-adventure flick, herself the heroine making the narrowest of escapes, and eyes widen around her. "Oh look, a deer!" she cries. They have emerged from the woods onto the bank of the pond, and everyone is so enthralled listening to her that they've forgotten to look for birds, let alone any other creatures. Now they hush at the sight of a beautiful brown doe, alertly watching them from the other side of the footbridge. It's the first time they have actually spotted a deer on one of their walks, and Melanie, who loves soft things, imagines how perfect it would be to put her arms around the deer's neck and gently hug her. Then someone's shoe snaps a twig, and the doe bounds away into the forest with a flash of white tail.

"Wow!" says Raven. "That was so cool."

They get back to birding. Goldfinch, phoebe, a flock of cedar waxwings. Both a downy and a red-bellied woodpecker. An eastern kingbird. Two warblers at a hot spot, a magnolia and a blackpoll. A white-eyed vireo that Lois identifies by its inflected call, *check the birrrd out!* Jane doubts she'll ever get to the level of identifying many birds by their vocalizations. For one thing, they don't stick to a single sound. The repertoire of an ordinary cardinal, according to her book, includes a metallic *chink*, an ascending *cheer, cheer*, a siren-like *wheep-wheep-wheep-wheep*, and a two-note *purdy, purdy*. Toss those notes into the exuberant sexual symphony of spring breeding, add the confusion of a mockingbird mimicking other species' calls, and how can anyone tell which is which? As they loop back through the woods, Jane relies on eyesight in hopes of catching an unusual bird.

"Oh, look," Raven points a fire-engine red fingernail across the field, "somebody's lost their pet parrot."

"Oh my gosh, a monk parakeet!" Hortense exclaims, as heads and binoculars swivel. They've been so fixated on finding warblers in the trees, they hadn't yet turned their gaze to the hedgerow where the exotic, foot-high lime-green creature is perched.

"Well, I'll be a horse's—" Roy stops himself. There are ladies present.

"What is it?" Raven asks.

"A monk parakeet," Hortense repeats, opening her book, and the group clusters around the illustration. "They're native to South America, but back in the nineteen-sixties they were being imported to the United States as pets and batches of them either escaped or were let loose. They established colonies in Florida and Texas and along the southern New England coast. Roy and I have seen them on day trips, but it's a surprise to have one show up here."

Roy's gaze has turned to one of longing. "If only I could count it."

"We're going to count it," says Jim, admiring the bird, and Lois nods agreement.

"Russ and I counted them when we saw them down by Bridgeport last year," Charlie affirms.

"Count what?" implores Raven. "Will someone please tell me what's going on?"

"Most birders keep a life list of the species they've seen," Jane informs her. "Once you see a new bird, you write it down."

"Okay, so if you've seen this bird before, why didn't you write it down then?" Raven demands.

Roy sighs. "Because it's originally an escapee, not a native wild bird, so the purists say it doesn't count."

"But it's wild now," Raven counters.

Roy nods.

"And not only is it wild by nature, it's wild by choice. Somebody tried to cage it, and it flew away to freedom." Raven flings out her arms. "It's like going into a zoo and opening all the cage doors and crying to the animals, 'Run away! Be free!'" Her glance gleams on the parakeet. "This is even better. It's a self-liberated bird!"

Melanie wants to shout, Hooray! Hooray! How she would love to free the animals in the zoo! She's going to count the parakeet. She has never seen one before, and when she writes it down she'll have a hundred and eleven birds on her list, which she keeps in a pink diary. It's her most treasured possession, and she tucks it safe in her dresser drawer because the one time she took it to school to show Ms. Shaw, the mean kids grabbed it away—nyah, nyah, try to get it back!—and she cried, snatching frantically, and they got dirty fingerprints on it. Like Hortense, Melanie writes special notes about her birds. *The robin was eating a worm. The house finch pooped on a leaf.* When she writes about the monk parakeet she will say, although she's not sure how to spell it, *A self-liberated bird.*

"You know, Roy," says Hortense, "it's been a good thirty-five years since the first birds escaped, and they do breed in the wild. It's quite possible this is a first-generation wild-born bird."

Roy hesitates, and even the newcomers, who only suspect the significance of the moment, join in the hush. Roy's list is sacred, a matter of honor. He has never, ever counted a bird he wasn't one hundred percent sure of or that wouldn't hold up to the scrutiny of his peers. He has stood all morning in pelting rain waiting for gannets to be blown in to shore by a storm. He tracked a veery through the under-brush on his hands and knees for an hour until he not only heard but saw the elusive bird. If tomorrow he reported the arrival of a passenger pigeon at his backyard feeder, his friends would rejoice at the miraculous reappearance of the extinct bird. Now here is the monk parakeet, sitting in plain view, as if it, too, is waiting for him to decide.

"Four hundred ninety-eight," says Roy softly, and around him a cheer goes up. Melanie hugs him, Hortense squeezes his hand, Russ and Charlie clap him on the back. Jane smiles, and Roy grins at everyone. Jimmy Stewart would approve.

"Good eyes, young lady," he congratulates Raven, "good eyes!"

"My pleasure," says Raven, sweeping him a curtsy.

The monk parakeet completes its inspection of the humans and flies away, and the birders troop to the front gate. As they begin to depart, the two young men ask if Raven needs a ride back to town.

"I have my car, thanks, but you come see my play." She turns to Jane. "I must say that when my therapist said go on a nature walk, I thought 'Right, I'll be hanging out with a bunch of cuckoos,' and you guys really are. But you have to be crazy to be an actress, and you were terrific to be so friendly and include me." Her voice aims for lightness, a breezy note. "Okay if I come again sometime?"

"Absolutely! You are a sharp-eyed young lady and an asset to our group," Roy proclaims.

"Please come," begs Melanie.

"Okay, see you soon!" Raven hops in her car and waves goodbye.

"My goodness," chuckles Hortense, as everyone else leaves, "she is flamboyant, isn't she?"

"That's an understatement," replies Jane, thinking she would prefer if Raven didn't show up again.

"Don't worry." Hortense reads the unspoken thought. "She'll either fit in or drop out. Besides, she's right."

"About what?"

"That we're cuckoo."

"We're *not* cuckoo."

"We'll all be here next Sunday, looking for that next bird to add to our life list. Won't you?" Hortense lifts a querying eyebrow.

"Yes," Jane admits.

"Cuckoo," says Hortense.

Chapter 9

On the last Saturday in June, eighteen artists gather at the front gate of Deerfield lugging easels, canvases, sketchpads, brushes and paints. It is Bella who greets them. She wears a dark green dress and the inevitable high heels, and she picks a spot to stand that offers an extra foot of elevation, so her height is more comparable to those gathered before her, including Jane.

"Welcome, everyone, welcome," she says. The weather is perfect for their plan, not only hot but so muggy that the saturated air falls on them like a damp wool blanket. Already she observes a sheen of perspiration on foreheads and cheeks, telltale circles of armpit sweat. Moreover, Jane has reported the presence of hordes of voracious mosquitos by the pond. "It does feel a bit like we're in the Everglades, doesn't it?" Bella sympathizes and gets an instant murmur of assent. Idiots! It's summer. It's supposed to be hot. What did they expect?

"We did think about postponing our little event to next weekend," she continues, "but who knows what the weather might be then? So it seemed best just to go ahead and let you decide whether to come. It's not too long a hike to the pond, is it, Miss Avery?" Bella turns to her, and Jane nods. "This is Jane Avery, our property manager. She'll lead you on the trail through the woods. I hope you all have appropriate footwear and brought hats and sunscreen as we suggested?" Again, there is a general hum of agreement, although naturally there are four or five who shrug it off because they're the kind of people who never believe the rules apply to them.

"Miss Avery has extra sunscreen and insect repellant if anyone needs it," Bella adds, proving she and Charlotte have spared no thought to make this a safe, enjoyable outing. "We have also placed ice chests at the pond containing juice and bottled water, sandwiches, cookies and fruit. We had hoped to be a little more elegant, cheese, wine, pâté, but in this heat we naturally have to be concerned about food spoilage, and the health experts do warn that alcohol consumption can be dangerous in such temperature conditions. So please drink plenty of water and take advantage of the folding chairs Miss Avery has carted to the pond. She really deserves a round of applause for trekking back and forth numerous times and doing so much to make you comfortable on this sultry afternoon."

The artists clap, and Bella wraps up her presentation. "The painting session is scheduled from noon to five to give you plenty of time, but you mustn't feel obligated to stay the entire five hours. If you feel at all tired, simply let Miss Avery know, and she will escort you out. Don't overdo it, because it's a bit of an uphill slope on the return and you will have your belongings to carry. Now off you go to create some wonderful paintings and sketches to thrill us at the art association."

Cheerily, Bella waves them off. It's not really inhospitality on her part that puts her in this position. During Charlotte's three marriages, in what Bella considers the good old days, they had marvelous parties and entertainments at Deerfield and at their residences in New York, and Bella excelled in organizing these affairs. Caterers, musicians, florists—oh, she made them jump. She orchestrated the guest lists, the table seatings. She designed the invitations, sent printers scurrying. Many of the events were crucial to maintaining the position of Charlotte and her husbands in their ring of society, receptions for visiting artists, cosponsoring charity balls for the nonprofits on whose boards Charlotte and the husbands served. But the good old days are gone, and it's not nearly as much fun planning entertainments when you're in reduced circumstances. And where they once hobnobbed with curators from the Metropolitan Museum of Art and conductors from the New York Philharmonic, they are now stuck with these provincial dabblers.

Bella sighs and clumps back to the house, her spirits rising in anticipation of a pleasant lunch with Charlotte in the mansion's one homey room, a cozy dining nook. The sandwiches, fruit and cookies awaiting their artist guests were ordered from the gourmet market and shouldn't displease anyone. Bella kept the pâté, cheese and chilled wine for Charlotte and herself, and they celebrate the afternoon's auspicious beginning with a toast. They had been obliged, on second thought, to modify their original group profile of twenty aging painters with heart problems and arthritic hips; having artists drop dead all over the property might be viewed suspiciously. More ingenuity was required, and they rose to the challenge. Bella began by contacting the director of the art association to make their generous offer. The director and trustees, highly gratified and burnishing visions of Deerfield coming eventually to the art association by bequest of Charlotte's will, readily concurred that it would be wise for this occasion to limit the number of participants. Bella sent out the announcements; a total of forty-seven eager replies was received. Then the real creativity began.

First, they chose four of the oldest and most feeble artists, two of whom phoned this morning to cancel, intimidated by the heat. So sorry, Bella consoled them. Another time perhaps.

Second, they chose a smattering of the worst painters. Whether they stick it out for five hours or not, the results will be so dismal no one else will think the property worth visiting.

Third, they included two sourpusses, disliked by the

entire membership, grouchy company even on the best occasion.

Fourth, they picked two very snooty women, the ones who insist on wearing gold bracelets, crisp blouses and tailored pants while they paint, the kind of women who can't enjoy themselves unless their hair and makeup are absolutely perfect. One of them was already patting at her hair in frustration at the gate, agitated by the effects of the humidity.

Fifth, an inspiration by Charlotte, they chose two quite excellent painters who also happen to be lushes, then made sure the invitation stated that refreshments would be served. It's well accepted that most art association events and gallery shows in town will serve wine. "You'd have to be drunk to think some of it was art otherwise," Bella once snorted. When she was forced to confess it would be water and juice today instead of alcohol, she observed how far the faces of the two lushes fell. She and Charlotte have another giggle over this as Charlotte replenishes their goblets with a delightful chardonnay.

Finally, they reserved five spots for decent artists/nice people, who may even survive this heat and produce passable art. Being honest, this group will also make it clear that no matter what any of the others say, Miss Deerfield went out of her way to accommodate her guests.

Everyone at the art association, meanwhile, assumes the slots were filled on a first-come basis.

"It's almost as if we've created a painting down there at the pond," observes Charlotte, "our own *Sunday Afternoon on the Island of La Grande Jatte*. And hasn't our property manager has been helpful in staging this, hauling those ice chests and chairs."

"She had help," Bella quickly reminds her. "When the market delivered the food this morning, I paid the driver extra to assist her."

"Nevertheless, I think we should give her a tip."

"No, she'll come to expect it. It sets a bad precedent."

"She fixed the lawn mower, too."

"That's nothing special. She's an engineer."

They had taken turns with the binoculars observing the latter feat. One of Jane's regular duties, since adding gardening around the mansion to her job description, has been to mow the expansive front lawn. When the old riding mower sputtered to a stop, she procured tools from the garage and spent a grease-stained hour manipulating it back to life.

"I bet it was a man," says Charlotte suddenly.

"What are you talking about?" Bella responds crossly. She isn't feeling quite well again. The rich food? A little too much wine?

"It was a man that drove her out of California or wherever it is she's from. An affair. He broke her heart. Ah, he was married." Satisfied with her deduction, Charlotte helps herself to more pâté.

"No." For a minute, Bella sulks at this easy answer. She prides herself on being able to find out about people without their knowing it, but she has had no luck so far and no time lately to pursue her investigation of Jane. The idea that it could be anything as simple as a broken heart, which would not show up on the Internet, defeats her.

Charlotte shrugs and pours herself another glass of wine. She doesn't care who Jane is or what she's done, not when her retrospective upstairs is going so well. Magnificent, really. The inspiration for the next series depicting her marriage to Morton Fischer came almost immediately when she recalled his reaction the morning she walked in to breakfast in their Park Avenue apartment and announced she was initiating a divorce.

"Oh," he said, looking up from the *Wall Street Journal*, "do you mind if we hold off liquidating some of the stocks until the market recovers?"

And there it was, the flash, the vision that makes this next series particularly brilliant in conception. A cold, emotionless being, Morton was, and he nearly turned her into an icicle as well. So for her self-portrait at age sixty-two, the last year of the marriage, she has painted a beautiful woman in a crimson ball gown imprisoned in a block of jagged bluish ice. A rim of water is accumulating around the base of the ice; some inner fire, burning to emerge, is causing it to melt. At age fifty-nine, the ice is so hard frozen the woman looks like a glacial mummy in an iceberg. At fifty-six, the canvas she's doing now, the ice is clearer and only half as thick, and you can see embedded in it the accoutrements of her life: ballet and symphony tickets, a winding staff of musical notes. At fifty, the ice will be but a glaze that drapes her from head to foot like a glamorous opera cape, its weight not yet felt. At forty-five, the age she married Morton, all the viewer will see is the beginning of a frost on her shoulders, glittering like diamond dust. Five portraits in total, telling the story of her own personal Ice Age.

Bella has left off grumbling about Jane, and for a minute they go on eating in quiet. Despite the heat outdoors, it's not uncomfortable in the house. The stone walls keep it cool inside, and the dining nook is partially shaded by a willow tree that allows dappling patterns of sunlight to play across the room. A sense of companionship steals into the air.

"Bella," says Charlotte, "would you like to go to Italy this fall?"

They stop eating, probe each other with their eyes, doing their best to let no emotion show. Every few years they ask themselves this question, bring it out to examine and see if it's still alive, although the years between questions have gradually grown longer.

"To Capri?" asks Bella cautiously.

"No, I don't think so. I don't suppose there's much left of the villa anyway. Rome would be enough. We could see great art in Rome."

"We could see great art in Paris."

"Yes, but in Rome you could see the Pope. Maybe we could get you a private audience. We could go in October, now that we have a caretaker to look after the place…"

Charlotte's voice trails. Bella isn't responding. Sometimes they're angry at each other over the past, and sometimes they're sad about it. This time, it's sadness. They have
been to Paris, London, Athens, Madrid, Amsterdam. They
both know it has to be Italy or nothing, because Italy is where
it began.

"Let's think about it," advises Bella, and their faces
clear. They might do it this year, who knows? They might go
and find they can both be forgiven. Bella rises, pressing her
hand to her abdomen as a pain catches her off guard. "I don't
feel well," she murmurs.

"It's the heat. Go lie down," Charlotte urges. "I'll
clear the table." She stands and begins stacking dishes to take
to the kitchen sink where Bella can attend to them later. As
her secretary clumps off, Charlotte calls after her in a joking
voice, "I'll keep watch in the studio as our bedraggled
visitors come trailing back from La Grand Jatte."

Which, although it's only one-thirty, is exactly what's
beginning to happen.

"This is too much! We're being eaten alive!" One of
the snooty women throws down her brush, swatting at the
hordes of mosquitos that are tormenting the artists. Her hair
is in an abominable frizz. "If Charlotte was going to invite
us, she should at least have provided a tent."

"This is nature painting," one of the decent
artists/nice people gently points out. "Why don't you try
some of the insect repellant? It seems to work."

"I'm not getting any of that sticky stuff on my
clothes, and I'm certainly not going to the theater tonight
covered in insect bites." The woman packs her supplies and
starts to huff off.

"I'll show you the way," says Jane, holding out her
hand in an offer to help carry, and the woman thrusts the
entire lot into her arms. The other artists roll their eyes, yet
by the time Jane returns from this escort duty, the two oldest
painters are also ready to pack it in.

"We're so sorry," they apologize. "It was very kind of

Miss Deerfield to host us, but in this heat we old folks just don't have the stamina we used to. You don't have to show us out. We can find the path."

"No, I'll take you. It's no trouble," Jane answers, determined there will be no lost senior citizens or casualties from heatstroke on her watch.

"You know," another of the decent artists/nice people speaks up, drawing everyone's attention, "it's unfortunate about the weather today, which is why we need to be considerate and not put Miss Avery to endless trips back and forth. If anyone else needs to leave now, they should, and after that we could do two more groups, one at three-thirty and one at five. Is that all right with you, Miss Avery?"

"Yes, thanks, and please call me Jane." She acknowledges the plan with a grateful nod to the speaker, a handsome, heavyset woman.

"And anyone who can, carry a folding chair out with you," the woman adds.

The two lushes, having already pawed through the ice chests and verified they do indeed contain only water and juice, opt to join the current exodus, as does one of the sourpusses. At three-thirty, the other sourpuss and three of the bad painters depart. The remaining eight stick it out till the end, and that last hour and a half turns quite pleasant. A breeze picks up, the humidity begins to dissipate, the mosquitos recede into the woods. A great egret lands in the trees on the far side of the pond, and several of the painters abandon their palettes and flock around Jane as she offers the binoculars from her knapsack. She takes a lingering look herself; watching the stately white bird crook its long neck and rustle its showy breast feathers is a study in nature's own artistry. When she lowers the binoculars, some of the artists are already incorporating the egret into their paintings.

"Tell me," she says, a little surprised at her impertinence, "is Charlotte Deerfield considered a talented artist?"

The reactions range from muffled snorts to tentative nods to shoulder shrugs. The heavyset woman who suggested the exit strategy gives a measured sigh, and the others defer to her to answer.

"Charlotte definitely has had training none of us can match, in New York, in Europe, and she can travel to study art wherever she pleases. Her grandmother was an accomplished portraitist, and her mother—"

"A beautiful lady! You should see the portrait of her in our museum!" several voices interrupt, although none of those present are old enough to have known Clarisse Deerfield personally.

"As for Charlotte," the first woman resumes, "maybe the question for her, for any of us, isn't whether she's a good, bad or mediocre artist, but whether she *is* an artist."

Heads bob, exchanging glances.

"It's something we discuss a lot," says a long-haired man.

"Hey, we know some of us have more talent and technique than others," one of the bad painters admits.

"We don't kid ourselves, even the best of us, that our pictures are ever going hang in the Louvre."

"But we try to improve, we try to learn. Don't you feel there's tremendous satisfaction in the process itself?"

What makes great art? They're off and debating. Technique, subject matter, strokes of the brush and strokes of luck, being in the right place with the right concept at the right time. If it's a portrait, you want to feel it's more than just someone's picture, you want it to communicate something vital about who that person was, you want to see their soul. You want to interact with the art, be it a canvas or sculpture or photograph, a watercolor landscape or a gritty black-and-white print. You want to be moved to admiration or understanding or tears. But what about that guy in Boston who did a sculpture of four blue metal cubes, exactly four foot square on each side, placed exactly four feet apart? The critics raved, even knowing that to get the cubes exact, the artist didn't cut them himself but had the work done by a metal shop. And some people are moved by velvet Elvises.

They groan and laugh.

"It's just that we can't *not* paint," the long-haired man explains to Jane, "because it takes what we feel here," he motions with both hands, as if coaxing meaning from his chest, "and brings it out."

"But what about Miss Deerfield?" Jane persists. "What did you mean, *is* she an artist?"

Glances run again around the group, then settle on the heavyset woman as spokesperson. She taps a finger to her lips as if cautioning her words to be truthful before they come out.

"Please don't think we're mean-spirited or ungrateful," she says finally. "We know we wouldn't be here today or even have an art association without the Deerfield family. On the other hand, Miss Deerfield doesn't hesitate to wield her influence to further her art at the expense of others, and you can understand that would cause some resentment. But I guess what bothers us most is that art is a sporadic thing for her. There would be years she was off in New York, on the social circuit, not caring what happened at the art association and not painting anything herself."

"Leaving us much better off," the long-haired man mutters, and around him heads nod.

"Then she would come back," the woman continues. "She'd *decide* to be an artist again, usually by copying someone else's style. I think great art involves courage. You take risks, you reach out to make that connection with the viewer we were talking about. Whereas Miss Deerfield's paintings, even though they're technically proficient, don't seem to be trying to speak to anyone but herself. They're just selfish somehow. Excuse me, I've probably said too much."

"No, it's all right." Jane waves a reassuring hand, bends to help one of the older artists collect her belongings. "I'm new here, and I have a lot to learn, including about art. I hope you can come again."

She leads the painters to the front gate, where they depart with effusive thanks. Then she makes a last trip to the pond to collect the empty ice chests. It's been a long after-noon, and her clothes are soaked with sweat, her damp hair plastered to her forehead and neck. Yet she's not exhausted. Three months of daily hiking and outdoor work have taken over for the aerobics and weight training that used to keep her fit for flight. She sits on the log bench beside the pond, sipping the last bottle of water from the cooler.

I feel at home here, she thinks. I am finally beginning to feel good.

A brilliant blue dragonfly hovers, then darts out of sight. From the footbridge comes the trickle of the dam. Jane lifts the bottle and splashes cool water over her head. A few birds are flying from tree to tree, and the sun, westering, casts gold onto the pond.

Chapter 10

They say there are five stages of grief: denial, anger, bargaining, depression, acceptance. Originally, these five steps applied to terminally ill patients confronting their impending death. You disbelieve and protest the fatal prognosis, rage at its unfairness. Why me? Why? Those with faith in a higher power then bargain: Let me off the hook and I'll be in church every Sunday from now on. When that fails, they become depressed. Finally, acceptance; thy will be done. Those without faith can skip right to life's a bitch, then you die.

The formula can also apply to other life-changing events, the loss of a promising career, the breakup of a marriage, a crippling accident. The five stages are convenient for everyone, the griever, their friends and family alike. It gives them the illusion they can understand and manage the tragedy, and progress through this process is viewed as healthy and desirable. No one likes it when the griever gets stuck in one stage for too long. But if you skip a stage, it makes everyone suspicious. What do you mean, you don't feel anger? Let it out, so you can move on. Yet it's really a lot more complicated. Sometimes all five stages get bunched into one—or none.

Take Melanie.

One day she was a pretty, slender, popular honors student. The next she was a barely breathing body, an unconscious lump in a hospital bed. Then she awoke, her brain no longer connected in the old way, and now she is an overweight eleven-year-old in special education, who loves soft things like pillows and hugs and eating whole bags of marshmallows. Except for that vague memory of tumbling over and over, she can't recall any specifics of the accident a year and a half ago, and she still doesn't guess its cause. In the summers, splashing with her friends in the country club pool, she couldn't know those were Long Island iced teas her mother was constantly sipping as she waved from the chaise lounge. She never imagined there was always rum in the cola, vodka in the orange juice. When she hopped into the car that New Year's Day for the drive back to her father in Manhattan, she smelled her mother's familiar Chanel perfume but not the whiskey on her breath. Melanie's mother was an elegant, impeccable, steady-on-her-high-heels drunk, a functional drunk people suspected but couldn't quite catch out.

So Melanie got into the car, and when the tumbling was over, her brain damage cushioned her from everything but the vaguest sense of depression and loss. It could be said she went pretty directly from accident to acceptance with no steps in between. Besides, her father did it for her, except he only got to the anger stage where he has been stuck ever since. Peter Babcock knew about his ex-wife's drinking. He *knew*, but he was busy, and he chose to overlook. The accident happened in broad daylight, no ice or obstructions on the road, no other traffic in sight. There is no one else to sue this time, no one else to blame.

Jane not only went through the five steps differently, she went through them twice. First, she grieved for Jill, and here denial and bargaining were pointless. They were both experienced pilots, and as Jane pulled up from her dive and saw the flaming wreckage below, she knew there was no hope. Guilt substituted for anger and depression, although the official inquiry did not find her at fault. *I killed my best friend, I may have killed my best friend, I contributed to the death of my best friend.* How could she ever be sure which was most true? Yet she accepted that Jill was gone and that she herself would get back in the cockpit and fly. It was precisely because she did accept that she was totally unprepared for what happened the first time she walked back on the field toward her plane. That locking of her knees, the closing of her windpipe, the intense trembling of every limb, heart hammering, frozen, paralyzed. She stayed in California and fought it, denying and furious at her weakness. Then she fled across country, bargaining not with any deity but with distance and time. If I get so far away, geographically and chronologically, will it work? When it didn't, there was nothing left but to accept the permanent loss of her past life.

But now something else has happened, a sixth stage of grief some people experience: rebirth. They lose a child to a vicious crime or an insidious disease, and they turn their energies to new legislation to prevent similar tragedies or to fundraising for a cure. They suffer a wrenching divorce or a catastrophic business failure, and after the crying is over, they put on a fresh face and get back in the game. In a way, Jane has already entered this sixth stage, inviting Burt and Hortense to the cottage, buying the binoculars and bird book. That Saturday afternoon when the artists leave and she sits alone by the pond, baptizing herself from the water bottle, she is ready to embrace this new life.

She acquires a library card and picks up a copy of the local summer events calendar. With recommendations from Burt, she reads up on the town's history, the Native Americans, the colonial settlers, the China trade. She adds to her knapsack a pocket guide on the identification of trees. She visits the small beach at the south end of the shore road and introduces herself to the teenaged girl, Elizabeth, who sits reading Chekhov while she collects parking fees at the entry booth. Although it's not really her job, Elizabeth says sure, if she sees anyone trying to sneak into Deerfield, she will tell them it's private and encourage them to come for the Sunday walks instead. Jane buys a tape of bird calls and listens to them rather than the radio while she's gardening around the estate. This is her job now, this is where she lives, and as she hikes on her daily patrols, she is taken aback not only by the large but by the small beauties of Deerfield, the roots of a massive tree flowing like a tangled river down an exposed slope, the psychedelic orange of a mushroom, the startling blue of a blue jay's feather lying on the ground at her feet.

By the end of June, warbler fever has passed and along with it "warbler whiplash," Hortense's term for the crick birders get in their neck from peering diligently upward into the trees. The composition of the weekly group also begins to change. In March and April it was the hardy regulars. From May to June, serious birdwatchers homed in. Now school is out and the summer people are arriving, residents or vacationers in town for the art shows, families with children looking for an educational hike. Most will come once, rave about the beauty and tranquility of nature, vow they're going to do it more often and never come again. Jane, security guard, tour guide, amateur naturalist, budding historian and camp counselor, opens each walk with what is now a well-polished routine.

"Hello, welcome to Deerfield, I'm Jane Avery, the property manager. Let's go around the circle and introduce ourselves and say where we're from."

"I'm impressed," admits Tim Hennessey, who has shown up that morning and worked his way along the line to join Jane in the lead. "You have over twenty people today. Has it been as steady as that?"

"Between twelve and twenty," she confirms. Crowd control continues to go smoothly, although she doesn't always have her full complement of regulars to help out. Russ and Charlie take turns coming; business is good at their café. Jim and Lois make it when they're not golfing, sailing or playing mixed doubles at the country club. Burt shows up in between chapters of the Great American Novel. Today she has only Hortense, who has posted herself midway along the line, and Roy and Melanie as always bringing up the rear.

"You're happy we're getting more people?" she asks Hennessey.

"Yes, although it was never the goal to attract hordes. At least," he makes a slight grimace, "it was never my goal. You have to strike a balance. If you're going to foster public awareness and concern for land preservation, you have to make the land accessible. You can't say to people, just give us your financial support and stay out. The flip side is that too many visitors causes wear and tear on the environment even when they're perfectly well behaved."

"Then what will happen if Deerfield does eventually become a full-fledged nature preserve? Would you clear trails, put up interpretive signs?"

"Not me. I'd leave it as wild as possible. But there would have to be a comprehensive plan, and that won't happen for quite a while. After all, it's still Charlotte Deerfield's property."

"I'm glad someone recognizes that." Jane pauses to fulfill from her knapsack a request for sunscreen by one of the mothers, who slathers it on her complaining five-year-old. "I was getting the impression people were trying to carve up Deerfield while the owner was still very much alive."

"There has been a lot of politics involved," Hennessey concedes. "It's not my thing, politics, committees, bureaucracy. I just want what's best for the environment."

He runs a hand through his hair in ill-disguised frustration, and Jane recalls Hortense's comment about decisions being reached behind closed doors. The land trust, the art association, the town council—different entities harboring different agendas forced to present a united front for negotiations with Charlotte. None of this would be palatable to a scientist like Tim Hennessey. Interesting man, she thinks, reassessing him. Quick-minded, late thirties, sharp blue eyes, his curly, dark red hair the color of a weathered penny. In the woods, his movements are almost graceful. Then several more plaintive peeps interrupt her.

"Mommy, I'm hot." "I'm tired." "Where are we going?"

"To a special pond," says Jane, putting a finger to her lips, "but we have to be very quiet and stay on the lookout, because you know what we might see? A deer!"

Deer! That revives them, and even if they don't spot one, she can always count on a few sunning turtles which, unlike birds, stay put for everyone to observe at length through the binoculars or Hortense's scope. With a murmured, "I'll let you get back to your job," Hennessey recedes down the line, and Jane embarks on a mini-lecture on the fascinating habits of turtles. The advent of the summer people has brought a change in both the pace and the route of the Sunday walks. Where the birders were happy to stop for fifteen or twenty minutes at a hot spot, the summer visitors prefer an overall hike, and Jane takes them over the bridge, through the woods, and out onto the ridge. The kids scramble right up, the adults lend each other a hand.

Last come Roy and Melanie. Roy prefers the rear anyway, especially when there's a crowd. Kids are fine, and it's important for them to learn about nature, but with the trees in full foliage it's often hard to spot birds, and few youngsters have the patience to focus until a tiny blue-gray gnatcatcher pops out among the leaves. Moreover, the mass shuffling of a fair-sized group of amateurs quickly alerts any birds to their presence, and they melt out of sight as the crowd approaches, reappear once the people pass. Hang back a bit and you may have a better chance of a good sighting at the rear. His winter aches and pains warmed away by the sun, Roy manages the ascent up the ridge and gazes gratefully over the wooded slopes, the blue ocean on the far horizon. Sometimes you can almost feel young again.

When they finish the tramp back at the front gate, Jane receives compliments for the tour and whispered kudos from several of the mothers. "Thanks for wearing the kids out. Maybe they'll take a nap this afternoon!"

Tim Hennessey lingers. Something on his mind, Jane thinks. Yet when he does speak, there's a slight awkwardness to him, as if he's more comfortable peering into a microscope than into someone else's eyes.

"Look," he says, "if there's any assistance I can render you, I mean, you're obviously becoming well versed in the ecology here, but if you need help locating resources or information, well, you could contact me."

"Thanks." Jane accepts the card he offers from his wallet and with it the unspoken apology for his past disdain. This is his way of trying to explain that his objection to her was never personal. "I hope you'll come again, Dr. Hennessey."

"Call me Tim?" he asks, and looks relieved when she nods. "Okay, see you soon."

Then at the beginning of July, Raven reappears. No flimsy sandals today. She's gone in for pink high-top sneakers, red bicycle shorts and a white scoop-neck tee shirt with the word "DIVA" in sparkling rhinestones across her ample chest. A pink baseball cap sits atop her cascade of dark hair. Why doesn't she just wear a flashing neon sign that reads, "Look at ME!"

Hortense, Jim and Lois rush to greet her. They've seen *Cat on a Hot Tin Roof* and swear it's excellent. The reviews in the newspaper and tourist guides also overflowed with praise, although Jane, now that she regularly reads the local publications, has gathered that any happening in town from the dance troupe's latest performance to an origami demonstration will be positively promoted. After all, those whose endeavors are being reviewed are often the news-paper's own advertisers and possibly neighbors of the reviewers. Raven breathlessly tells about two recent auditions she's had in New York.

"One is for a TV movie. I'd play this cocktail wait-ress who overhears a drug deal going down and gets her throat slit." She makes a slicing motion with her forefinger, sticks out her tongue and closes her eyes, eliciting a round of laughs. "Then there's this really great part in an off-Broadway show by a hot new playwright…"

Jane moves away to get the walk started. Raven stays in the center of the group, fascinating Charlie and the two families who have come that day with tales of an actress's life. One of the little girls is convinced she's talking to a movie star. Raven hushes whenever Jane halts the group to show them a tiger swallowtail butterfly or to point out a squirrel's nest, but it's a slow day bird-wise, and whenever there's a lull, the others barrage Raven with questions. She answers merrily, tossing her hair, eyes sparkling as brightly as the rhinestones on her tee shirt. Even Roy keeps his ears tuned in.

"You know who was a great actor?" he says, as they head back from the ridge. "Jimmy Stewart."

"Are you kidding?" says Raven. "He was the greatest. I love Jimmy Stewart!"

"*It's a Wonderful Life*?" says Roy.

"I watch it every Christmas," Raven swears.

"*Harvey*?"

"Too funny!" She drapes her arm around an invisible rabbit in a tipsy buddies pose. "And you know the one I really love? When the plane crashes in the desert, and they have to rebuild it from nothing, and there's the German guy who claims to be an airplane designer, but it turns out he's only a designer of model airplanes. Oh, why can't I remember the name of it? Help me, Roy! Help!"

"*The Flight of the Phoenix*," says Roy, grinning.

"Yes! You know, Roy, sometime you and me are going to get together and rent a whole stack of Jimmy Stewart movies, and we'll watch them and eat popcorn all night long."

"Me, too?" asks Melanie, gripping Roy's hand. She has no idea who Jimmy Stewart is, but Raven makes everything sound so exciting. Please, please, let her be included.

"Of course, you, too." Raven tousles her hair, and

Melanie goes warm with happiness.

When they arrive back at the front gate, Raven admonishes everyone to come see her play.

"It's fantastic, I'm fantastic, and it's only going to be on two more weeks before we start a new production. Besides, we starving actors need your support. We'd be nothing without an audience."

Roy says he'll talk to Melanie's father and ask if he can bring her to the show that very night. Charlie vows he and Russ will attend. The families echo they'll try to come also; they just have to secure babysitters. Jane smiles and nods, holding back any specific promise.

"Great! See you next week!" Raven calls and waves goodbye.

Up in the studio, Charlotte gestures impatiently to Bella for the binoculars. "Have you figured out who the hussy is?" she demands.

"Yes, it's coming to me."

Bella goes to her desk and picks up a flyer from the playhouse; as the town's premier resident, Charlotte is naturally on every mailing list. Bella points to a photograph of Raven in a sultry pose with a handsome young man. Under the title *Cat on a Hot Tin Roof* is the verdict: SIZZLING! A list of performance times and ticket prices follows. Charlotte compares the photo on the flyer to the view through the binoculars.

"An actress. She's gaudy. She sleeps around."

Bella doesn't answer. The pronouncement on Raven's sexual habits may or may not be correct, but at the moment she's more concerned as to why an actress has come on the nature walk, not to mention all these families with children, plus a handful of the usual birdwatchers. The novelty of Deerfield being open should have worn off by now and the crowds decreased, but today there were fifteen in attendance. There has not, however, been any repeat request from the art association for painting at the pond, and Bella chuckles to recall the success of that plan. Still, she and Charlotte must begin some summer entertainments if they are to uphold their position in town. If only she could get Charlotte to focus and, more important, to drop this latest endeavor, the so-called "Retrospective in Retrospective" in which she will paint her life backwards. Oh yes, Bella knows about it now. First those youthful self-portraits, then this disturbing series of the woman in the ice block. What are you up to? she demanded, and Charlotte told.

Bella stares regretfully at the depiction of the marriage to Morton Fischer, a union she still wishes had never ended. What is the point of getting divorced at age sixty-two? Why, after seventeen years, couldn't you stick it out to the end? Morton was a good, if unexciting man, a Wall Street financier, and they had enjoyed a most satisfactory existence that included a Park Avenue apartment and a chauffeured limousine. He loved music, and he quietly donated more than anyone realized to the symphony and to scholarships at Juilliard. Late at night, after the concerts and operas and parties were over, he would come to Bella for a game of chess. Then he would go to the office the next morning and spend all day in dry financial calculations because that's what his brain did best. He knew the divorce was coming, and what he said, as he looked up from the *Wall Street Journal* that day at the breakfast table, was not so much a heartless comment on their breakup as a last helpful piece of financial advice: "If you can wait until the market rebounds, you'll do better on your stocks." He died a year after the divorce.

Now, to hear Charlotte tell it, her marriage to Morton was an entombment of her artistic spirit in the ice of cold commercialism and the false glitter of society. Oh come on, Bella thinks. Morton never asked you to give up painting. You chucked it of your own free will, thinking you had something better in hand, and for many years you did. You liked his money and your gowns and jewelry fine. But then you had to be "fulfilled," you cast everything off to pursue your art, and has it brought us any more happiness? No.

Bella turns away. This whole retrospective is a bad idea, bad, bad, but there's always the hope it will sputter and die as so many projects have before. Stay away, she tells the muse, stay away or better yet, tempt her to try being Monet again. Really, those pastel water lilies weren't so bad.

Charlotte is still spying out the window, and Bella goes to her desk, switches on her computer and listlessly checks an astrological website. She's feeling unwell again today, but it comes and goes, indefinable, so it can't be anything serious. Perhaps she ought to get back to mass again; it's been a few weeks. Denial. Bargaining. Bella doesn't know it yet, but she is about to enter her own five stages of grief.

Chapter 11

Raven is *on*.

Never mind that she got word today that she didn't land the part of the cocktail waitress in the TV movie or the off-Broadway play by the hot new playwright. Never mind that she has waitressed from six a.m. till six p.m. this Saturday evening because her checking account is near empty again and she needs every last dime in tips she can pocket. Never mind that she's thirty-six—old, old, old!—although she can still get away with telling men she's twenty-nine.

Raven is *on*.

When she steps onto the stage, she is Maggie the Cat. No one, not Elizabeth Taylor, has ever done it better. She's a cat who can make a hiss seductive, a purr menacing; the merest flick of her tail is a tease. She's a feline who knows the reason you have nine lives is to prowl with panache through every last one. Her feet, her tender paws, are already singed from that hot tin roof, but she digs in her claws and hangs on. When the curtain goes down and the applause bursts up, Raven has to blink and remember, feel Maggie draining out of her. She stands on stage, bowing with her fellow actors, and as her eyes readjust to the audience she had forgotten was there, she sees Jane Avery clapping. Their glance meets, both looking surprised. Raven could have sworn Jane didn't like her and never meant to come.

Jane hadn't meant to come, except that as the week

wore on, she felt more and more uncomfortable about not going. Roy, always true to his word, would no doubt already have taken Melanie. Ditto Charlie and Russ. What if, come Sunday morning, Raven arrived for the bird walk and Jane was the only one who had failed to see the play? It's guilt that brought her to the theater tonight where she fully expected to endure two hours of Raven prancing and flirting on stage in a low-cut dress and an exaggerated Southern drawl. Well, the dress is low-cut, but within ten minutes Jane has forgotten this is Raven at all. Instead, she watches a passionate woman named Maggie tenaciously play the hand she's been dealt, cream in her whiskers, steel in her claws. She is *good*. Why hadn't she believed it was possible, Jane wonders, as she rises to join the ovation. Then their eyes meet, and Raven mouths the words *Wait! Don't leave!* Jane is standing diffidently by her seat, most of the audience departed, when Raven rushes up and clasps her hand.

"Jane! I'm so flattered you came. You look really pretty." She gestures and smiles at the lavender top and floral print skirt.

"I bought it today. I didn't have much else but jeans." Jane spreads the skirt in demonstration. The purchase is another sign she has moved forward; she can wear the outfit to other events in the summer calendar.

"It's perfect, and it looks great on you because you're so slender. Goddess, I wish I had your figure! Come have a drink, okay? Some of us in the cast are going out on the verandah for a beer."

She takes Jane's hand before she can demur, and in a minute they're on the verandah where Raven rattles off introductions. Big Daddy and Big Mama, real names Bucky and Eileen, are local residents and playhouse veterans. Dan and Amy, who play Big Daddy's unloved son and daughter-in-law, last starred as Alice and the Mad Hatter at Disney World. Brandon, the actor who plays Brick, has credits that include Shakespeare, children's theater and a touring pro-duction of *Grease*. Jane remembers the latter details from the program notes. You don't forget the resume of a guy that good looking, especially when Raven is pushing you into the chair next to him.

"Jane is my friend from the place where they do the nature walks," Raven tells everyone, "and she's fantastic! She knows all about birds and butterflies and how to look for ticks so you don't get Lyme disease. Brandon, pour her a beer and somebody send that plate of nachos my way. I'm starving!"

"You were all great tonight," says Jane, surprised at the reference to the tick inspection ritual that closes the Sunday walks. She hadn't thought Raven was paying attention.

"We're always great," says Brandon, pouring her a beer as ordered from the pitcher on the table. This revives a discussion that was apparently underway when Raven and Jane interrupted, Eileen talking about the play's pacing and the others chipping in with requests for Bucky to stop stepping on their lines. Also, some of the local kids playing the no-neck monsters really are getting pretty full of themselves and that one stage mother should be strangled. They talk about past roles, botched auditions, asshole directors, box office receipts, the bars they've tended, where to get good head shots, where to crash cheap in New York. Bucky and Eileen are married, not to each other, and took up acting after their kids were grown. Dan and Amy are a couple and plan to leave it at that. It's chancy enough getting parts from one month to the next. You can't be tied down.

Jane listens, absorbed into their world, tentatively sipping her beer. It's been a long time since she drank alcohol because there are strict rules about alcohol and flying, and since she used to be up in the air either practicing or performing almost every day, it was simpler just to abstain even when the regulations would have allowed her to slip one in. The beer tastes unfamiliar but good; being in this easy-going company is fun.

"We'll talk half the night if you let us," Brandon

whispers to her in an aside as the others keep on. "So you're the bird expert."

"Hardly," she replies. Brandon has deep brown eyes, chestnut hair, a nose that's slightly beaked but which on him looks just fine. He's not overly tall, but he doesn't have to be. On stage as Brick he was dissolute and aloof. In person he has a palpable charisma, and Jane feels it enveloping her as she tries to explain her position at Deerfield. "I kind of fell into it. I'd left another job in California and was ready for something different. Anyway, I look after the estate grounds, and on Sundays we give guided nature walks." She shrugs sheepishly. It sounds so lame, and besides she's having trouble not staring at him, although technically she's allowed to because they are having a conversation.

Brandon isn't put off by her explanation. Jumping from one gig to another is what actors do all the time. "So you're educating people about nature, that's terrific. I go back and forth to New York a lot and I love the city, but it's nice to be in a place where green isn't confined to a park square or a rooftop or a window box. Didn't you see some kind of rare bird a few weeks ago, a parrot, I think?"

"A monk parakeet, and it was Raven who first spotted it."

"Well, it really made her happy. Listen, I don't know anything about birds, but maybe I could come sometime?"

"Sure, any Sunday morning, eight o'clock."

"Great, I'll try to make it. Got to run now, though. I promised some friends I'd hook up with them. Nice to meet you, Jane." He shakes her hand, his voice mellow. It's hard to tell from his frank tone whether he's developed a sudden interest in birding, in her or both. Does he look into everyone's eyes that way? She wouldn't mind finding out. A few minutes after his departure, the others drain their glasses and also bid goodnight.

"Don't go." Raven touches Jane's arm as she's about to rise. "I still have half a beer left, and if I sit here alone, it's a foregone conclusion I'm going to get hit on." She rolls her eyes to indicate the crowd on the verandah. Some are left over from the audience at the play, but the wraparound porch and generous seating capacity make the restaurant a popular watering hole in its own right, and there are plenty of singles on the bar stools and mingling around. "In fact, with you here," she laughs heartily, "it's twice as likely the guys are going to move in. But don't worry, I know how to handle them. Unless you want to get hit on...? By the way, what do you think of Brandon? Isn't he melt-in-your-mouth gorgeous?"

"He's very nice," says Jane, feeling a little out of her depth. Not since the accident has she hung out socially with anyone, and back then it was mostly with other pilots, replaying their flights, swapping opinions on airframe modifications, "hangar flying" as it's called. It's been an even longer time since she was hit on. As she didn't frequent bars, most of the men she met were other performers or production people on the air show circuit, and two transient lives, she learned the hard way, don't add up to one happy one.

"Ladies, you look lonely." Two men have materialized, mid-thirties, smooth talkers. "Can we get you another round of beers?"

"Oh, thanks, no." Raven presses her abdomen and lets out a martyred sigh. "You wouldn't happen to have any Midol, would you?"

"Midol?"

"These cramps, they're killers. My friend and I were just saying what agony we're in, and the drugstore is already closed."

She kicks Jane under the table, and Jane jumps, then clumsily imitates her gesture and groans.

"It's like a bowling ball pressing on your stomach, and booze doesn't help," Raven continues, waving at the empty pitcher. Her face brightens. "I know, maybe we ought to try more Prozac. I'm sure I have some in here somewhere." She begins rummaging in her woven tote bag, and the two men beat a hasty retreat. Raven sits back jauntily in her chair, grinning.

"Hey, you were good at that!" she congratulates Jane.

"Raven, that was crazy." Jane, flustered, doesn't know whether to laugh or scold.

"No, that was improv. Just try not to be so jerky in your movements next time."

Jane makes an exasperated sound, and Raven is instantly contrite. Her therapist said she should try to develop new interests, be around normal people, and the very way Jane has rebuked her reinforces that imperative. Jane is so grounded, so steady, so down-to-earth sane. Raven needs a friend like that.

"I'm sorry, force of habit. Sometimes I don't know when to stop acting. We'll tell the truth next time and just say no thank you, okay?" She keeps the pleading out of her voice.

"Okay. Actually, it was kind of funny." Jane looks after the two men who, unabashed, are chatting up a trio of women at the bar. "Maybe we should move to a smaller table, though. With these empty seats, it may look like we're inviting company."

"Oh right, sure," Raven agrees, and in a minute they're reseated at a table for two. "Of course, now you realize everyone here thinks we're lesbians."

"Oh no." Jane sighs. Can't two women, or two men, just be friends anymore? It wasn't so long ago that a pair of unmarried females in their thirties would have been written off as asexual old maids.

"Well, we did just brush off a couple of decent-looking guys and move to a table where we can be alone," Raven observes. "We could talk a little loudly about your broken engagement, if you want, and I'll be the sympathetic friend who's consoling you." She tips her head toward the other tables, willing to help Jane create whatever impression suits her. Everybody is always thinking something about you anyway, judging you, jumping to easy answers. So don't give them time, get right in there and hit them hard with the version you want them to believe. That's Raven motto; at least, it's one of them.

"That won't be necessary," says Jane firmly, opening the program from the play. "Look, I didn't realize you had this long list of credits. TV commercials—"

"I was a dancing aspirin, a customer choosing paint colors in a hardware store."

"—stage plays in New York—"

"So far off Broadway people had to pack a change of underwear in case they couldn't get home the same night."

"—modeling—"

"A lingerie catalog. I did bras. It's all in the boobs." Raven looks down her chest, eyeing what most producers and directors consider her best asset.

"But you were so good tonight." Jane shakes her head, puzzled.

"I was terrific," Raven vows. There's no point in being too self-deprecating. Besides, it's hard for people like Jane, who aren't in the theater, to comprehend how you can be very good and yet not succeed at the level by which they measure success, namely that you've starred in movies or a television series. How can you be an actor if no one has ever heard of you? "Wait till you see our next play here. It's a hilarious British bedroom farce, and I have a really juicy role. Plus, I'm lining up more auditions in New York, so lots could come of this summer. Keep your fingers crossed for me!" She holds up both hands, fingers crossed, and Jane matches the gesture.

"That's wonderful," she says, and Raven, glad to have dispelled any gloom before it can become catching, is *on* again. She tells funny backstage stories and promises to bring Brandon the next time she comes for the walk. She's seen the way Jane reacted to him, and since she herself has slept with him only twice, there's nothing serious between them.

"Except I can't come tomorrow. I have to work the

breakfast shift at six a.m."

"Six a.m.?" Jane checks her watch. "Raven, it's almost one now. You should be asleep. I didn't mean to keep you up talking."

"Oh, I'm fine." She waves it off, but in truth it's nice to be told, *Sleep. Go to bed.*

"Do you live nearby?" Jane asks. "Do you need a ride?"

"No, I have my car and a place in town with Dan and Amy. Thanks again for coming, Jane."

They walk to the parking lot, and she watches Jane drive off in her truck. Please, let her like me. Raven knows she is sometimes too exuberant, comes on too strong. She's been trying to tone it down. She backtracks over their conversation, hoping she didn't brag too much, but she didn't want to mope or bemoan her life either. She spends enough time doing that with her therapist. She noticed Jane didn't talk much about herself, and perhaps that's something she, Raven, should emulate, except that as an actor you have to believe in yourself completely or no one else will. Especially not the people who matter, who can turn thumbs up or down when all you wanted was to play a stupid cocktail waitress who overhears a drug deal and gets her throat slit...

Then Raven feels it happen, that sense of deflation overtaking her. When she steps out of Maggie at the end of the play there's a buffer while the applause still clings to her and the cast lingers in camaraderie. Now she's herself again, and the real sense of loss sets in. Because who, after all, is Raven? Who has ever heard of her? Sometimes she feels like a ghost no one can hear or see. To keep up her spirits, she interviews herself as she drives home. "Raven, how does it feel to be holding your first Oscar?" "Tell us the truth, who is your favorite leading man?" Dan and Amy are making love in their room when she gets in—you can *hear* them—and she's tempted to bang on the door and shout, "Don't get pregnant in there, you two!" Then she's tempted to shout, "Yes, get pregnant!" because when do you quit? When you do realize it's not going to happen for you and move on? Most of her friends her age already have, but hey, she's a character actress, not a star; she's got longevity.

She goes to the fridge in the tiny kitchen for a bottle of water. Her voice coach in college, before she dropped out, was always urging her to stay hydrated, and she may not have the leading role in the British bedroom farce, but her part is a saucy one with the potential to steal a few scenes. Two plays back to back, she's on a roll. Except she's been on rolls before...

Raven hugs herself, looking out the window at the warm summer night. Then she reaches for her tote bag and begins rummaging. Wallet, keys, makeup, hairbrush, tissue. She knows the Prozac is in there somewhere.

Chapter 12

By the middle of July, Deerfield and all of New England are deep into one of the most beautiful summers in memory. Waking day after day to unadulterated sunshine and blue satin sky, it's hard to sense time actually passing. Maybe some enchantment has fallen on the world, and it will stay this way forever. To be sure, some moan it's too hot, and others grumble that the infrequent bursts of rain aren't sufficient to keep their lawns lush and green. But the sailors and golfers and beachgoers love it, the tourists are flocking to town, the merchants gladly stay open till ten o'clock, and the children, who more than anyone know what summer is really about, arise each morning to face the serious challenge of playing themselves into exhaustion by bedtime.

On the estate, Jane continues her chores and undertakes more bushwhacking, over the first ridge, down its western side, and up onto the second ridge that abuts the state forest. She follows the deer trails, narrow but navigable. Sometimes she sees deer, and once, a coyote on the run. It must have heard her coming; all she glimpses is a furry caramel-colored shape that was definitely not a dog disappearing into the trees. The muddy path around the pond has dried up since the spring rains, and when she makes forays north of the pond she comes across the remains of stone walls overgrown by bramble bushes and vines.

"Colonial farms," Burt confirms when she stops in at the library to ask him. "That land was cleared and farmed into the early eighteen hundreds by a succession of families, most notably the Gardiners and the Mowrys. The stone walls could be part of property boundaries or sheep pens."

The Sunday walks continue as well, and even with the spring migrants gone it's not uncommon on a typical Sunday to chalk up twenty to thirty species. Many are everyday birds, cardinal, robin, song sparrow, but since every new species is a first for Jane, the life list she's begun jotting in her notebook is growing rapidly. Now the words "rare bird sighting" make her ears perk up and her mind leap to the possibilities. Hortense was right—start listing and you're hooked.

One Sunday they see a partial albino fawn, or so they determine afterward. At the time they simply stand gaping at the apparition, a small white deer mottled with reddish-brown patches, frozen in terror at the sight of them. The vision comes to life with a crash as the fawn bounds away in panic through the woods. Roy and Hortense research at the library and on the Internet, and Jane phones Tim Hennessey for his opinion. True albino deer with pink eyes are rare, he says after hearing her description, but partial albinos, called piebalds, are more common. Unfortunately, their conspic-uous coloring puts them at a disadvantage. They're easily spotted by hunters and predators and shunned by other deer.

"Let's hope your little guy makes it," he says, and his tone changes to one of longing. "I'd really like to come to Deerfield again, but I've been stuck behind my desk for weeks. Damn, I hate paperwork."

Melanie didn't get to see the fawn. Her father was having another busy weekend in the city, and he brought her to stay with him. When she returns and hears from the others about the deer, she is heartbroken. A white deer! It had to be magic, a fairy tale, and for once, to everyone's surprise, Melanie isn't a sweet, pliant child. She's angry, not at them but at life because it wasn't fair—not fair!—that such a beautiful creature happened and she didn't get to see it. She doesn't realize she's whimpering, shuddering, her raised fists shaking as if there is someone in front of her to battle. She can't hear Hortense's soothing voice trying to calm her down.

"Melanie, Melanie," Jane touches her arm, "I know what we'll do. Remember the first time you came and you threw coins into the pond like a wishing well? We'll do it again, and you can make a wish that the deer will return. Does anyone have change in their pocket?"

Coins are quickly pressed into Melanie's hand by a half dozen of the day's walkers, and her face clears. When they reach the pond, she tosses the coins into the air and watches them tumble and splash into the silent cool green. There, that's better. Now the white deer will come again.

At the end of the walk, a tall man takes Jane aside and introduces himself as a special ed teacher from a neighboring school district. "You handled that very well with the little girl," he observes, "and I think the other children on the walk also learned a lot today. Is there any chance the estate might be open for class field trips in the fall?"

"Field trips? I don't know." Jane weighs the idea. "We haven't tried anything like that yet."

"It wouldn't have to be a formal presentation. My kids don't have long attention spans. But the kind of program you gave today, explaining about the birds, the trees, the importance of preserving nature, that would be a very positive experience for them. Could I call you in September and see what your situation is?"

"Sure," Jane says, although she's fairly certain that Charlotte's reaction to an invasion of Deerfield by a horde of schoolchildren will be a gasp of pure horror. She also hadn't realized she was giving a program, but the man's compliment is a nice one all the same.

Raven comes on the walks whenever she's not waitressing the breakfast shift. Even when she's trying to be inconspicuous and stay toned down, Raven stands out. One week her fingernails are magenta, the next jade green. She talks with her hands, uses body language that's all over the place. She says "Oh my goddess!" instead of "Oh my god!" and she shimmies when they identify a new bird for her list, which she has started at Roy's suggestion. Everyone is eager to know what she's doing, and Raven is not one of those people who, when asked "What's new?" ever answers "Nothing much." She might get a part in a Coke commercial, she did a voice-over for a radio ad, the bedroom farce opens this week—promise you'll come see her!

Burt confides in her as they walk about his Great American Novel. He's twenty-seven, Raven discovers— "Why, I'm twenty-nine," she says—and he has no idea how hard the road ahead will be. She smiles and listens attentively to his naïve dreams, silently praying, Please, goddess, let it happen for him. Let someone make it big on the very first try. And please let me get that Coke commercial. She would sleep with Burt if he asked her. She can tell he's attracted. But Jane seems to like him, too, and she won't make a move until she's sure Jane's interest is purely platonic. Brandon hasn't yet made it to a Sunday walk, and Raven wants to give Jane first choice, Brandon or Burt. That's what friends are for. But the main reason she's so vibrant, so sparkly, is because for these two hours on Sunday mornings, Raven is truly happy.

"It's such a beautiful, peaceful place, and everyone is accepted there," she tells her therapist at one of her sessions. "No one's judging your performance or rejecting you for your looks. They're just glad to have you along."

"That actress is here again," Bella reports to Charlotte from the studio window, "most of the usual birders, a handful of strangers. No children today but that fat girl."

She offers the binoculars, but Charlotte, paintbrush in hand, waves them away. There have been far too many distractions lately, brunches and luncheons and receptions at this or that gallery, an unavoidable wedding last weekend, a Red Cross fundraising gala the weekend before that. Last night took the cake. An abominable woman, some friend of the director of the art association and a newcomer in town, attempted to make a splash by hosting an elaborate fiftieth birthday party at the country club—*for herself!* How tasteless can you get? Charlotte shudders. This is what happens when trash comes into money, and it makes her wish she had a clone or a double to send to such events. Perhaps Bella in a red wig...? The image prompts an inward chuckle. Of course, she's had to do her own share of summer entertaining, but by keeping her dinner parties small and select, she not only reduces her costs but makes her invitations the more sought after.

Meanwhile, she is poised to start the third series backward in her retrospective, the years of her life from age forty-four to thirty-nine, and once again genius reigns. Thus far, she has five youthful self-portraits in the first sequence, then another five for her Ice Age, and she had balked at the idea of getting locked into a specific number of paintings per series. It's inartistic; moreover, it's time consuming. She is already too late to have her whole life done by the annual members' show in August, and she'll have to speed up if she is to exhibit by Christmas. So to depict the years between her third and second marriages, she zoomed in on a single vision. What did she do in that period? Painted. She reclaimed her maiden name and painted. She had to do something other than grieve when her second husband Robert Drayton left her, to hold up her head and not let the world, her peers, her social circle, know he'd broken her heart. She had loved Robert beyond measure, fully expecting theirs would be a union unto death, and when he left, when he left...

Charlotte cuts off the memory, cold ashes in her mouth. How foolish to think anything will last. Except art— and this second time she was serious, no naïve young creature dabbling in pretty watercolors but a mature, fascinating woman who would take the art world by storm. By day she painted passionately, by night she attended openings and glib cocktail parties all over New York. She wore dramatic long-sleeved black dresses and high-heeled boots, her long red hair fire-balling down her back. She rarely came to Deerfield, ignored this provincial town. Bella worked and schemed behind the scenes to promote her. They knew by now they were stuck with each other for the long run.

Yet there was no blazing fame to show for it, and as she approached forty-five Charlotte was beginning to feel desperate, a joke. What was she to do? She smoothed in vain at the tiny crow's feet wrinkling the corners of her eyes. She awoke one morning and discovered three gray hairs. Then Morton came along and offered marriage, and she said yes, not to him but to the opportunity to exit under acceptable pretenses. Bella, too, breathed a sigh of relief. Becoming Mrs. Morton Fischer gave them both built-in job descriptions for which they were qualified and experienced, and they did good works in support of others' music and art.

And her own paintings from that second artistic interlude? Looking around the studio at the ring of canvases littering loveseats and chairs, stacked in layers against the walls, Charlotte can hardly remember what she painted then, although that passionate outpouring must be buried in there somewhere. A joke—and therein the very inspiration she required. She will paint for this series a single portrait containing two figures. One is a red-haired woman in a harlequin outfit, a black-and-white diamond-patterned suit with a ruffled collar and fuzzy snowball-sized pompoms down the front. On her head is a jester's cap, the belled peaks flopped over at foolish, foppish angles. The harlequin extends a paintbrush toward a full-length, gilt-framed mirror, but in the mirror, in the place where the reflection should be, is a woman in a dramatic black dress and high-heeled boots, a tumbling inferno of hair. Her pose is calculated to be both striking and nonchalant; a cocktail glass decorates one hand.

Will they get it? Will those fools at the art association understand when her "Retrospective in Retrospective" goes on display? Charlotte draws back, doubt gnawing. Maybe she'll have to dictate captions for the pictures for Bella to type, spell it out in words: Both women are *me*. For five years I looked in the mirror and saw this intense, fascinating creature where the reality was a fool with a paintbrush in her hand. You will notice there's no silly grin on the harlequin's face; discovering you are a joke is no laughing matter. Now do you comprehend? They won't, they won't, and at the futility of it Charlotte almost throws down her brush.

"Your use of black is too stark," observes Bella from her desk.

"It's not stark, it's dramatic."

"No, it's not. No color looks as dramatic in a mirror image as it does in real life. It should look glassy."

"I suppose you think you can do better?" Charlotte scowls. This would go faster if Bella didn't keep criticizing and interrupting. Come to think of it, it's also Bella who insists they hold the dinner parties and attend every trivial summer event, not that she ever gets to dine with the town's elite or sit in the center box for the tennis tournament. Bella is a servant. She knows her place. She prefers to watch from behind the scenes and scoff at rich people's pleasures, the little hypocrite. Those who can spend, do. Those who can't must munch sour grapes. Charlotte decides it's time to put her secretary to work. "My exhibition will need a commentary for the program," she says. "I'll dictate it to you while I paint."

"Very well."

Bella types at her computer as Charlotte recalls the angst of her harlequin period. It's another "woe is me" tale, but Bella lets her utter what she wants. She rewrites everything Charlotte dictates anyway. She saw, too, how Charlotte nearly threw down her brush, a promising sign. Charlotte rarely sees anything through to the end, or in this case, back to the beginning, and what she has painted so far has been easy. Soon, the story will turn difficult. Perhaps Bella can subtly assist the demise?

"You know," she says, "I'm afraid your concept of 'A Retrospective in Retrospective' may confuse people. You should call it something simpler, like 'A Woman's Journey.'"

"'A Woman's Journey'? You like that?"

"No, I think it's trite. However, it's a popular way for unexceptional women to view their lives. They convince themselves that whatever disappointments they encounter in their marriages or children or careers are part of a journey of growth and self-discovery that will lead to enlightenment, presumably before they die. They'll relate to your paintings if you call the exhibit that."

"I don't want anything trite associated with my exhibit! Besides, if I call it 'A Woman's Journey,' they won't know it goes backward. They'll think they're meant to start viewing the paintings from the earliest age."

"They'll think that anyway. People's brains naturally move forward chronologically. Maybe you could call it 'A Woman's Backward Journey' or work in the word 'chron-ological.'"

"No! I like 'A Retrospective in Retrospective.' The program will make it clear the paintings are to be viewed in reverse order. If people prove extremely stupid, we'll mark arrows on the floor."

"Yes, we could do that. I was only trying to be helpful."

"Well, you're not."

Charlotte tries to resume her painting, but she's nettled, and the brush sticks in mid-air daubed in black paint. Is her life trivial? It's far from the first time she has asked herself that question, but the answer keeps changing, it's inconsistent. It peels off in layers, like these paintings, as she tries to get to the core of it. She didn't think each period of her life was trivial while she was living it. It's only when she looks back…

Bella watches Charlotte's brush stuck in the air. *Stop*, she thinks, *stop now. Haven't I confused you enough?* And don't ask me for answers because I have none. I doubt God himself knows, he left loopholes in the Bible big enough for an army of Philistines to march through, and all the elucidations and reinterpretations over the centuries have only made it worse. In fact, the only person in the history of the world who ever got it completely right was Mary. She did one thing, gave birth to a child in a manger. She got it right the first time, and now she's revered for all eternity.

"Bella, do you think if only we had—"

"No," Bella cuts her off. She knows that bruised, longing tone of voice. Artists, actors, writers—neurotic, the lot of them, with their insatiable need for love and approval, their craving for answers to the meaning of life. Bella knows the meaning of her life: God just keeps her around for a joke. "No, I don't think anything. I was wrong about the black. Go on, paint, paint."

She flicks her hand at the canvas. It can't matter, it can't go much further. Slowly, Charlotte's brush returns to the portrait, and dab, dab, dab goes the black paint. Bella sighs. Just think if she'd had a gifted artist to work with. Just think what she could have accomplished.

Chapter 13

On the last Sunday in July Brandon comes.

And—hallelujah!—no outsiders.

All the regulars think this with a little relief. For whatever reason, the day too hot, kids at summer camp, some event in town, the only ones to show up at the front gate are Hortense, Roy, Melanie, Jim and Lois, Burt, Raven and Brandon. It means Jane gets a break from the role of tour guide and can relax her vigilance about keeping fifteen strangers informed, entertained and safe from venturing into poison ivy or tripping over tree roots. It means Roy and Melanie can take the lead, since everyone knows about and will forgive Roy's gas. It means they can stop as long as they want to coax out of the undergrowth a wood thrush Lois has identified by its flutelike *ee-o-lay!* Come on, come on…They can hear it scratching and hopping about on the ground, but like other members of the thrush family, the wood thrush prefers dense cover and refuses to appear. Hortense relates a story she once heard about how the bird got its beautiful call.

"It was told to me as Native American lore," she says, "although I don't know if that's correct. According to the tale, the Great Spirit promised to give the most beautiful voice to the bird that could fly highest into the sky. Naturally, every bird wanted the honor, and each strove to fly higher than the next. When it was the eagle's turn, he spread his mighty wings and took off, confident of winning the prize. But the wood thrush jumped on the eagle's back, and by that trick he flew the highest of all. The Great Spirit fulfilled his promise and gave the thrush his voice, but he made the thrush so ashamed of his cheating that forever after the bird has hidden out of sight."

The story meets with approving laughter, and Roy reminds everyone who doesn't yet have a wood thrush for their life list that they can still count it by sound.

"Did you count it?" Jane asks, guessing the answer.

"Well, no, but I already have one on my list," Roy replies.

"Which I bet you didn't count until you'd both heard and seen it and were one hundred percent sure?"

"Well, yes," he admits, and his friends chuckle because there it is again, the sacredness of Roy's list. Honor. Duty. No cheating. Jimmy Stewart wouldn't cheat, you can bet on that. "But there are some birds you pretty much have to count by sound," Roy allows. "Nocturnal owls, for example. I've counted one or two of those by sound alone."

Jim and Lois nudge each other, winking. "Do we have a story about that," says Jim, and they take turns telling it.

"We were in southern Arizona, and we knew it might be our one chance to get a western screech owl for our list," says Lois. "So we got up at three a.m., wasn't it, dear?"

"Three-thirty," says Jim, "but either way, it was a moonless night, very dark."

"Right, and we were using our tape to lure it out—"

"Your tape?" Raven interrupts. "You catch birds with tape?"

"A tape recording of bird calls," Lois explains. "If you play the call of a particular species and there's another bird of that species nearby, it will usually answer."

"Some places forbid the use of tapes," adds Jim, "but we were out in the middle of nowhere so we figured it would be all right."

"Why are some places opposed to tapes?" Burt asks.

"Because if you have a rare bird hiding in a bush and

every five minutes someone is playing a fake call just to make it pop out, that would be unduly stressful for the poor bird," says Jim.

"Anyway," says Lois, and Melanie, whose attention has been bouncing back and forth between everyone talking, nods eagerly as if to say, Get on with it! She knows the etiquette about bird tapes already, and she can tell by the grins Jim and Lois are wearing that there's a funny story coming. "Anyway," says Lois, "we use the tape, *hoo-hoo-hoo-huhuhuhuh.*"

"And very faint, we think we hear *hoo-hoo-hoo-huhuhuhuh,*" Jim echoes, imitating the eerie, accelerating trill.

"So we sneak a little closer in the direction of the sound." Lois holds up an imaginary tape recorder and mimes pushing the play button, and she and Jim exchange a second round of tremulous owl alarums.

"Now we're ninety-nine percent sure," says Lois. "We want just one more *hoo-hoo-*"

"*Hoo!*" hoots Jim, "and then six U.S. border patrol agents came crashing through the dark with flashlights and guns. We'd sneaked right into a stakeout for illegal aliens."

Amid gasps and laughter, Lois finishes the tale of how they were unceremoniously escorted out of the area by the disgusted lawmen. "But we did get our western screech owl," she concludes.

"Yet you all look like such sane, respectable citizens," says Brandon. "Who would have guessed bird-watchers lead such perilous and clandestine lives?"

"I told you they were cuckoo," says Raven in a loud stage whisper, eliciting more laughs. Having come with Raven, Brandon isn't an outsider, and his easygoing conversation has made him welcome with everyone as they amble along. Melanie is already in love with him. He's handsome!

They climb the first ridge and find seats on the rocks, Raven next to Burt. Brandon sits down beside Jane.

"So this is your gig." He nods at the treetops in the valley below. "What a place to clear your head. Great therapy."

Jane looks askance. "Therapy? Is that what you think this is?"

"Sure, the healing power of nature, the aura of a protected place. A refuge for the bruised and battered of body and soul. Hortense and Roy have both lost lifelong mates, not that Hortense's husband is dead, but with advanced Alzheimer's..." Brandon shrugs, keeping his voice low. "Melanie, poor kid, this is a haven from her father and school, a place where she can be accepted just as she is. Burt is recuperating from a wrestling bout with his novel. As for Raven, it's a chance to get away from a world where everything is make-believe and sit down in a place where everything," he pats the rock ridge beneath them, "is real. Not that she doesn't love the make-believe."

"What about Jim and Lois? They don't need therapy. They're not running away from anything." Jane stops at the words "running away." She was happy to see Brandon when he arrived that morning. No, face it, her heart stepped up a beat, and sitting beside him is only making it beat faster. But his stream of talk is leading her into uncomfortable territory, and by the sudden sharp look in his eyes he's picked up on it.

"No," he says slowly, "Jim and Lois don't need a refuge. They have each other."

Their gaze travels to the couple, Jim untangling a twig from his wife's honey-brown ponytail. Brandon is right. Jane would like to have that someday.

"Well," she concedes, "you certainly seem to have found out quite a lot about everyone in a very short time."

"It's what I'm good at, getting into other people's heads. I wouldn't be much of an actor otherwise. Except yours. You don't want to be figured out, do you?"

"There's nothing to figure." Jane tosses her head, realizing too late it's a bad imitation of Raven. "Besides, if this is therapy, why are you here?"

"I said I'd come." Lightly, he touches her hand. "I'm sorry if I offended you. That wasn't my intention."

"It's all right." She shrugs off the touch, instantly regretting its loss. Lois and Hortense are both pretending they didn't see it, and remembering she's still on the job, Jane raises her voice inquiringly. "Anyone see anything interesting?"

Melanie points upward. She's been lying on her back, nestled in a mossy pocket among the rocks, feeling warm and lazy in the sun. She sees no need to say anything. She just points straight up.

For ten seconds, no one else spots the bird.

Then Hortense says, "Oh yes, there, quite high. Good eyes! What do you think, Melanie?"

"Red-tail."

"Attagirl," says Roy.

"Get out!" Raven gives Melanie an admiring punch on the arm, and as Roy opens his book to show how Melanie could make the identification, Jane watches the soaring bird. She doesn't want to, already her chest is tightening, but against her will she's hypnotized. It was a red-tailed hawk she saw on that very first walk with Roy and Hortense when she started to fall apart. She hears Roy's voice.

"…broad wings, wide tail, but raptors in flight are often too fast moving or too distant to rely on field marks like color or belly bands. So you go for overall shape, size, silhouette, flight pattern, whether they're soaring or flapping or gliding. You have to *feel* the bird."

Jane does, more than anyone can guess. She feels the way the hawk is flying. She feels the way she's not. No, she pleads, her throat going dry, no, this can't be happening. I can't freeze here the way I did at the airport, not when everything has been going so well. Her head starts to spin as she follows the bird's circling flight, up, up, dizzyingly high. Her heart tugs out of her chest after it. She can't tear her sight off the red-tail, yet she can't see it for the tears gathering in her eyes.

"Do you think," asks Raven, "that if there were no birds, it would ever have occurred to human beings that they could fly?"

The nonchalant question makes everyone's gaze swing her way, and Jane quickly wipes the corners of her eyes.

"I mean, think about it," Raven insists. "Suppose there were no birds on this planet. Would we have imagined we could fly without some example in front of us?"

"Insects," offers Jim. "Dragonflies, butterflies. Bats."

"Too small." Raven shakes her head. "Besides, they don't fly very far or very high. It would have to be something big. How big are that red-tail's wings?"

"About a four-foot wingspan," says Roy, not needing to check his book.

"A bald eagle can be over seven feet," adds Hortense.

"Bigger than me." Raven stretches her arms to their widest to prove it. "And what are those birds that fly really far, almost from the North Pole to the South Pole and back again?"

"Arctic terns," Lois supplies.

"Right! That's what we wanted, the freedom to travel great distances, and birds gave us the inspiration."

"But people already had the ability to cover long distances before air travel," observes Burt reluctantly. He's loath to disagree with anything Raven says, but the historian and truth-teller in him can't help it. "They had trains, boats, horse and wagon. They had their own two feet. Look how far Marco Polo got by overland caravan, and the Vikings in their longships sailed to the Mediterranean, Russia and the New World."

Jane opens her mouth to second Burt's statements, anything to divert the topic to history or Norse culture, all too aware of Brandon's gaze alternating between Raven and her.

"I'd guess the inspiration was simply to break free of gravity," says Jim, picking up the thread before Jane can speak. "When Leonardo da Vinci drew those flying machines, I don't think he necessarily wanted to go anywhere. He just wanted to fly."

"Personally," says Raven, "I think Leonardo was totally bogus. I mean, sure he was a great artist, but everything else he did was only an idea. Did he ever try to build a real flying machine? Did he ever glue himself up with feathers and jump off a cliff? No, he was too busy being a genius putting fancy notions down on paper."

"He was a *live* genius," Brandon teases, momentarily releasing Jane from his gaze. "He didn't end up at the bottom of a cliff with a broken neck."

"I think there were English monks trying that as far back as the tenth or eleventh century," Burt chips in helpfully to make up for any appearance he may have created that he wasn't on Raven's side.

"See? That's exactly what I mean." Raven points emphatically at Burt, then jumps to her feet while everyone else is still sitting on the rocks. She has an audience, this is outdoor theater, and her voice projects, her eyes flash, her body electrifies. Raven is *on*. "Leo's in his ivory tower, genius at work, solitary, noble, no time for real life." She crosses her wrists in front of her chest, fists clenched, imagining the tower around her, the confinement of knowledge. "But far away in a monastery on the sea-swept coast of England, a brown-robed monk is watching the seagulls wheel in the sky. He collects feathers from the beach, whole armfuls," Raven scoops up the imaginary bounty, "then he glues and ties them to a rickety wood frame and straps it on." Her arms lift slowly at either side, trying to float against the invisible weight, no grand gestures, not yet. It's her voice, her conviction, her *belief* that makes them believe it, too. She's half aware of Jane staring at her, horrified, but she can't stop the performance, it has a life of its own. "The monk stands on a high cliff above the sea, salt wind blowing into his face, waves crashing on the rocks below. Then he starts to run."

In a flash, Raven is running along the ridge, the loose

sleeves of her gauzy white blouse fluttering like wings, Jane shouting something after her that she doesn't heed. When she leaps in a triumphant arc it almost feels for a split second as if she really will take off into the air, but there's still a long length of ridge before her, and of course she comes down, stumbles on a rock, lands on both hands and one knee. Burt rushes to make sure she's not hurt, but she is already picking herself up, brushing grit from her palms. For a minute, everything really came together there, voice lessons for proper projection, a rapt audience, six years of ballet. Sometimes, being Raven, it's hard *not* to be on.

"Anyway," she says as she rejoins the group, "what I mean is that Leo may have been bursting with brains, but that crazy monk had the real guts. He had faith."

She resumes her seat on the rocks, the others still a little amazed by her performance, except Brandon, who takes it as quite natural, and Jane, who isn't saying anything.

"Angels have wings," says Melanie. It has taken her brain a long time to reach this statement. She has a vague memory of someone asking for examples of creatures with wings, like at school when Ms. Shaw asks for an example of sharing or how could we build a robot. Some kids shout answers right away, although not necessarily good ones, and often by the time Melanie has a reply, the class has moved on to a new topic. And of course she had to stop thinking altogether while Raven was going to fly. She didn't want to miss that. Now the angel answer has flown into her head, and since everyone else was quiet, out it popped.

"Heaven?" Hortense wonders. "Is that what people were really seeking through the pursuit of flight? They aspired to reach the divine?"

"Like building a Gothic church spire as high as possible to reach up to God," Burt seconds.

He and Hortense, Jim and Lois begin talking excitedly. Does anyone remember exactly how angels are described in the Bible? Are all souls ascending to heaven given wings? Lois cites mythology, Pegasus, Cupid, Mercury the messenger god. What about the winged lions on Assyrian, or is it Babylonian, temples? Icarus, don't forget Icarus, and they're off on the subject of hubris, not pausing to wonder how they got from simple birdwatching to philosophical ground.

Melanie listens happily at the way she has drawn people into a discussion. In school, Ms. Shaw would smile and put a plus beside her name for "Class Participation." Beside her, Roy isn't saying much, and hoping he doesn't feel left out, Melanie slips her palm into his. Roy winks and points upward, enjoying the hawk everyone else has forgotten. The red-tail circles higher and higher, out of sight.

Raven comes to sit with Brandon and Jane. "I'm sorry, Jane," she says. "I'm sorry I didn't stop when you yelled. I wasn't anywhere near the edge of the ridge, and I wouldn't have jumped even if I was. I'm not that suicidal, honest." She laughs imploringly. Oh goddess, she's done it again, shown off, stolen what was supposed to be Jane's show, made her worry someone was going to get hurt on the walk. No wonder she looks angry and upset. No wonder she's not speaking.

"She wasn't yelling at you to stop," Brandon informs Raven. "What she shouted was, 'Wrong way!'"

He regards Jane quizzically, one eyebrow lifted in an invitation to explain. Jane stares back mutely, watching their expressions shift from curiosity to concern when she fails to reply. She didn't freeze completely this time, not like at the airport, but everything today seems to have conspired against her. The soaring red-tail, that feeling of flight, Raven's outrageous performance, angels, Icarus, Brandon's assessment that they're all here to escape something painful left behind. It's no one's fault, this unintentional reopening of a wound they don't realize is there. Even Hortense's amusing story about the thrush flying on the eagle's back, disgraced, hiding out of sight, doubles back on her now with a vengeance. Please, don't let her cry. She has to say something.

"Planes," she says, and her throat knots around the

word, "airplanes take off *into* the wind. You were facing south, and the wind today—it's just a breeze, you probably didn't notice—the wind is coming from the north." She smiles raggedly. It was the only thing she could think, Raven poised with arms aloft, gauzy wings spread, and she blurted it in warning. *You're taking off the wrong way!*

"Really?" Raven perks up at the information. Jane isn't mad at her after all. "Why do planes do that? I mean, I just get on them and fly and never think about it. Wouldn't it make more sense to take off with the wind at your back so you'd get an extra push?"

"No, it's lift, airflow over the wings." She wants Raven to stop now, and she answers as briefly as she can.

"Hey, everybody," Raven interrupts the others, who are deep in a discussion of Genesis, "did you know that planes always take off into the wind? Tell them, Jane." She steps aside, smiling, giving Jane back her show as well as a chance to impress Brandon.

"Sure," says Jim, unwittingly sparing Jane the need to answer, "it's Bernoulli's Principle. When you have airflow over a specially shaped surface like an airplane wing, the leading edge separates the flow so the air above travels faster than the air below. The resulting pressure differential between the upper and lower surfaces creates lift. It's high school physics."

"Well, excuse me," says Raven with mock affront, "but while some of you were acing physics, others of us were vying for the role of Eliza Doolittle, which went to that snotty Allison Hooper instead. *I* didn't know any of that." She turns back to Jane, determined to give her the spotlight.

"And a bird's wings work the same way?" she demands.

"Yes," Jane surrenders, "you can think of them as planes."

And there it is, the thought she didn't want in her head, the connection she had been avoiding. It seems so obvious. How could anyone look at a bird and not compare it to a plane, marvel at the freedom to fly? Yet until now, they hadn't. Sparrows flitting from bush to bush, warblers darting from tree to tree. That isn't flight. But when a hawk or eagle goes into aerial display, when it skims the clouds and mounts the wind, when it disdains the earth and climbs the vault of heaven, you must stop breathing, you must, for one aching moment, feel your heart cease to beat.

"Well," says Brandon, casually, "I don't know about the rest of you, but it's quarter to ten, and unfortunately I have to head back. I'm bartending the lunch shift, and aren't you waiting tables?" He gives Raven a significant look.

"Oh my goddess, yes," she sighs. "The never-ending glamour of an actor's life."

The others rise with murmurs about getting back to chores or lunch or plans for the afternoon. As they trek through the woods and past the pond, Hortense, Jim and Lois resume their theological discussion while Raven pairs with Burt. Roy and Melanie take the lead. Brandon walks in the rear beside Jane.

"Don't mind Raven," he advises. "She means well, although she does tend to give actors a bad name."

"No, it's fine," Jane replies, too quickly, wanting only to put the memory of the soaring hawk behind her.

"You sure? You seemed upset by her performance. It was a bit over the top. You see, Raven isn't extravagant *because* she's an actress. She's an actress because she's naturally extravagant, and acting is her way of channeling it. Most actors, myself included, are much more stable."

"I'm glad to hear it." She nods to Raven and Burt, a little ahead. "She seems to be enthralling Burt now."

"She'll no doubt hitch a ride home with him," Brandon agrees, "but don't worry, she won't hurt him."

Sure enough, when they reach the front gate, Raven bounces into Burt's car with a wave goodbye. Jim and Lois thank Jane for a most interesting morning. Hortense, Roy and Melanie promise to see her next week. Brandon remains.

"I hope you enjoyed the walk," she says, a limp

statement. Brandon is regarding her with more than friendly attention, and she's aware again of his magnetism. But he also said he was good at reading people, and if that's all he wants from her, another live character to study...? She doesn't know what she wants from him.

"Would you like to go out sometime?" he asks, and Jane says simply, "Yes."

"Then I'll call." He smiles and gets in his car.

She walks to her cottage, feeling somewhat better, and when she risks a glance above the horizon, no hawk meets her eye. It occurs to her that in her four months at Deerfield, she has subconsciously been keeping her gaze low, rarely above the tops of the trees. She'll have to overcome that, teach herself to look high into the sky without flinching. She must accept that birds fly and she doesn't, that the air is no longer her element. Standing on the ground, she must learn to take pleasure in their flight. There may be, as Brandon said, healing power in nature, but it hasn't healed her yet.

Chapter 14

Nature doesn't care about healing Jane. All nature cares about is that you survive and procreate.

It doesn't care whether Raven is a talented actress, a waitress in a restaurant, a borderline manic-depressive who subconsciously understands what a succession of therapists can't seem to grasp, that she has to act, she *has* to, because one life isn't nearly enough. Nature does care that Raven wants to fling herself at Burt. There is possible procreation in that.

Nature doesn't care that Burt is a shy librarian, who, although he optimistically believes otherwise, is not writing the Great American Novel. It does care that Burt, after luke-warm romances with two or three young ladies of remarkably bland temperament, can't believe his good luck that a vivacious, electrifying woman like Raven actually seems interested in him. There again, the possibility of procreation looms.

Nature is encouraged that Jane is attracted to Brandon, although Jane is at present unsure she wants to enter any relationship. It's wise to be selective, courting rituals are essential to vet potential mates, but don't procrastinate. In nature, he or she who hesitates is genetically lost. Nature is immensely pleased with Brandon, whose attitude toward sex is, What's all the fuss about? It feels good. We like it. Your place or mine?

Roy, Hortense, Jim and Lois have already fulfilled their procreative function, and to them nature says Bravo! Now don't take up too much more time and space on the planet, will you? As for what to do with Russ and Charlie, nature is at a loss. Nature gave Charlotte a chance, and soon Charlotte will be painting about that. Melanie will be deprived of her chances not by nature but by those who decide what is best for her.

Nature has never had any use for Bella.

Jane isn't thinking exactly along these lines the following morning when she sets off on her usual patrol, yet more and more an awareness is seeping into her that beneath Deerfield's appearance of a leafy, idyllic retreat lies a fiercely complex structure wherein beauty is not careless and every detail carries a life-or-death consequence. There is purpose here, intensity, and she comes a step closer to comprehending it each time she learns some new intricacy of an animal or plant. She studies to answer questions, not great overarching questions for now, but the vital little ones that arise on the Sunday walks.

How many eggs does a robin lay? Three to four, and did you know that if habitat and food resources are abundant, robins, wrens and some other species will raise two and even three broods in a single season?

Which is bigger, a fox or a coyote? A coyote, they generally weigh thirty to forty pounds, whereas a red fox is tiny, a mere fifteen pounds.

What kind of tree is this? A white oak—see the rounded lobes on the leaves?—whereas a red oak leaf has points. Think white man's bullets, red man's arrows. This helpful, if politically incorrect, memory aid comes from yet another woodland guide added to her knapsack, and each time she slips the knapsack on, Jane welcomes its growing heft and weight, its solid feel against her back. All this new knowledge displaces the life she has lost, and if every once in a while a soaring hawk does tear at her heart, this, too, she will master. She will steel herself to look up and watch the hawk with dispassion. She will break her connection to the sky.

Today she is mastering a new trail, an ancient trail to the Native Americans who once walked it, the white-tailed deer before and after them. It's on the wooded northwest side of the pond, an area that had seemed too thickly overgrown ever to be breached by trespassers or to merit exploration. Yet today there is an impression of a passage through the thicket and a bird call she can't identify luring her on. She pushes back bull briars that snag and tug on her long-sleeved tee shirt and jeans, necessary attire for bushwhacking despite it being the end of July; she has learned how deeply even small thorns can rake into bare legs and arms. The day is a little on the cool side anyway, the breeze verging on gusty, the blue sky leaching to a gray whiteness as a summer storm threatens to move in. Jane can hear the bird moving ahead of her from bush to bush, sees the flutter of leaves and a glimpse of a long tail each time it lands. Bigger than a sparrow, she judges, more the size of a catbird, a distinction she would never have imagined making just a few months ago coming to her automatically now. It is not, however, a catbird's call. She tries pishing, but whether she hasn't Melanie's knack or whether the unknown bird has abandoned this game of hide-and-seek, no response and no further movement are heard.

She stays on the trail—or makes one, she thinks wryly, ducking under a hefty tree trunk that has splintered at shoulder height and toppled at an angle. In a short distance, she reaches a low stone wall. She has come across remnants of them in other out-of-the-way places on the estate, and they're always a bit of a surprise, these leftovers from the days when Deerfield was a cleared patchwork of small farms. Jane never knows whether to marvel more at the dogged persistence of some colonist in knee breeches, hewing down and uprooting tree after mighty tree, piling stones to build a wall, or at the plants' rampant reclamation of their territory, the forest's ability to recreate itself from a few wind-blown seeds or acorns conscientiously patted into the earth by an industrious squirrel.

She sits on the wall and runs her fingers over the surfaces of the rocks, their slight graininess contacting her skin like varying degrees of sandpaper from gritty to ultra-fine. Their shapes are round, oblong, flat, their once-tight fit worked looser over the centuries by prying vegetation and the battering of wind and rain. Vines weave in and out among the crannies, like curiosity seekers that can't resist poking into every nook, and ants crawl unconcernedly over the terrain, decorated by lichen doilies in patches of pale green lace. The wall runs for perhaps thirty feet, tapering and crumbling to an end in a wild blackberry bush. Except there's another stone half-hidden beyond the bush, an upright gray slab about two feet high with a rounded top...a grave?

Jane rises, the distinctive silhouette already confirmed in her mind. Two more headstones stand to the left, two to the right, and a second row behind. *Sacred ground.* She's not sure why the words enter her head, since she doesn't profess any established religion or entertain spiritual notions of the goddess sort that Raven tends to spout. Yet the discovery of this long-forgotten cemetery makes her stop and look around, as if seeking permission to take the next step forward. Then curiosity gets the better of her, and approaching the nearest stone, she kneels and carefully pulls away enough of the weeds and briars to expose the inscription on the dark gray slate. *Mehitable, wife of Isaac, 1724-1759*, it reads, along with some lines of verse or tribute too dirt-encrusted to decipher. *Isaac* is one grave to the right, surname *Mowry, 1720-1799.*

Jane sits back on her heels to overview the site. The plot is perhaps twenty-five by fifteen feet, eight stones in two uneven rows, another fragment of stone wall at the rear. It's not hard to place the name Mowry. Burt had mentioned them as colonial farmers, and it probably wasn't uncommon for a family to have its own burial plot on a quiet corner of its land. Does he or anyone else involved in local history know of the cemetery's existence? Jane wonders. Should she tell them? The last thing Charlotte will want is an army of amateur historians tramping over her land to examine and catalog the site. Does Charlotte herself know it's here? Jane pauses, guesses not. It may be best just to let the dead rest in peace.

She retreats from the cemetery and hikes thoughtfully back. What will happen to this estate when Charlotte goes to her grave? The logical outcome, if indeed there are no heirs, would be to preserve it in some self-sustaining format, and with the introduction of the Sunday walks Charlotte has grudgingly taken a first step. But wouldn't it be wiser to plan now, to specify in writing exactly what you want to occur? Jane backtracks a little guiltily. What right has she to mentally dispose of someone else's property, especially when there is already a town full of people eager to stick their fingers into that pot? Then she comes to her own defense. She has a right to be concerned, she's the property manager and—the realization hits her full force as she stops on the bridge—the one person truly intimate with the land itself. Not Charlotte or Bella, who never set foot by the pond or among the trees. Not the land trust crusaders and scientists like Tim Hennessey who have multiple properties to oversee. Not the art association members whose main consideration is, will it make a pretty landscape to paint? She is the one person with the least valid reason to be here at Deerfield; now she's beginning to feel the most responsibility to protect it.

By the time Jane reaches her cottage, the first raindrops are spitting out of the sky. Upstairs in the studio, Charlotte watches the drops tap on the diamond-shaped panes. There doesn't seem to be any pattern to the way they fall. She chooses a diamond, and when the next droplet hits, she touches her fingertip to that spot on the glass, then the next and the next, as if she's playing a game of connect-the-dots. But when she tries to predict and leap her finger ahead, the raindrops elude her guess. There are getting to be too many of them anyway, and she turns back into the room. She has finished her harlequin portrait, and look how good it is, look! If only she could have painted like that back then…She drifts around the studio, fingering this object and that. Marriage, art, marriage, art—pick something and stick to it. Because that's the real story, isn't it? You have to find a way to occupy your life. A person has to have something to *do*.

Take Bella, the little monster, the little gargoyle.

Charlotte settles her gaze on the empty computer desk. Bella has gone to the bank and to confer with their accountant. She isn't happy about some of their investments, and she will straighten out their portfolio. Bella has invitations to RSVP, correspondence to answer, phone calls to make, issues and politics to keep abreast of at the art association, charities to hold at bay, the arrangement with the land trust and the Sunday walks to monitor, accounts to maintain with the local establishments, investigations to pursue on her computer. Bella is constantly busy, she has many things to do, and Charlotte would be lost without her. Yet where would Bella be without Charlotte to generate a life for her? Bella needs her as much as she needs Bella, and to sustain that symbiosis they need Charlotte to be doing something, be it her marriages, her social life or her art. If she were to stop right now and do nothing, both she and her secretary would be rendered useless. But does Bella ever say thank you? Why isn't she here at this critical point?

Alone, Charlotte faces her new, blank canvas. It's time to paint her second marriage to Robert Trevor Drayton, her life from age thirty-eight back to thirty-one, and so far all she has done is pace the room and distract herself with raindrops on the windowpane. Why did she begin this project anyway? What it will accomplish? If she stops, who will know or care? She waves a hand in flippant dismissal at the self-portraits already completed, then shivers as they stare back. If she stops, they become meaningless. They tell only half a story, they don't make sense. She can't exhibit them at the art association. She'll have to add them to the ring of canvases around the wall, another layer closing in around her, gathering dust.

Charlotte whimpers, a small, muted sound. It's been fun till now, rewarding. It's been easy. But she knew this was coming. What did she expect? Just try it, she coaxes herself. Maybe it won't be so bad. You can paint the story any way you want. Try just one portrait of age thirty-eight. Pick up the brush.

Her hand obeys the order, the brush smears paint on the palette. Smiles, that's how she would paint herself at that age, a woman swathed in smiles. Smiling face, smiling hair, smiling clothes. Except there would be tears in her eyes— maybe it's the increased tempo of rain hitting the windows that makes her think of this. There might also be tears on her arms and in her heart, and all those smiles, if you looked closely enough, would be clenched. How to depict this, though? She paints one tiny smile in the middle of the canvas and feels a little better for it. Some pale blue teardrops follow, flicked lightly over the surface, then some soft red waves to represent her hair. Maybe it will become an abstract series; no one said the art had to conform to one particular style. Yes, abstract, and it will consist of three paintings that even after so many years, it hurts to think about. Three visions of an indistinct pelvic bone, and within each one a swirl of dark red, a tiny hand reaching out for help as it's sucked into the maelstrom, clinging desperately to a trailing, pulsating umbilical cord. Three miscarriages. Then she couldn't even get pregnant anymore, and Robert, whom she loved, who she thought had loved her, divorced her though she begged him not to.

"We don't need children. We'll live for each other," she pleaded. Wasn't their marriage otherwise perfect? Wasn't his career in his father's publishing firm assured? They traveled yearly to London to seek rare books for his collection and sailed in the summer on his yacht. But by that third failure to produce a child, Robert was in shock. Rich, handsome, nothing had ever gone wrong in his life.

Beautiful children who would grow up to be just like him were his due, and soon after, married to another wife, that's exactly what he got. So you see, it wasn't any shortcoming or lack of manliness on his part. Whereas Charlotte knew by then she was cursed. She didn't speak to Bella for months after the divorce, except to spit at her. Bella spit back. They both knew whose fault this was.

The thing is, she would have been a good mother. She wanted those babies as much as Robert did, and she would have rocked them in her arms and sung them lullabies. She starts to paint hearts in amongst the teardrops, not fake red Valentine hearts but tender green curled-up capsules. She can't tell why at first, that's just how it feels to her. Then gradually she recognizes them as buds that will never open. Maybe she doesn't need three different paintings, maybe one canvas will tell it all. Maybe one is all she can bear to paint. She spatters more tears over the blurry picture. This is getting to look like a clumsy imitation of Jackson Pollock. She'll have to take it out and shoot it.

Outside, the rain pours down.

Chapter 15

The storm intensifies around midnight with a boom of thunder so violent Jane starts awake wondering what exploded. Rain slashes at the windows. Trees thrash in the wind. Far down at the beach she can hear the pounding of surf, the weight of waves repeatedly hitting the sand and receding in a gritty hiss. Once, in such weather, she would have worried about her plane. Not every airport at which they performed had adequate hanger space for transient aircraft, and in advance of a blow, she and the other air show performers would hurriedly contact nearby airports to see where they could squeeze in. Right now at that little airfield north of here, the small planes on the grass are taking a beating, their wings and tails secured by ropes to tie-down rings cemented into the ground. Even so, a plane can break loose and be plucked up by a tearing gust to go tumbling away like a battered toy. And if a plane, so a bird, and now it is the wrens and robins and woodpeckers Jane finds herself worrying about, the deer huddled in the forest, the frogs and turtles and frail butterflies at the pond. Yet they know more than humans do about surviving a storm, and all over Deer-field creatures have scattered to burrows and hollows and empty tree cavities. Jane listens to the dark, whipping wind, the rattling windowpanes. It's gale force outside, and she won't be surprised if that stony, clattering sound overhead is her roof shingles falling.

The rain and high winds continue the next day,

though thankfully no power lines come down. In the studio Charlotte has placed three canvases of varying sizes on three easels side by side. She paints smiles backward, clenched, trembling, hopeful. She paints pelvic bones helplessly encircling, vainly cradling dark red maelstroms, little hands and feet swirled away into nothingness. Tiny green bud-hearts hold false promises, blue tears come and go. Sometimes the tears rush into a river flowing through the bones. When she finishes, the three canvases will overlap like a collage. She isn't sure how yet, but you've seen that effect, they do it with landscapes, it's trendy, it's in. At times like this, Charlotte understands that artists, writers, poets are monsters. They will eviscerate their own lives and anyone else's to feed their version of the truth, and it may be that in this ruthless re-visioning, she is closing in on being an artist after all. Bella, meanwhile, stays out of her radius. One look at that first canvas when she returned from the accountant's yesterday, and she knew what Charlotte was up to. She makes herself scarce.

By that night the sky is finally clearing, the rain tapering to petty, intermittent tantrums. Yet even the third day is rough and windy, albeit bright, and Jane postpones yet again her routine patrol. Branches are down everywhere around the cottage and the main house. Charlotte hasn't had the trees thinned of their dead limbs in almost a decade, and the wind has unerringly found and pruned them.

"You see?" She lords it over Bella as they watch Jane collecting the dead wood in a wheelbarrow. "I told you there was no need to pay an expensive so-called arborist to lop a few branches."

Bella grunts. Penny-wise and pound-foolish, she would like to retort. Suppose one of those limbs had smashed through a window? Suppose the gale had uprooted one of those old beech trees entirely and it crashed onto the roof? A pretty repair bill they'd have had then. But she can't say anything because Charlotte will only smugly point out that those extreme scenarios didn't happen, and there is Jane uncomplainingly hauling away the heavy branches and debris. Any of the other caretakers they've hired and fired over the years would have demanded extra money for the task. Why doesn't she? And suddenly, Bella gets it. All this extra work, the diligence to the nature walks, the initiative to make contacts with the summer staff at the beach, the local police.

"She's ingratiating herself," Bella announces.

"What?" says Charlotte.

"She's making herself useful."

"Isn't that what good employees are supposed to do?" Charlotte raises a sarcastic eyebrow. "You're the one always complaining that the people we hire don't work hard enough."

"No, you're the one who complains that," Bella counters. "You want them to work for nothing, then take offense when they won't."

They glare at each other. Some days it isn't important what they're glaring about.

"She's sized us up, and she's trying to make herself indispensable," Bella repeats. "We should have seen it coming. The smart ones, not that we've had many of them lately, always get around to it."

Charlotte weighs this truth. Her money isn't what it used to be, but it attracts people nonetheless. They calculate how old she is, see she has no husband, no obvious heirs, no concerned nieces or nephews calling to check up on dear Aunt Charlotte. If they happen to be in her employ when she dies, wouldn't it be natural for her to leave them a generous bequest? Of course, that usually depends on length of service, and most are too impatient to stick around to reap their unjust rewards. They steal and run instead. But it is possible to hit it big in this racket, and Charlotte and Bella eye each other, mutually recalling pathetic, real-life instances that have earned their disgust. The buxom young nurse who marries the drooling, ninety-three-year-old widower and who, to the relatives' fury, inherits a fortune for sixteen months of devotedly pushing his wheelchair and cooing into his ear. The rich, befuddled old women who adopt shameless, grown adults as their son or daughter and leave them ocean-front estates, the directorship of their trust, and a passel of bereaved, pampered dogs.

"I'm not going to adopt her," Charlotte snorts. "You have nothing to worry about."

"Nevertheless, she's been here almost five months," says Bella. "We should determine her future intentions."

"And how do you propose to do that?"

"I'll go down and talk to her."

"Well, whatever you do, don't scare her off. I don't care what she's done in the past or if she's run away from an affair with a married man. She works hard, she works cheap, and she isn't dealing drugs out of the cottage like that last scum…You've double-checked on that?"

Bella nods.

"Well, don't run her off," Charlotte repeats.

Bella leaves the studio, clump, clump, clump down the stairs. It's still very windy out, and she stops at a closet near the front door to drape a sheer black scarf over her topknot. In truth, it wouldn't matter to her now if Charlotte did take it into her head to adopt Jane or anyone else. Once, years ago, she might have been frightened of being kicked out, cut off. Once, she might have worried that if Charlotte predeceased her she would be left homeless and penniless. Those eventualities have passed. They recognize what they have done for each other, and each will live up to her share of the debt.

Bella walks out the front door and clumps toward Jane, who is halfway between the mansion and the cottage, wrestling a branch out of a privet hedge.

"Hello," says Bella.

"Hello." Jane stops and nods in greeting, a little surprised to see the secretary out in this weather, arms folded protectively against her chest, her crooked body hunched against the occasional buffets of wind.

"I've come to ask if you need any help," says Bella, "if you'd like me to hire a man to remove some of these large limbs."

"No, it's fine. I can manage. I phoned the town maintenance department, and they're sending trucks around in the next few days to make a special collection of the storm debris. I just have to get the branches down to the end of the service road. Unless you'd like some firewood?" She gestures to the chain saw she's been using to cut the more unwieldy branches.

"We use artificial logs, cleaner, easier to carry," says Bella, noting how here again Jane has taken charge, stepped forward without permission to make arrangements for waste removal. "About your job—"

The wind snaps the scarf off Bella's head, and she grasps futilely after it as it whirls over the hedge.

"I'll get it." Jane sprints after the flying scrap of black and catches up with it near the cottage, Bella clumping after her. When she turns to hand the scarf back, Bella is patting at her flustered, wind-torn topknot in an attempt to restore her disheveled dignity. *About your job,* Bella had begun, a hint in her tone that she wishes to talk seriously, and meanwhile Jane can't shake the impression that this wind will somehow break the little secretary like a dry twig.

"Would you like to come inside?" she asks, forcing the matter by opening the cottage door.

"Thank you."

Bella steps in, hiding her surprise at the unexpected offer of hospitality. She's not surprised to see the cottage neat, clean and in far better condition than the last tenant, the amateur drug dealer, left it three years before. Fresh eggshell-white paint, pristine windowpanes, a new chrome lighting fixture above the kitchen sink, the refinished wood floor. Another project is in progress on the newspaper-covered dining table where a small bookshelf sits amidst scraps of sandpaper, a can of mahogany wood stain and a paintbrush soaking in a jar of turpentine. The furnishings and curtains are still ugly faded florals, but they have been aired and cleaned and the musty smell is gone. Library books and a laptop computer rest on the coffee table before the couch. In all her life, Bella has never had a home of her own, only a room in someone else's, and in a raw minute of longing, she imagines herself living in this cottage, a place that is hers alone.

"About your job," she says, confused, recalling her sense of purpose, "you're satisfied with the position so far?"

"Yes."

Jane indicates the sofa and Bella takes a seat, sitting forward a little self-consciously so her feet won't dangle. "We wondered how much longer you might be staying," she continues.

"I don't know," Jane replies cautiously. Bella's question seems polite and innocuous, yet it has almost the tone of a host tactfully inquiring the departure plans of a guest who has overstayed her welcome. "Are you saying you're terminating the position?"

"No, no, not at all." Bella waves her hands to show she meant no such thing. She doesn't know either why she and Jane must always be on their guard with each other. "It's only that we often have trouble keeping good people." The outspoken compliment surprises her, and she hurries to cover the remark. "I mean, it's not a glamorous job, the pay is minimal...Perhaps it's lonely here for you." She shrugs to indicate not the cottage, which hardly feels lonely at all, but their immediate surroundings, the semi-isolation of the Deerfield estate.

"I like it," says Jane, "I like the work, and if I did decide to leave, I wouldn't just go. I'd give you notice and stay until you could hire someone."

"We hope that won't happen," says Bella, again confusing herself. Jane isn't scheming to be adopted then. If she were, she would have protested that she loves Deerfield and wouldn't dream of going elsewhere. Bella's gaze travels again around the first floor of the cottage. The framed landscape prints and few ceramic knickknacks are the cheap decorations that have been part of the cottage for ages. Aside from the library books and laptop, Jane has added nothing of a personal nature; she hasn't claimed possession. "So you foresee being here until perhaps Christmas at least? Miss Deerfield and I were thinking of taking a trip to Europe in October, and if we could be assured that we had someone reliable to look after the property in our absence…?"

"Europe," says Jane, "that sounds nice. Yes, I'll probably be here then."

"We might go to Italy," Bella adds. "It's where I'm from, although I left long ago after the war."

They pause. It's the first time Bella has offered Jane a personal statement about herself, a seemingly harmless remark that slipped off her tongue, and Jane is willing to take her up on it. But Bella can't talk about her remote past any more than Jane can about her immediate one, and suddenly they know this about each other, see in their eyes that they are each withholding something painful, a part of their story that says *Do Not Touch*. Bella doesn't even know why she began talking like this, talking too much. It wasn't to pry out tidbits she could use to further investigate Jane; she'll stop that now for good. She just wanted to talk and have Jane speak in return. A conversation, a real conversation about computers or books or how they pass their days. All Charlotte ever wants to talk about is herself, and although occasionally in years past they did have a cook or maid or butler in the house with whom Bella could converse, even then she had to be careful not to get too friendly or Charlotte would accuse her of siding with the servants. It's lonely for *me* here, Bella wants to tell Jane. I'm busy, I try to keep busy, but you can see I don't have any friends.

"Well," Bella pushes to her feet, adjusts her spine to standing position. She must make the vertebrae realign like so many mis-stacked dominoes each time. "Miss Deerfield and I would like you to know that you're welcome to have visitors stay at the cottage, family or friends who may come from out of town."

"Thank you. My family is pretty far flung, but I do have a few friends among the birders I'd like to invite in from time to time."

"Of course." They're back on safe territory now, reassurance in their voices, and as Jane graciously opens the door, Bella firmly knots the black scarf under her chin. "Look," she says, stepping out, "there's a little bird hiding in that hedge. The wind must still be too strong for him."

She clumps away. Jane watches her hitching gait progress back to the house, then spares a glance for the sparrow sheltering deep in the hedge.

"Stay down," she tells the bird. "It's not a good day for flying."

She works until late afternoon clearing the fallen branches, then mixes instant iced tea and sits down at her laptop. Nudged perhaps by Bella's comment about having visitors, she begins an email to her family. They are none of them great correspondents, although they would rally immediately in an emergency. When Jane had her crash, she had to dissuade them all from jumping on planes to California, a revelation the psychologist pounced on with alacrity. Aha, she wanted to distance herself from her family, and her father was retired Air Force, perhaps an ace pilot whom Jane had adored and strove to emulate, and now the crash symbolized her failure to live up to his expectations. No, she replied, her father wasn't any kind of pilot but a procurement officer who processed requisitions for uniforms, blankets, toothpaste, soap. And the family wasn't racked by constant upheavals during his military career, they moved only twice in her childhood and never out of the country, the majority of her father's service spent in an unassuming office in the Pentagon. Finally, her parents' divorce wasn't acrimonious but amicable, and her sister didn't run away to Australia to escape nonexistent family tensions but because she fell in love with an Australian businessman to whom she remains happily married.

"Look," Jane told the frustrated shrink, "it's simple. I went to college, I got a degree and a job in engineering. Then one day for a date a boyfriend arranged a scenic flight at a small airport, and by the end of that hour I knew I loved flying more than engineering and the boyfriend combined. I loved to fly. *I lived to fly.*"

Abruptly, Jane stops typing, closes the unfinished email, walks a few restless steps to the window seat. She ought to make some dinner, she thinks, staring out, when a shape in the hedge attracts her eye. The little bird is still in there, hiding. Was it injured in that storm? She fetches her binoculars and bird book but can't spot anything as obvious as a broken wing. True experts can ID a multitude of sparrow species with a single glance at the head, but beginners call sparrows LBJs, little brown jobs, for their indistinguish-ability. Nevertheless, with this one sitting put, Jane has a chance.

She starts by trying to narrow down the categories. Does it have a clear or streaked breast? Does it have wing bars or not? After that it's a matter of head and throat markings, eye stripe, short, long, rounded or notched tail. Be careful! Chipping and clay-colored sparrows both have brown ear patches in fall and winter. An immature swamp sparrow can be misidentified as a Lincoln's. But even with binoculars, Jane can't see the bird fully. All she glimpses when the wind rustles the leaves is a brownish head and orangey patches on the shoulders and wings. She works her way patiently through every one of the forty-five pictures of sparrows in her book. No, no, no, no. She rings Hortense and gets her answering machine.

"Hortense, there's a little bird outside the cottage I'm having trouble ID-ing, maybe an immature sparrow. If you get in and have any tips, please give me a call."

Next she phones Roy, who answers with a tentative hello.

"Hi, Roy, it's Jane," she says.

"Eh, who?"

"Jane at Deerfield." She shouts a little. "I have a bird I can't identify."

Roy's hearing improves immediately at the words. You never know, when you first answer the phone, if it's going to be one of those blasted telemarketers. "What kind of bird?"

"I think some species of sparrow, but I can't match it to anything in the book." She gives him the description, still rather vague, although she's positive about the orangey color.

"Are you sure it's a sparrow?" Roy reaches for his collection of bird guides. "It's late in the season to be seeing warblers, but some of them have orange patches. Check the blackburnian and the bay-breasted, especially the females. Does it have a warbler's bill?"

"Hold on." Jane thumbs through the pages. "No, it's not a blackburnian. It's not the throat that's orange, it's more down on the wings and the sides of the breast. Oh wait...I think it's a female bay-breasted. Let me take another look."

She raises the binoculars. From what she can see of the bird, the coloring for a bay-breasted looks right. Then the wind tosses the leaves aside, and the little head peeks out. The bill. Warblers, insect eaters, have thin needle-bills, she recalls from the spring migration. Sparrows and finches, seed crackers, have bills that are short and thick.

"Short and thick," she reports to Roy.

"You sure it's not a house finch? They're usually pretty obvious, red not orange, but it could be the late afternoon lighting or a case of dull plumage."

Jane flips pages to the house finch. "There's something called an orange variant, but it shows only an inset of the head."

"I better come out there."

"Oh no, Roy, I don't want to trouble you when it's probably something very ordinary."

But Roy is on a mission, there's an unidentified bird, and he's on his way with binoculars and an armload of books. Let him come, Jane thinks. He might not have anything else to do tonight, and for that matter neither does she.

"Don't go away," she tells the bird.

She removes the bookcase, wood stain and newspaper from the table and searches her cupboards for something she can fix Roy for dinner. Cooking is hardly her forte, but she can make tuna casserole, and it's likely that Roy, an elderly man living alone, doesn't always eat as well as he should. He's at the door before the macaroni has finished boiling in the pot.

"Okay, where's our bird?" He rubs his hands enthusiastically, and Jane beckons him to the window seat and points out the sheltered form. Roy peers with his binoculars, runs his finger through pages of sparrows, and frowns. "Don't recognize it," he says. "When did you first spot it?"

"Mid-morning, only I didn't see it first," Jane corrects. It's very bad form in birding to take credit for someone else's sighting. "It was Miss Deerfield's secretary who pointed it out to me."

"Has it made any kind of call?" Roy rapidly thumbs more pages.

"No, it's been entirely quiet."

Roy's finger slows on a picture, then stops. He goes from the book to the binoculars to the bird and back again several times. His finger stays put. Onto his face comes a dawning look of joy.

"It's a brambling," he whispers, as if the very naming of it might cause the creature to disappear.

Jane studies the proffered page, while Roy quickly weights opens several other books and consults them. His smile grows until he's grinning like a boy possessed of a dime in a penny candy store.

"It's a female brambling, Jane!"

Jane reads the description: a six-inch-long Eurasian bird, member of the finch family, found mainly in birch forests from Scandinavia to eastern Siberia. The name means "little bramble bird," although they generally prefer trees and have been known to appear at backyard feeders.

"What's it doing here?" she asks.

"Probably blown off course during a migration, although this isn't the right time of year." A tinge of doubt enters Roy's voice as he acknowledges the quandary of accounting for the bird's arrival. Maybe it actually appeared in North America the previous fall or winter, up north or out west, and has been riding the prevailing winds toward New England? He's sure it's a brambling. "We have to get someone to confirm it," he says, "see if it's been reported."

"I called Hortense and left a message," Jane offers.

"Let's call her again." Roy heads for the cottage phone. "Hortense!" he shouts into the receiver. "We got a brambling here at Jane's house! Get over as soon as you get home and get this message!"

A scorched smell comes from the stove.

"The macaroni!" Jane dives for the pot, the water boiled away, curls of burnt pasta stuck to the bottom of the pan. "Roy, I was going to make us some dinner. How do you feel about tuna sandwiches?"

"Fine." At this moment, Roy would eat worms. His eyes alight with a gleam on Jane's laptop. "Mind if I use your computer?"

"Help yourself."

He's clacking away before the words are out of her mouth. Amused, she turns to the sink, scraping out the blackened macaroni with a spoon. She drains a can of tuna fish and chops celery and onions, while Roy, eyes riveted to the screen, talks at her over his shoulder.

"There was a brambling in New England five years ago, spotted a few times between January and March. One in Portland, Oregon, four years ago in December. The first-ever sighting in the United States was in Washington in 1967. I'm not finding any log-ons of recent sightings."

"Could it be an escapee like that monk parakeet?"

"Unlikely. It's not the kind of bird anyone would

have as a pet, besides which, it's illegal to possess any migratory birds." Roy types, scans, types some more.

"Roy? Eat?" Jane brings him a sandwich on a plate and a glass of milk. He nods, but when she sets the plate beside the computer, he ignores the food. She fixes a second plate for herself and takes it to the window seat, watching for further movement in the hedge. The brambling sits un-moving, feathers trembling in the dying wind, a winged creature bruised and battered, out of its season, far off course.

Hortense arrives, breathless, a few minutes later, and she and Roy creep to the window seat together.

"Yes, yes," she whispers, as between the binoculars and the books, the two of them strain to reconfirm every detail and rule out other species. They ache for it to be a brambling, yet they don't dare make it into something it's not. A sighting doesn't count if it has no integrity, if it isn't true beyond all doubt. They debate going outside and pishing but don't want to risk scaring the bird away. Then as if the brambling itself is ready to be known, it edges out of the leaves and perches quietly in full view. Roy sees it and knows in his heart. Hortense slowly exhales and smiles. Jane gazes through her binoculars, beginning to catch their awe. What a strange, passionate world she has entered where the appearance of a six-inch bird seems to rival the discovery of a new galaxy or a previously unknown sonnet by Shake-speare.

"Oh, Roy, a brambling. What a feather in your cap!" Hortense laughs at the bad pun. "If only it will stick around a few days so Melanie and the others can see it. A brambling and your four hundred and ninety-ninth bird!"

Roy beams as if it's Christmas, his birthday and the Fourth of July all rolled into one.

The next day, all hell breaks loose.

Chapter 16

Jane wakes about five-thirty, imagining she hears voices, then movement outside the cottage. Warily, she slides out of bed and edges to the window, anticipating prowlers. The sun is just above the horizon, filtering through gauzy clouds, and she puzzles at the sight of four, no five, figures creeping around her yard in the obscure dawn. What on earth—? They aren't behaving like professional burglars, more like a contingent of amateur bunglers whispering and beckoning to one another as they tiptoe around the walls. Her memory flashes to the snooping antiques dealer who showed up for one of the spring nature walks, and she gasps in anger at their nerve. Jane slams on jeans, tee shirt, boots, bolts down the stairs, and ambushes them from the front door.

"Excuse me!" she demands loudly. "What do you think you're doing?"

"Shh!"

The five invaders have fanned out, starting toward the field, and two of them, a tall woman and a bald man, turn and angrily shush her. Jane strides out to confront them.

"Stop right there! This is private property!"

"Keep your voice down, you'll scare the bird," the tall woman hisses, and suddenly Jane recognizes her and the bald man who appears to be her companion. They're the same pair she caught trespassing earlier that spring who obstinately claimed she was interrupting their scientific pursuits. The woman has dishwater blond hair pulled into a ponytail and wears camouflage gear. The man, dressed in khaki, resembles a bad imitation of a safari hunter. The other three, all middle-aged, are outfitted as if for an expedition in an assortment of army surplus jackets, Australian bush hats and waist packs hung with canteens and water bottles. All wear binoculars around their necks and one of the men carries an expensive spotting scope. It would be funny if not for their presumption. Jane plants herself in front of the angular blond woman.

"I've told you before. This is private property. We do nature walks every Sunday morning from eight to ten a.m. You're welcome to attend. Right now, you're trespassing. Get out."

She points tensely, although there shouldn't be any question which way is the exit.

"You reported a brambling," the woman insists. "You can't make a rare bird report and not expect people to come see it." She looks Jane scornfully up and down. "You have no idea how important this is, do you?"

"I have an idea it's illegal." Jane holds her ground. "Now you can either move off this property or I'm phoning the police. In fact, I'm phoning the police anyway."

She turns and marches to the cottage, furious. Behind her, the three unknown birders confer among themselves and nudge each other toward the gate. The blond woman and the bald man refuse to budge, relentlessly scanning the hedge, trees and field, keeping one eye and ear alert to the road as if gauging how long they might have before they're forced to make an escorted exit. The nerve of these people! Jane thinks, outraged that they've ignored her, hitting the number for the police on her phone. To their credit, a squad car is there in six minutes, by which time the three more law-abiding birders are already back on the shore road outside Deerfield's gate, trying not to look guilty. The bald man and blond woman hurry to join them as the black-and-white approaches, and Jane steps up to the officer as he emerges.

"Okay, folks, what's going on here?" the cop says, eyeing the group. Camouflage outfits? Bush hats? It's barely six in the morning, way too early for a bunch of nut cases.

"A very rare Eurasian finch has been seen on this property, officer." The bald man, prim and prissy, pulls a paper from his pocket, inserting himself before Jane can speak. He unfolds the quartered sheet and thrusts it at the cop. "It was reported last night on the Internet."

"If you didn't want it known, you shouldn't have reported it," the blond woman seconds in a so-there tone, adding a vigorous nod of her head for emphasis.

"I *didn't* report it, this is *private* property, and you're *trespassing*," Jane repeats, steaming. She turns to the officer. "I'm Jane Avery, the property manager. I'm the one who phoned."

The officer beckons her a little aside, and together they peruse the paper. More a query than a report, the printout gives a detailed account of last night's sighting and identification of a female brambling at Deerfield and asks for confirmation of any other brambling sightings in the area. It's written and signed by Roy.

Jane's breath goes out in a long sigh. "Roy is one of our regular birders," she explains to the cop. "I asked him over to help me identify the bird, and he was using my laptop to verify it."

The cop nods and walks back to the group, the two leaders no less defiant. He takes off his hat and runs his fingers through his short, sandy hair, exasperation on his fleshy face. Jeesh! Some days you'd think he was a kinder-garten monitor.

"Okay, so somebody may have seen a rare bird," he says. "I don't see anywhere on this paper that there's an invitation to enter the property and search for it. Why don't you all head home now and get yourselves a canary."

Indignant grumblings arise among the birders.

"This is a public road, isn't it?" demands the tall woman.

"Yes, the shore road is public, but the estate is not. See the big wrought iron fence, see the lock on the front gate?" The cop gestures.

"Well, there's no gate on the road up to the cottage," the bald man chimes in.

"Sir, you're trying my patience. That road is clearly a service drive to the cottage, and the cottage is clearly part of a private estate. Now just so there's no further misunderstanding, I want everyone to listen carefully."

The three timid birders hang their heads for a scolding, the two leaders shuffle sulkily.

"This," says the cop, pointing both index fingers at the pavement beneath their feet, "is a public road. Everything on the west side of the road," he pushes his palms repeatedly toward Deerfield, "all the way south to the beach, is private property, whether there's a fence, a gate, no trespassing signs or not. Everybody with me so far?"

They nod, two grudgingly.

"This strip east of the road," he pushes his palms toward the narrow stretch of shore and ocean beyond, "is public property. You can stand there all day staring out to sea with your binoculars if you've a mind to. But you can't obstruct the road, leave litter, create a nuisance or noise disturbance, and, one more time," he pauses for effect, "you can't cross onto Deerfield property. Got that?"

The ringleaders huff a little, then draw their confederates onto the shoreline to regroup. The cop turns to Jane.

"Nut cases!" he says. "Miss Deerfield's not going to like this."

"I know. Thank you for coming. I can't believe I woke up and found them crawling over my lawn." Jane makes a rough attempt to finger-comb her still unbrushed hair.

"You want to file trespassing charges? You can, you know."

"I have a feeling that would only provoke them and

make matters worse. Do you think it's safe for me to leave them for a few minutes while I get properly dressed?"

She indicates her rumpled clothes, and the cop nods sympathetically. "Sure, you go ahead, and I'll stick around. I have to call in a report anyway."

"Thanks, officer. Can I bring you a cup of coffee? A bagel?"

"Black, two sugars. If you happen to have any cream cheese for that bagel, I'd consider myself a lucky man."

Jane walks back to the cottage, the adrenaline surge beginning to ease. The nerve of those people! She realizes she has said, or thought, this several times already, but she still can't get over their blatant disregard for trespassing. And the cop is absolutely right—Charlotte isn't going to like this one bit. Jane groans as she changes her clothes. Then she descends to the kitchen and is toasting bagels—one for the cop, one for herself, and yes, she does have cream cheese— when a thought hits.

Where is the bird, the brambling? Where is it?

The early morning mist is quickly evaporating, and she takes her binoculars to the window seat and scans the hedge for the bird. It isn't where they saw it last night, and the five invaders, with however much ground they covered before Jane awoke, apparently didn't catch sight of it either. She hopes it has flown away safely, although the rest of her regulars will be disappointed not to add it to their life lists. But Roy did, and Hortense confirmed it. The others are younger; they'll have more chances.

The toaster oven dings, and Jane spreads cream cheese on the bagels, pours two mugs of coffee, and carries a tray down to the cop, who chats amiably as he eats.

"Going to be a hot day, I heard, and there they are in that commando gear, out in the sun, no shade." He chuckles. "Wonder how long they'll last."

Jane relaxes at the wisdom of this, and the cop departs with thanks for the breakfast and a reassurance that she can call again if anyone gets pushy. She sits on a rock by the front gate to sip her coffee, but it isn't long before the approach of rapid, clumping footsteps makes her jump to her feet.

"What's going on?" Bella stares at the five outland-ishly dressed birders camped opposite. "I saw a police car leave. I came as quickly as I could."

"They're hoping to see a brambling," Jane keeps her voice calm, hoping to break the news gently, "that bird you saw in the hedge yesterday. It's somehow flown here from northern Europe."

"Europe? Oh no! How do they know about it?"

"I invited two of the Sunday birders over last night, and one of them went on the Internet to see if there had any been any other local sightings."

Bella's crooked body stiffens. Her face drains white. "You didn't post it on the Internet?"

"No, not exactly. Roy was only asking if—"

"No, no! Oh, how could anyone be so stupid! Don't you realize what these birders do? The Internet is like a magnet for them. They jump in their cars at the merest rumor of a rare bird, and they'll overrun anything to see it. It will be the Chinese seagull all over again!"

"Please…" Jane stands bewildered by Bella's agita-tion. The appearance of five trespassers, although unsettling, hardly seems a major crisis. But within a few hours, she's beginning to understand. The five birders are now thirty, and the strip of shoreline is becoming an encampment. By noon, the crowd has doubled to sixty or more. The original invaders have stripped off their jackets to reveal more comfortable tee shirts, the newcomers have brought folding chairs, and the sunbathers en route to and from the beach at the south end of the road stop and add to the gawkers. The heat doesn't seem likely to drive them away anytime soon. To Jane's immense relief, Roy and Hortense arrive with Melanie on the chance of showing her the bird, and when she beckons their car up the service drive, the tall bossy woman shouts, "Hey! Why do they get to go in?" Jane ignores her, and her three friends cover for her at the front gate while she goes to the house to face Charlotte. Bella escorts her up to the studio and clamps her hands over her ears.

"You're fired!" Charlotte screams. "Fired!" She hurls a paintbrush at the windows—a mob at her gate!—and Jane flinches as the brush bounces off a pane and lands on the wide sill beside a pair of binoculars. Binoculars? Since when have Charlotte and Bella become birdwatchers? Then she recalls the accuracy with which Bella always comments on the head count at the Sunday walks, how she knew Hortense when Hortense has never met her. Is this how Bella knows? She and Charlotte spy on the gate, on the cottage…on Jane? She blinks at the thought, jerks her gaze back to the two women before her.

Bella looks broken and fragile. Charlotte rants about security and break-ins, but she's trembling, her voice shakes, and Jane begins to comprehend that what she's seeing is not wrath but fear. Two old women living alone in a big house while outside the barbarians muster at the gate. How easy to slink back after dark and break in here! Any first floor window could be smashed with a pipe. Sleeping in the upstairs bedrooms, Charlotte and Bella wouldn't hear. Even if the alarm did sound, anyone who knew what he was doing could be in and out quickly, disappear into those three hundred acres of woods behind the house. Deerfield must contain any number of objects and jewelry worth stealing, or the plain thrill of rape and murder.

"Miss Deerfield, three of our Sunday regulars are out front to help," says Jane, shaken by the perception, "and I'll call the police again to see what they recommend." It doesn't matter that she's fired. She is responsible for this mess, and she will clean it up somehow. A sense of loneliness grips her, she doesn't want to leave another place in disgrace, and then, more deeply, she feels a second wave overwhelming her. She doesn't want to leave *here*. "I'm very sorry, Miss Deerfield. I had no idea when we first saw the bird yesterday that anything like this could result. I'm sure most of the people out there are just curious and will go away soon."

"They have no right to be here, no right!" Charlotte cries, hugging herself. "I feel like a prisoner!"

"I'll take care of it," says Jane firmly. "Just stay inside."

Back outside she finds a squad car already parked in the service drive. It's not the same officer as this morning, but a wiry woman with close-cropped brunette hair.

"I stopped by to monitor the situation," she tells Jane, as they walk toward the gate together. "Any problems so far?"

"Only that Miss Deerfield is very upset. Can't you order them to leave?" Jane sweeps her hand at the crowd, although the size is holding steady.

"We've considered it, and the chief is aware of the situation, but unless there's a real threat or disturbance, it's usually better to let these events run their course. Last summer we had a dead right whale wash up on the beach on the other side of town. Decomposing, stank to high heaven, but you wouldn't believe the people who drove to see it and dragged their kids along. I suppose they thought it was an educational experience, and we did get a delegation of scientists in to study it and arrange for the removal. We set up a perimeter around the carcass, instituted traffic and parking control, and other than that, it blew over within twenty-four hours."

"I hope so," Jane sighs.

Across the road, Hortense is speaking to the birders. "Yes, it was very exciting," she tells them, smiling, "although you could see the poor creature was spent by that storm. No, we haven't seen it since. By the way, I've been hoping to pick up a yellow-billed cuckoo for my list this year. Would you have any suggestions as to where my best chance is?"

Immediately, she's bombarded with remonstrances, go here, don't go there, not all of which may be on the up-and-up. Rabid birders aren't above lying or misdirecting a competitor to the wrong site to keep a rare bird sighting to themselves, rather like a jealous cook who omits the secret ingredient from a recipe before passing it on. The bossy blond woman, naturally, has seen more yellow-billed cuckoos than anyone else, and she's quick to let everyone know she has almost nine hundred birds on her life list. She begins an argument with a mustached man over whether a Florida great white heron can be counted as a separate species or whether it's simply a color morph of a great blue. Hortense slips back to Roy, Melanie and Jane, who are chatting with the cop.

"Consorting with the enemy, were you," chuckles Roy.

"Certainly not," Hortense replies. "I was endeavoring to win their confidence and plant the hint that they ought to leave our little storm-tossed brambling to recover and depart on other ornithological pursuits. I don't think I succeeded."

"Tell me," says the cop, "in a situation like this, would it actually be better if the bird did appear so they could get a glimpse of it and go home? Or could you shoo it deeper into the woods and tell them it's flown off?"

"Roy and I could go take another look around the cottage," Hortense offers. "If there's no sight of it, that may prompt the less serious ones to leave."

"What if it is there?" Jane asks.

Hortense and Roy exchange glances. Jimmy Stewart isn't going to like this.

"We'll lie," says Hortense.

Jane's shoulders droop. For all the worry and annoyance the situation has caused, she's begun to understand how much it means to Hortense, Roy and Melanie, to the nut cases across the road, to see this particular bird. Crazy as it seems, it meant something to her to see it last night. It's like getting to view the Mona Lisa or witness that record-breaking home run or, once every seventy-six years, to marvel at Halley's Comet streaking across the sky. It makes you feel special, and that's all the people on the other side of the road want, to feel special. So if the brambling wants to hang around and make an appearance, why not?

"Look, it doesn't matter to me," she says. "I've already been fired by Miss Deerfield."

"What? No! She can't!"

Hortense and Roy break into exclamations, and Melanie, who has been lazily listening to the grownups' conversation while she watches the funny people across the road, is suddenly alert and distressed. Fired is a bad thing. It means you did something very wrong and you have to go away. She clutches Jane's hand. She's sure Jane is not a bad person. Whatever she did, it must have been an accident.

"No, don't go!" she cries.

Roy sizes up the situation and takes command. "This is my fault. I posted that sighting, and I shouldn't have done it without Miss Deerfield's permission. You are not going to lose your job over this, Jane. Hortense, we'll lie. You sneak up to the cottage first with Melanie while no one across the road is looking, and I'll follow in a few minutes. If the brambling is there, we'll let Melanie get a peek."

"But it's a secret, Melanie." Hortense cups Melanie's face in her hands and looks straight into her eyes. "If we see this little bird, it's a secret. Do you understand?"

Melanie nods solemnly, crosses her heart. "A secret," she repeats. "Don't tell."

"Attagirl, off you go." Roy scoots Hortense and Melanie away, then rocks on his heels, whistling nonchalantly should anyone glance their way. Lying to save a lady's honor—or her job—well, Jimmy Stewart would approve of that. Two minutes later, he sneaks off toward the cottage. On the shoreline, a few people are beginning to yawn and some of the sunbathers straggle off. Fifteen minutes later, the reconnaissance trio returns.

"No brambling," Hortense announces, relieved to be telling the truth.

Roy seconds it with a nod, Melanie third. She's not disappointed they haven't seen the bird. Somehow not seeing it makes it an even better secret.

Hortense flexes her shoulders and clears her throat as if she's about to step onto a stage. She strolls across the road, a genial smile on her face, and listens for several minutes to a debate over the credibility of a razorbill sighting last December. The prissy bald man contends that the couple who reported it were novices and it was never confirmed by anyone else.

"Yes," sighs Hortense, as if she's been present all along, "and I wish I could tell you for sure it was a brambling we saw here last night, but we've just had another search and there's no sign of it. Hopefully, it has recuperated and is safely on its way home."

The news is met with groans. Then a car pulls up, and a young man hung with cameras and lenses gets out.

"I'm a photography intern with the newspaper," he says eagerly. "We heard there's a rare bird here, and the editor sent me to try and get a shot of it. Where is it?"

"It appears to have left," repeats Hortense casually, and her shrug seems to convince even the bossy woman. It's inconceivable that a birder would forgo the chance to publicize their sighting of a rare species and earn glory among their fellow birders.

The intern ruefully scans the sky, although he has no idea what the bird looks like.

"It was nice meeting you all," says Hortense, waving goodbye to the group. "You know, I had some good luck with shorebirds last week at that cove past the creek outlet."

She strolls back to Jane and reports.

"Right," says Roy, taking Melanie's hand, "if we leave now, that should seal it. And don't you worry, Jane. I'll come back first thing tomorrow and personally explain to Miss Deerfield that this was my fault."

They head for Hortense's car. Across the road, a few others are packing up scopes, water bottles, field guides, backpacks. Sweat stains their sticky tee shirts. It's one-thirty, and stomachs are rumbling. Cars begin to pull away.

"Brambling! There!" the blond woman barks, her arm shooting up. Her finger quivers like a divining rod at a small brownish-orange bird perched on the branch of a maple tree on the edge of the property beside the road. Instantly, the crowd reverses direction, everyone hustles back, scopes snap into place, the photography intern's camera goes *whirr, whirr, whirr*. The bird is in clear view, and despite the flurry of noise and attention, it doesn't startle. It merely sits, looking a little baffled, as if it has been waiting for some time to be noticed.

"My sighting!" claims the blond woman. "I saw it first!"

"You did not!" Roy gasps. Halfway into the car, he unfolds his skinny body out again as quickly as he can. "You did not! I saw it yesterday, and I put my name on that rare bird alert."

"You only queried, you didn't positively ID it," the blond woman shouts.

"I did!" Roy shouts back. "I ID'ed it, and this young lady right here saw it first." He puts his arm proudly around Jane's shoulders.

"Well, no, it wasn't me actually, it was Miss Deerfield's secretary," Jane begins, because the photographer is rapidly jotting notes, and she remembers even in this commotion that in true birding etiquette you never take credit for someone else's sighting. Around her, people are jostling and shushing each other, everyone trying to get closer.

Melanie looks up at the brambling, small and quiet, brown and orange, a pretty color like cinnamon toast, its feathers softly fluffed out. Melanie likes soft things.

"Is that the secret bird?" she asks Hortense.

"Oh dear," says Hortense. "Not anymore."

Chapter 17

The story and color photos of the brambling appear in the newspaper the next day.

"You? You saw the bird first?" In the studio, Charlotte turns on Bella, gripping the article in disbelief. "How could you do this to us? Why didn't you keep your mouth shut?"

"How was I to know?" Bella pounds her temples in frustration. "It was just a little bird. I only pointed it out by way of conversation."

"You aren't supposed to be having conversations with the servants! Just make them behave, that's your job!"

"She's not a servant, she's an employee."

"I don't care what she is, she's not even supposed to be here anymore. I fired her! What are they doing out there?" Charlotte grabs the binoculars and stares at the gate. It's only nine a.m., and already the crowd on the strip of shore opposite Deerfield numbers about a hundred. "I can't paint," she pleads, rubbing her hands up and down her arms. "How am I supposed to paint, to do anything, when those people are besieging us?"

"It's not us they're besieging, it's the bird," says Bella, but there is no comfort in the statement. After the brambling appeared late yesterday for its photo op, it flew right toward the house and out of sight. Given half a chance, those birders would pour over the property like a tidal wave to flush it out. And who knows how many of those now peering through the gate aren't thinking of bramblings at all but calculating to themselves, I didn't know this mansion was here, all alone, easy pickings, wonder what they have inside...?

Bella kneads a hand on her abdomen—the anxiety is making her stomach aches flare up again—and looks out the window to the service drive where a squad car is now permanently stationed. Jane is handing the officer a mug and a donut or something on a plate. She has also called in her Sunday morning regulars and posted them along the border of the property to prevent incursions by the outsiders. Bella recognizes Hortense, Roy and Melanie through the binoculars, those two men who seem to belong together—gay, no doubt—and that busty actress, who has brought along a handsome man and is flirting with the crowd. Whatever commotion Jane has set off, she is vigilantly controlling it, and Bella thinks a little sadly that she and Jane did have the start of a real conversation the other day in her cottage, and it was pleasant.

"I'll go find out what's happening," she says bravely, and it is bravery on her part, because in a crowd she is the one who will get trampled or picked on. She's the Quasimodo.

She clumps downstairs and steps outside. The mood isn't as fearsome as she expected, and as she moves tentatively forward she doesn't feel threatened. The crowd, although large, appears mostly patient and good-natured. The cop, a fleshy-faced, sandy-haired man, is munching a bagel with cream cheese Jane has brought him. Jane gives her the latest report: no brambling this morning.

"I phoned the land trust yesterday afternoon to alert them to our situation, and they're very concerned," Jane adds. "They didn't foresee anything like this occurring. Would you like to meet the Sunday regulars who are helping with crowd control?"

"Yes, please." Bella nods, and Jane takes her to Hortense, who beams and pumps her hand.

"So you're the one who first spotted our errant avian visitor. Good eyes! Though we are sorry for the disturbance this is causing." Her faces lapses into an apology.

"It seems all right," says Bella slowly. Good eyes. What does that mean? No one has ever said anything like this to her before, especially not with her right eye permanently, glaringly bloodshot. Yet Hortense clearly intends this as a compliment. Jane takes her along the line to meet Raven and Brandon, who warmly urge her to come see them in the British bedroom farce at the dinner theater, to the two men, Russ and Charlie, who offer her a cranberry-orange muffin from a box they've brought from their café, to Roy and Melanie, who sit in lawn chairs in the shade playing checkers on a magnetic board.

"Pleased to meet you, madam," says Roy, unkinking his joints to rise and doff his baseball cap. "Congratulations on being the first to sight the brambling, although I do have a few words to say as to what has transpired as a result of that." He clears his throat with several phlegmy ahems. "It was I who posted the report that has subsequently drawn this crowd, and I wish to make an appointment with Miss Deerfield to clarify my responsibility. I understand she has fired Ms. Avery, and I cannot allow Ms. Avery to lose her position on my account. Moreover, you would be losing a highly efficient property manager who is a credit to your estate."

"I'll see what can be done," says Bella, making a slight formal nod in keeping with this unexpected speech. It's unduly courtly and old-fashioned, yet the chivalry of it awakens a longing note. Why does it so often seem that only old men know how to be gentlemen anymore? She glances to Melanie, who has watched this exchange with undisguised interest. Melanie doesn't know what to make of Bella; there is no one like her in special ed at school. She looks and talks like a grownup, but she comes only a few inches above Roy's elbow. She resembles a gnome or a dwarf from a fairy tale, or maybe she had a bad accident and her bones didn't get put back together right, the same as happened to Melanie's brain. But whatever the cause, you mustn't judge people by their looks, no one knows this better than Melanie, and she holds out her hand for Bella to shake. Bella looks startled, then slips her dry palm into the child's plump, moist one. Melanie points to the checkerboard, which Roy brought this morning when he picked her up.

"I have a queen," she says. Checkers is a good game because the rules are simple and you can be red or black. When you get a piece all the way across the board, you get to say "King me!" and be crowned with another piece; those little ridges click-fit together just like a set of teeth. And Roy said they could change it to "Queen me!" which makes more sense because Melanie is a girl. She pushes a red checker forward, the round plastic disc stamped with a fancy royal design. This is a perfect day, what with shady trees, a secret bird, and a chocolate-chip muffin from Russ and Charlie's café. Also, Mrs. Egan, the housekeeper, packed a turkey sandwich and potato chips and juice for her so she can stay as long as she wants.

"I'm going to walk toward the beach and make sure no one is sneaking in from the south," Jane tells Bella, aside, "and about what Roy said, don't worry. I'll leave as soon as this blows over."

"No." The word comes quickly from Bella's mouth, and she means it. "Please don't. Miss Deerfield sometimes doesn't mean what she says."

"Well, I do," says Jane. She turns and heads along the line of regulars to inform them and the cop where she's going. Raven nods. She and Brandon have been chatting with a bespectacled man who is a Yale ornithologist, and as Jane starts away Raven gives Brandon a none-too-subtle nudge. The ornithologist is demonstrating to her the peculiar mating behavior of the male woodcock, turning around in place and at each quarter turn uttering a nasal *peent!*

"You call that foreplay?" Raven demands, her laugh descending into a sexy chuckle, and the ornithologist grins like a love-struck schoolboy. She does have a thing for intellectual types, she isn't sleeping with Burt yet, and what the hell, a man in the hand...

Bella watches Raven wrinkle her nose in laughter at the ornithologist, notes Brandon catching up to Jane. The crowd on the beach has been diverted to watching seagulls and a flock of little shorebirds that skitter along the tide line like mechanical wind-up toys. Bella glances to the house, suddenly reluctant to return. Perhaps she should stay here in her official capacity as secretary in case there are further developments. She wanders back toward Roy and Melanie, the cranberry-orange muffin, fragrant and sticky, cupped in her hand, a child on the fringe of a game longing to be invited in.

"I was wondering...I noticed some little birds running on the beach..."

"Sanderlings," says Roy. "You like birds? Here, have a seat."

Jane and Brandon head south toward the beach, walking on the shady side of the road. Traffic is light, a few cars crammed with teenagers, a muscular bicyclist in purple spandex pumping by, no evidence of guerilla birders trying to breach the estate. Jane's initial, purposeful pace slows as the mini-circus at Deerfield falls behind them and the lazy August day takes over.

"Well," says Brandon, strolling beside her, "I was going to call you, and now here I am on bird patrol. It's just as well because otherwise I have the play every night this week. If I can rustle up a free ticket, will you come and applaud your local starving actor?"

"Are you any good?" She matches the slight tease in his tone.

"Extremely. Also, I take off my shirt in Act II."

"And that sells tickets?"

"You bet. You'd be surprised how many busloads we get from out-of-town women's clubs looking for a hot night out."

What can she do but laugh? Except there's something not funny about the way Brandon affects her. Two minutes in his company and she's warm, she's picturing him with his shirt off. She would really like to know, a bit irritated with herself, whether her reaction to him has any substance or is it going to be merely physical?

"Attendance is good then," she says, damping the banter to a more platonic level, and Brandon agreeably takes the cue.

"Yes, but it could be better. The play's fun, the cast is great, but it's the management of the theater I find discouraging. I don't think the owners appreciate how much time and money it really takes to put on a show."

"Who are the owners?"

"Summer people from New York, would-be impresarios. The theater dates back to 1910, and it's had its ups and downs and periodic closures. The present owners took it up on a whim about five years ago, but they're rarely here now. I think the plays could go year-round if they'd hire an experienced manager and put some cash into it, not that I expect to get rich there."

"What do you expect? What do you want out of acting, I mean?" He's chosen to accompany her, so she doesn't hide her curiosity.

"What do I want?" He scoops up a small, dusty feather and hands it to her as they walk. "Back-to-back Oscars, a sex scene with Gwyneth Paltrow, a five-million-dollar home in Hollywood, and my picture on the cover of *People* magazine as the Sexiest Man Alive. Seriously, I'm grateful just to be working on a steady basis." He gestures at the feather she's stroking between her fingers, ash gray with a black oval patch on one side, downy whitish fluff at the base of the stem. "Can you tell what kind of bird it is?"

"No, but did you know that most feathers have tiny barbs on them that hook together to form an interlocking structure that's essential for streamlined flight? When a bird preens, it's not vanity. It's cleaning the feathers and rearranging and relocking the barbs. It's preflighting."

She holds the feather toward him, and he slips a thumb and forefinger along the silky shaft.

"I don't feel any barbs."

"You won't, they're microscopic. And see how the tip of the feather is a little worn?" She touches the blunted upper edge, smoothing it with a fingertip to coax back a rounded shape. "Feathers regularly get broken and damaged, so most birds molt at least once a year to renew them. As the new feather begins to form in each follicle, it gradually pushes the old feather out. It can take four to eight weeks for a complete molt to occur, and the timing is linked to a species' breeding and migration patterns. Some birds will start a molt before migration, suspend it during the long flight, then resume the molt when they reach their destination. That's because flying and molting are competing processes—you can't fly at maximum capability when you're shedding feathers—so nature separates them because survival is dependent on both processes being completed successfully." She stops stroking the feather and looks up, embarrassed. "I'm sorry. I've been reading too many birding books. Weren't we talking about your acting aspirations?"

"We were, but never mind. That's interesting. I've never hung around with a bunch of birders before."

"I've never hung around with a bunch of actors. Anything special I should know about them?"

"Just that we're ordinary people who earn our living by pretending to be other people, and contrary to popular belief, we're not shallow egotists who can't resist checking our reflection when we walk past a mirror."

"I never thought—"

She halts in the road, protesting the stereotype, but Brandon laughs.

"Sure you did. Maybe not this minute, but everyone thinks it at one time or another when they're introduced to an actor. You have to admit it's pretty suspicious, grown adults running around playing make-believe, and it makes you wonder, is he acting now with me?"

"Okay, maybe I did wonder that," Jane admits, walking again. "And the answer is...?"

"That I never act off-stage any more than anyone else does, and probably less. I think you'll find most actors are pretty grounded people."

"Like Raven?"

"Okay, you got me there." This time they both laugh, then Brandon continues. "Bottom line: I like what I do, I'm good at it, and I've had enough success to encourage me to keep going, although I'd hate to think I'll still be playing Android #4 or Man In Café when I'm fifty. Those are some of the impressive TV credits on my resume, in case you aren't aware. What about you? What's your life plan?"

He tosses a look her way, and Jane caresses the feather in her hand. He can't have any idea how deeply the question cuts, how starved she is for a true answer, especially now.

"Well, for a start I guess I'm leaving Deerfield. I've been fired over this brambling incident."

"Why? That's totally unfair. You've done a lot for this place, and people would miss you."

"Hardly. I haven't been here long enough to be missed."

"Raven would. She often talks about you at the theater. And the Sunday morning walkers think quite highly of you."

"That's nice, but they'll find someone else."

"True, we're all replaceable."

"I thought you were encouraging me to stay?" She cocks her head at him in exasperation.

"I'm being honest, no acting. Isn't that what you want?"

"Yes, and it's irritating. Come on," she beckons to pick up the pace. "I'm supposed to be protecting the estate from intruders."

"Why? You've been fired, and you're leaving."

He catches her wrist to stop her onward stride, and the momentum of the pull brings her up against him. He doesn't exert any further pressure, letting her decide. It's the feel of him that's irresistible, Jane thinks as they connect, that recognizing in each other's scent and sensations that you have a match. The kiss is good, their bodies pressed in that pleasurable cell-by-cell exploration when every touch is a first, and standing in the cool shade, the heat they're generating beats anything the August day can pump out. And now they're relaxing into it, his hands easy on her hips, an inviting sway between them. When his mouth leaves hers, they know they'll be taking this up again at a more convenient time.

"Now," says Brandon, "I suggest we continue on to the beach, so you can fulfill your responsibilities as property manager. Because I don't believe you really want to go." He tweaks the feather she's still pinching between her thumb and finger, and as they walk, Jane smoothes the plume, restoring its shape, rehooking the invisible barbs to make it seamless and sleek.

"Hi!" Elizabeth, the teenaged girl in the entrance booth, looks up at Jane's approach, then shoots her a second, more deliberate glance as she takes in Brandon and his arm around her shoulder. Lucky you, her look says. She closes Chekhov with her finger holding the place. "What's happening with your bird up the road? I passed the crowd when I got here early this morning."

"No sign of it," says Jane. "We came to check if birders were camped down this way or giving you any problems."

"No, in this heat people just want to jump in the water." She motions to the swimmers, then a sudden worry creases her forehead. "What should I do if that bird does turn up here? I'm by myself, the town doesn't even provide a lifeguard at this beach. I can't control a crowd swarming in here."

"Call the police. Call me if you can't get them. You

have a phone?"

Elizabeth nods, producing it from her canvas tote, and Jane gives her the numbers to program in.

"Thanks, although if I see that bird, I'm just going to keep quiet," Elizabeth decides.

"Good plan, wish I'd thought of it. Hopefully, by tomorrow this will be over…" For an instant, Jane's mind sticks on the words. Tomorrow is Sunday. "We have to get back," she says abruptly, grabbing Brandon, and with a quick goodbye to Elizabeth they start up the shore road.

"What's wrong?" he asks.

"Tomorrow, it's Sunday."

He shakes his head, not getting it.

"The weekly walk. There are a hundred people outside the gate, and tomorrow morning at eight o'clock we're obligated to open the property."

"Cancel it. It's extraordinary circumstances. You'd be justified."

Jane nods, walking rapidly. Canceling the walk is her first instinct, and Charlotte and the land trust will undoubtedly support it. Allowing a horde to trample the estate in search of a single elusive bird won't serve either of their interests. But the town council and the chamber of commerce might feel differently. Already the stream of birdwatchers and curiosity seekers has meant increased business for the shops and restaurants, the bed-and-breakfasts where the die-hards took up overnight residence to be on the stakeout early this morning, the drugstore selling sunscreen, sun hats, visors, sunglasses, bottled water. It usually takes an art fair to get this much attention. Now the same effect has been achieved by one little bird. And when the front gate of Deerfield comes in view, the crowd has swollen again, and a musical truck is selling frozen lemonade and soft ice cream cones. Jane looks for the cop. He's slurping a lemonade in the shade with the mayor. She spots Raven. She's mesmerizing both the besotted Yale ornithologist and Tim Hennessey as she seductively licks a swirly chocolate cone.

Tim's gaze lifts, a hitch in his expression as he sees Jane and Brandon coming to meet him.

"I just got here," he says. "What's the story? Is anyone in charge?"

"I am," says Jane, and Brandon touches her shoulder.

"Listen," he says, leaning close, "you have a situation to handle, and Raven and I have to get to work. Besides, if I don't pull her out of here soon, that Yale guy's going to melt in his shorts." He casts a bemused glance at the shameless flirting nearby. "I'll call you tonight after the show. Don't lose your feather."

He leaves and tugs Raven away, and Jane smiles in spite of herself, the well-traveled little plume secure in her fingers. "I'm glad you came," she says to Tim. "We should go talk to Miss Deerfield's secretary, if she's still out here."

She leads Tim to where she last saw Bella, then pauses to register the strange sight. Bella is sitting in a lawn chair, playing checkers—no, it's chess—with Roy.

"Where's Melanie?" Jane asks cautiously, though what there is to be cautious about, she isn't sure.

"Hortense took her to your cottage for lunch and a nap," says Roy, not looking up.

"We thought the heat might be getting a little much for her," adds Bella, not looking up either.

The two of them stare intently at the board arrayed in chess pieces. Ah, chess, what a wonderful game, the intricate moves a fusion of tactics and choreography! Bella hasn't had a chance to play like this since Charlotte divorced Morton Fischer, it's simply not the same on the computer, and Roy spares a thought for his sweet, late wife Myrna, who laughingly confessed no head for the game and yet tried so hard to take it seriously so they would have one more pastime to share. Roy's hand hesitates over his bishop and Bella hunkers forward, neither of them fully attending what Jane is trying to communicate with some urgency.

"The Sunday morning walk, eight o'clock," Jane repeats firmly, and Bella lets out a small, despairing "Oh!" as the words begin to penetrate and the chess game dies from her mind.

"How many of the people out there know about the walks?" Tim asks, frowning.

"A few, at least." Jane points out the tall blond woman and her four companions, still as much on alert as ever. "By now, she's probably spread the word to everyone in the crowd."

Tim shakes his head. "No, it's probably just the opposite. The really sly ones will keep mum because if there is a walk tomorrow, they won't want a troop of amateurs in their way. They'll want that brambling all to themselves. I suggest we wait. As long as the brambling doesn't reappear, a lot of people will drift off, and by tomorrow you may be down to a manageable group. If not, we'll cancel then. Either way, I'll stick around to give you a hand."

"Thank you," says Jane, and Bella seconds with a thank-you of her own. It seems a good plan. The only problem is, it doesn't work.

Despite the continued absence of the brambling, the crowd continues to increase over the course of the afternoon. A minibus of birders arrives from Massachusetts, a van from Vermont, a bird club from upstate New York. They've set out fresh this morning for a great Saturday adventure, and like fans at a rock concert, they're willing and eager to wait for a glimpse of the star. From the chatter on their cell phones they're also contacting every other birder within a three-hundred-mile radius. Every time it seems a few people leave, more determined reinforcements arrive to enlarge the ranks. When the cop takes a stand about vehicles parked on the verge, the birders begin democratically organizing a shuttle service, sending the majority of the cars to park in town and teaming up in vans to ferry people and supplies back and forth. The cop radios for two more squad cars. By three o'clock they have a half dozen police and nearly two hundred birders clogging the shore, along with TV cameras and newspaper reporters.

"This isn't supposed to be happening," Bella moans, beseeching Jane for help.

"I know," she agrees, at a loss. "They're supposed to be getting bored and leaving, not bonding."

"I'm sorry," says Tim. "I thought this would work."

"I don't like it," mutters the sandy-haired cop, standing beside them and giving the scene a once-over. The mood is still friendly, but people are beginning to bump shoulders for lack of space, there's a sharp "Hey!" as an expensive scope gets knocked over, and a strident "Excuse me! You're pushing!" rises above the crowd. "I'm going to talk to the other officers and put in a call to the chief," says the cop. "We've got valid public safety issues here, and I think it's time we broke this up."

He heads away, his ominous tone throwing a fresh blanket of anxiety over those on the Deerfield side of the road. What happens if the birders get ugly? Jane wonders. It sounds incongruous—these are sane, gentle people, aren't they?—yet the act of ordering them to leave and enforcing a dispersal is bound to cause arguments and bad feeling and increase the chance that someone might accidentally get hurt. Then the velvety purr of an engine begins to make itself heard from up the road, and as heads rotate in that direction an exhalation of pleasure and admiration swells through the crowd.

"Oooooh!"

A classic red roadster prowls toward them, sun glinting off its low-slung lines, its occupants a sixtyish couple looking about in bewilderment. The man, chubby-cheeked and white-bearded, wears an English driving cap, a short-sleeved yellow shirt open at the neck, Bermuda shorts in a madras plaid, a chunky gold watch and a diamond pinky ring. The woman's hair is rolled up under a broad-brimmed straw hat, her sleeveless ivory linen dress belted at the waist with a turquoise sash. Both appear taken aback and not a little frightened at the scene they've stumbled into, and the woman taps her husband's shoulder and points to the approaching police officer with her white-gloved hand. Their faces clear at this sign of authority, the relief that they haven't fallen into a mob. The birders edge closer, one of them knowingly proclaiming the car to be a Jaguar XK-140.

"Sorry, folks, you can't park here." The sandy-haired cop gives the car's fender a rueful pat. He sure wouldn't mind a longer look.

"My dear sir, I assure you that wasn't our intention." The man steps out to greet him, fumbling with an accordion-folded map. "My wife and I are looking for property in this area and appear to have taken a wrong turn. We didn't mean to intrude on any gathering."

People are pressing forward to see the car, and the sun-hatted woman, a little nervous at the scrutiny, exits the car and shies around to stand beside her husband. The cop waves dismissively at the birders.

"It's just some rare bird showed up," he says, moving closer to peer at the burl walnut dashboard. Man, what he wouldn't give to take a spin in this beauty, midnight black leather seats, soft as a glove to the touch.

"Oh, a rare bird," says the wife, her fears alleviated. "You mean there are two of them?"

In the instant of silence that falls, you could hear a feather drop. The birders gape at each other.

"Two?" the bossy blond woman demands. "You saw another brambling? Where?"

"Here, here," says the gentleman a little huffily, interposing himself between his wife and the crowd. "Mind your manners." The cop gives the nearest birders a menacing look, they back down, and the gentleman continues. "Yes, there's some little bird that people are watching at a park in town."

"A sweet little bird, wasn't it, dear?" the woman adds helpfully.

"What did it look like? Did you see it? Was it this one?" Bird books are thrust forward, fingers pointing to the wished-for answer.

"H'mm, yes, I think so," says the gentleman, as he and his wife peruse the pictures and confer.

"Rather like an English robin, wouldn't you say, dear?"

"In size, yes, but not quite such solid colors."

"It had a small patch of orange here."

"Do you think so? I didn't get the clear view you had of it."

"My, isn't this a helpful book. What nicely done illustrations."

"And what is the rare bird you've seen here?"

The lady and gentleman look up but get no answer.

"It's the brambling!" the Yale ornithologist shouts, and in a gallop the birders snatch up their books, backpacks, binoculars, scopes, water bottles, and bolt to the nearest vehicle they can find.

"My goodness, what strange people," the polite woman murmurs, clutching her straw hat to her head as the exodus swirls past her.

"Go ahead, my good man, slip in," the gentleman says to the cop, opening the car door. "Lovely area, this. Grew up by the seacoast in Dover myself, and we still visit Mother there once a year. You wouldn't happen to know of any reasonable seaside properties, would you, officer? In my experience, the best places aren't always advertised."

The woman affectionately taps her husband's shoulder, a reminder they must keep to their schedule, and after another minute they head back north. The remaining onlookers stand at loose ends, like hangers-on at a party after the best guests have departed. Then in twos and threes, they begin to wander off. In fifteen minutes, the shore is clear.

"Well, matters seem to have resolved themselves," says the cop affably to Jane and Bella, as the squad cars take their departure. "I think I'll mosey into town and see if there are any parking tickets that need writing. Adios."

Russ and Charlie shove off, and Hortense fetches Melanie, yawning and rubbing her eyes, from Jane's cottage.

"I better get you home or Mrs. Egan will be worried. Coming, Roy?"

"No, you go ahead." He clears his throat and shuffles his feet slightly in the direction of the interrupted chess game on the board beneath the tree.

Bella follows his glance. In the forty-eight hours since she spotted the brambling, she has been scared, angry, upset, intrigued, fascinated, entertained, complimented by Hortense, offered a cranberry-orange muffin by two nice gay men, shaken hands with an actress and a handsome actor, helped babysit the child Melanie, played chess with Roy, who also bought her a frozen lemonade, strategized with Jane, and been taken into their circle without question or qualm. She has been made to feel…welcome. And it was her, Bella, the insignificant secretary who knows nothing about birds, who first sighted the rare brambling. Good eyes!

"Don't leave," she says to Jane. "Miss Deerfield will rescind the firing."

"Don't spy on me anymore," Jane replies. She lifts her head in the direction of the studio window where she's sure Charlotte has been with the binoculars most of the afternoon.

Bella's mouth opens, then she nods, shamefaced. "I'm sorry. We won't." Roy invites her to the chessboard where they take seats opposite each other in the lawn chairs. In ten minutes Bella is ruthlessly winning.

"You got fired?" Tim asks, his face clouding.

"And rehired, it seems. Don't worry, it's just a small misunderstanding. Thank you for coming." They're the last two by the front gate, and Jane mops her forehead with her tee shirt sleeve. It's been a steam bath of a day, and her clothes are stuck to her skin with perspiration. "Can I get you something cold to drink? Iced tea? Soda?"

"No, thanks. You look pretty beat. I mean, it looks like you've been working hard." He tries too late to shift the balance of meaning, but Jane only laughs.

"Nothing a long, cool shower won't cure."

"Then I should go." He shrugs.

"Come again some Sunday."

"Sure, I'll see if I can."

They walk to his car, and when he's gone, Jane enters her cottage. The interior greets her with a welcome flush of coolness, and she pulls a juice can from the refrigerator and swallows a long drink. Then she picks up her phone.

"Brandon? Sorry to call you at work."

"No problem. The bar is quiet at the moment."

"Thank you."

"For what?"

"You know very well for what." She can hear him grinning at the other end of the line.

"Bucky wasn't too much of a ham?"

"Well, maybe a little. It took me about five minutes to recognize him. He didn't have a full beard when he played Big Daddy, just a goatee, and that driving cap was covering his bald head. I must say the madras shorts were a colorful touch. And Eileen was perfect as the doting wife. But where did they get that car?"

"What car?"

"You don't know about the Jaguar?"

Brandon laughs as Jane fills in the details. "Trust Bucky to make an entrance. He must have borrowed it some-where. The only coaching Raven and I gave them was to act like lost tourists, although Bucky did insist on having an English accent. The car, the costumes and anything else was strictly their own invention."

"So Raven was in on this, too?"

"We plotted it on the way back after we left you. And it worked? Everyone's gone?"

"The birders took off like a buffalo stampede." Jane stops with the juice can halfway to her lips. "Oh no, what's going to happen when they get to the park in town and the brambling isn't there? They'll turn around and come back again."

"I don't think so." There's a chuckle at the other end of the line.

"Why not?"

"Because as the thundering herd arrives, they're going to be met by two very dejected birders who had a rare brambling in sight and then lost it as it flew away northward."

"And those birders would be?"

"Dan and Amy. What a cast! What a show! What synergy!"

They spend a long minute laughing, then wind down to a moment, each recalling where they left off that afternoon. Jane's voice brushes the phone.

"Brandon?"

"I could be there by ten-thirty. If I act fast, I could be there by ten-fifteen."

They hang up, and Jane goes to the bathroom, unlaces her boots, pulls off her socks, sweaty tee shirt, bra, shorts and underpants. As she tosses them toward the wicker basket she uses as a laundry hamper, a small gray feather flutters out of the wad of clothing and lands by her bare feet. She picks it up, wondering. Though she doesn't remember doing so, she must have put it in her pocket after she got back from the beach with Brandon. Carefully, she preens the feather, restoring its curve, rehooking the invisible barbs. She glides it in a whispered touch over her face and down her neck, stopping as she catches her reflection in the mirror.

"I'm molting," she says, a little surprised, as if it's someone else to whom she must explain. "I came here to molt because I had to give up something I love and become something else. I have to grow a different set of feathers."

It's the truest answer she has been able to give yet, and in response a grip lets go inside her. She holds the feather near her lips, blowing gently to fluff the down at the base of the stem. New feathers. She rather likes the way they're coming in.

Chapter 18

The brambling is not seen again. Those who glimpsed it count themselves lucky or, in the case of the bossy woman, entitled. Those who didn't are disappointed, wistful, a little envious, yet mostly optimistic that another day will bring them an equally wondrous sight. A few onlookers will decide this birding stuff can be a lot of fun and will enrich the local stores with purchases of birdfeeders, seed, binoculars, field guides and hiking boots before they lose interest. A few will rediscover a pleasure in nature, pausing to observe a pair of ordinary white butterflies in a fluttering *pas de deux* or slowing their car past a row of tawny orange day-lilies lining a roadside.

For Jane, the brambling brings a sense of gratitude, a confirmation that she has passed another milestone into a new life. She has already thanked Brandon, asleep naked beside her the next morning. She reaches over to touch his shoulder, cautiously reaffirming possession, at least for the time being. She's never slept with an actor before, and despite his claims that he's as straightforward as the next guy, she couldn't help thinking when he arrived last night, Now we'll see some stagecraft. Who doesn't pretend a bit when getting into bed with a stranger for the first time? But their lovemaking didn't start out as quite the smooth scenario she expected. Caught up in hotly undressing each other, he forgot to remove his watch, and when he reached to pull a pillow beneath her angled neck, the watchband snagged in her hair, causing her to yelp and him to crush her collarbone with his elbow as he started back in reaction. He apologized, contrite at his clumsiness, and she apologized because it really hadn't hurt as much as her startled gasp implied. After that it got very good, very fast. He was sly with his hands, keeping her wet, teasing with a probing finger until she was close, closer, *oh please!* then backing off to let her panting subside while his hardness grew hotter inside her pumping fist. He smelled and tasted faintly of cinnamon; not an after-shave or cologne, it seemed to be part of the russet hair on his chest, in his armpits, down there. When they were spent and sweaty in the summer night heat, they laughed at themselves.

"You smell good," she said, nuzzling him. "You smell like fresh-baked cookies."

"I love your ass," he countered, cupping it in both palms. "It's cute and squeezable and just the right size. Think about that when I'm strolling along behind you on the walk tomorrow morning."

They fell asleep in the timeless pose, her head on his shoulder, his arm draped protectively and contentedly around her waist. In her early teens, Jane had often wished to be taller, five foot six would have been ideal, but if there is an advantage to being petite, it's this, that even a man of average height like Brandon can give her a sense of being sheltered, as if under a tree or an eave. It was nice in the dark to accept that sensation, not something she could acknowl-edge back in her old life when she had needed to be seen on a level with the men she used to know, pilots and engineers.

Now she eases out from beneath the sheet and dresses quietly. Brandon sleeps on, and she wonders if there is a predisposition for theater people to be night people, at their peak in the late hours. She decides not to wake him for breakfast, and when he's still not stirring at five to eight, she leaves a pot of coffee and a note on the kitchen table. After that comment about her ass, it might be preferable if he misses the Sunday walk. How will she concentrate on distinguishing a downy from a hairy woodpecker if she's imagining the workings of his mind as he's nonchalantly eyeing her rear? At the front gate, Jane finds her regulars and a handful of newcomers, still on hopeful brambling alert, but the total is a manageable fourteen, and she greets them with a smile. As they start up the service drive past the cottage, Bella, dressed for mass, is about to enter the garage. Her hand climbs in a tentative wave, and Jane signals back. Roy and Melanie, at the end of the line as the group treks away, spot her and wave, too.

Up in the studio, Charlotte cranes to observe this exchange of greetings between Bella and the birders. If only she still had her binoculars on the windowsill! But Bella took them away when she came in late yesterday after the brambling and the birders were gone.

"We're not to spy on Jane and her friends anymore," she ordered.

"'Jane and her friends'?" Charlotte huffed. Not "Miss Avery"? Not "the nature freaks"? Now it's "Jane and her friends"? And presumably Bella thinks she is one of these friends, because Charlotte saw how she spent the afternoon out there, playing chess and drinking lemonade, talking with people, the little traitor.

"It's a condition of her staying," Bella stated.

"She isn't staying. I fired her."

"No, you didn't. We need her. We want her to stay. I've already fixed it."

Bella strode out, leaving Charlotte in disbelief. Now, *sans* binoculars, she stares forlornly out the window as Jane leads her troop away. Despite being born into a family where a housekeeper, cook, maids, butler and gardener were the norm, she has never acquired the knack of managing subordinates. In her younger days, she had wanted them to see her as good and kindly and to be devoted to her and always speak her praises, as they did of her mother. When they saw the young lady instead as spoiled and frivolous, she tried being preemptory and issued temperamental commands. Charlotte tells herself the animosity isn't her fault. It's the nature of the servant class to be jealous of the very wealth and power that provides the employment to put food on their lowly table. They've swallowed the myth that they're just as good as their employers, it's a democracy, everyone is equal—not true or they wouldn't be servants, would they? Finally, they're resentful that if they do have to labor as underlings, it's not for a better family, someone really rich, like the Astors and Vanderbilts used to be. Yet Charlotte suspects that even the maids and footmen in Buckingham Palace snicker and gossip behind their servile, smiling faces, their prompt Yes, sirs and No, ma'ams. Which is why she relies on Bella as a buffer between herself and them, to issue instructions and ensure they are carried out efficiently. Bella can do it because she doesn't mind if the servants dislike her or if the people at the art association roll their eyes behind her back. Bella is used to being scorned.

Charlotte paces to the other end of her studio, bereft of purpose and occupation. The affair of the brambling has unsettled her and sidetracked her art. It's like losing an end of yarn in a basket of tangled skeins and trying to find the right one to pull out to get the project moving again. It's particularly hard at this next stage of her "Retrospective in Retrospective," the years from age thirty back to twenty-five, the first time she tried to declare herself as an artist. Of course, she'd had conservatory training and tutors in watercolors and oils. Young ladies of a certain class were expected to excel in a dilatory way at something, and like her mother and grandmother, Charlotte did have an acknowledged talent.

So when her first marriage ended—widowed this time, please note, not divorced—painting was the natural fallback. Except what kind of time was the late 1950s to be an artist? It was too late to emulate the realists of the thirties and forties, and anyway, what business had a wealthy young woman painting gritty and lonely city scenes à la Edward Hopper? Nor was it credible that she could cast off her lineage and become an abstract expressionist, a spatter-hack like Pollock or a swatch painter like Rothko. Maybe she could launch a new movement—café society art—and she tried filling canvases with the same scenes of people drinking martinis at exclusive parties and charity balls that regularly turned up as photographs in *Vanity Fair*. No one paid any attention. Even in her own circle, no one took her seriously. Everyone but her knew the art was just a hobby to keep her occupied until she married again, which she did to Robert Drayton, for love.

Charlotte stares glumly at the blank canvas on her easel, then at the ring of canvases around the studio. Those café society paintings are in there somewhere. Should she pull them out and insert them in her retrospective? It would change the ground rules; so far everything else is a new painting looking back and viewing her life from the perspective of her current age. But why not, who is making the rules for this retrospective if not herself? Besides, she has to keep up the pace if she and Bella are going to bully the art association into a December show. If she decides to put in old paintings because they still accurately reflect her life, that isn't cheating. But those paintings aren't portraits either; she isn't in any of those martini-drinking scenes. Charlotte gnaws on the dilemma. Art is a lot harder than most people think.

"I was trying to put myself into the company of the greats," she announces to the room at large, and the instant she says it, her frustration clears. That's it. She will paint herself in the company of the great artists throughout history, she will fill this canvas with head portraits of all the painters she has ever admired and tried to copy. She'll set Bella to finding pictures of them to work from, and right in the middle she will paint herself.

"Bella!" She turns, expecting to find her secretary at the computer, then she remembers and dashes to the window instead. "Bella, wait! Come back! Don't go to church!" she shouts, but there is the car leaving the driveway. Charlotte slumps into a chair and mutters. Now she'll have to wait for Bella to get home.

For an instant, Bella almost does turn around, but not because of any mental interception from Charlotte. It was that wave from the birders, the acknowledgment touched her, and as she heads up the shore road, she ponders an inclination to skip church and join the walk instead. She could do it, return to the house, change from her constant high heels to one of several pairs of sturdy, flat-heeled footwear lying dusty in her closet. Why does she always wear the high heels anyway? Because they make her two inches taller, two inches closer to looking an adult in the eye, two inches loftier in her own self-image. Besides, for all her crooked spine and stunted growth, Bella does have nicely shaped albeit short calves, which the high heels accentuate. Vanity. She exhales a long sigh. This is the lesser reason she needs to go to mass today, to be cleansed of such conceits.

She drives to St. Joseph's but doesn't park in one of the three designated handicapped spaces, though no one seeing her emerge from the vehicle would object. She could probably qualify for a handicapped license plate. But it isn't pride or defiance that stops her, merely a recognition that there are others in this world who are truly feeble, whereas Bella is perfectly capable of walking, clumsy as her steps may appear. She enters the church and settles into a middle pew. She could be walking along with Jane and the birders right now, she reflects, picturing them heading through the forest to the pond. The terrain that far isn't rough, and the nature lovers, always pausing to study a bird or plant, won't walk fast. Bella used to walk that way relentlessly day after day, to the pond, across the planked footbridge and beyond, one spring nearly sixty years ago when she and Charlotte were very young. But not since. Bella separates the image of herself from the company of the birders and makes the clumping figure turn and walk back toward the house. She can't go there, not in person, not in her mind. The banishment is total, the sin unforgiven. Eden is closed.

Ah well, you could have become a nun, Bella flippantly reminds herself, as old Father McCaffrey drones on. It's what they did with ugly daughters back then in the old country, maybe still do for all she knows. A rush of air comes up her chest, and she ignores the people rising around her for a hymn, as she's suddenly nailed to her seat, sucked back into a powerful, unwilling memory of the one and only pilgrimage she made to Rome. The singing congregation politely avoids any glance in her direction; they assume it's too much for her to keep popping up and down in the hard pew. But no, it's the memory. God has it in for her now.

She was sixteen, and it was the autumn the war was finally over. Her mother had died on a night two months before, murdered by local thugs who broke into the Deerfield villa on Capri to plunder decorations and silver. Unfortunately, the loot wasn't there. Charlotte's parents had packed up and shipped home most of their valuables when the war in Europe began, and they hadn't yet returned to the villa, even though Capri had become, after the Allied invasion and Mussolini's fall, a recuperation site for American soldiers and was thus relatively safe and open to rich foreigners. It had been safe enough till that night for Bella and her mother, who had served the Deerfields as housekeeper for as long as Bella could remember and who was always accorded favored status among their servants. But the men broke in, and thwarted of profits, they caught her mother by her long black hair as she screamed and fought in her tangled nightgown, screamed at Bella to flee out the door. Bella scrubbed the dark, dried blood off the floor afterward, and Charlotte's mother, the lovely, kindhearted Clarisse, cabled in great sorrow and agitation that she was wiring money immediately for the funeral and that the family would return to the villa soon. Bella was taken in by peasant relatives meanwhile, until one sunny day in October her uncle Antonio, a gross, mustached man who smelled of cigarettes and vinegary red wine, announced he was taking her to St. Peter's.

They set off on the ferry to the mainland, her uncle in good spirits, ogling the women on the boat. From Naples, they took the train to Rome, where they stayed overnight at a cheap inn. Bella drank in each new sight—she had never been off the island—yet she kept mindful of their mission to offer special prayers for her mother's soul. Her mother would need them, for she had been both a good Catholic and, at the far spectrum of her talents, a good poisoner. When Charlotte taunts Bella as a little Borgia, she's not far off the mark. Perhaps some drop of famed Lucrezia's blood did pass on, mother to daughter, along with whispered concoctions for love and fertility potions, herbal brews to dull pain, swift draughts to eliminate an enemy, merciful relief to permanently close a sufferer's eyes. But the next morning when they stepped into the magnificent piazza of St. Peter's and stood with the crowd awaiting the pope's appearance on the balcony, it was of Bella's own future that her uncle began to speak.

"It is time, Bella," he said, "to look around you and see the glorious path that lies ahead."

Bella looked, uncomprehending. What did this coarse and often drunken uncle, a man who never had any use for her before, intend her to see here? She gazed around the milling throng, and her focus gradually narrowed, her peripheral vision contracting as she systematically cut out of the picture those images not pertinent to herself. Well-dressed Romans, prosperous business owners smart enough to make a quick economic recovery, chic wives on their arms. Poor city families carrying wide-eyed children. Handsome young couples holding hands. Tourists flocking back to art and culture, country people come to pray and receive a blessing, disciplined contingents of black-robed priests, tonsured monks, twittering nuns…

Nuns. They smiled back at her in shy invitation while the rest of the crowd ignored or jostled or pushed by her. A few of their faces were truly lovely, lit by faith's glow, but most were plain, mousy girls. Finally, trimming more and more out of the picture, Bella saw the disproportionate number of sisters who in some way resembled herself—

birthmarked, deformed, pinched ferret faces, a withered arm, eyes askew in a misshapen skull. They might, they might become saints, their devotion entirely real. Yet Bella recoiled and gaped in shock. No, no! That no man would ever marry her, that she would never bear children, she accepted. But surely there were other possibilities? She would not spend her life in a sisterhood of ugly, unwanted, unmarriageable girls. Stunned by the betrayal, she turned appealing eyes on her uncle and saw this was not his doing alone but the joint decision of a rough peasant family who had no room for another mouth to feed when a time-honored solution was at hand.

"No!" Bella screamed, there in the piazza of St. Peter's, defiling the holy place with her shrieks. "No! Not me!" The nuns huddled back in consternation, while others in the crowd snickered at the panicked, bellowing, comical creature. She screamed it again when her uncle dragged her in front of the mother superior with whom the appointment had been made the week before. The mother superior was stooped and whiskered, her teeth either missing or yellow, and in her right eye like an exploding ruby a crimson bloodshot filled the milky white next to the pale blue iris. She laid a hand on Bella's quaking arm, locking the girl's terrified eyes to hers.

"No," she said firmly to the uncle's furious protests that his niece was calm, obedient, submissive, only reluctant to leave her family, that's all. "No," the mother superior said again, "this is not for her." The uncle took the journey home to grow drunk and slap her. Ingrate!—*smack!* Witch's whelp!—*smack!* You'll be a whore like your mother! Bella didn't care how much his callused fingers stung and rasped her cheeks or how his liquored oaths blasted hot in her ears. She would escape, run away. She would not be locked up in some convent to become a lonely old woman with only God for company. When the boat docked at the harbor on Capri, she eluded the inebriated uncle and begged a ride in a donkey cart to the Deerfield villa. None of her peasant family came to look for her, and when the Deerfields and their retinue arrived later that month, debonair Vincent, lovely Clarisse and their now sixteen-year-old daughter Charlotte, they were delightfully surprised to find little Bella in a spanking clean villa, aired, dusted, polished, swept, bouquets of fresh flowers on every table. Bella knew where her future lay. One way or another, she was going to America.

And yet, and yet...Bella comes back at last to the mass, now almost over, and looks around at the people shifting in anticipation of release. And yet here she is, a lonely old woman in a church with only God for company. You could laugh at the irony of it, if you had a mind to. But no laughter comes, only a low dread as Bella presses a hand to her abdomen, the real reason she has come to St. Joseph's today. There's something wrong, God, isn't there? For over two months, she has shoved aside the vague discomfort, the backaches she attributed to too much time hunched at the computer, the intermittent stomach pains and bloated feeling she assumed were indigestion or anxiety. Consult a doctor? Maybe, but if you're going to do that, you should know what's wrong first, know if there's a possible cure or what's the point? Otherwise, you become a medical curiosity as they poke and manipulate and violate you, call in a gaggle of green interns to stare at your goose-bumped, naked body under the guise of science and those unforgiving lights, prescribe chalky pills and rigid braces and bone-cracking exercises that don't straighten your spine but only torture it until you cry in bed at night. Bella did try once, you see. When she came to America with all its marvelous medical science, she did try.

Well. She glances around the emptying church, listens to the cool silence as the last footsteps leave. Don't answer then, God. She will begin researching on the Internet this very afternoon. Bella slips out of the pew and hobbles out the door to her car.

Chapter 19

August mellows into a contented, somnolent month. The mad drive of June and July—school's out, summer's here, vacation trips, go, go, go!—is over. In August, beers get sipped more slowly, dogs pant in the shade, people grumble complacently about the heat as if it will last forever, as if they won't be yearning for its return come frigid February. The grass gets a little dry, the green leaves start to turn leathery, the hours of sunlight shrink a few minutes each day. In town the shops and restaurants and art galleries, still experiencing a steady clientele, are nonetheless scheming ahead for ways to extend the tourist season into autumn. Boating regattas are planned through September; an October-fest celebration will coincide with the fall foliage tours. The leaves may turn crimson, garnet and orange, but dollars are always green.

At Deerfield there are still birds to be seen, brilliant yellow goldfinches chirping *potato-chip, potato-chip!* in undulating flight, great crested flycatchers that advertise their presence with a loudly whistled *wheep!*, ruby-throated hummingbirds, the only hummingbird species to breed east of the Mississippi—although Roy has photos to prove that a rufous hummingbird native to the western United States once spent half a winter at the feeder in his backyard. Green herons stalk fish at the pond, and iridescent blue-green tree swallows and rust-breasted barn swallows skim the water, the latter the only swallow species with a true, deep-forked swallow tail. One morning a blunt brown bomber passes over the field, a short-eared owl, unusual because Roy claims such owls normally don't appear in their area until October. Monarch, viceroy and painted lady butterflies add to the flight list. On one hike everyone stops stock still as a two-foot garter snake wiggles unconcernedly between Melanie's sneakers and slithers into a pile of dead leaves.

By now, the nosiest of the local residents have made their one-time trek to peer at Deerfield, and the transient birders, ever in quest of rarities, have gleaned what the estate has to offer and moved on. Even some of the regulars begin to drift off. Hortense and an old college chum take a two-week trip to England and Ireland. Russ and Charlie are busy revamping the menu at their café. Jim and Lois have joined a golfing foursome and are serving on the organizing com-mittee for a tournament at the country club to raise money for muscular dystrophy. One Sunday morning, quite unexpect-edly, Jane finds herself alone.

She stands by the front gate, checking her watch and wondering. Raven and Brandon are probably working the breakfast shift at the playhouse restaurant. Though Jane and Brandon are seeing each other several times a week, he's irregular about calling and Raven even more so. She either bursts upon you or she doesn't, with or without Burt, and Jane still doesn't know if what she and Raven have is a normal friendship or if, being such diametrically opposed personalities, they're rummaging for a bond that really isn't there. Melanie might be away with her father today, whom Jane has never seen since that first time he delivered his daughter to the estate along with a lecture on her disabilities. Yet he does come from the city most weekends, because Melanie will report excitedly that they have been to a dinosaur museum or a horse show or an amusement park where she ate pink cotton candy. And Roy, where is Roy? A fine lot they are to stand her up like this!

She laughs at her chagrin for their desertion, her mother hen-ishness in wanting to account for every member of her flock. Then with a Sunday morning suddenly open before her and a whim to do something different, she recalls the old Mowry cemetery deep in the woods northwest of the pond. She stops at the garage, exchanges her knapsack and binoculars for work gloves and garden tools and hikes to the spot. It takes a few turns in the wrong direction to relocate it, but once she does, it feels right to be here, sunlight dappling through the trees, and she begins clearing bull briars and choking vines of bittersweet, rooting down to graves long forgotten. A few are carved with an angel's head or a simple floral design, but most bear an inscription only. Isaac Mowry merits the longest epitaph, a tribute to his patriarchal status and *Long Life of Christian Duty*. When Jane removes a glove and sits down to scrape her fingernail into the lines on Mehitable Mowry's stone, the words *tender Mother* emerge from the crusted dirt along with a seeming reference to death in childbirth...*innocent Babe who shares this grave*. Sad, but probably not uncommon in those days. Nor did it take Isaac long to remarry; a second wife is buried on his other side.

Trowel in hand, Jane digs in. It will take several sessions to expose all eight stones and perhaps copy down the inscriptions for posterity. Beyond that, she's not sure what her objective is, since the vegetation will surely grow back once she's gone. She pauses to reflect on the thought. Much as she's come to love Deerfield, she will go eventually, probably by Christmas. This haven will have served its purpose; look how far she has already come. When she arrived in March, she was walking wounded, in need of shelter, and here she found sanctuary. Now she has emerged from the worst and is starting to plan ahead. She'll never go back to flying, but she's young, ambitious, no strings, and in possession of an engineering degree. If there's some way to stay in the area, near Deerfield and her new friends, she'll consider it, but more likely, she'll have to cast a wider net to bigger cities to find a job, and that could mean anywhere across the country.

The next Sunday everyone is back, glad to see her,

glad to be there. Each week the mood changes with the composition of the group and the presence or absence of birds. When newcomers appear, Jane invokes the usual ritual of welcome and the circle of introductions, then cites the collaboration between Miss Deerfield, the town and the land trust that makes it possible to open this *private* estate—she still stresses private—to the public on a limited, chaperoned basis. In mentioning the collaboration, she doesn't mention the reduced tax rate, and increasingly there is a sentiment percolating that Charlotte Deerfield is indeed a generous benefactress to the town. When serious birders arrive, Jane and her regulars do their best to flush out a decent count of species, although by August most birds have fledged their young, and both adults and juveniles have departed as separate travelers on the wing, leaving only an empty nest behind.

One Sunday late in August two rabid birders from California show up and quickly and repeatedly let it be known their life list tops twenty-one hundred, including St. Lucia parrots found only on that one Caribbean island, Darwin finches in the Galapagos, and bowerbirds in Australia. There seems to be no limit to the distance they'll travel to bag a new species, but their attitude makes it clear that whether it's fifty miles or five thousand, they expect birds to be there, and Deerfield is an extreme disappointment. The regulars are heartily glad to be rid of them at ten o'clock.

"The snobs! If they're such experts, they should know August is not a peak month," sniffs Hortense, usually so forgiving and magnanimous of spirit.

"Twenty-one hundred," humpfs Roy. He's still on the lookout for his five hundredth, trying to be patient, yearning to find it. It doesn't have to be anything as unusual as the brambling, although he has accounted for virtually every other species likely to pass through New England. Please, one more bird. That's all he wants.

Raven strolls along hand-in-hand with Burt. They have become boyfriend and girlfriend, Melanie understands, curious and envious at the same time. Do they kiss? What does it feel like to have a boy kiss you? Raven still hasn't told Burt she's not twenty-nine but thirty-six. Burt drinks chocolate milk with his cookies at lunch, he's never really been hurt by the world or anyone in it, and in a summer when every audition Raven thought went spectacularly has resulted in a bored "Don't call us," she feeds on his innocence and mothers his optimism when it's often she herself who needs mothering.

Jane and Brandon don't hold hands on the walk. To them it's silly, unprofessional for Jane, and unnecessary. Usually, they've already made love the night before. He comes over after the play, which Jane has seen three times, and she'd swear the temperature in the audience does rise when in Act II his shirt comes off. Her temperature does. Then late one Tuesday afternoon Raven phones. The play isn't on that evening, she and Brandon are off duty at the restaurant, and Burt has reached an impasse on the Great American Novel and needs creative rejuvenation. How about the four of them hike out to the ridge at Deerfield and watch the sun set?

"You know, a loaf of bread, a jug of wine and thou." Raven's voice descends into a husky chuckle. Oh, it's fun to be a muse, tickling along your captivated poet with your goddess-given powers like the coy mistresses in those English sonnets. If she can't break Burt's writer's block, trust her, no one can.

"I'll ask," says Jane, not averse to the implications for Brandon and herself and fairly sure no permission is required. She's welcome to have visitors in the cottage, and these past weeks Charlotte and Bella must have seen, even without binoculars, Brandon's car parked outside overnight and made no objection. Taking her friends onto the property after hours shouldn't be a stretch, especially given Bella's reaction to the role the actors played in dispersing the brambling seekers. She laughed aloud when Jane told her, the first time Jane has ever heard such an unrestrained sound escape her lips. In fact, the whole affair of the brambling has been a turning point. She and Bella chat several times a week now, usually when Jane is outside working on the grounds. August is a busy entertaining month at Deerfield, so it's natural for Bella to stroll over and apprise Jane of forthcoming events. Luncheon and dinner parties are frequent, caterers and florists come and go, and at month's end Charlotte will host her annual lawn party to benefit the art association's scholarship fund. They talk as if they are new neighbors, Jane pausing to lean on her rake. Today when Jane knocks on the front door, Bella immediately grants the request for an evening hike.

"Ah, Miss Avery, I thought I heard your voice." Charlotte leans over the railing of the staircase, her tone honey-dipped. "Might we trouble you to come up to my studio for a few minutes? There's a matter of art Bella and I have been discussing, and we would value your opinion."

"Well, yes, although I'm hardly qualified...," Jane begins, but Charlotte's face disappears, compliance is expected, and Jane has a sudden flashback to her first introduction to Deerfield, that strange meeting in which Bella tried to trip her up on Jackson Pollock. Except Bella herself seems caught off guard by the command, and she turns to Jane not with animosity but apprehension in her eyes.

"It's all right," says Jane cautiously, though it's clear she has walked into the middle of something, most likely a viper's nest. The air left in Charlotte's wake hisses and slithers past her as she and Bella mount the stairs. She finds the studio cluttered as before with canvases and the spattered drop cloths on the floor, and there is the silver tea service on a side table, dainty gold-rimmed china cups, lemon slices in a small bowl, sugar-dusted jam cookies and iced buns on a plate. Back when she assumed there were servants in the house, Jane had thought the tea an elegant holdover from bygone days. Now that she knows it's only Charlotte and Bella, it seems a disturbing anachronism. Ominously, the cookies and frosted buns sit untouched. Still more ominous is the large blank canvas in the center of the room. For the moment, however, Charlotte ignores it.

"I trust the property management is going well, Miss Avery?" she inquires, instantly appalled by the stupidity of her question as Jane offers a polite recital of projects in progress. Shouldn't she, the owner of Deerfield, know exactly how the property management is going? Shouldn't she be on top of it, snap to it, this displeases me, how much will these new shrubs cost?

But Charlotte, too, has fallen into the trap that is August, this month of drowsy indolence, an infuriating trap when you're trying to get something accomplished. All day she stews and stirs, yet nothing gets cooked. Part of it is the missing binoculars. How can anyone feel on top of the management of their estate when this vital tool has been forbidden and confiscated? She's at a loss without them, can't spy, can't know in advance, which magnifies her inherent unease with servants. Worse are the repeated distractions and interruptions to her retrospective, the obligation of parties and entertaining to pay back those whose invitations she accepted the previous month. When she does snatch time for the present series, her life from age thirty back to twenty-five, the spark of inspiration she had almost three weeks ago to paint herself in the company of the great artists is failing to ignite. Just look—

Starting at the upper corner, she has painted a line of faces from left to right, petering out after a row and a half. There's swarthy bald Picasso, fox-faced Vincent Van Gogh in his straw hat and blue smock, pouchy-cheeked Rembrandt in his saggy beret, Norman Rockwell peering from behind his glasses and cozy pipe—a perfectly good *artist,* let's have no more of this demeaning *illustrator* label. But who are all these other faces? Does anyone know what Cezanne, Manet, Monet and Renoir look like? Oh, they might get little Toulouse-Lautrec in his overcoat and bowler hat. And what about women? There's Georgia, of course, in her black sombrero, and Frida Kahlo with her one eyebrow; thanks to a recent Hollywood movie, she's very popular at present. But here Charlotte has painted a perfectly lovely image of Mary Cassatt and who will recognize her? Why aren't there more women artists anyway? She's going to have a canvas full of nineteenth-century Frenchmen!

And that, fifteen minutes before Jane knocked, is how the argument started.

"The idiots at the art association won't recognize half these painters!" she despaired when Bella bore up the tea service. "We'll have to provide some kind of graphic key, one of those silhouette outlines beside the painting with a list of identities below, and then it will look like some atrocious paint-by-number, like the cover of that record album, that Beatles album, Sgt. Pepper."

"Maybe you should put it aside for a while," Bella soothed.

"I can't! I've already let it be known to the director I'm getting ready for another one-woman show!"

"But there's no deadline, no hurry. Put it aside a while and next spring—"

"I can't wait till spring! I have to keep at it, it's taking forever as it is, all these mini-portraits to paint. I can't let my 'Retrospective in Retrospective' lose momentum when everything so far has been sheer genius. You can see that, you can see that!"

Their voices rose, Bella's in a renewed hope she dared not show, disguised as empathy, consolation, wise advice, take your time, you've been painting nearly nonstop, take a break; silently begging, Please, let this project falter and die now, please, no further back. Charlotte's rose in anguish and fear; how could the inspirations rolling so abundantly off her palette thus far suddenly desert her when she finally has a real vision, a real ache, she feels flat, collapsed, empty, what is an artist if she's not creating art? Rising voices, rising anger that terrified them both, until Charlotte shrieked, "I'll leave the damn canvas blank!"

"Blank," she repeated, testing the word, and suddenly

it made sense. She never succeeded in putting herself in the company of the great artists, and between the difficulties of portraying so many unrecognizable faces and the acute possibility that the art association dunderheads, recognizing her self-portrait in the center, will totally misinterpret the canvas to mean she actually does rank herself in this esteemed pantheon...

"Blank, Bella." She grabbed a fresh canvas, slapped it on the easel. "Why not? When I think of those frivolous, wasted years, there isn't one true or decent thing about them to paint. Blank—symbolizing my start in the art world, the purity of optimism, the dazzling white light of unattainable dreams. It will be daring, outrageous! So what if no one gets it? If you tell people a painting or novel or play is brilliant and they don't get it, they generally think themselves to be stupid. Wait, maybe I will paint the canvas, solid white, so it actually has paint on it. Remember the artist who got away with that? Huh, a whole canvas solid red or purple or something, and it got hung in Boston or New York!"

"No, please!" Bella begged, anything to stem the frenzied flow of words, Charlotte viciously squeezing white paint. "We'll look like fools, we'll be a laughingstock!"

The words dropped into silence, Charlotte turning slowly to face her.

"Are you saying I'm a laughingstock?"

And in that awful moment while they stared at each other came Jane's knock at the front door.

"We wish your opinion, Miss Avery," says Charlotte now, composing herself to dispel any leftover tension in the air. Bella is glancing glumly, accusingly, in her direction. She thinks so much of Jane and her friends lately. Very well, let's have a neutral, unbiased opinion from an intelligent member of the general public. Charlotte gestures peremptorily to the easel. "What would you think if you walked into an exhibition in an art museum and among the other canvases you saw one that was painted over in solid white?"

"Solid white," Jane repeats. She has already decided

on the simplest solution: Tell the truth. "I would suppose the artist wants me to imagine it's snow or winter…or an absence, death, innocence, a clean slate. What does the caption, the title beneath the painting, say?"

"It doesn't say anything!" Charlotte's hackles rise. "You're supposed to *know*, not guess."

"How can anyone know?" Bella leaps to Jane's defense. She has tried to remain patient these past few weeks while Charlotte muttered in the studio, ignoring the arrangements for the lawn party, growing increasingly snappish when Bella interrupted to apprise her of menu choices, decorations, music requiring her approval, pestering her instead to locate the likeness of this or that dead artist. She can't bear the bad impression this scene must be creating on Jane. They might, Bella thinks, become friends.

Jane says nothing. She has given her opinion as asked. This war is silent now, Charlotte and Bella exchanging looks she can't begin to read, looks that have a long history in which no one else has a part. The tea steeps untasted in the elaborate silver pot, the iced buns and jam cookies sit prettily on the doily-covered plate, the succinct lemon slices overlap precisely in their dish.

"Thank you for your opinion," says Charlotte haughtily, and Jane smiles a polite goodbye to each of them and heads downstairs. She isn't halfway down the staircase when she hears the voices rise.

"Stop it, stop it now!" Bella begs.

"I can't! It's art! It's suffering! It's art!"

It's *crazy*. Jane shakes her head and closes the door behind her. In an effort to dispel her own unease, she relates the episode to Brandon, Raven and Burt as they hike out to the ridge that evening, breaking her usual policy of not spreading telltale stories that might violate Charlotte's privacy. She tries to downplay the bizarreness.

"Two bats in a belfry," Brandon concludes. Life is amusing, so long as it doesn't concern him, and the only matter that concerns him right now is a laid-back night of very enjoyable sex.

"You might walk into a similar argument backstage with a group of actors working out their parts," Raven offers. "Like once, I was playing Ophelia in Seattle, and this director wants the usual limp female, 'O my sweet lord, how can you treat a poor maiden so,' et cetera." She drapes a hand to her forehead and as always, it happens, she's *on*. Well, who wouldn't be on a gorgeous summer night with the sun melting down to the horizon like a tangerine lozenge and her best friends and lots of wine and laughter ahead of them, who wouldn't be? "So I said, 'C'mon, let's be different, let's make Ophelia an aristocratic slut, a sex-addicted mead-swigger who's already had a taste of it with randy Hamlet and can't give it up.'"

"You'd play the Virgin Mary as a slut if you had the chance," says Brandon, giving her a teasing whack on the rear with the rolled blanket he's carrying, a gesture that Burt takes askance, although maybe this is how actors behave among themselves. So he and Jane let them have the stage as Raven launches into a horny Ophelia and Brandon supplies a stud Hamlet. They're all laughing by the time they sit down at the end of the ridge, and after they drink their wine and watch the sunset, Raven slyly leads Burt off. She's always wanted to make love in the woods, well, actually, she has made love in the woods, but not this woods, not with Burt, and she bets he's never done it outdoors period, about which she's right. So when she pushes him into a mossy nook just as it's getting dark and slips her hands into his pants, Burt gets the fastest erection he's ever had and practically falls off the ridge trying to get his pants over his tennis shoes. To hell with writing the Great American Novel. He has never gotten laid like this before.

"Quiet over there!" Brandon shouts at them, then chuckles as the only response is a panting, urgent uh-uh-uh.

"She's crazy, you know," he says, slipping his arm around Jane as they sip fruity sangria. "Crazy but fun."

"Does she ever calm down?"

"Sure, occasionally, infrequently, rarely…no, maybe not. You just have to take her or leave her. Now, what about us?"

He offers her one hand to rise, catches up the blanket in the other, and they walk back along the ridge to a grassy spot sheltered by a clump of short pines. Brandon pauses and listens. "Out of earshot," he whispers, and Jane listens, too, no more sounds of Raven and Burt. Brandon spreads the blanket, undresses her, she undresses him. They take their time. Jane and Raven may try to be friends, Brandon and Burt may attempt to share a camaraderie, but friendships take second place when sex and desire come along. Each in their pocket of darkness, the two couples make love, and nature, in this ripe month of August, is pleased. It would be even more pleased if it could understand that Raven and Burt, intoxicated by wine, lust and heat, have made contact without protection, closed flesh on flesh while Burt was still trying to rip open the packet. When they make love a second time, giggling and now with a condom in place, they're blissfully unaware that it's too late, the accident has occurred, reproduction has begun.

At the end of August, Charlotte's party for the art association scholarship fund is a splendid success. Nearly three hundred people mingle in the huge tent staked on the rear lawn, munching the sweet-and-sour chicken kabobs, crab quiche and stuffed mushrooms offered by roving waiters, grazing at buffet tables laden with fancy arrangements of fresh fruit, gourmet cheese and pâté, cold beef and smoked salmon, lining up at the cash bar for a pinot grigio or vodka and tonic in the name of a good cause. An extensive silent auction is displayed on decorated tables where people may bid on a sunset cruise for eight on the charter schooner *Windhawk*, a dinner for two at the Black Horse Restaurant, a basket of pampering bath products from the Mist & Magic Spa. Police officers provide security, and at the front gate a valet parking service relieves guests of their cars.

Jane, having volunteered her assistance, is assigned to

the caterers who loan her a spare bow tie to complete her outfit of white shirt and black pants. She navigates through the tent with a tray, collecting lipsticked wine glasses and empty plates and transporting them to the kitchen where an assembly line of dishwashers and waiters quickly replenishes the hors d'oeuvres platters. It's fun, a fly-on-the-wall experience of traveling between the guests in the tent conversing about their golf scores and their latest trips to Europe to the kitchen staff cracking rude jokes and sneaking out on the back steps for a smoke. It's also the first time she has seen the rear of the mansion, the working half, and she sidesteps the bustle at the monster cast iron stoves, the deep double sinks, the massive oak table in the center of the room. Entertaining on a grand scale is what the huge, old-fashioned kitchen was designed for, and tonight Deerfield is fulfilling its mission in glory. This is how it was meant to be.

For Charlotte, although she claims to scorn the social hubbub, there's nothing like being the star of it. Wearing a champagne lace gown, she is warmly introduced by the director of the art association and applauded for her pre-eminent role in fostering the local arts scene. More good news: Her "Retrospective in Retrospective" is back on track. Forget the white canvas, a stupid idea if ever she had one. She was right the first time about trying to put herself in the company of the greats; it was the execution of the concept that was boring and flat.

Now, instead of a canvas of silent heads she will have a collage of great artists and their works. This solves three problems in one brilliant stroke. First, it renders unnecessary any kind of silhouette identification key. Intelligent viewers may not recognize a particular artist's face, but they'll certainly zoom in on a picture of *Water Lilies* and say, Aha, Monet! Second, it relieves the visual monotony of nothing but heads by interspersing landscapes, still lifes, Maxfield Parrish fairies, Degas ballerinas, Dali clocks. Already, she has Bella busy scanning and sizing and printing out from her computer the paintings she wants to incorporate. Third, this collage idea is a great saver of time, fewer square inches of canvas to paint. And Jane was right, her paintings will need titles and captions, long captions if necessary, so that nothing is misinterpreted, so that even a dolt is forced to understand what each picture means. She will call this collage *One Hundred People I Longed To Be*, retaining the small portrait of herself in the middle, and in the caption she'll dictate to Bella she will speak of the craving of every artist to be loved and acclaimed, to achieve immortality. Tonight, circulating among her guests, accepting their congratulations on the enchanting party, Charlotte does feel loved, she is happy, caught up in compliments and a heady sensation of viewing life from its peak.

Bella, in a violet dress, gold necklace and earrings, smoothes over the minor flusters of the evening before they're noticed. A broken glass? Dispatch a waiter with a dustpan. An inebriated guest? Summon a taxi. The tent, the caterers, the lighting, the music by a string quartet, the security, the parking, the auction. Who arranged all this? She poses the question without resentment, watching the laughing company. She can't seem to help being efficient, wouldn't know how to take a day off or stop working if she tried. In fact, so well-organized is Bella that in between the party planning and producing the art prints Charlotte wants for her collage, she has researched her symptoms of illness on the Internet, arrived at a diagnosis, visited a doctor and this morning received confirmation that her opinion is correct. Well, God, she thinks, idly shooing a fly off a cake on the dessert table, what took you so long?

Chapter 20

And now summer is slipping away from all of them, running through their fingers the way sand in an hourglass seems sedentary until it suddenly funnels into a miniature whirlpool that swirls the grains away.

Labor Day comes, and Elizabeth of the beach shack and the Chekhov is gone. Jim and Lois are readying their sailboat for the return voyage to their winter home in Florida. Burt, having overcome his writer's block with Raven as his muse, pours every spare minute into the Great American Novel. It's been five years since he graduated from college, and the bestseller list can't be far off.

Melanie turns twelve and starts middle school. Within the first week she gets punched, her backpack is stolen, and a horrible boy shoves his hand down her pants. The kids who were the troublemakers in grade school are merely bigger troublemakers in middle school, the boys taller and heavier, sprouting unsightly facial hair, the mean girls have breasts and one of them doesn't wear underpants to class. The teachers can't control them and aren't allowed to hit them even when they hit each other, and overall there is very little "education" left in special ed.

All of which her father shouts angrily at the principal, a really bad thing to get mad at the principal as they're sitting in conference in her office. Melanie's father is angry he had to take a day off work to deal with this and about his tax dollars and his daughter shouldn't be in special ed anyway, she is not a special needs child, she is recovering from an accident. The principal with grim pleasure accedes to his demand that Melanie be mainstreamed into regular classes, where within a week she is so far behind her head hurts at night from trying to remember the lessons she learned that day and already forgot. And with each successive day the burden of lost information grows, until Melanie cries for her old teacher at elementary school, nice Ms. Shaw, who says of course Melanie can come back to her class and envelopes her in a warm hug. Melanie is happy again, starting back mentally where she did last September, where she will start every September for the rest of her life.

The British bedroom farce ends its run at the dinner theater, and Dan and Amy head for New York, try again, try again. Brandon crashes with them when he's in Manhattan doing TV commercials. In one, he's the customer admiring his new look in a department store mirror as the voice-over extols the fall line of tailored wool suits, and even in the three seconds his face appears on screen, Jane is startled by his sexiness, his photogenic quality and the ease with which he conveys the picture of a man confident he could not look one iota better. Two or three nights a week, if he's in town, he shows up at the cottage. They're alike, Brandon and Jane, both smart and work oriented, he as committed and passionate about acting as she once was about flying, and he fascinates her. When he rehearses lines for her, he can change the portent of a sentence by a look, a gesture, the inflection on a single syllable. When they make love, he makes sure she's satisfied, enjoying her pleasure before he lets himself go.

As for Raven, there's a fair-weather friend. Jane was beginning to enjoy the friendship they started. Now Raven disappears from the Sunday walks, and Jane misses that flamboyance, that crazy energy that ricochets off invisible walls and bounces around to bombard everyone in the vicinity. And where is Raven? Waiting tables, pursuing auditions—please, goddess, let the phone ring! Try Hollywood again? She barely has the money for plane fare, and if they didn't want her at twenty-five, who's going to want her at thirty-six soon to be thirty-seven? Even famous actresses start running out of roles by their forties, until they're resurrected a decade later for guest appearances on TV sitcoms playing the mother of some perky young star.

Then Raven hatches a brilliant plan. Maybe she can make a career by combining acting and theater administration, persuade the absentee owners to let her run the playhouse year-round? She and the other actors have talked about it from time to time. Moreover, there's been a renaissance in regional theater lately, even some of the Hollywood crowd branching out to establish their own venues. Why not her, why not here? She doesn't have a box office name, of course, but she was popular in the two plays this summer, she has a foothold. Maybe she could be the driving force behind building the playhouse into a reputable twelve-month operation? It would coincide with the town's plan to extend the tourist season, offer another attraction to the leaf peepers on their bus tours through New England, perhaps entice the Christmas shoppers to stay overnight— shop, dinner, theater, brunch—instead of limiting their stay to a single afternoon. They could throw in the Sunday morning walk at Deerfield for the nature types.

Once the idea takes hold, Raven can picture it as easily as she's always pictured herself accepting her Oscar. They'll stage *A Christmas Carol*, the perfect holiday play. She confides her scheme to Brandon, Bucky and Eileen, to the chef at the theater restaurant, to the bartenders and wait staff. Go for it! they tell her. They need jobs, too. Raven phones the playhouse owners in New York, makes inquiries with tour companies, schedules an appointment with the director of the chamber of commerce. Everyone is enthusiastic—See what you can make of it! they exhort—and she plunges into the arrangements, not realizing it's only her own enthusiasm the others are caught up in that's boomeranging back at her. Because when she's *on*, Raven truly is a driving force, she's so believable as a theater entrepreneur she convinces everyone around her. She doesn't realize she's just being a great actress. Only her therapist treats the plan coolly, but Raven hardly needed her all summer, so why absorb her negativity now? Exhilarated with her new project, not yet aware she's pregnant, Raven cancels future sessions and throws her Prozac away.

At Deerfield, the fall migration begins, a different tempo than in spring. During April and May it was a sex-driven rush, when over a few short weeks the birds streamed through wearing their most vivid plumage, a feathered frenzy of hormones on the wing. There was an imperative to claim territory, build nests, mate. The males sang to advertise to the females: Here I am, ladies, check out this voice, this plumage, this DNA. Do your offspring a favor and choose me!

But in autumn the sex is over, the young have gone their separate ways, the migration is quieter, less cohesive, more drawn out. It can begin as early as late August when flocks of tree swallows in the tens of thousands start gathering in staging areas and continue until early November when a last few warblers straggle through. It's all about food now, about gobbling up insects and berries to put on as much fat as possible to sustain themselves for the long flight south. Since there's no longer any competition for territory, the birds travel in mixed flocks, kinglets with chickadees and juncos, robins, blue jays and grackles amicably sharing the same stand of trees. Absent the competition for mates, some species lose their colorful plumage entirely, and Jane discovers two pages in her bird book she has previously overlooked. Headed "Confusing Fall Warblers," they depict over two dozen small birds in subdued shades of yellow and olive-brown. It's hard enough telling them apart in the book, let alone when they're hopping about in a forest full of amber leaves. Hortense and Roy can do it, but not Jane. And here she thought she was getting the hang of this, feeling proficient and smug.

One other, less obvious aspect of the fall migration begins as well, a phenomenon most people never notice. They hear the Canada geese, their approach heralded by loud, unglamorous honks, and look up at the long, wavering Vs flying south. At backyard feeders they observe the departure of songbirds from their neighborhood. Along with the turning leaves, cooling temperatures and dwindling daylight, these are all the signs they require that autumn is on the way. Even beginning birders may go an autumn or two before someone points it out to them: September and October are the migration months for hawks.

Jane doesn't notice it at first either. Most hawks are solitary; they don't travel in formation or noisy flocks. They don't need the seeds or suet the kind people put out. While you're seeing the world at eye level, they glide silently overhead, climbing up the wind, hollow-boned, honed for flight. Nor do they use flight merely for transportation from one place to another. For them, the air itself is a destination, a place to be. They soar where other birds flap; they drift in effortless circles, controlled by the tipping of a wing. They can balance so perfectly they hover in one spot at minimum controllable airspeed, ascend on an impulse, descend on a whim, plummet like a self-propelled arrow, engage in an aerial ballet. In autumn, the hawks are everywhere—over fields, forests, suburban neighborhoods. You have only to look up.

Jane looks up, and it's finally all right that they're beautiful, that they fly. As she once could distinguish any type of plane by a glance at its silhouette overhead, now she concentrates on learning hawk species. Buteo hawks, like red-tails, are stocky with broad, "fingered" wings and fan-shaped tails, built for soaring. Accipiters, like the Cooper's and sharp-shinned, are forest dwellers with slender profiles, short, rounded wings and narrow tails that allow them to flash with unerring precision between the trees. Falcons are streamlined with pointed wings and long tails.

Sitting out on the ridge on her daily patrols, Jane

waits and watches for the hawks to fly over. She knows how the earth below appears to them, knows as closely as another species can how these wind-borne beings feel. When hawks appear on the Sunday morning walks, invariably someone will wish they could fly like that, and she'll find herself explaining to the group just how it is a red-tail can make that kind of maneuver, the ratio of wing length to fuselage, the turning axis, the similarities between tail feathers and an airplane rudder, between the configuration of a hawk and a plane in the landing flare. One week someone says, "You sure know a lot about planes!" *I used to be a pilot*, Jane almost replies, and suddenly she knows she could say it aloud, explain calmly about Jill and the accident, accept their initial shock at the revelation and move on. Yet now that she can say it, there's no longer any need. Confession is for sin, guilt, penance, absolution. Jane is finally at peace.

      Peace is what Bella desires also. On the last Sunday in September, she gets out of bed and dresses in a burgundy turtleneck sweater, nubby black pants and a long-unused pair of sturdy brown oxfords. The clothes feel strange as she slips them on, a different skin than the unvarying style of dress she has worn almost every day of her adult life. Sweaters are not entirely foreign; she has cardigans to wear with her dresses, plain for everyday, beaded or embroidered for evening affairs, lightweight or heavy for summer or winter warmth. But this sweater is a ribbed turtleneck that smothers her long, undone hair as she pulls the snake-like garment over her head, the folded-over collar snugging up to her chin. The body is just loose enough to hang around her torso without looking baggy at the one extreme or accentuating her distortions on the other. It's a girl's, not a woman's size sweater, and she ordered it from an on-line catalog so no prying eyes need watch her fumbling to find such a garment in the local stores. For a like reason she cut and sewed the pants herself and lined them for substantiality and a quality feel. Otherwise, where in any store would you find garments tailored for a spine-twisted, four-foot-four woman?

Bella knots up her hair, then ponders her appearance in the bedroom mirror. She doesn't look like a woman who's dying of ovarian cancer, does she? But an ultrasound has detected the presence of a large abnormal mass, and a blood test has confirmed a raised level of the chemical that is a tumor marker for ovarian cancer. The doctor insisted a biopsy was necessary for one hundred percent certainty; she mustn't despair. Bella doesn't despair, she *knows*, and the clarity of her knowledge is hard as a diamond inside her. She has refused the biopsy and the procedures that will follow: a hysterectomy to remove as much of the cancer as possible, then chemo and/or radiation that will leave her weakened, nauseated and bald. After which, she'll die anyway. The doctor grew angry at her pessimism and blustered that with aggressive treatment there was still hope. He's lying. Bella has done her research, both on the Internet and in medical books. The early symptoms of ovarian cancer are so vague and nonspecific that the vast majority of cases aren't diagnosed until it's too late, and the abdominal bloating she mistook for indigestion means the disease has already spread. Just keep me out of pain, she ordered the doctor. Come on, be a fighter, he cajoled. He doesn't understand that Bella is a fighter. It's just not her life that she now chooses to fight for.

She smoothes her hand over the new clothes, then walks downstairs to the kitchen, puts a kettle of water on the stove to boil, and heats a frozen waffle in the toaster. It might be better if she leaves before Charlotte comes down, let her assume Bella has gone to mass early. Nevertheless, Bella is prepared to face her. She's holding the waffle in her fingers, dipping it in a puddle of syrup in a saucer, when Charlotte walks in.

"Bella?" Charlotte eyes the strange outfit of sweater and pants, her eyebrows raised mockingly at first, then in apprehension. Something is up. "Are you going to church?"

"I'm going on the nature walk. It's time we took a firsthand look at how these excursions are being conducted."

"What? We never—What are you talking about?"

"I'm going on the nature walk. It's our responsibility to know what is happening on the property. I doubt there's any cause for worry, but if Miss Avery—"

"'Miss Avery'? I thought it was 'Jane and her friends'?"

"Miss Avery," Bella repeats. "If she is allowing visitors to over-exert themselves or leading them up steep trails where they might fall or twist an ankle, I suppose we could be liable."

"No, we couldn't. You know perfectly well it's written into the agreement that people come at their own risk. Bella, what are you—"

"Besides, you don't need me today anyway. You'll be finishing your collage painting. I do think it's remarkable."

She brushes past Charlotte to the sink, and Charlotte pauses, bewildered but not convincingly sidetracked. Yet the last comment deserves inspection because Bella doesn't lie about her artwork. Mostly she criticizes, but when she compliments, it's genuine; there will be at least a grain of truth in it. And that is Charlotte's curse, or one of them, that she *is* good at art with flashes of talent that rise above the ordinary. It's why she has never been able to quit completely. So now she focuses on Bella's unsolicited praise of the collage multi-portrait she has created of *One Hundred People I Longed To Be*. Bella has been indispensable in researching this for her, locating self-portraits and photographs and famous paintings by those artists to be represented, and Charlotte has diligently and cleverly worked them into a jigsaw-like collage that will keep viewers clustered around the canvas trying to identify each piece. She stops, her senses hardening…Wait a minute—what if all Bella means is that the painting is indeed a curiosity, a brain teaser, an oddity to briefly widen your eyes, that it is, in short, *remark*-able.

Bella, at the sink, rubs her teacup with a smidgen of dishwashing liquid on her finger, rinses it in hot water, and leaves it in the rubber dish drainer for next time. Charlotte stares daggers at her back, the stiff topknot the only familiar aspect of this gnomish figure in turtleneck sweater and black pants. Bella is dissembling, her reasons for joining the nature walk are an excuse, yet she behaves as if she expects Charlotte to swallow this.

"I need a change from church," says Bella abruptly, turning to face her.

"Oh, really?"

"Yes, really."

"No, not really, Bella. I'm not quite the fool you think."

Bella opens her mouth, but no retort comes out. Charlotte's look already says she isn't buying it, and with a heavy exhalation of breath that is the end of resistance and the beginning of defiance, Bella comes clean.

"We have to decide about the future," she says, "the future of this estate after we're gone."

"No!" The recoil and recovery are as automatic as if Charlotte has been shot but wears a bulletproof vest. "Why? You don't want anyone to have it any more than I do. Besides, we have years yet, we only did this for the tax break. I won't allow the negotiations to go any further. We have to keep playing them off one against the other. You like doing that, Bella. Isn't that the whole point, to manipulate people so you can feel superior to them? Now you're siding with the birders, the land trust, is that it? Why? Because they were nice to you?"

"Yes!" shouts Bella. "Yes, they were nice to me!" And this is true, this is one of the reasons she wants to go on the walk today, why she perused the on-line catalogs to find the turtleneck sweater, why she labored so meticulously to pattern and cut and sew these pants.

"*I'm* nice to you."

"When? When are you ever nice to me?"

"Always! I brought you here! I gave you everything you asked for!" Charlotte's hand sweeps wide in demonstration. "You got far more than you deserved. Poisoner!"

"You wanted it! You begged for my help! I should

have asked for more! I should have had what I'm entitled to!"

"What more are you entitled to? What good would anything more have done you?"

"Nothing, nothing! It wouldn't have done any good at all!"

Fury distorts Bella, threatens to make her crooked bones crack apart, but it's not only fury at Charlotte, but at herself, at all the lies, at the stupidity of this quarrel while the clock is ticking toward eight and what she yearns for is more of the human contact that began the day the cursed little brambling appeared and the birders welcomed her into their circle. She didn't know how to follow up on it, couldn't invite them into the house because Charlotte was still incensed over the episode, couldn't fathom another way to play chess with Roy or show up at the walk in her dress and high heels. And then she was busy arranging the August lawn party and sneaking off to those doctor's appointments. Now she needs to get the future settled. She needs to know how this will end.

"We have to decide about the estate," she insists, grounding herself on the single most important issue, focusing her energy on one task. "If you leave it up in the air, if you don't make a clear decision, someone else will make the decision for you. That's not what we want."

"Yes, it is. We want them fighting at each other's throats." Charlotte shakes her head, confused. They had a plan, Bella helped her concoct it. Stay as rich as possible as long as possible, then when you know the end is near, surprise them all and find a way to take it with you. Hand out the money to beggars on the street, donate this painting to that museum, that painting to this. Disperse of it piecemeal until there's nothing left but a shell of a house, a property so overgrown it's impenetrable. Then let the stray dogs fight over the scraps, the art association, the land trust, the city, the tax collector, whatever impossibly distant relatives might crawl out of the woodwork. If she can't leave her own art legacy, she won't leave anything at all. And Bella was her partner in this, until this revolt in a turtleneck sweater and pants. What on earth does Bella want?

"Rome. We'll go to Italy. You'll go to Rome," Charlotte promises, suddenly guessing. It's not what on *earth* does Bella want, it's what in *heaven*. "We'll go to Rome. It's not too late. Catholics can always be forgiven. You can book tickets on the computer. You know how to do that."

"Yes." All Bella means is Yes, I know how to book airline tickets at discount rates on the Internet, not yes to going to Rome or any of the argument that has preceded it. But that yes suffices to soften the rancor. That yes gives them a plausible truce. After so many years, they know not to push too hard for fear the whole edifice will fall. They can't let that happen while they're still inhabiting it.

"Good," says Charlotte, "now stay and keep me company."

"I can't."

Bella pats Charlotte's hand and offers her a sad smile. Then she clumps away down the hall. It's too late for any pilgrimage to Rome, for confessions and forgiveness. It's too late for religion, church, faith. Bella has passed through her five stages of grief and arrived at acceptance. All she wants before the end is a little human-ness.

Chapter 21

At the front gate, Jane spots Bella coming toward them. Her eyes register the secretary's attire from her sweater down to her shoes and her jerky, determined gait, and Jane's mouth opens in astonishment. Bella laughs, a short nervous laugh they're too far away to hear, to cover the awkwardness she's about to precipitate.

"I was wondering if I might join you this morning, if I may?" She starts politely, then ends on a hesitant question.

"Yes, of course," says Jane, too quickly.

Bella smiles her thanks. Of course she can come, they can't exactly deny her. Yet she can't help but wish Jane had weighed her answer a brief second, let Bella see in her eyes whether she really wanted her along. Nevertheless, she's in, and the others rise gamely to the situation.

"Good morning," says Roy to Bella. "You've got the birding bug, have you?"

"It's wonderful exercise," adds Hortense, then stops, flustered. Retired gym teacher that she is, she's always encouraging people to get more exercise. But given Bella's deformity, even an ordinary walk might pose a challenge, and Hortense's face shows instant remorse that her words might appear insensitive.

"I'm sure I'll enjoy it," agrees Bella, endeavoring to put everyone at ease.

"Well, then," says Jane, picking up smoothly, "since we have some first-time visitors this morning, why don't we go around and introduce ourselves? I'm Jane Avery, the property manager."

Around the circle, they speak their names, Hortense, Roy, Melanie and three women who are from a birding club in Massachusetts. Bella says, "I am Bella, Miss Deerfield's secretary," and in that one sentence, so often spoken, is the sum total of her life. Jane gives a brief explanation for the newcomers as to the hows and whys of the estate being open, the trail they will cover, and off they go.

Once again, the dynamics of the walk shift to suit the group's configuration. Jane, with no forewarning of Bella's participation, can't help but wonder at the motive. Some sort of job review? An embassy from Charlotte to gather ammunition for renewed negotiations with the town? Hortense and Roy also become a bit more formal, automatically dropping to the end of the line, though they would do this anyway to give the three out-of-state visitors the first crack at glimpsing any birds they might startle up. Yet even the newcomers, a friendly trio in their forties, step back to give Bella precedence. They aren't sure whether her attendance is a regular occurrence, but they have quickly understood that she represents the owner. Moreover, all of them instinctively recognize that her official position aside, Bella's physical constraints must necessarily set the pace.

Only Melanie has failed to grasp these subtleties, and forgetting her responsibility to keep Roy at the rear of the line when company comes, she plants herself at the head with Bella and Jane. She wants to ask Bella questions. Why are you grownup but short? Why is that red blotch in your eye? Does your body hurt to be crooked like that? Were you in an accident, too? Do people tease you? Did you have to go to special ed when you were in school? Melanie knows regular people aren't allowed to ask hurt people such questions, but hurt people are allowed to ask other hurt people, and sometimes when you share the hurt, even though there are two of you, twice as much hurt, somehow it feels less.

Walking beside Jane, Bella is more aware than

anyone of the ripples her presence is creating, but they are all, including Bella herself, going to have to deal with it. Including the hiking, which is harder going than she expected. The route they're on has the faint impression of a human trail being worn into the forest by the mass effect of Sunday footsteps and six months of Jane's patrols. Yet there are still irregularities in the ground to throw her off, and with her illness already weakening her, it's an effort to haul her legs along, the pain encroaching despite the drugs. She prays not to trip and fall and make a fool of herself. Fortunately, the birders don't go far before stopping to look and listen, cover another short distance, stop and listen again, and the more they get into their birding, the more their inhibitions about her presence drop off.

"Hear that?" Roy points for her to look upward as a honking squadron of Canada geese passes overhead. "You wouldn't guess it from the racket, but that's actually two distinct sounds they're making. Canada geese form lifelong pair bonds, and when the male says *honk!*, his female gives an answering *hink!* It helps keep the pairs together, like they're holding hands in flight."

"And when you do hear Canada geese, it's always worthwhile to look up at their passage," Hortense advises. "Occasionally, a snow goose will mix in with them, and there, streaming along in the V, you'll see a slightly smaller white goose flapping away as if nothing is amiss."

"They can fly pretty high, too," one of the Massachusetts visitors chips in. "I've read that migratory geese go up to five thousand feet, and there are records of snow geese cruising along at an altitude of twenty thousand."

"Thank you, I didn't know any of this," says Bella, amazed at these revelations about the secret, romantic lives of geese.

"Do you work at the estate every day?" another of the newcomers asks her. "It's such a lovely place!"

"I live here," Bella replies, and at their appreciative murmur, she adds, "I have lived at Deerfield most of my life," thus beginning the same cautious process of self-disclosure Jane entered into last spring, this tentative making of friends.

"How lucky you are!" the third woman says. "Imagine having a whole estate as your backyard to stroll in!"

Jane and her regulars exchange a look. They know how extraordinary Bella's presence here is, though even they can't suspect how truly long it has been. Bella herself responds with a smiling, noncommittal murmur. To these people it would be unthinkable to let such a property lie idle and not be roaming all over it, and it's gratifying that already the newcomers have overlooked her disability far enough to assume she strolls regularly in the woods. She must be holding up her effort well.

"Miss Deerfield prefers to devote her time to painting and her patronage of our art association," Bella adds in an attempt to balance her own half-truth with one for Charlotte, and this information is greeted with another approving "ahh!" as Charlotte's reputation as local benefactress continues to grow.

In a few more minutes they come upon the pond, and from the newcomers arise gasps of pleasure. The oaks and maples wreathing the rim are tinged with the first infusion of autumn orange, red and gold, and swift-winged tree swallows dart above the water feasting on insects in mid-air. The sunlit surface reflects the forest around it, as if the trees are looking into a mirror, and the burnished blue of the sky belies the coolness of the air in that delicious mingling of autumnal crispness with the last heady warmth of summer. As the birders train their binoculars on a black-crowned night-heron perched on a rock, Jane steps a little apart. Once, when she first came here, the pond held trepidation, suspending her in fears. Now it offers her a beauty so vulnerable, she would clasp it to her chest. The season is different, of course—how can any landscape in barren March compare to the emerging blaze of late September?—but Jane knows she is different, too. She had felt then the pond was like a heart trapped between beats, but it was her heart on hold, wasn't it? Now the beat is a swell, stepping onto the bank of the pond feels like coming home, and the idea of leaving Deerfield at Christmas is suddenly, impossibly hard.

"Please? Where do you go from here?"

A halting footstep sounds beside her, and there is Bella.

"Oh, well, lately we've been going out on the ridge to watch for hawk migration." Jane comes back to the Sunday walk, then pauses as she grasps the unspoken import of the question. Bella has managed the terrain thus far, but the ridge is rocky and steep in places. "We have another trail that loops back to the field," she quickly offers.

"No, no, stick to your route. I didn't really come to see the birds, just for a little fresh air and exercise. I've probably gone far enough for today." Bella speaks con-fidingly, silently pleading not to have an issue made of it. Just this short time in their company has given her a sense of comradeship, and she doesn't want it spoiled. Besides, the ridge isn't where she needs to go. She raises her voice and calls to the others still observing the heron. "Thank you for sharing your binoculars with me. I'm going to sit by the pond awhile. Do go on and enjoy your hike. It was a pleasure to meet you."

"I would be happy to escort you home," says Roy, stepping forward.

"No, thank you, I'll be fine. I know the way." Bella waves breezily toward the house, though it's well out of sight. For a moment they waver, dubious at leaving her alone, but what can they do but respect her decision? In this enlightened age, no one wants to be accused of treating a handicapped person in a patronizing fashion. They file along the bank toward the footbridge, and as her charges cross into the next stretch of forest, Jane glances back, her expression misgiving. It takes a last ebullient wave from Bella to send her on.

Oh, God.

Bella sinks onto the log bench, the brisk bravado of her forced pace, her smile and the cheery insistence of her voice gone. It's not exhaustion or pain, however, but the convulsion of memory that brings her down. Nearly sixty years since she last came to this spot. What do you want, Bella? Why have you come? She stares at the pond, no longer aware of its details of birds and leaves and turtles basking on a log. She doesn't see it as a heart as Jane does, nor as a childhood swimming hole for Roy, nor as Melanie's wishing well. Bella sees it as an eye, an unequivocal pupil-less eye that stares back at her. And she had once thought it would be so beautiful! As a child back on Capri she would hear Charlotte's fragile mother Clarisse speak of "boating parties on the pond," and she pictured ladies in white dresses holding lace parasols and gentlemen in straw hats paddling rowboats on a lazy summer afternoon.

But when she arrived that spring after the war, when she made Charlotte bring her to America, that pretty picture was already forgotten, and neither a contemplation of nature nor a desire for exercise propelled her excursions over the property. She was in urgent need of plants, herbs, and she combed these woods, paths or no, scratching her face and hands on thorns, losing her footing and stumbling on the ridge, searching the dense thickets to the north of the pond. Once she lost her way and wandered off the estate into the forest beyond, off course for several hours until the track of the sun moved from overhead to westward and gave her a basic sense of direction. She clambered back—failure again!—berating herself because Charlotte had already fulfilled her half of the bargain. Bella stares at the water of the pond, a blank eye that watched her come and go that spring in increasing desperation, a blank eye that watches her now, nearly six decades later, still neither judging nor condemning. She can do that well enough herself.

Bella wipes a tear from her cheek. The bridge is there, waiting. She needs to cross it soon, while she still has the strength, but today it's too dangerous, she might run into Jane and the birders on their return, better to come here another time, alone. She starts back toward the house, taking each step slowly.

The birders are already on the ridge, having picked up their pace after Bella's departure. The wind is still today, however, and no hawks appear, so one of the newcomers ventures to inquire more about the estate. How old is the house, how did the family make its fortune, who lives there at present? Jane by now has pat, tour-guide replies that achieve a fair balance between answering the questions and protecting Charlotte's privacy, and she concludes with the information that the house "is still in the Deerfield family" as a way of not advertising their isolation. Privately, she's still hoping Bella made it back safely, and she's relieved when the group begins to retrace its path. "What's that?" asks Melanie.

They stop and look around, but instead of pointing to a bird, Melanie puts one hand to her ear to signal a sound. In the ensuing silence, they hear a faint *pop, pop, pop*. Puzzled, their faces examine and discard the possibilities. Not a bird or an animal; an artificial noise, a distant car backfiring?

"A gun," says Roy, not surprised that after all these years, he still knows that sound, how it echoes from a distance, startles at middle range, how a whole barrage of guns becomes a terrifying fusillade when you're sent into it, although by then it's not the guns you hear anymore, it's the blood pounding in your ears. The memory doesn't haunt or torment him. It's just a sound you don't forget.

"Deer hunters in the state forest?" asks Hortense. She nods to the vast expanse of trees west of the estate.

"I don't think deer hunting season starts this early," one of three new women replies. "Besides, it came more from the north."

"We aren't anywhere near it, are we?" another of the women says with a shudder. "There's no hunting on this land?"

"Oh no," Jane reassures them, "there's no hunting allowed at Deerfield. Let's continue on." She points to the trail that leads to the footbridge, disguising her unease. The noise stopped almost as soon as they heard it, but there's no fence, no marked boundary line between their property and the state forest, and deer season or no, she has no desire to lead her visitors into the vicinity of anyone with a gun. Yet a deeper worry is gaining on her, a dread feeling that the *pop, pop, pop* echoing in her memory came from the direction of the Deerfield house.

"It's okay, Melanie. We're safe," she says, taking the child's hand, for in these few minutes of trying to decipher the mystery no one until now has noticed the fright on Melanie's face. Hortense pats her shoulder, but it's not herself Melanie is afraid for. It's the deer. It's Bambi's mother. They don't show it in the video, but you know that's what happens. Bambi's mother gets shot. Melanie knew it before her accident and she knows it even more after, because when you lose your mother like she did your whole life changes, things turn bad, and despite Jane's clasp of her hand and Hortense's pat on her shoulder, Melanie feels anger wrestling inside her. Nobody should hurt deer, nobody should shoot them. They're soft, beautiful creatures who would never hurt anyone, little fawns with white spots like snowflakes and brown-eyed does and stags crowned with antlers. She wants to pull free and run go save the whole deer family, but Jane is firmly leading her along.

When they cross the bridge, Jane drops Melanie's hand and asks Roy and Hortense if they would mind escorting their visitors to the gate. It's probably nothing, but she wants to run on and make sure everything is all right at the house. She sprints off, although there's no more of the disturbing noise. That's because what the birders heard out on the ridge was the end of it, the last three shots.

Bella, on the other hand, heard the whole rampage.

Pop! Pop! Pop! She had left the pond and completed the slight ascent up the trail to the field when the first gunshots fired. Then *blam! blam! blam!* and in the pause it takes Charlotte to reload, Bella starts running. If you can call it running. Her legs jerk, her arms flail, the crooked tilt of ordinary becomes a hideous lurch like a marionette that's had half its strings severed. She trips and lands on one knee, starts to push up, catches the toe of her shoe on a straggling root and falls flat, the breath knocked out of her useless body. *Blam! Blam!* Bella struggles up and lumbers on, a pain in one ankle adding an extra hobble to her gait. She's lost track of the shots, only knows she must get there quickly. There might be cars passing on the shore road, someone might hear and call the police, explanations would be necessary. Stop, stop! she cries silently, ignoring the twisted ankle to keep up speed. Bella has a cut on her cheek she's not aware of, and her topknot is lopsided and unraveling. Anyone watching would simply burst out laughing, it's so funny, so ridiculous. She hurries toward the rose garden behind the house. *BLAM! BLAM! BLAM!* It's these last three shots the birders hear as disembodied *pops* out on the ridge.

"Stop it!" Bella shrieks at Charlotte. "Stop it!"

Charlotte doesn't lower the gun. There is her collage painting, *One Hundred People I Longed To Be*, completed only a half hour ago, propped against a rose bush and riddled with bullet holes. Not one bullet has missed its mark; Charlotte is, as she told Jane, an excellent shot. She has blown a hole in Picasso's bald head, another in Van Gogh's ear. She has executed Rembrandt, Renoir, Winslow Homer and Dali. Poor little Toulouse-Lautrec she has let live; there he is, painted in at the last minute fleeing off the right side of the canvas, terror in his face, just as Bella ran away this morning and deserted her. She'll show everyone just whose artwork is *remark*-able.

"Put the gun down," Bella says because they both know she has to say, request, order it. So far, no one else has heard the shots, there's no wail of a siren approaching. Yet Charlotte can't relinquish the situation. She has to appear, even between the two of them, most importantly between the two of them, to be torn and persuaded.

"No." Charlotte turns on Bella a taunting look and points the gun to her own temple. Everyone always talks about the agony, the suffering, the anguish of the great artists. What about the little artists? What about them? They suffer. They sacrifice. They try, they try! They try and weep and try again. They know every agony the great artists know and one more, the agony of failure, of mediocrity, of not having been blessed. They don't even have the courage to pull the trigger; they are doomed to long, prolific and unrewarding lives. If she could only squeeze that trigger...

Bella knows she won't. Weary to the bone from this morning's exertions, weary to the soul of this monumentally insignificant drama, Bella clenches her fists. She *does* understand. She has a whole lifetime of regrets and guilt and unfulfilled dreams, but she bears it. That's the difference. Bella *bears* it. In a mood most hateful, she screams at Charlotte.

"Go ahead! Blow your brains out! I don't care! Nobody does!"

And in the next instant Charlotte turns the gun on Bella and blasts the ground six inches in front of her feet, sending up a small explosion of dirt. For a full minute, Bella quakes from head to toe, not at the narrowness of her escape but at the closeness of her release, denied her by Charlotte, who is an excellent shot. Oh, that was mean!

"Well," Bella recovers her equilibrium with a weighted intake of breath, "are you happy now?"

"I do feel better."

"Then put the gun down," she orders, and this time Charlotte complies. They both stare at the mangled painting. "You'll stop now," says Bella, "give up the retrospective."

"No." An automatic refusal that wavers, then hardens, because Charlotte, too, is bitterly tired of this.

"Please, Charlotte, don't make us go back any further. It was so long ago. Paint something else if you must. Flowers, what about flowers? No, you did that, I know, Georgia

O'Keeffe." Bella glances toward the painting. O'Keeffe is blasted through her black sombrero.

"No." Charlotte has a stake in this, too. It's her art, her idea, the most original concept she has ever put on canvas. And Bella must understand this, Bella who would be nothing without her. Can't she see Charlotte is doing it for them? "It might be great art, Bella, maybe not each piece singly, but when you put them together. All the last months will be lost if I stop now, all our lives wasted."

"No, if you stop here, we will be *saved*." Bella gestures imploringly at the bullet-riddled collage. "Let this painting be the beginning of the retrospective, when you first really tried, and now it's expressed, the effort and the anger. I understand, I understand!" She's almost crying, unheard of because Bella never cries. But she aches, her legs, her spine and her head ache, and oh, the cruel pain in her abdomen!

"But I wouldn't have been forced to try if things had gone differently before that. I'd have something else to do now." Charlotte waves helplessly at the painting. They hate the way their lives have turned out, but there's nothing for it but to carry on till the end. And she, Charlotte, still claims the superior privilege of suffering, because she has to suffer for both her art and her sin, whereas Bella has only her sin for which to pay.

"All right then," Bella surrenders, "finish the retrospective." She can put up no more fight, only try to get matters settled before her part in it is over. "Is the gun empty, by the way?"

"I think so." Charlotte aims into the air, and the gun makes a useless, metallic *click*.

"Miss Deerfield! Bella!" Jane careens into view. "We heard shots, shouts, I thought intruders—"

She comes up short at the sight of Charlotte's gun, then her startled gaze goes to the assassinated painting. *She only uses the gun when she's come to hate her paintings*, Bella had advised that day Charlotte flourished the pistol before Jane's face in the studio, *then she takes them out into the rose garden and shoots them.*

"Oh, Miss Avery, I'm so sorry!" Charlotte's face pulls down in genuine contrition. Imagine, Jane was actually dashing to save her! "It was the impulse of an artistic moment. I'm so sorry you were frightened."

Bella smiles feebly, and Jane takes several deep breaths to restore her heartbeat. To think she ran all this way imagining who knows what, only to find this false alarm. She holds out her palm.

"Miss Deerfield, give me the gun. I don't care how good a shot you are, it was completely irresponsible to fire a weapon without giving me any warning and especially when we have visitors on the property."

"Yes, yes, you're right." Meekly, Charlotte hands over the weapon. Jane has probably forgotten she has other guns stashed in drawers if she needs them. Besides, a new thought is dawning. She picks up the canvas and studies it, her face brightening. Shooting it has vastly improved it. Why not include it in the retrospective as is, a testament, as Bella said, to all her failed attempts? In fact, Bella has unwittingly come up with the perfect title for the painting, *The Effort and The Anger*. Less direct perhaps than *One Hundred People I Longed To Be*, but definitely artsier, and if a further caption is required for explanation, so be it. That crew of hapless hacks at the art association can't help but get this one, and even intelligent non-artists like Jane, who had asked, "What does the caption say?" will begin to get a glimmer.

"We are deeply sorry, Miss Avery," Charlotte repeats. "I assure you, I won't be shooting any other paintings, will I, Bella?"

"No, we're very sorry," says Bella, ashamed.

"Good," says Jane, stalking off.

Charlotte pats her canvas fondly. You could only get away with one shot-up picture per exhibition anyway.

Chapter 22

October may be the most beautiful month in New England, especially on the southern coast. All summer the sun heats the ocean, and that reservoir of retained heat, along with the Gulf Stream curving up the coastline, conspires to impart a lingering warmth to the shore. Land temperatures may still be in the balmy sixties at the same time the trees are phasing from green to ripe yellow and orange. Foliage snobs will argue the colors are more brilliant and crisp in the northern forests where the cold snaps its fingers and the leaves burst into flame, but in southernmost New England you will still be playing golf or tennis or gardening in shorts, surrounded by the mellowness of Indian summer.

For the birders, the fall migration continues, although gradually diminishing. "I think we're beginning to feel a little limited," Jane confesses to Tim Hennessey when he shows up one weekend with a casual explanation that he wanted to check in on behalf of the land trust. They're standing on the ridge with a handful of Sunday visitors watching a circling red-tail. "We have only a few trails on the lower half of the property and another around the pond that's pretty rough. The hard-core birders don't mind it, but when we get the more touristy types…"

She nods discreetly in the direction of two women wearing smart wool blazers, pleated slacks and polished loafers, for heaven's sake, as if dressed in faithful adherence to some clothing catalog's depiction of an autumn walk in the woods. They must have imagined a stroll on a sun-dappled path with rustic signposts and leafy trees vaulting overhead. To their credit, they're not complaining, but although they've made it up the ridge without scuffing their expensive shoes, they're clearly not getting the thrill out of the swooping hawk that's mesmerizing the true birders and seem instead to be politely puzzled by this close encounter with nature.

"Well, I can't exactly take them bushwhacking, can I?" Jane concludes.

Tim laughs, also discreetly, then clicks his tongue as he glances down the trail from the ridge. It's nowhere too steep for anyone in average health, but it does involve picking a way over exposed tree roots and up the rocky side of the ledge. Roy can make it, for example, but not without a touch of breathlessness.

"Snow and ice are going to make hiking this ridge problematic in winter," Tim agrees, "although in bad weather most people will stay home anyway. But you can always cut the walk short or cancel it at your discretion."

Jane nods. She hasn't seen or heard from Tim or the land trust since the brambling that summer, and she's glad to have him as an ally. He doesn't come to Deerfield with any political agenda or ulterior motives. What—or who—does he care about besides his work? she finds herself wondering. Then she brushes off the thought and continues to another matter on her mind.

"I'm also concerned about deer hunting in the state forest." She gestures westward, not mentioning the incident of Charlotte's gun that first raised the issue. "I made a few phone calls and learned the season doesn't begin until late November, but when it does there's no fence or boundary markers to alert hunters they might be crossing onto private property. So I'm going to post NO TRESPASSING signs, like I did at our south boundary with the beach, and I'll just take my best guess as to where the property line lies. Meanwhile, I should probably notify the land trust that we're starting to get requests for group tours during the week."

"From who?"

"One from the art association. They want to paint the fall colors." Jane pauses over the memory of the disastrous painting party at the pond that steamy day in June. The request this time is for a smaller, select group, and both the size and the weather should be manageable. "The other came from a special ed teacher who visited this summer and wants to bring his students on a field trip. He has eleven behaviorally and mentally challenged kids, and he promised to supply adequate chaperones. Miss Deerfield said yes to both visits, which really surprised me. Is there a provision for that in her agreement with the land trust and the town?"

"It surprises me, too." Tim pauses, perplexed. "Our only stipulation so far is that the estate be open for public access these Sunday mornings. Otherwise, it's her property, and if she wants to allow other organizations or individuals to visit, I guess she can. But she's always fought that, tooth and nail. Is there some change of heart going on?"

"I don't know...I hope not. I must be turning into a tree hugger, Tim, because I certainly don't want to see this place spoiled or overrun. Even you just said the Sunday walks are your only stipulation *so far*." She eyes him accusingly, ready to downgrade her earlier, favorable assessment. Then she glances around the heart-piercing view, imploring him to see what she feels. Deerfield on this beautiful morning makes you yearn to bottle and save it against the day the landscape is so developed your soul will cry out for an oasis of leaves and light, of flawless blue sky, of rustling sounds and damp earth scents, a treasure trove of birds.

"I know," says Tim, quiet for a moment as well. "I only meant we're keeping the door open in case Miss Deerfield eventually wants or needs us to take a more active role. And some on-site educational programs would be good, Jane, or how are we going to raise another generation of people who care? But believe me, neither I nor the land trust want to turn Deerfield into a campground or amusement park."

"And the town?"

"I think they view the present arrangement as a first step to get their foot in the door and eventually charge admission to the house and garden for tours. They could run a gift shop, rent out the premises for weddings and corporate events. I know, I know," he holds up his hands as her mouth opens in protest, "environmentalism makes strange bed-fellows. But you have to understand that if it's done right, Deerfield could be their biggest tourist attraction."

"Over my dead body," Jane mutters. She still has Charlotte's gun, after all. Yet she can't deny compromises will be necessary, and perhaps Charlotte's acceding to the artists' and the schoolchildren's visits is a sign that she recognizes this also. Bella, meanwhile, has not returned for another Sunday walk, and Jane wonders if she ought to issue a specific invitation. Bella seemed to want something from her.

"Look, I'm sorry I upset you," says Tim. "Nothing drastic is going to happen in the immediate future, and the number of visitors will probably drop off soon. Mild as the weather is now, *The Old Farmer's Almanac* is predicting a stormy winter."

"And you believe it?" Jane allows a small smile onto her lips. When he warms up, Tim isn't quite the rigid scientist he appears.

"I don't disbelieve it. Between the fur on woolly bear caterpillars and bird migrations and leaves turning, nature knows a lot more than we do. How about this: I'll propose we put a moratorium on the Sunday walks for January and February to prevent any injuries on icy trails. Then we can take those two months to revisit our intentions and assess how well we've met our goals." He grimaces at the language, but that's the way you have to talk if you're going to persuade bureaucrats to preserve a wetland or save an endangered toad. "Meanwhile, I'll recommend the land trust post a notice on their website that Deerfield is open 'Weather Permitting.' That will back you up in case there's a week you feel it's prudent to cancel."

"Thanks." Jane tips her head at the red-tail drifting off. Hortense and Roy are attempting to engage the two wool blazer women in conversation, and she has left her duties long enough. "Okay, time to start back," she says.

Roy sighs to himself, takes Melanie's hand, and brings up the rear. No sign today of that five hundredth bird, and with the migration winding down, so are his chances for another year. Does he have another year? Of course, as the songbirds and hawks depart south, ducks and shorebirds will begin arriving from farther north for the winter. When you summer near the Arctic Circle, as do eiders, oldsquaws, harlequins, brants, black-bellied plovers, purple sandpipers and more, the unfrozen sea off New England is your Florida. But Roy's list already includes every usual species plus rarer prizes, including a Barrow's goldeneye, a black guillemot and a glaucous gull. Checking the bird alerts on the Internet, nothing new or very unusual has been posted lately, so it will take a real rarity to qualify. And once winter socks in, will he be able to make these expeditions? Summer is so good to his brittle bones, stiff joints and withered muscles, warming them into a false sense of vigor, that when the frigid weather does hit, he's shaken to discover how quickly he loses the sensation in his fingers and toes, how audible becomes the creaking in his left hip, how his spine rattles with every shiver. He smiles at Melanie and holds her hand more tightly. Come winter, he'll be clasping her hand not to keep the child safe but for the sureness of her grip steadying him and for that pocket of warmth between their mittened palms.

"Keep your eyes open, Melanie," he whispers, because even more important to Roy than seeing his five hundredth bird is having his friends see it with him. Their happiness for him would make him happier than the appearance of the bird itself.

When they reach the front gate, Jim and Lois say their goodbyes for the year and exchange hugs all around. They're sailing to Florida via Bermuda, and everyone wishes them bon voyage.

"We'll see you next April or May," Jim promises as they drive away. "If you come to Florida this winter, look us up in Cocoa Beach."

"Wouldn't we love to be sailing south for the winter," sighs Charlie to Russ, and for a minute everyone succumbs to the natural curiosity of seeing a lifestyle based on more money than one's own and wondering, How did they do it? Is there any way I could do it, too?

"Well, I guess I should be going," says Tim, lingering. There seems to be something more he wants to ask Jane but doesn't know how. "Do your, um, actor friends still come on the walks? I was thinking how ingenious they were when the brambling was here, that charade, you know."

He fiddles with the focus on his binoculars, and Jane does a quick rearrangement of her thoughts. So that's it, that's why he's come, an ulterior motive after all. *Raven.* Raven who hypnotized him that day the brambling came. He must have been hoping ever since to meet her again and couldn't get up the nerve to give her a call. And here she was beginning to think...never mind. Jane clears her head. Brandon is sleeping in at the cottage this morning as usual, and he'll have coffee and French toast waiting for her before he draws her back to bed.

"Maybe next week," she says, wondering if she ought to take a hand in it. She hasn't seen Raven in weeks, Brandon reports she's wrapped up in her theater administration project, and Jane assumes she's still dating Burt, a relationship that seems too mismatched to last. Raven and Tim as a couple don't seem any more likely, but it can't hurt to bring them together and let them take it from there if they wish. "I hope you'll come again."

"Oh, okay. Right, thanks."

He waves and drives off, and Jane goes into her cottage. She won't see Jim and Lois again, not if she leaves at Christmas, but she couldn't say that in front of the others, who as yet have no inkling of her plans. Nor does Brandon, but then he always has plans of his own. She smiles at him across the breakfast table—right now he has bedroom on his mind—and it doesn't take much coaxing for her to join him. But as Brandon slips out of bed and kisses her goodbye, she reflects that it's time to revise her resume and start looking into engineering jobs, and Tim has, unknowingly, just given her a further push. If, as makes sense, they close Deerfield to the public in January and February, what better time for her to depart? That will give Charlotte, hopefully with the advice of the land trust, two months to hire a permanent, experienced property manager and for all parties to lay out a comprehensive plan for next year. Meanwhile, she'll use her remaining time to wind up the autumn chores on the estate and complete the carpentry and repairs to the cottage so the next occupant won't find it in the dilapidated condition she did. She spends the afternoon planting daffodil and tulip bulbs in the flower beds around the main house. The staff at the nursery, ever ready to pad Charlotte's account with purchases, had raved to her about their bulbs and the profusion of flowers that would burst forth next spring.

"I'll ask Miss Deerfield if she's interested," Jane had answered them, and as always asked Bella instead because she's learned by now that's what it means to ask Charlotte, you ask Bella.

"Bulbs for next spring," Bella replied wistfully. "Yes, why not? I'll order them over the Internet, however. It will be cheaper than that pirate at the nursery charges."

When the bulbs arrived, the quantity was excessive.

"I thought you might like some extra to plant around your cottage," Bella explained, and as Jane sets the first bulbs into place, six inches apart, six inches deep, she ponders this small flare of generosity and adds it to the growing list of rapprochements between Bella and herself. The way the secretary mitigated, then revised Charlotte's firing of her over the brambling incident, their informal conversations as Jane works on the grounds, Bella's appearance on that one nature walk. Yet the warmth never quite kindles into anything permanent. It's as if Bella is a fire of near-dead ashes, old coals that glow up briefly, then fade out, not enough heat at the core to reignite any flame, if ever one was there. In between these brief visitations of warmth Bella looks withdrawn and even more impenetrable than when Jane first met her, her eyes stony, a hardened twist to her mouth. Are she and Charlotte fighting again? Once, pruning a shrub near the front door, Jane thought she heard quarreling voices from the studio above, but the heavy door and the leaded glass windows were shut, and they'd have to be screaming for any sound to penetrate those fortress-thick stone walls. Whatever the argument, it seems to do with Charlotte's art and some long-ago grievance neither one can forget. Jane pauses, a brown-sheathed bulb in one gloved hand, a trowel in the other. Does everyone have something like that in their past, a loss or grief forever planted deep in their heart? Surely, she will feel that way about Jill's death, regret all her life that it happened, wish she could have changed it somehow. Yet she can encompass that regret and live with its flowerings. This month is one year since the crash, a year she never thought she could survive. Did nature heal her after all?

Later that week, when the special ed children come, she revises her usual introduction. "Good morning, welcome to Deerfield. I'm Jane Avery, the *sanctuary* manager. Do you know what a sanctuary is?" Eleven heads shake at the unfamiliar word. "It's a place where no harm can come, not to the plants, the animals, the trees, the pond."

Not true, her brain corrects immediately. Hawks swoop in to pluck off pretty songbirds and scurrying voles in the field, songbirds eat insects and delicate butterflies in turn, ancient trees are split by lightning strikes, snapping turtles in the pond reach up and drag fuzzy ducklings down. Life and death are the warp and woof of nature, which honors no form of sanctuary, and Jane reworks her theme. Some of the children are docile and blank-eyed, a few are already fidgety and in the firm grip of a chaperone. All are about Melanie's age, and she imagines it is to Melanie she's speaking.

"People have sanctuaries, too. In some religions, churches or temples are sanctuaries. It's a place you can go to, not to hide—because people know you're there—but a place everyone has agreed shall be free of hurting."

She shapes her hands to indicate a sphere, still searching for a convincing explanation. When Brandon said on his first visit that she was seeking sanctuary at Deerfield, she bridled at the notion, yet it applied more than she was willing to admit. She has found here a refuge from grief and guilt, a last resort for salvation. She wraps up lamely, the three chaperones nodding, the children staring at her in confusion.

"Only humans can create sanctuaries, whether for themselves or other species, so you must remember as we take our walk today that this is a special place, it's the animals' and the trees' home, and we are only visiting."

It's hard to tell if the children get anything out of the trip, until a few days later she receives a package of teacher-prompted notes and crayon drawings. Most say, "Thank you for the nice walk." But one says, "I don't like being hurt either."

When the artists come for the foliage painting session by the pond and when the walkers come on Sunday, Jane again introduces herself as the sanctuary manager, this time without further explanation. The artists don't notice the change in title from when she was the property manager, nor do the new Sunday visitors. But Roy and Hortense do, and at the conclusion of the walk they stay behind with Melanie.

"Has there been some revision to the agreement between Miss Deerfield, the town and the land trust?" Hortense asks. "Is she definitely going to bequeath the land for a nature preserve?"

"No." Jane relates her experience with the school-children. "I'm just trying out the word to see if it might have more impact, impress on people that this isn't merely a property but a haven, a refuge. Do you think it sounds presumptuous? Does it imply Deerfield has some sort of protected status, which isn't yet the case?"

"Puts a little respect in folks' minds, if you ask me," says Roy, "these days when people drop litter everywhere, run red lights, think they own the world. You say 'sanctuary,' Jane, that'll set them straight."

"I think most people who come here are pretty respectful," says Hortense, smiling at Roy's crankiness, "but I do agree there's power in the word. Who wouldn't long for a place where they feel protected and the world's in harmony, even if it is an illusion."

Melanie listens carefully to their talk. She already knows what a sanctuary is, a place where she feels happy. Now Jane says Dr. Hennessey wants to close Deerfield after Christmas, but that's okay because Roy says they'll go other places to look for ducks in the winter and Deerfield will reopen in the spring. Then she hears something that makes her even happier. Hortense is explaining to Jane about the Christmas Bird Count.

"It's an annual Audubon census that began in the year 1900," says Hortense. "Back in those days of indiscriminate shooting, it was traditional for the gunners, as they were called, to go out on Christmas Day and see how many birds they could bring down simply for sport. So the Audubon Society encouraged people to go out and count live birds instead. It runs from mid-December to early January, and if you want your results to be included, you can register and be assigned to a group. We do it unofficially, just for fun, trying to visit as many spots in a day as we can. Do you think Miss Deerfield would let us include the estate?"

"Sure, I'll ask," says Jane, and Melanie's heart lifts. She didn't get to go on last year's Christmas count because it was only shortly after she started birding with Hortense and Roy, and her father refused. His daughter was not allowed to be out all day in the cold, piling into cars with strangers and driving in a rush from place to place to stand in more cold searching for birds. Hortense tried to assure him that every-one would drive carefully, they never stayed out too long, they always stopped for donuts and hot chocolate and brought lunches, and any time anyone got cold they could warm up in the car. Melanie was planning it would be a maple-frosted donut with her hot chocolate when her father said no again, and it caused her to have one of those rare bad times when she got angry and screamed and cried and wanted to hit people. Hortense had to bite her lip, as Jane is doing now. Why is she doing that? She looks a little sad, and nobody should look sad if they live at a sanctuary where, if Melanie is happy on Sunday, Jane ought to be happy all the time.

Impulsively, she flings herself into Jane's arms and hugs her, nearly knocking her down, because Melanie is almost as tall as Jane, and she weighs more, being fat. The adults laugh, Jane included; Melanie can feel it in her slight body as she hugs her. So she's surprised, drawing out of the hug, that although the rest of Jane is smiling, there's a glimmer like tears in her eyes. Melanie doesn't know. Hortense and Roy don't know. Jane hasn't told them she'll be leaving.

Chapter 23

When she reviews the paintings in her retrospective so far, Charlotte is not entirely satisfied. Oh, the paintings are good, perhaps very good, perhaps brilliant…well, perhaps just very good. It's the size and number of them that concerns her. First come those five flattering self-portraits in which she successively un-aged herself with her magic paint wand. There followed the five Ice Age paintings of her union with Morton Fischer and the single harlequin portrait depicting her artistic New York years. Next the tearful womb series, the three overlapping pictures of the miscarriages during her marriage to Robert Drayton.

Finally, the large collage canvas, *One Hundred People I Longed To Be*, deftly shot with bullet holes and renamed *The Effort and The Anger*. Charlotte has come to like this pocked painting exceedingly. It explains everything. How can any other artist, on seeing it, not grasp immediately the eternal anguish of the creative soul, criticized, mocked and destroyed? This single painting is so powerful, she's contemplating revisiting all the previous series and reducing them to one picture apiece, either by picking the best of each lot or by painting a fresh canvas that embodies the whole episode. That would also enable her to refine and advance a comprehensive vision of the retrospective, which she didn't have when she accidentally began it with that first self-portrait early in the new year.

This is where the problem with size and numbers begins.

Thus far she has a total of fifteen completed paintings, make that thirteen if you count the overlapping wombs as one instead of three. If she does only one picture for her first marriage, covering years twenty-four to eighteen, and one for the final series at age sixteen, that makes seventeen canvases at the maximum, a barely decent number to adorn the smallest of the three exhibition rooms at the art association, even if you stage some plants like those tall potted ferns in between. If, however, she goes back and reduces the multi-painting series to one apiece, the total becomes seven, not enough to exhibit, period—unless she repaints them much larger.

Charlotte pauses, tapping a finger to her lips, contemplating the bare canvas on the easel before her. Bella has gone out—"On an errand," she said vaguely—but Charlotte can't be bothered too much about the little traitor's whereabouts, however strange she has been acting lately, not when she herself is in the grip of an artistic dilemma. So, paint them larger? It's not necessarily a bad thought or a philistine one. A painting like David's *Coronation of Napoleon in Notre-Dame* derives magnificence from its huge twenty by thirty-foot size, whereas Dali's *The Persistence of Memory*, those famous melting clocks, strikes you as positively insignificant when you see it in person and discover it's a mere thirteen inches wide. At least that's what Charlotte thought when she viewed it years ago. Why would anyone make a fuss about that dinky thing?

So, size matters, but can even seven large paintings in a room be big enough, powerful enough, to be considered and valued as a retrospective? Maybe more is better. Maybe, along with everything she has painted so far—and they are good—she should augment from the canvases layered around the studio? Of course, she can't use any of the old ones with bullet holes. Those she assassinated because even she couldn't delude herself they were in any way redeemable.

Au contraire, they were atrocious. Still, she couldn't quite bring herself to throw them out. She has never in her life been able to throw out a single one of her paintings, which is why they're huddled in lonely layers around this room. What if she flipped through them, picked out the best, and inserted them in their appropriate era within the retrospective? Then she could easily fill the walls of all three rooms in the art association, and what could they say about that? Ha!

Charlotte smiles at the notion of flooding the entire museum with her work. The art association people are getting pushy again. First, they have asked her to renew her sponsorship of the winter lecture series from January through March. Very well, she's funded it for a dozen years, and it's not that expensive, punch and cakes and speakers' fees for six lectures. Second, they pestered to come on the property again to paint, which she agreed to after some bullying by Bella and which admittedly went off without a hitch. But third, and here's the rub, they have sent a letter inviting her to an estate planning seminar they're holding as a "service" for their most valued members. Charlotte has had similar solicitations from other charities in the past, always in the form of a cordial personal letter. The seminar is to be presented by an esteemed financial consultant, and since everyone can benefit from expert advice on estate planning, they're sure she will find it informative. There will be no hard sell or attempt at persuasion, only sound, up-to-date advice for those who wish to "protect the value of their estate." In other words, give us the money so the government doesn't get it when you croak. The overture would be infuriating were it not so laughable. Who else can they possibly have invited of her financial caliber? No one, that's who. It's her fortune and land they want to get their greedy paws on, and anyone else in attendance will be there merely as props. Sometimes she wishes her grandmother had never founded that damn art association. They're like spoiled children who refuse to grow up, leave home and support themselves. Oh, if only she'd had a real child!

Charlotte closes her eyes and swallows painfully. Some days, painting this retrospective, she doesn't know who she is anymore. Reliving her life backward, as Bella warned and tried to stop her, has been no joyous romp. But surely not all of her life was bad? When she started this, she expected to find some beauty amidst the dust. Her lifetime of donations to music and the arts is praiseworthy and of no measly amount. And Robert Drayton did love her, at first, for a while, until she failed to produce a living heir. As for the ending of her first marriage, widowed at age twenty-four, that was perhaps a blessing for both herself and poor Lawrence Chandler. Neither of them quite understood what went wrong in a union that was supposed to make everything right. Charlotte picks up her brush and begins to paint a beautiful Titian-haired young woman in a widow's dress.

While Charlotte paints, Bella sits on the log bench beside the pond. The weather has grown cooler, and she wears a navy blue wool jacket over the ribbed turtleneck and black pants. She stares down at her brown oxford shoes. She needs to make a journey but can't quite bring herself to move. The autumn colors encircling the pond are at their peak, amber, gold, orange, crimson, russet, with here and there a holdout of green leaves for contrast, as if the trees are boasting, See what we can do! Bella picks up two fallen maple leaves from beside the bench and idly examines them. It has been a few days since the artists were here for their landscape painting session, and Charlotte has already re-ceived a gracious thank-you note from the group leader that extolled the natural beauty of the setting, the shifting colors as the breeze stirred the leaves, the changing reflections in the water as the sun moved four hours across the sky in prismatic slants of light. It didn't strike Bella as the usual effusive bread-and-butter letter but as a deeply felt ex-pression of what had moved the writer, yet staring at the pond, she can't summon any similar emotion in herself. When she read the letter to Charlotte, Charlotte merely sniffed and said, "There were seven of them, weren't there?

I should have had seven thank-you notes."

Bella twirls one of the maple leaves by its stem, holding it up to contemplate its scarlet hues. She and Charlotte are not nature lovers, although for very different reasons. Charlotte, because she owns nature. Here, she owns three hundred acres of forest, ridges, valley, meadows, pond. In the apartment they used to have in Manhattan, she owned an excellent view of Central Park. In those long-ago days when the Deerfields used to winter in Capri they owned one of the most desirable villas on the island and land that encompassed vineyards and tenant fields. That's not to say people necessarily take what they own for granted; Charlotte's mother Clarisse, who asked to have this crude bench built, who, when she was well enough, paddled herself in a wooden rowboat on the pond, cherished this same land. It's only that for Charlotte, the satisfaction is in the proprietorship; whether it's a plot of nature or a piece of jewelry, the pleasure rests on the word "mine." Which is why Charlotte will never gladly surrender her land for a nature preserve or an art school or a tourist museum. She *owns* it, whereas if you *love* something, as Clarisse did, then even when it's in your possession you never truly feel it belongs to you alone.

Bella twirls the other leaf, sere brown and shriveling at the edges yet still harboring a tiny flash of green at the heart. She can't be a nature lover because her heritage is to use nature. Nature exists to cut and clear, to plough and seed, to provide timber and grazing, to harvest when crops are ripe and curse when the rain or soil fails. To love nature is a luxury those who depend upon it for their livelihood can't afford. So it was for generations in Bella's peasant family, and although she left it long ago, that childhood knowledge remains. In a dispute between loggers and spotted owls, Bella would side with the lumberjacks; between cattle ranchers and wolves, she prefers the roast beef on her plate. She thinks of the people who have come on the Sunday walks, those she spied on at first with the binoculars, those she met during the brambling incident and the one time she joined the hike. Every last one a professional or city person in search of an idyll, who loves nature on Sunday morning, penciled in from eight to ten. And yet, these leaves are beautiful…

Bella shakes herself out of an unwanted sentimentality. She must go on, she must make this journey, before it gets any more difficult, before her time runs out. She stands and holds up the two leaves, and on the next swirl of breeze she releases them to spin over the water and float down onto the surface of the pond.

Fifty feet back up the trail, Jane lets out her breath. When she first glimpsed the figure on the bench, its back to her, her automatic reaction was alarm that some child was lost on the property. Almost instantly, her brain corrected the impression, only to have her curiosity deepen as she remained stopped in place. What was Bella doing here? She seemed in a contemplative mood, examining first one, then the other of two maple leaves in her hands, and Jane imagined what anyone might on seeing such a scene, that Bella, taken with the beauty of her surroundings, couldn't resist the urge to touch and wonder at nature's intricate designs. Her lifting of the two leaves to set them free only confirms Jane's trite, forgivable assumption, and to avoid intruding on the sacred moment, she takes several noiseless steps backward until she's out of sight. Then she re-proceeds down the trail, making sure to scuff her boots in the dry leaves littering the path. This ensures that when Jane comes into view, Bella is alerted to her arrival and nonchalantly watching a flock of robins on the far side of the water. It also gives both women time to adjust a smile on their faces, an uncompromised look in their eyes.

"Hello!" Jane calls first as she nears. "Beautiful day, isn't it?"

"Indeed," says Bella. "I suppose we won't have many more like it, so I thought I would play hooky and take an hour off." Play hooky—how juvenile that sounds. She mimics a carefree laugh, never having been carefree in her life.

"I'm going up to the ridge, over it actually, to post these signs. They were just delivered." Jane holds out a box containing the PRIVATE PROPERTY–NO TRESPASSING signs that will mark their western boundary.

"Ahh," says Bella approvingly. She feels the pond staring at her, like an eye, as it felt that morning she came on the walk, a flat glassy eye that prods you to gaze in and acknowledge your reflection.

Jane feels the pond like a heart, as she has since the first time she walked down the path and it opened before her, a heart that won't accept the burden of your secrets, it has enough of its own. Why is it tugging at her and Bella now?

"Tim Hennessey has suggested closing the estate to the public in January and February," she says to make conversation, and for a minute they discuss the idea.

"I'm sure Miss Deerfield will agree that's a wise decision," Bella concludes. "I'll tell her. I should probably start back now anyway." She nods up the path.

"Yes, I'd better go take care of these signs," says Jane, then halts. Something is wrong here, and it's not merely the stilted conversation prompted by their unanticipated meeting. She recalls the image of Bella tossing the leaves to the pond—an offering, a reconciliation?—recalls her impression that Bella has seemed subdued and saddened lately, as if she's longing for something but doesn't know what it is. Jane doesn't know either, but she offers the one thing she can.

"If you're free to come on another Sunday walk, we, I, would be happy to have you. We're still seeing some late warblers and woodpeckers, and the hawks are magnificent."

A warmth softens Bella's face, and she tilts her head in acknowledgment of the invitation. She won't come on another walk. It's impractical, though they would accommodate her handicap. More important, it's unnecessary. She isn't here to seek communion with nature as they do, and although it was under camouflage of the group that she came to the pond before, she has now proven she can get this far alone.

"Thank you," she says. "I'll see if my schedule permits."

Jane smiles, waves and hikes on. Bella watches her go. She's having good days and bad ones, and although today is relatively good, she can't cross the bridge and continue to her destination now. There's too much chance of running into Jane on her return. And maybe she doesn't yet have the resolve to make it anyway. Otherwise, she would have marched straight on, not allowed herself to dawdle to no purpose, playing with leaves on this side of the bridge. Bella wearily turns back, her stumping steps crunching on the dry leaves underfoot.

Jane strides on, carrying her NO TRESPASSING signs, one of the tasks on the checklist she has assigned herself before she departs. Finish the yard work, plaster the cracks in the cottage bathroom and repaint, compile for Tim Hennessey a summary of her tenure as sanctuary manager for use during the review in January. She has already revised her resume and started researching engineering firms between Boston and New York, and it would be nice if Brandon gave her an extra reason to stick around. If not, the possibilities stretch far and wide. She feels a nudge of conscience that she hasn't told Bella she'll be leaving, while Bella, slowly making her way toward the house, wonders if she dare confide anything of her plans to Jane. They continue in opposite directions, having talked about what will happen in January, both thinking, Come January, I'll be gone.

Chapter 24

Raven is back.

In the fading afternoon, she arrives at Jane's cottage and knocks on the door, a figure in a long skirt, unruly dark hair, clutching a paper grocery bag and casually swaying her hips as if to let everyone know she can wait, no problem, she's fine. Come on, Jane, come on.

Jane is replacing tools in the garage. She has just finished clearing out the old Mowry cemetery northwest of the pond—chopped down the last of the invasive bittersweet and bull briars, pulled out spiky weeds by their tenacious roots, raked decades of dead leaves from among the headstones—another task she can cross off her private to-do list before she departs Deerfield. That morning she finished planting the daffodil and tulip bulbs Bella ordered, both around the house and the cottage, and still she has a sack of bulbs unopened. It strikes her suddenly what to do with the extras—plant them in the cemetery so Isaac, Mehitable and their family may have the unforeseen pleasure of flowers when the sun shines on their graves next spring. This first week in November shouldn't be too late to plant bulbs, should it?

It's only five-thirty when she emerges from the garage, but with the artifice of Daylight Savings Time stripped from the calendar, the sun is already below the trees and a gray twilight is closing in. The air has a muffled quality, the high overcast that gathered in the afternoon gradually descending and bringing down a chill. Busy working, Jane hadn't noticed it. Now she feels that first hint of winter coming, the trees going bare, the nights steadily lengthening. There's a sense, too, of isolation as she walks past the main house. You'd like to imagine and envy a life in this place, chandeliers ablaze in a great hall, sconces lighting the wall up a grand staircase, crackling flames in a fireplace, elegant dinners, music and parties to fill the winter nights. Instead, Deerfield looks and is, in truth, half deserted. Save for a few lights in the front rooms, there's little sense that anyone inhabits this stone fortress, as if squatters have moved in and closed off the rest for economy's sake. As for her cottage, it's completely dark, except for someone half hidden in the doorway. Her pace and her heartbeat quicken. Brandon? She hasn't seen him in a week, he must have steady work in New York, and it surprises her how glad she is—

"Hi!" Raven waves as if she's stranded on a desert island, signaling a ship at sea. "Can I come in? I brought dinner."

"Sure," Jane replies, not unfriendly, but perplexed. She's had no word from Raven since August, and even making allowances for her involvement in the theater's new winter season, you don't make a friend, then drop them. Yet Jane hasn't been diligent about staying in touch either, leaving it to Raven, the gregarious one, to lead the friendship along. A little guiltily, she drops the resentment provoked by Raven's appearance, the disappointment that it's not Brandon, and gives way to curiosity instead. Raven must be here for a reason.

"What's up?" She opens the door and invites her in.

"Nothing much. Well, I'm still waiting tables at the restaurant, although the crowds are down from summer, but then two bartenders quit so we were short staffed, and you can't imagine what a project the theater is turning into! I mean, I'm not dumb, I've worked enough plays that I know what everyone's role is supposed to be, the stage manager, the lighting director, the set designer, but now I have to supervise these people, and they're all convinced they know the one and only way to do it. Plus Bucky is on my case wanting to play Scrooge, and it just won't work, Jane. You can't have a fat, jolly Scrooge, and he's gone all sulky about it."

Raven unpacks the grocery bag, plunking Styrofoam takeout boxes on the kitchen table, her voice picking up speed, and as Jane opens her mouth to offer a consoling remark, she barrels on.

"And costumes, okay, we've found a few in stock that are suitable, but if you want that real Dickensian flavor, you have to get an authentic look for the whole cast and the right mixture of colors or you end up with a stage full of shabby brown coats. And Brandon, I don't know if I can count on him for Bob Cratchit. He says he will, but he's here, he's there, he's off to New York."

Is he? thinks Jane. She doesn't sit around waiting for Brandon to call. She has never sat around waiting for any man. Nor has she let the thought of Brandon deter her from sending off her resume this week in response to several job postings on the Internet, none of them in New England. They're long shots, requiring different experience than she possesses, but she'd take them if offered. Yet she wouldn't be averse to staying for the right relationship with the right man. Is it him?

"So I thought of calling Dan and Amy to come back from New York and be the Cratchits for me," Raven continues, a flutter of paper napkins escaping from her hand, "but I can't guarantee them any money yet. I can't guarantee any of the actors how much they might make because the playhouse has never done a winter season before, and here we are in November and I figure we need to run every weekend in December, Friday through Sunday or maybe Thursday through Sunday to break even. I'm trying to work with the bus tour companies, but naturally they want a discount, and what about Saturday and Sunday matinees?

Would it bring in enough of a family crowd or would it be one of those disasters where I have more actors on stage than people in the audience?"

Raven pops open the Styrofoam containers. Greek salad, nachos, onion rings. The lunch cook is being nice to her because he thinks she's going to sleep with him, and she doesn't know why men always get that impression about her but they do. And what if Brandon does bail on her? He will if he gets a better part, who wouldn't? If she got a break again, she'd be gone so fast, she'd walk off stage in the middle of a line if it came to that. There's just so much wrong right now, so much hitting her all at once, and she pulls out forks and spoons she borrowed from the restaurant, bottled water, and she can't tell if she's depressed or stressed or both because her therapist is on vacation. And what good could she do anyway because Raven can't take anything, she can't even drink now, and she can't pop the top on this container of ravioli, damn it, and then her thumb punches the Styrofoam so hard the box flips out of her hands and lands upside down, sauce and pasta splattering over Jane's kitchen floor.

Raven, what's wrong?

Raven hears the question as if it's trying to swim to her brain through water, sees the expression on Jane's distant face, not angry about the mess on her floor but furrowed with worry, and she knows she's really in trouble this time.

"I'm pregnant," she says and sits down on the couch and cries.

Oh, Raven, no.

Oh yes, oh yes. The home testing kit confirmed it. Except the pregnancy isn't the real problem. She's always wanted kids, but she wanted them in the context of a career and financial security with a real husband and father for her children. How old-fashioned can you get? But at thirty-seven, another fatal birthday come and gone, she doesn't have that many years left, and maybe this accident was a way of telling her to get on with it. Frightened as she is, the tears that come to her eyes when she thinks of the baby growing inside her are genuine miracle-of-life tears, and it overwhelms her that she already loves this child. It's everything else that's wrong, that's making such a mess of it.

Is Burt the father?

Yes, that night the four of them drank wine on the ridge. That has to be it because it's the only time they skipped protection, and she hasn't slept with anyone else, honest, not since spring when she had those two nights with Brandon. Of course, that was before Jane met him, and as soon as she saw Jane was interested, she stepped aside and brought her and Brandon together like a good friend should. It's Burt. One time unprotected and look what happens. He gets his muse back, and she gets pregnant. Pretty stupid, huh?

How does Burt feel about it?

Burt doesn't know. Raven hasn't told him. He still doesn't guess she's a decade older than he is. Burt is a library clerk who thinks he's writing the Great American Novel, and he's infatuated with the idea that he has a girlfriend who's an actress. If she tells him she's pregnant, he'll gulp and go pale, seeing his life drain away before him. Oh, he might do the right thing and marry her, but she isn't truly in love with him either. He's a boy, and she needs a man.

What does the doctor say?

What doctor? Raven doesn't have health insurance. And she didn't realize she was pregnant at first because she had a period, sort of, after that evening on the ridge. Now it's too late for the abortion pill, though there's still the option of a clinic, but she can't trust her own decisions as to what's best. All this theater stuff is making her crazy, and she went off the Prozac back in September when everything seemed so great, and now she can't go back on it because of harming the baby. She's been trying to do everything right since she did find out, eat healthy, sleep, not even an aspirin, but she keeps throwing up, morning sickness, actually sometimes it's afternoon sickness and evening sickness, too.

"Oh, Raven."

This time Jane's voice comes through for real. She's sitting beside Raven, one arm around her shoulder, and the tears resume their flood down Raven's cheeks. Why can't she ever go through life without making a disaster of it?

"You better lie down, come on."

Jane helps her stretch out on the couch, brings a blanket and tucks it around her. The smells of spicy nachos and ravioli and deep-fried onion rings are perfuming the cottage, and although she has never dealt with a pregnant friend before, Jane does make the mental observation that a steady diet of restaurant leftovers is probably not the recommended nutrition for a mother-to-be. Warm milk, cocoa, seems more like it, and when she's made two cups, she sits down by Raven again.

"The first thing you have to do is tell Burt. It's his baby and his responsibility, too. Then you need to see a doctor to make sure you're all right, that this throwing up is normal. There must a Planned Parenthood chapter or some kind of women's health network you can contact for counseling."

Jane talks on calmly. There are enough public service announcements on radio and TV that you don't have to be pregnant yourself to recognize the basic steps to be taken. Raven knows, too, and doesn't protest the suggestions, just curls up in the blanket, nodding. It's over, you see. That's what was really so hard to admit. It's over and done. She is never going to have an Oscar, an Emmy or a Golden Globe, she's never going to be the best or even the best supporting. She doesn't understand how it didn't happen—didn't she work hard enough, aim for the top? Weren't all these little jobs supposed to pile up into something big any time now? Already she's clung to her dreams longer than most of her actress friends. And isn't it funny how perseverance is extolled when it finally blossoms into success and how that same perseverance becomes pathetic when success proves elusive. Give it up, grow up, move on.

Raven swipes at her eyes. Move on. You could say

she was already heading in that direction by taking on the theater management project even before she knew she was pregnant, and suddenly she clutches at that because without it, what else will she have? She'll be a single mother working as a waitress, and she wants better than that for her child, the child she's not yet sure she's keeping. She does still have options. But this is the trouble with being clinically depressed and off your medication and pregnant and tired and worried and then convincing yourself it's going to be okay and believing your own delusions. Is this real? Or is the bottom dropping out from under her and she doesn't recognize she's falling? Then she has to go throw up the cocoa. That's real enough.

Jane holds back Raven's hair as she retches into the toilet, insisting she's fine and doesn't need any help. Maybe cocoa wasn't the best idea. Maybe it should have been water and soda crackers? And what now? At some point she'll have to decide whether Raven's startling revelation about sleeping with Brandon means anything to her, but for the moment it seems too trivial for consideration. Meanwhile, she's woefully unqualified to offer much advice beyond the elementary suggestions she's already given. Hortense, wise and motherly, would have made a far better choice for Raven to confide in.

Raven spits into the toilet and looks up, sheepish and wan. "Can I lie down again?"

"Sure." Jane guides her back to the sofa, tucks the blanket around her, and sits holding her hand. In five minutes, Raven is asleep, her face exhausted. Jane glances to the cold food on the kitchen table, the ravioli and sticky sauce congealing on the floor. She'll make sure Raven gets to a doctor and quietly see to the bill. One more item to add to her to-do list before she leaves Deerfield.

Chapter 25

Raven doesn't tell Burt she's pregnant, not right away. She wants to get her act together first, sort out her own emotions before she dumps the news on him. When Jane phones to make sure she's okay, Raven sounds like her old self again, silly of her to panic like that, of course everything is going to be fine. Bucky is so cranky about not being Scrooge, he's actually cranky enough to be Scrooge, and they've shortened the schedule, the whole month of December was way too ambitious, it's going to be just the two weekends before Christmas. What's more, she made an appointment at Planned Parenthood and is no longer throwing up in the afternoons and evenings, it's only mornings now. So don't worry, Jane, just come see the play, we need a packed house, please, please, promise you'll come!

Brandon doesn't tell Jane he's seeing someone else in New York, because it doesn't occur to him he has to. They never said this was exclusive, and he wouldn't mind if she were dating other people, too. Besides, it's not another lover that's drawing him away. His career will always dictate his footsteps, and as his absence lengthens, Jane can sense for herself that he's moving on. Throughout the autumn he's been staying in Manhattan more often, crashing with Dan and Amy, picking up work in TV commercials and a small but semi-regular role in a daytime soap opera. His name is getting around. It would be easy for Jane to salve her feelings by writing him off as a shallow person, but Brandon never pretended to be anything he's not. Still, she'll be sorry when it's over. She enjoys his company, the sex is good, they're friends.

Bella doesn't tell Charlotte the real reason she's scheduling a new round of appointments with their accountant and lawyer. Ostensibly, if Deerfield is to be closed to the public in January and February, they should review their tax status in anticipation of negotiating an even better deal. Truthfully, Bella hasn't much time left, and if she can only coax Charlotte to declare her wishes regarding the eventual disposition of the estate, the lawyer can establish a trust or an advisory committee to assist her after Bella is gone. But Charlotte has become increasingly willful as her paintings reach farther back, almost to the beginning now, and she doesn't want to be bothered with meetings or decisions.

"I don't have time!" she flares, when Bella importunes. "My retrospective must be ready by December!"

"No, it doesn't," Bella pleads. "Art doesn't have deadlines. Why must you persist at something that will only make us miserable? Stop it, Charlotte, now, please."

"No! Look, Bella, look, I'm so close!"

Together they regard the two easels Charlotte has set side by side. One holds her portrait at age twenty-four, the year poor Lawrence Chandler died. She wears a widow's black dress and veil, and her hand at either side holds the hand of a ghostly child, a pale vision of a girl and boy, perhaps five and three years old. The children are dressed in Sunday clothes and rendered in swathes of white and gray as if seen through gauze or shrouds. The girl has red-gold hair, the boy blond. Those were the first two miscarriages when Charlotte, excited and expectant, leaped to imagine the family she and Lawrence would have. For the later three miscarriages during her marriage to Robert Drayton she forbade herself to do that, to get her hopes up, and yet each successive failure to carry a child was no less ripping for her willing the infant to be faceless. But these first two—how clearly she saw and had believed in them! Their births would have meant the mistake in Capri was behind her and never to be discovered. It would mean she and Bella had pulled it off.

Except the children died before they were born, and the marriage ended that should never have begun. In her sheer black veil, Charlotte's expression is unreadable, and the two ghost children clasp her hands as if all three are solemnly viewing a funeral cortege passing by. Lawrence drowned in a boating accident on a bright, sunny day off Cannes, knocked overboard by the boom in a tragic mishap—or, hopelessly drunk, he slipped noiselessly off the bow before anyone was aware. The story from his distraught friends was never clear, and in those days people were still kind enough to cover up unpleasant details, especially when rich Americans in foreign countries were involved. Charlotte wasn't in Cannes when the accident occurred. She and Bella were at Deerfield, agonizing over how to let it be known that she and Lawrence had separated. Then came the news, and since it was better in those days to be a widow than a divorcee, the announcement of their separation died with Lawrence as well. Hence the concealing veil over the young widow's face. Already there was so much in her life Charlotte could not reveal.

"I remember," says Bella sadly, and they turn their gaze to the second easel. It holds a painting in progress of Charlotte at eighteen, embarking on that first marriage. So far, she has painted the bride in an extravagant white wedding gown with a billowing skirt and a froth of veil, lying on her back on an altar. There's no background yet, no stained glass windows to indicate a church, although she and Lawrence were married in one in quite lavish style. Charlotte pauses, her paintbrush still tipped in the virgin white of the bride's gown. The image of the veiled bride metamorphosed almost immediately from the painting of the veiled widow. What better symbolism for the beginning and end of a union that deceived everyone, including the unlucky couple? But why did the bride insist on lying on an altar? Charlotte's puzzlement clears. Aha, this is society's altar, on which she was a willing sacrifice, because although her father wished it, no one can say she was forced into the marriage with Lawrence. On the contrary, she clutched at it, and suddenly she stops painting in white, switches brushes, and dabbles yellow on her palette.

"Bella," she says thoughtfully, "a yellow stripe down the back means what?"

"I don't know." Bella doesn't want to be sidetracked. She hurts, she's weary. Everything she has ever tried to do was for their own good, and it flashes across her mind that the one sure way to end all this would be to take every last canvas, the retrospective, the abandoned years of art ringing the studio walls, cart everything out to that field beyond Jane's cottage, heap it in a pile, and strike a match.

"Yes, you do." Charlotte's eyes narrow at her painting. "It means cowardice, the badge of a coward. But where did that symbolism come from? Some military tradition? Go find out. Look it up on your computer."

"I don't want to. It's not important." Bella eyes the canvas and sighs. She can guess what Charlotte is about to do, they've been together so long. "Go ahead." She nods at the painting, and Charlotte poises the yellow-daubed brush before the recumbent figure on the altar. The bride lies with arms crossed on her chest holding a bouquet, like a stone sculpture on a tomb. Starting under the shoulder, Charlotte runs a hairline stroke of yellow along the figure's underside down to the small of her back. They study the effect.

"It's not wide enough," says Bella. "It needs to be broader."

"It's wide enough," Charlotte counters. "Anyone with half a brain will get the point."

"No, they won't. Most people have less than half a brain to begin, and that line is so thin and pale they'll assume it's an indication of sunlight, as if you're being borne up on a golden light to your groom."

"I can't make it any darker or wider. It won't look right."

"Then you should paint the whole scene differently, you and Lawrence kneeling at the altar with your backs to the viewer. Then you'd have plenty of room for a big yellow stripe. Give him one, too."

"I don't want him in the painting! He doesn't belong! There's to be no one in these paintings but me!"

"Then tell the truth for once!"

Bella jerks the brush from Charlotte's hand and streaks a broad yellow swatch down the white-gowned bride's back. Charlotte gasps and Bella freezes, shocked at her own audacity. For a minute the room is so silent they can both hear the air pressing on their eardrums. Bella has never done anything like this before. Berated, belittled, criticized and mocked Charlotte's art, yes. Vandalized it, no. Charlotte is so stunned, she can't move. Bella, shaken but recovering, slowly puts the brush down. It's a good thing, she thinks in a far corner of her mind, that the brutal age is past when a servant could have a hand chopped off on the spot for such disobedience.

"I'm not sorry," she says.

Charlotte begins sniffling, and Bella relents a little because there were things no one knew then. If Charlotte's father had suspected, he would have taken enough time from his own drinking and amours to choose another suitor from those who presented themselves after her debutante ball, even though young Chandler presented the wealthiest, most socially advantageous match. If Charlotte's mother Clarisse had survived, she might have stroked her daughter's hair and fondly advised her not to rush into any marriage but to wait for true love to come along. But Charlotte wasn't granted those "ifs," and when she came to Bella after a month-long honeymoon in Paris and tearfully whispered, "He knows! He must know, Bella! He can't...we haven't..." Bella became frightened, her position in as much jeopardy as Charlotte's. Then she regained her cool head.

"He can't know, no one does. Did you get him drunk on the wedding night as I told you?"

"Yes, and almost every night after. He can't bring himself to touch me!"

Bella should have guessed then. On Capri, that island of pleasure where the perverted emperor Tiberius held court in the days of Rome, all manner of sexuality and prostitution had long been tolerated, and rich foreigners flocked to the island to indulge just such desires. Bella's mother, the good Catholic and poisoner, had also done a fair business in the making and selling of aphrodisiacs to enhance the potency of flagging English homosexuals, bored wives and beautiful young Romeos. But perhaps the very fact of its openness in Capri was why Bella didn't recognize Lawrence's homosexuality here in America where such tendencies were repressed. Nor did Charlotte, a sheltered girl of her class. Nor did shy, handsome Lawrence guess it about himself, for he, too, was bowing to convention by courting the woman his parents decreed he should wed. Like Charlotte and Bella, he had a secret to hide; unlike them, he didn't even know what his secret was.

They solved it by Charlotte plying him with more alcohol, now laced with the aphrodisiacs Bella had learned from her mother. Lawrence gratefully gulped the liquor down, and finally, two months after the wedding, he managed to consummate the union before passing out on the body of his unsatisfied young wife. After a year of such intermittent success, Charlotte was pregnant. But that baby miscarried, and two years later another miniscule fetus was rejected by Charlotte's womb, and by then poor Lawrence was a bleary-eyed alcoholic who couldn't bear to see his wife naked. Charlotte turned on Bella and Bella turned on Charlotte, and they made it a practice to hate each other thereafter.

Now they stare at the mutilated painting with the broad yellow stripe down the bride's back. Charlotte is beginning to like it. It's bold—shouldn't art be bold and dramatic?—but she won't admit that to Bella who has been such a pest lately, a little demon gnat whining at her to do this and that to protect the estate for the future when Charlotte wants it to crumble into dust.

"You've ruined my painting," she says, letting a sneer accumulate on her face, in her voice. "But then you've ruined everything for me, haven't you, Bella? You've ruined my whole life."

"No! You started it! You did it! I'm trying to make things right!"

"Right? When was anything about our lives ever right?"

Bella clamps her hands over her ears and marches out, as forcefully as anyone can march with her crooked spine and her crooked pain. At the bottom of the staircase, she sits on the lowest step and breathes. She knows what's going on above her head. The yellow stripe wasn't a bad inspiration, except that Charlotte lacked the courage to execute it properly. Now she's contemplating the painting and perceiving that Bella has unintentionally improved it. If only she won't ruin it by slabbing on still more yellow and overdoing the effect. Too bad, Bella reflects, that she and Charlotte couldn't have been condensed into a single person; they might have made one decent artist. Together, they have added a nice irony to the painting, cowardice signified by one bold stroke. But the viewers probably won't get that either. They'll have to put it in the caption and explain.

Bella sighs. When was anything in our lives ever right, Charlotte asked, and Bella knows the answer. At our death. The one time everything becomes finished and right is when you die. So let it come. She has only a few loose strings left to tie. A final confession, though not to Father McCaffrey at St. Joseph's; the poor old man would be so shocked and befuddled, he wouldn't know what penance to prescribe. Instead she will ask forgiveness of the one she wronged, as she started out to that day Jane caught her tossing leaves into the pond. Meanwhile, she'll meet with the lawyer and the accountant, tell them she knows Miss Deerfield's wishes, and direct them to draw up the necessary papers. Then it must be up to Charlotte to sign. She still won't tell Charlotte she's dying. Terrified of being left alone, Charlotte would beg and bully her into useless surgeries and treatments that would only painfully prolong the end.

But something has to become of Deerfield, and with nothing else to leave behind her, no marriages, no children, no art, Bella will create her own legacy, even if it never bears her name. The artists have the association founded by Charlotte's grandmother. The town does well enough with its historic waterfront and upscale stores. So Bella has decided for the land trust, the trees and the birds, the sky and the pond. She has as much claim to this property as Charlotte does. And she alone knows where the body is buried.

Chapter 26

Adapt and survive applies to birders as well as birds, especially in New England in late autumn. Take a case of birds first, robins in particular. Most people assume they all fly south for the winter, reappearing months later robust and red-breasted as harbingers of spring. Not necessarily. Why expend energy on migration when you have another trick up your wing? Instead, robins adapt. Insect eaters in the warm months, they switch their diet to berries come fall and simply melt deeper into the forest to forage. As long as the food source is sufficient, some will happily stay in northern climes. Go walking in the woods in January and you'll find them, along with other year-round species such as blue jays, crows, Carolina wrens, chickadees, cardinals, song sparrows and mewing catbirds. When robins do start popping up in suburban backyards come March, it's still a sign of spring, albeit with a slightly different explanation. Insects are once again buzzing, fat worms are churning in the ground, and the robins are ready to emerge from their restaurant in the woods.

Birders, if they wish to continue feasting their passion, must also change their diet and habitat come winter. Most of the songbirds that have delighted their palate from spring through autumn do head south, and in the forests and fields birders in search of a plentiful buffet will find only slim pickings. But the ducks arriving from further north offer a diverse new menu, and at the hot spots along the coast it's possible to sample a dozen species in one location, each in their separate niche. Harlequin ducks, so named for the male's brilliant paint box of colors, have a special tooth on their bill to scrape barnacles from rocks; if you see a raft of ducks riding the waves perilously close to the rocks, it's a good guess even before you raise your binoculars that they're harlequins. Surf scoters, nicknamed the "skunk duck" for their black-and-white coloration, ride the surf, just as their proper name tells. Elsewhere in the salt bays, you'll find eiders, goldeneyes, grebes, and red-throated and common loons, the latter unmistakable for their large size. Melanie loves the buffleheads; small, cute and cuddly, with a bonnet-like white patch on their puffy head, they're the teddy bears of the duck world. And these are only the sea ducks. On lakes and ponds, the marsh species take up winter residence, gadwalls, wigeons, pintails, teal, black ducks and shovelers. Gulls and shorebirds also increase in variety, although identifying the immature gulls with their many intermediate stages of plumage can drive you crazy. Even Roy sometimes says to heck with them.

To catch this influx, it's necessary to leave Deerfield and move on to new territory, a natural transition since the demographics of the Sunday walk have once again changed with the season. Gone are the autumn leaves and with them the leaf peepers. Now it's only a handful of birders who appear weekly at the front gate, and although Jane offers newcomers the option of exploring the estate, usually by mutual consent they carpool instead down the shore road to the empty beach. There they scan the tide line for ruddy turnstones and killdeer and hike around the end of the peninsula to a rocky bay frequented by ducks.

Meanwhile, the November weather continues mostly mild, with southerly winds commuting up the Atlantic coast and temperatures still bouncing up to sixty degrees. Remembering Tim's prophecy of a cold winter, Jane buys a copy of *The Old Farmer's Almanac* and consults the regional forecasts. Colder than usual in November and December, it predicts, with copious early snow. Not likely, she scoffs, when the very next morning, another warmish and this time foggy day, she's in jeans and an old shirt planting the last bulbs in the Mowry cemetery. Tim hasn't come for another Sunday walk, and of course there was no point in trying to set him up with Raven once she learned Raven was pregnant. Raven, along with Brandon and Burt, also seems to have vanished again from her life, which may be just as well. When Jane came to Deerfield, she put on her friendships slowly, like layers of clothing; now she has to shed them to move freely and leave. By their absence, they're unwittingly making it easier.

She works her trowel into the ground. Still without a single frozen night and damp after a recent rain, the earth turns up in clumps as she sets the tulip and daffodil bulbs among the eight graves. She isn't much of a gardener, and next spring when the flowers bloom, the mansion and her cottage will undoubtedly have too much purple here, too much yellow there, and no sense of order to the plantings. At least here in the cemetery no one will complain.

The fog that blankets the coast this morning brings a profound silence as well, and as Bella leaves the house and skirts wide past Jane's cottage, she hears no breeze or whispering of air, no faint patter of leaves falling from the nearly bare branches. Few birds call and fewer fly; they are invisible, solitary voices, hidden in the trees. Bella enters the woods and carefully picks her way, an omnipresence of soft, damp grayness obscuring her vision on every side. It would be easy to get lost, as happened to her that one time years ago, no marked trails, no orderly paths, only the narrow passages trodden by deer and this past year by the birders. Individual trees become important. A birch stands out for its whiteness, a twisted limb seems noteworthy, helpful signs if you became disoriented and found yourself going in circles. As Bella penetrates deeper toward the pond, her imagination becomes an accomplice to the fog. There is something medieval about the atmosphere, and she half expects a line of cowled monks to appear in prayerful pilgrimage to a distant monastery, or a mounted knight, his armor rusted with long wandering, pursuing a lonely quest for the Holy Grail. The fanciful notions surprise her; this isn't her usual cast of mind. Yet she feels pulled into the realm of lore, of witchcraft and spells, of hermits and abandoned shrines. Then she comes out on the bank of the pond, her heart double-clutches, and she emits a gasp.

Floating a foot above the surface, the fog rises from the water as if the pond is a cauldron of ghosts. Bella herself, were anyone there to see her, becomes a strange, stunted creature not quite of this world. What is she doing here? What mission is she on? She wears her turtleneck sweater and homemade pants, her stiff black topknot bobbing through the fog, her body moving like an awkward, limping bird. She forces herself to the footbridge but can't seem to step onto it. Her feet won't lift from the ground. Perhaps that first step up onto the wood planks presents too great an obstacle? But think of the staircase in the main house, Bella clumping up and down it in her high heels, no difficulty there. This step onto the bridge is no higher.

Then something about Bella's pose would tell you. The little secretary is frozen to the spot, her legs locked, body rigid, her ribs constricted and crushing her heart inside her chest. You can't see her face in the fog, but it's white and aghast, and her brain is reeling in her skull so that she must either black out or back down. If Jane, in the cemetery, saw her, she would know in an instant. *This is exactly how she felt every time she tried to cross an airfield to reach a plane.* Helplessly, Bella confronts the bridge while the pond stares at her, a flat, unyielding eye. The enveloping fog has allowed her to make it this far, the farthest she has come on the property in almost sixty years. It's why she finally made the attempt today. Blocking out any sense of what's in front or behind, she has only to concentrate on one step at a time. But the bridge is a clear boundary…

Help me!

With a silent, violent cry to the god she both hates and loves, Bella swings her right arm hard, grabs the wood railing, and hoists herself up. A rough splinter stabs into her palm, and she yelps and jerks up her hand. She quickly pulls out the jagged piece and throws it into the water, pressing her palms together to crush the pain. She's on the bridge, though, she's done it, and the blessing is that once again she can't see too far ahead, she can delude herself about what's coming.

She straightens her shoulders and moves on, instructing herself to think of happier times, if ever there was such a thing. Remember when she first came to this country, what dreams she had? Remember when she first came to this house? This was America, where all the people were as rich as the foreigners who lazed on Capri, and those who weren't, the people who lived in the measly houses Bella saw from the limousine as the chauffeur drove them from New York to Deerfield, well, it must be their own fault. They weren't clever enough or hadn't worked hard enough or had misspent what they earned. Whereas Bella was very clever—thwarting her family's desire to imprison her in a convent and conniving her escape to America proved it—and she planned to work and save diligently. In America, she would not be judged by her physical stature, her deformity, her ugliness, but by her abilities alone. Oh, poor Bella! To be so smart and yet so naïve!

A tear rolls down Bella's cheek that might be self-pity or fear or regret. It might be a mocking tear or a tear of sincere repentance. Even Bella can't tell at this moment; thinking of herself at age sixteen is so hard. She concentrates instead on her footing, picking her way around the west side of the pond. Dead wet leaves carpet the ground, and although she has never forgotten this particular route, she must beware not to trip on protruding rocks or knobby tree roots. She startles at a scampering overhead, wheels around, sees nothing. The sound fades off, and belatedly she tells herself it's only a squirrel, no reason to be afraid. To dislodge her fears, she occupies her mind with details for the gala opening of Charlotte's retrospective, scheduled for the fifteenth of December. Has she picked the right paper stock and font for the invitations? But of course she has. So, too, the flowers, the caterer, the selection of wines and hors d'oeuvres. The painting of the retrospective is nearing its end, and Charlotte has left the coward bride's yellow stripe unaltered, declaring that portrait finished as it stands. But what is she painting now, this very moment?

No, Bella shudders, *no*.

She must be almost at her destination when a half-fallen tree trunk blocks her path, bringing both her footsteps and her memory up short. She doesn't remember this. Thick as a battering ram, it has splintered about four feet above the ground and snapped over like a toothpick, frayed and graying. Worriedly, Bella gazes around. Surely it should have occurred to her that in sixty years there would be changes? Storms, nor'easters, more than one hurricane, lightning strikes. What if this isn't the way after all? Nature doesn't stand still, and in this fog…

She listens to the rustling of another unseen squirrel, then shakes off her confusion, stoops under the tree where it jackknifes at the trunk, and follows her instincts. The fogginess is around her, not in her head. She's medicated not too much, not too little, just enough to quell the pain for today's effort. And to think her mother, the good Catholic, the maker of poisons and aphrodisiacs and charms, had to rely on primitive herbal concoctions where Bella nowadays has a veritable pharmacopeia of drugs, legal and illegal, at her fingertips. It's true—you can get anything on the Internet. She smiles a bit vainly at the thought. Ingenious Bella to master such technology when Charlotte can't even send an email, resourceful Bella who has solved so many problems in their past, sharp-eyed Bella who on a journey long ago spotted this crumbling stone wall now emerging a dozen paces ahead in the fog and beyond it the gray arch of a headstone—

Bella shrieks, a wail so eerie and deformed, it's like

no cry of animal or bird Jane has yet heard. She drops her trowel and falls back on her rear, and there standing before her is the little secretary, face contorted in terror, fists clenched.

"What is it? Are you hurt?" Jane starts to rise, too taken aback by the apparition to question how or why it got there, but Bella brushes past her and crumples to her knees, crawling crazily toward the exposed earth of Mehitable Mowry's grave. Her frantic hands pat down the dirt.

"Bella, what's wrong?" Jane demands, stunned at this grotesque spectacle, determined to grab it back to reality. She reaches for Bella, but Bella shakes her off and pats, moaning, at Mehitable's grave, trying to recover with more earth and leaves the bared spot where Jane has been digging.

"What have you done? What have you done? We told you, no clearing, no pruning, leave the woods alone."

"I...I haven't cleared any paths in the woods. Just this cemetery. I came upon it by accident, and it didn't seem right to leave it so overgrown. I've been clearing other flower beds for you, back at the house—"

"Not here, not here!" Bella squeezes her eyes tight, dizziness threatening to overcome her. "Who else knows?" she asks, a silent rage building. "Who else knows?" she demands in a rising cry.

"Knows what?" Jane replies. "No one, no one."

"The birders? You haven't brought them here?"

"No."

"The land trust, the artists?"

"No."

"Just you then." Bella spits the words accusingly. "You had to go interfering, you had to pry. I thought I could trust you."

"You can." Bewildered, Jane shakes her head. "Bella, I found the cemetery by accident, it was covered in thorns and thicket. I was curious, I admit, so I cleared it, dug out the roots and planted the last of those bulbs you gave me. But that's all and besides—"

She's about to say the cemetery might have historical significance, that the information on the headstones should be recorded, but Bella's skin has bleached even whiter, and her face is bony and hollow, a death's head.

"You dug up the graves?" The words whisper out of her mouth.

"No, of course I didn't dig them up," Jane protests, then slows. "Bella, what is it? What are you afraid of?"

"Nothing." Bella draws back, a stiff movement that bumps her up against Mehitable's stone. "Nothing. You shouldn't disturb a graveyard, that's all. It was safer covered over. If people know about this, they'll want to traipse in here to see it, and then we'll have vandals, littering." Her manner becomes belatedly righteous and self-justifying.

"But you knew about it." Now it's Jane who is softly accusing.

"Of course. When I first came here, I explored all over this property that was going to be my home."

A half second of silence passes. Jane could stand and walk away, forget this bizarre encounter, get out of the fog. She'll be leaving soon anyway. What does it matter what Bella has buried here, because suddenly Jane knows Bella has buried something. Jewelry? Documents? Something a thieving servant would covet or use for blackmail? Bella, despite the mild temperature, has begun shivering; she, too, wants to get up and leave, pretend this hasn't happened. But there is real pain now, in her crooked spine, in her gnawing abdomen, and she can't rise.

"Please go away," she whispers, summoning a show of small authority.

"No, I'm not leaving you like this." Frustrated, concerned, Jane spreads her hands. "What is it? What's buried here, Bella? Can't you tell me?"

"Nothing. Old graves. Nothing."

"But maybe I can help you. What's buried here? What's wrong?"

"Nothing! Go away! You're fired! I mean it this time!"

"What did you bury here, Bella?"

They stare at each other, Jane with no idea how cruel she is being. She thinks it's some long ago trinket, some inconsequential love letter. What can it matter now, if it hasn't mattered in sixty years? But it does matter, and Bella begins shaking in earnest, whimpering, and in uncomprehending sympathy with whatever this anguish might be, Jane opens her arms.

"Bella?" she asks, and Bella falls into her embrace, sobbing, and begins her confession.

Chapter 27

His name was Niccolo. He had eyes the color of dark sweet chocolate, curly hair that was almost black, a sensuous mouth and olive skin, and his bare chest, the first time Charlotte saw him, was as smooth and flat and gracefully muscled as a sculpture. He was seventeen, a boy of Capri, and Charlotte was just sixteen that autumn when her parents deemed it safe to return to the island after the war.

In fact, as Bella could have told them, Capri had gone through the conflict relatively unscathed. There was a loss of tourist income and shortages of food and supplies, and to go hungry is never pleasant. But unlike the mainland and devastated Naples a mere twenty miles away, Capri never endured any bombing or invasion battles. On the contrary, Il Duce had decreed early in his Fascist regime that Capri was to be a showplace where he could offer recreation to foreign VIPs, and he directed extra money be sent the island's way to improve the harbor, pave the main roads, and complete other public works projects. The garrison on the island consisted of some ill-clad and ill-equipped Italians and some rather better-off Germans who operated a rest camp for their own soldiers, and their spending at the local establishments was not unwelcome. When the victorious Allies moved in, Capri became a stopover for American airmen, whose salaries were even more generous than the Germans and who freely handed out food and chocolate, cigarettes and chewing gum. No wonder Bella had imagined that even average Americans were rich and that in the United States prosperity and ease were the rule for everyone.

Thus, given Capri's semi-exempt status from the war, the island's hotels and restaurants and entrepreneurs were in a position to recover quickly once the peace was signed and the wealthy foreigners returned. Sun, fun and beautiful young men like Niccolo were in demand.

Charlotte didn't know he was a prostitute. Who would have told her? Her mother Clarisse, frail as ever, had been further weakened by the long journey to Capri and spent most days painting in the garden of their villa, recuperating in a lounge chair when fatigue overcame her. Because she was a lady in the old-fashioned sense of the word, even the most gossipy guests never sullied her ears with the truly juicy affairs of the island. She thought Niccolo was a gardener, that's what he came for once a week, to water the flowers and trim shrubs at her direction. Charlotte's handsome, dashing father couldn't have told her either. Vincent Deerfield was too busy resuming his own island amours, and the family was barely settled into the villa when his eye fell upon the buxom daughter of a tavern owner. He thought, without much dwelling on it, that Niccolo was a gardener and a fisherman, since he sometimes saw the young man helping his father launch their wood boat or mend nets on the shore.

Bella knew who Niccolo was, a gardener, a fisherman, and a prostitute for both men and women. She neither approved nor disapproved. In the lotus-land of Capri most people earned their living by catering to the tourists, although exploiting them might be a better term. You were glad to see them come to your hotel, café or shop and gladder to see them leave with their wallets empty. Bella's mother had always felt that way about the Deerfields in the days before the war, and she had passed that healthy attitude along to her daughter. God, Bella's mother said, had put the Deerfields in their path expressly to be exploited.

So after her mother's murder and the terrifying revelation of her future that day at St. Peter's, Bella fled back to the villa sustained by a crafty hope. She would prove herself such a loyal, industrious servant that the family would find her indispensable and beg her to sail home with them the following spring. Once in America, she would persuade them to set her up in business; perhaps she would own a shop or run a fine restaurant or hotel. Meanwhile, if Niccolo showed up once a week to help Clarisse tend her garden, it was nothing to Bella's plans. Niccolo might be beautiful, but she was farsighted. He would still be trimming hedges and mending fishing nets and bending over for some flabby, panting Englishman when she was living in luxury in America.

All sixteen-year-old Charlotte knew or cared about Niccolo was that he made her body flush in unbearable, secret places, and she believed he loved her.

Charlotte recalls this as she stands at her easel. The cowardly bride painting is finished; that yellow stripe does the trick. Now how to paint this final picture in her retrospective? She needn't go back any further. Her life before age sixteen, before Niccolo, was so ordinary for a rich girl that she can't think of a single incident worth commemorating, not even the pony she didn't have to ask for. No, Niccolo was how it started, and although she swore to Bella there should be no painting of anyone else in this retrospective but her, why is it that each time she tries to lift her brush, what she pictures on this last canvas is Niccolo's sensuous face and sculpted body, the beautiful thighs and the hot, dark cluster between his legs. Do you assume old women don't think like that? Charlotte gives a scoffing laugh.

What to paint then? What to paint? Her first sight of him was his curly head bent over the flowers, snipping a fragrant bloom and kneeling to offer it to her mother, their two faces meeting in laughter as they sniffed the petals. Charlotte had no idea this was Niccolo's way of ascertaining whether her mother might be seducible, extra money to be made there, and even when a glance into Clarisse's eyes told him that such a liaison would never enter her head, Niccolo carried through the little charade with all the finesse at his command. What lady does not like to be treated charmingly? And sure enough, Mrs. Deerfield tipped him generously and made him feel his attentions gave her an innocent happiness. Niccolo was not a vicious exploiter. He was a thoroughly gallant one. He was also an adequate gardener, and when he went off to fish with his father, that was fine, too.

Charlotte, meanwhile, dreamed of Niccolo presenting a flower to her. But she was shy and sheltered, and she knew these romantic impulses she was feeling for a servant were terribly inappropriate. She alternately painted in the garden, hoping he'd pay court to her, then the next week she would hide when he came, peeping out a window to watch him with her mother. A delicious tingle swelled her flesh at each sight of him, and when she touched herself, stroked, the feeling intensified and throbbed into a paroxysm that left her damp and exalted. Never having imagined the act of masturbation, she discovered it for herself by fantasizing about Niccolo.

She had to have him then. This was love, wasn't it?

Charlotte strokes paint onto the canvas, two bodies, two outlines entwined, one pink, one olive brown. She doesn't know where Bella has set off to today in this fog and doesn't care. Maybe she will paint Niccolo, paint the boy-girl couple in an erotic pose over one large canvas, paint them making love in her mother's garden, although they never did make love there. Niccolo knew all sorts of other places, actually any convenient location would do, as would any girl. So when Charlotte, emboldened by the discovery of her own sexual desires, began to flirt furtively with him, easygoing Niccolo didn't scruple to bed her. Give the foreigners what they want, that was his motto, and although Charlotte didn't pay him for his sexual favors, he had only to wish aloud for a watch or a fine shirt or film for the new camera another American woman had bought him, and she would fulfill his desire. Besides, she was young and pretty, and since sex cost Niccolo nothing, he could afford to be generous. He liked the strawberry smell of Charlotte's red-gold tresses, liked sucking the pinkish nipples on her small mounds of breasts, liked the way she pushed his head down between her legs and squirmed in pleasure as he lapped his tongue into her. He had been deflowering the local girls since he was thirteen, and he knew when the flesh was ripe and the juice bursting to flow.

Charlotte adds a wave of red-gold hair to the pink outline, a patch of the same color between the thighs, half-concealed by the olive-brown silhouette of the other figure. Then in a shade almost black, she bestows upon the latter two corresponding tangles of curly dark hair. She doesn't give the lovers eyes. They didn't see what was coming.

"Pregnant! I'm pregnant!" she cried in a piercing whisper to Bella. There was no one else to tell. Even if her mother's health hadn't taken a turn for the worse, even if her father, renouncing the tavern owner's buxom daughter, wasn't totally preoccupied by his wife's deteriorating condition, she could never have revealed this shame to her parents. She wanted to tell Niccolo, who would marry her and make everything right. Of course, she would be disgraced and disowned, never allowed back into respectable American society, but she'd have the man of her desire. She would beg her parents to give them this villa, or if not, they would live on their own in a little house, and she'd paint, he'd fish. They would be poor but in love forever.

But Niccolo vanished before she could tell him, and there was no one to ask where he'd gone except Bella, twisted little Bella, the funny monkey who curled up in a back room of the villa and always scampered to make herself useful, cleaning up spills, running errands, brewing soothing herbal drinks for Charlotte's mother. Mrs. Deerfield felt sorry for the girl and kept her on for the sake of past services by her murdered mother, and Charlotte, although she mostly ignored Bella, felt sorry for her, too. Now she needed her.

"You have to find Niccolo for me," she pleaded, and Bella brought back word that he was on a fishing voyage with his father and they hadn't yet returned. Charlotte waited, each day chewing her lip and wringing her hands, telling herself, Be patient, you'll be married soon. It was February, then late February, and still Niccolo didn't appear. Her mother's health grew worse, neither Bella's herbals nor the doctors brought over from Naples could help, and by March Vincent Deerfield was ordering they pack up to leave.

"No!" Charlotte tugged on his sleeve as if that could stop him.

"Of course we're leaving." Impatiently, her father brushed her off. "We're returning to America to get your mother the best medical care."

"Then let me stay here to look after the villa for you. I can take care of it for you, Papa. I can do it."

"You can't stay here alone. Why would you want to do that, Charlotte?"

To wait for Niccolo! But she couldn't say that, and her father was much too worried to pursue the matter. At three months, Charlotte's condition was barely beginning to show, and it would never have occurred to him in any case that his daughter might be pregnant. Frantic, Charlotte went again to Bella.

"He's gone," said Bella flatly. "He and his father found a bigger boat in Naples, and they signed on to make more money there."

"No!" Charlotte cried. "He has to come back for me!"

"He won't return," said Bella, "but don't worry. Take me to America with your family, and I'll take care of you."

I'll take care of you. Charlotte remembers the words as if Bella has just spoken them, as indeed Bella has spoken them in response to one misfortune after another for the lifetime they have spent together. *I'll take care of you.* It was all she needed to hear. People had been taking care of her for her entire life; it was her role to let them. And here was the pledge they made to each other: Charlotte would persuade her father to bring Bella to America, and in exchange, once in America, Bella would prepare potions learned from her mother—the good Catholic, the good poisoner, the good abortionist—to make the baby go away.

Charlotte's side of the bargain transpired easily. Her father, distraught over his wife's illness, agreed without a second thought to Bella accompanying them, and Clarisse Deerfield smiled weakly and praised her daughter's selfless spirit to wish to ameliorate the life of another girl her own age yet so much less fortunate. They arrived in New York on the boat, then rode to Deerfield in the chauffeured limousine, and why should it be surprising if still no one guessed Charlotte's secret? The spring was cold; bulky sweaters were everyday wear. Moreover, it was clear now her mother was dying, and all attention, from her father to every last servant, focused on the sickbed. If anyone observed that Charlotte, too, often appeared pale and unwell, what more natural than to assume she was grieving for her mother? When Clarisse finally did let go her frail life in mid-May and Charlotte locked herself in her room crying and refusing to see anyone but Bella, this solitude was not denied her. Vincent Deerfield was crying alone in his room as well. The fact that he had philandered throughout his marriage didn't controvert the fact that he had also loved his wife dearly.

Contemplating her painting of the two lovers, wondering what brush stroke to add next, Charlotte grimly recalls those mourning weeks after her mother died. She didn't dare show herself, the swelling of her abdomen had become obvious, and still Bella hadn't accomplished her half of the deal. She had brought with her from Capri the herbs necessary to effect an abortion, but they hadn't worked, only made Charlotte violently ill, and behind her bedroom door fights began to break out, screaming matches hastily hushed when any servant's footsteps came near.

You promised!

I'm trying!

Get rid of it!

It's your fault in the first place!

Poisoner!

Slut!

Help me!

I'm trying!

Bella clumped frantically over the estate in search of more herbs, combined them with shelf medicines from the drugstore and pills filched from the leftover prescription bottles on Clarisse Deerfield's bedside table. Stop eating, she commanded Charlotte, take long hard walks, drink brandy until you vomit. Her stomach in anguish, dazedly stumbling through each day, Charlotte thought, I'll be dead soon myself. Bella made long scouting trips through the forest, around the pond, out to the ridges, snatching up berries, plants, mushrooms, anything that might work. There was no Internet then to look up a solution, no cyberspace repository of answers.

Then one night in June when Charlotte was six months pregnant, cramps began, dull cramps like the onset of a menstrual period. This was it, it was happening, by morning it would be over! They hugged each other, rejoicing, and crept down to a dark corner of the basement to see it through. But it was too late to be an abortion. It was a birth. Bella realized it first—not a bloody disposal of tissue, but the increasing, insistent contractions of a child striving to be born. Charlotte, doubled in pain, hands clamped to her mouth to stifle her cries, read in one glance at Bella's face that this was not going to be the outcome they had intended. Then they were just two terrified sixteen-year-old girls, alone in the dark basement of a great stone house, weeping in anguish and clutching each other's hands.

The baby came out dead. They told themselves that afterward. It couldn't have survived, not with Bella's repeated poisonings and Charlotte's starving herself, not at barely six months with no prenatal care, no sterile delivery, no attendant doctor. Charlotte couldn't bear to look, couldn't face what had come out of her, and was close to unconsciousness. She closed her eyes, ready to die, vaguely aware of Bella wrapping up something and getting to her feet. The last thing she remembered before she passed out was hearing one faint cry.

Charlotte stares at the painting of her pink-and-gold silhouette entwined with Niccolo's Mediterranean brown one, her brush motionless in mid-air. What else is there to paint or explain? Her retrospective is complete. There's not another stroke needed, no redress, no redemption. She gazes at the eyeless lovers. *I'll take care of you.* The blind promise of one human being to another, the blind willingness to believe it. This is what she'll title the painting, and for once she's sure no caption will be necessary. Even an idiot will understand.

Chapter 28

The baby did cry once.

Bella can still hear it, like the mew of a tiny kitten, a plaintive whimper of loneliness and fear. Horrified, she tried to clear the infant's face so it could breathe; she knew enough to do that. But they hadn't expected a live baby. Constantly ill from Bella's potions, the fetus itself undersized and weak, Charlotte had never felt a telltale kick. Expecting only an expulsion of unwanted tissue, Bella hadn't brought to the basement any fluffy blankets or hot water, only a metal basin and some towels. She wrapped the baby in one of them and hurriedly wiped the mucus from its nose and mouth with a corner of her cardigan, the only soft material on hand. But the baby didn't make any more sound or movement, didn't breathe, and it was so tiny that cradled in Bella's arms the child created, if anyone had seen, the illusion that Bella herself was of normal size, a mother tenderly holding her newborn.

"What did you do then?" Jane, sick to her stomach at the story, doesn't really want to hear the answer. She's afraid she already knows, and when Bella points to the ground at Mehitable Mowry's headstone, that confirms it.

"It was nearly dawn by that time," says Bella tonelessly. "I had come upon the cemetery when I was searching for herbs to make the pregnancy go away, and it seemed the best place."

She traces with her finger the carved lines on the

headstone, the reference to Mehitable's death in childbirth and the unnamed infant sharing her grave...*tender Mother ...innocent Babe.*

"But no coffin, no nothing?"

"I wrapped it in my sweater."

For a long minute they sit in the enfolding fog, saying nothing, while Jane's mind reels. What do they do now? Dig it up? Call the police? Do Bella and Charlotte get arrested? The thought of a tiny skeleton buried unblessed and un-marked in this neglected spot makes her shudder, although she ought to be immune to religious sentiment or queasiness. The only thing about death a pilot needs to know, the joke goes, is that in the event of a crash, walk toward the light. These months of observing the life-death cycle around her at Deerfield have further attuned her to the briefness of the former and the permanence of the latter. More than once, she has stepped over a dead vole or squirrel on a trail, the debris of feathers where some predator has made dinner of a sweet songbird. Nature doesn't hold funerals. It simply, quietly, reclaims.

"What about the boy in Capri?" she asks.

"We never went back," says Bella. "After Charlotte's mother died, her father wasn't the same."

Indeed, at a time when smarter men were finding myriad ways to take advantage of the new peacetime economy, Vincent Deerfield seemed incapable of doing any-thing right. When he made decisions, they were bad ones, and the family fortune, already diminished over the years by his mishandling, began to disappear in alarming chunks. The villa on Capri was sold to cover debts, and Bella was glad to see it go. Safely in America, she had no wish to maintain ties with the family that had tried to relegate her to the cloister. As for Niccolo, Bella did imagine him sometimes, a fisher-man like his father, married to some once-pretty island girl, a brood of squabbling children swarming around their legs. For all his beauty and ingratiating charm, Niccolo was always content to hook the little ones and never had the brains to land one big fish.

Bella reaches out to smooth the broken earth of Mehitable's grave. The dirt is dark and rich, decades of dead leaves composted into it, and crumbs stick to her fingertips. There's a sense of relief in having made her confession at last. Odd how a secret, a nothingness, can weigh so much. Yet confession alone isn't what she sought when she pulled herself onto the bridge and made her feet take this path. Jane's presence forced it out of her, but the baby, abused and unwanted, betrayed and murdered, already knows its own story better than anyone else. It's forgiveness Bella craves, and Jane, still half in shock, can't give her that. Her hand stops its smoothing and lies quiet on the earth.

"Didn't you tell anyone?" Jane has to say something to break the silence or they will be swallowed up in it.

"Who could we tell? Charlotte's father was in mourning, he was useless. There were no near female relatives. It would have raised a scandal and ruined her chances for marriage, it wasn't like it is now. For an unwed girl of prominent family to have an illegitimate child..." Bella vigorously shakes her head. Even in the days following the baby's birth, death, the one overriding emotion for both Bella and Charlotte was relief. *No one knows. We got away with it.*

"But what about Charlotte?" Jane asks. "Wasn't she sick or hurt? There could have been serious complications."

"She was fine."

Indeed, with the baby gone, Charlotte's body and spirits recovered in short order. Some whispered that she recovered too quickly, from her mother's death, that is, still believing that was the reason Charlotte had taken to her room in the first place. The following spring her debutante party was held in New York, an old friend of the late Clarisse Deerfield hosting the event for the motherless girl, and the marriage to Lawrence Chandler soon thereafter secured a perfect fairy tale ending. Except Lawrence couldn't bring himself to touch his new bride. "He knows! He must know

I'm not pure, Bella!" Charlotte wailed on return from that loveless honeymoon, and they doped the unwitting bridegroom with Bella's aphrodisiacs and plenty of liquor to get the marriage consummated. The first miscarriage had seemed a sad happenstance, no reason to lose hope. But at the second one, Charlotte grew frightened, and when, in her marriage to Robert Drayton, three more fetuses were spontaneously ejected from her womb, she grew more heartsick and wrathful each time.

"We killed something inside me," she wept, clutching her abdomen, desperate for it not to be true. She had expert physicians for all her married pregnancies and the best prenatal care money could buy, and when the doctors examined her after each loss, they assured her they could find nothing physically wrong. But five miscarriages by two different men—it had to be her fault. "I'm poisoned, you poisoned me forever," she sobbed, not hurling the accusations but planting them like land mines around the two of them, creating a battlefield they could never step outside of no matter where they went.

And Bella, who had come to America with such heady dreams of independence and success, found she had nowhere else to go. Lacking a formal education and marketable skills, tied to the secret she and Charlotte shared, she stayed on at Deerfield and became Charlotte's secretary. Nor did she ever inflate her title to personal aide or administrative assistant when the terms became popular. *I am Bella, Miss Deerfield's secretary, the one who keeps her secrets.* Over the years she would shrug to herself that she had actually done very well. She lived in a fine house, ate the best food, had access to if not acceptance by the best people and society, some things are too much to ask. She applied her talents to further Charlotte's artistic goals and charitable causes and earned commendation in the eyes of their world. She attended mass and tried to believe in a god who could cleanse her sins with his love. But will there be a place in heaven for her?

No.

Bella can't explain why she knows this is the answer, why nothing she has done or can do in the short time remaining will atone. Jane's face, pale and drained, tells her the same. Lucky girl, Bella thinks, you've never had to keep such a secret. Whatever brought you here, a broken marriage, a nervous breakdown, some minor crime, it can't be as bad as the murder I have done. She doesn't guess that half the reason Jane looks so stunned is because her secret is of the very same nature, a death for which she feels accountable, a loss of life before her eyes. Bella lifts her hand from the grave and brushes her thumb over her fingertips to dust off the last grains of soil. What do they do now? she wonders, looking at Jane, who has no answer. Bella, it's always Bella, who must solve things.

"Go back to the house," she suggests.

"No, I'm not leaving you here alone," Jane replies.

"I'll be fine. I'll get up in a while and walk back."

"But it's wet and foggy. You'll catch cold."

"It doesn't matter. Please, I need to be here by myself for a while."

Jane hesitates, then nods her understanding. After they scattered Jill's ashes over the sea, she went back to the beach to stand there alone.

"What should we do, about this I mean?" She gestures at the grave, as if there were anything else to which she could be referring.

"Do whatever you feel you must."

Jane tries to think. There's such an urge to do something to make it right, to go back in time and prevent it, to apologize and explain. If you could rewrite just one episode in your past…but you can't. Bella will always hear that faint, mewling cry. Jane will always feel that *thunk* on her airplane wing.

"I planted bulbs here," she offers. "I didn't know, but I planted the flowers you bought."

"Thank you." Bella nods slightly. That does help

somehow. Then because Jane is still searching her face for some clue as to what she wants done, Bella adds, "I think it would be best if you let this cemetery grow over again." She glances around the small clearing, and Jane nods. Come spring, the weeds and grasses will return and run rampant, the cut-back brambles and briars will surge in from every side. Sun and rain will feed the soil, and leafy vines will creep in exploration over the headstones. In two or three years at most, this well-intentioned human touch Jane has felt moved to impose will revert to the untamed tangle nature intended. Deep in the thicket, a few unexplained tulips and daffodils may bloom.

"Go on now," says Bella, and after another moment, Jane turns and departs. Bella watches her disappear in the fog. She hasn't told Jane everything.

"I looked at you before I buried you," she whispers, her eyes traveling to the grave.

When she fled the house that dawn nearly sixty years ago, clasping the baby wrapped in the towel, Bella had no clear idea where to go. *Get rid of it*, was her only thought, *get rid of it, bury it, throw it away*. She stumbled through the woods by instinct until she reached the pond, and there she stopped, a strangeness overtaking her. The pond was looking at her, its flat eye lightless as a corpse's, the world around her still formless and pale. It knew. The pond knew everything. All spring it had pondered her comings and goings, now its deep curiosity was satisfied as it focused on the small bundle against her heart. Then a new sensation began, a compulsive twitching in Bella's arms, she could feel the rough texture of the towel prickling up against her hands. Her body understood what was happening before her brain did, and she started to sway unsteadily and to moan.

The pond wanted the baby. It had drawn her feet here, now the water was trying to tug the bundle from her arms. She could hear it in her head, *Throw it in, it will sink, you have to get rid of it somewhere, isn't that why you came?* Her arms began to quiver, and her breath came in whimpering sobs. No, no, it's too cruel! But how could it be any crueler than what she had already done? She could feel her fingers unplucking themselves from the lump of towel, her grip loosening. *Throw it in, Bella, then it will be over, the sun's not even above the trees, throw it in and you can go home. Do it quickly and blot it from your memory. There's nothing inside that towel, nothing.* To the east, the sun was rising; each minute the sky grew a little lighter and the shadowy trees on the far side of the water began to take on leafy form. Once she saw colors, it would be too late. Once green crept over the branches, once the sky whispered a sheer blue, once the water dappled in bright sunlight, she would no longer be able to convince herself it was all a dream.

Throw it in, Bella, and throw yourself after it...

Bella spat a curse at the pond, hugged the baby and ran, over the bridge, wildly through the woods. She reached the cemetery without thinking, or so it seemed. There Mehitable's grave appeared before her, and she knelt, panting, and dug a clumsy hole. She used a sharp-edged rock, and she prayed as she dug, fearful of hitting the coffin, visions of rising ghosts filling her head and chilling her nape as she scraped into the dirt. *Please, you must have room for one more innocent child.* The little bundle lay on the dewy grass beside the opened earth, no movement or sound, the daylight fast growing. When it came time to put the baby into the grave, Bella could hardly bear to touch it again. But she had to know it was real, and she had to be sure it was dead. If there was the slightest chance it still breathed and she buried it...Oh God, if she buried the child alive! She waited until her hands stopped shaking. Then she unwrapped the towel, bloody and sticky with mucus and the birthing fluids, and there it was, a bluish imp not twelve inches long. Six months, perhaps two pounds, its eyelids still fused—even in the best hospital in those days such a premature infant would not have survived. And this infant was already deformed.

Bella hadn't seen it in the dark basement, the child quickly concealed in a towel and hurried out of the house.

There in the full morning, she gaped at the sight. Spine twisted like a miniature snake, the shoulders crooked out of alignment—it was Bella, or might have been if carried to term. And first Bella cried, and then she took off her sweater and wrapped the baby in it because the towel was so rough and unkind. She remembers the color and texture of the sweater exactly, a lightweight blue cotton with fake pearl buttons. Before she put the baby in the earth, she cradled it and sang a wavering lullaby. The song kept unraveling as it left her throat, and she had to stitch the words together to get through a verse. As she laid the bundle in the grave and covered it, she murmured to the little girl, "It's better for you this way."

It wasn't until an hour later, repassing the now placid pond, emerging from the woods, catching sight of the roof of the Deerfield house, that it struck Bella what this meant. A second deformity like hers could be no coincidence. Back on Capri there had been a blind child, an idiot or two, a boy born without a little finger on his left hand. But no one else with Bella's particular affliction until this child of the Deerfield line...

She stopped, staring drop-jawed at the house. Vincent Deerfield, who had spread his amours all over the island, had he spread them to Bella's beautiful witch of a mother as well? Was her favored status at the villa, always a step better treated than the other servants, not only for her occult knowledge and herbal powers but for the gratification of lust? A whore like your mother! the drunken uncle had shouted at Bella on that abusive return journey from St. Peter's, while her mother counseled that God had put the Deerfields in their path for whatever benefits she and her daughter could wrest. If Vincent Deerfield was her father, had he passed on some hidden defect of blood and bone to her, and had the same defect descended through his daughter Charlotte to the infant just buried in the woods? Or were both deformities the result of poisonings by a mother intent on ridding herself of an unwanted pregnancy? Had Bella's mother tried and failed to abort her?

There were no clear answers then, and there are none now as Bella clumps back from the cemetery, past the pond, and stands staring at the roof of the mansion appearing through the fog. If she could shape the story her way, it would be this: Vincent Deerfield was her father. Her mother accepted his advances, money and favors; she accepted the pregnancy as an inevitable consequence. Witch, whore— what difference? Vincent passed on some genetic defect, not manifest in himself and Charlotte, severe in this infant grandchild and his other daughter, Bella. This version would make Bella and Charlotte half-sisters, a thought Bella still rejects. But this version means her mother refused to abort or abandon her illegitimate child, but kept her and loved her and named her, in spite of her deformity, Bella, she who is beautiful.

Bella completes the trek to the house and opens the heavy front door. It might be half her house, her property, her fortune, but though she's lived here her entire adult life she can never put forth a claim. She has everything but the name, Bella Deerfield. And she never tells anyone, and she never told Charlotte.

Chapter 29

In the days following Bella's confession, Jane tries to concentrate on her chores. She has put the cottage in good shape, likewise the grounds around the house. As a final project she is cleaning out the garage where decades of tools and garden implements lie in various stages of disuse and rust. She will sharpen and oil those worth salvaging, create a basic tool box, install pegboard and hooks on which to organize rakes, clippers, shovels and hoes.

But while she works, Jane's mind strays to the grave-yard, wondering what condition the bones are in. Experts can tell a lot from bones, diagnose arthritis and injuries, solve murders from bullet holes or traumatic blows to the skull, determine sex, age, nutritional deficiencies. What could they tell from the tiny skeleton resting with Mehitable Mowry? Does it still lie curled in its fetal position? Could they determine without a doubt whether the infant was born alive? Is it still there? Wrapped only in a sweater, flimsily buried in a shallow grave, it's surprising Jane didn't uncover it as she hacked out the stumps of thorn bushes and planted the bulbs. Possibly the corpse was carried away the very night it was buried, by some scavenging animal that scented a fresh death. The thought of a raccoon or coyote carrying off the remains creates shivers, yet that is nature, nothing wasted, everything reclaimed. She would almost like to go back, dig and not find it. But if it is there and her spade shatters the little bones, she will have desecrated a grave.

Tell someone. The urge arises frequently, only to die down again in futility. What good would it do anyone to know this now, other than to add a titillating layer to the local gossip about the Deerfield family? Early on, when she first met Burt, he claimed to have discovered scandals in the family's history that were better left unsaid, but Jane doubts he knows this. Such a rumor about the town's leading citizen would be too delicious not to become widespread, and she would have heard it from someone at the art association or the land trust or at one of the stores in town that have long held the Deerfield accounts. Now it's a secret that has outlived its usefulness; the knowledge of it confers no power. On the contrary, it's disempowering, causing only a turbulence of emotion without resolution. Knowing something doesn't necessarily require doing something about it. The truth doesn't always set you free; it just compromises the beliefs that enable everyone to get along.

So days pass, and the inner debate fades, and though Jane looks for opportunities to speak with Bella—to say, "It's all right, I understand"—those opportunities never come. Bella must be avoiding her; in her position, Jane would probably do the same. Then, near the end of November, she is summoned to the studio. To her surprise, Charlotte isn't painting, the easel is empty. She sits instead at an antique writing desk near Bella's computer, looking quite pleased with herself.

"Ah, Miss Avery, how are you? Well, we hope? We have a special request for your assistance. It's time to set up our holiday decorations, evergreen wreaths on the front door and the gate, electric candles in the windows, white lights on the trees flanking the portico. Bella has ordered a ten-foot pine for our Christmas tree. We're going to erect it in the great room, and we'll need your help to string the lights and arrange the ornaments. You're not afraid of working on a ladder? No, of course not. I recall how adeptly you cleaned out the cottage eaves."

Charlotte smiles magnanimously. At last, everything

is coming together perfectly!

"The opening of my retrospective at the art association will take place on Sunday evening, December fifteenth, from four to six p.m.," she continues, "and it will be open to the general public. Afterward, I'm hosting an invitation-only Christmas party here at Deerfield for approximately a hundred and fifty people. It's my annual tradition, and each guest brings a present for a needy child, which we turn over to one of the social service agencies for distribution. It's all going to be splendid, the best event of the season! I'll instruct Bella to send invitations to your birding friends, if you like."

"Yes, thank you. That's a nice tradition, very generous," Jane replies, a little caught off guard by the gracious offer. She glances to Bella at the computer, wondering if it's really her doing, and draws in a breath at how unwell Bella looks. Her face is sallow, her eyes unlighted; only her topknot, sprayed stiff, clings to its old authority. *Don't worry, I won't tell*, Jane wants to assure her, this image of Bella so different from the haughty secretary who tried to sabotage her at that first meeting in March. Today Bella says nothing, and when Charlotte begins hectoring her about the menu and musicians, she takes the orders meekly. Jane, ignored and deeming the interview to be over, departs with a murmur that she will supply a list of the birders' names and addresses.

When she walks down to the front gate the next Sunday morning, she finds her friends in a buzz over their invitations.

"My daddy's going to come. He's going to bring me himself!" reports Melanie.

"What should we wear?" frets Hortense. "Is it formal attire, Jane?"

"I don't know, but I'll find out for you."

"What type of present should we bring?" Russ and Charlie ask together.

"It can be anything a child would like," Jane answers,

"a stuffed animal, a board game, puzzles, books, toy trucks."

"I rather hope it is formal," Hortense decides. "Everything is so casual nowadays, wouldn't it be fun to get really dressed up for an evening?"

She strikes a fancy pose, as if she's a grande dame hoisting a cocktail glass in one hand and a cigarette holder in the other, six-foot Hortense in her anorak and mittens and red wool stocking cap. Everyone laughs, but they're all intrigued at the idea of stepping inside the house. Even Roy, who wouldn't normally admit it, is feeling a bit of curiosity to see how the other half lives.

"Will there be a band and dancing?" Raven demands. Prompted by the invitation, she has made an appearance, and in reply to their welcoming chorus of "You're back! Where have you been?" she bubbles about *A Christmas Carol*, synergy, a fantastic cast, everyone promise to come see it! Under her jacket, her pregnancy doesn't show, but she catches Jane aside and whispers, "No more morning sickness, hallelujah!" and Jane can only assume all is well.

"They've hired a pair of musicians who play harp and flute, so there will be background music but no dancing," Jane informs them. "From what I heard, the menu will be pretty elaborate, a catered buffet. Also, I'm sure Miss Deerfield expects you all to attend the opening at the art association first."

"Wouldn't miss it," everyone chimes.

For the day's birding, they bundle into two cars and drive to the beach to search for ducks and shorebirds. Tim Hennessey invites Jane to his pickup to join the small caravan. His appearance was unexpected, and he kept quiet while the others spilled their questions about the invitation.

"I was rather surprised to get mine," he confides as they follow Hortense's car along the shore road. "It doesn't appear anyone else from the land trust is invited."

"Miss Deerfield asked me for a list of the birders. Since you've come a few times under that heading, I put your name on as well."

"And neither Miss Deerfield nor her secretary took it off," Tim muses. "That's a good sign. Three years ago when I first contacted them they were slamming down the phone on my calls. It would be nice to think they no longer view me as their enemy and that we can have some productive discussions come January. You'll be there, of course?" He regards her a little anxiously, and for a moment she isn't sure whether he means at the party or the January meetings. She says yes and lets him think it's both, if necessary, and he smiles, relieved. "Good, that will make it a little friendlier. Schmoozing isn't exactly my forte. I promise you I'll treat it strictly as a social occasion, not an opportunity to bend anyone's ear about a land preservation agenda."

"Thanks," she says, although he doesn't have to promise her anything.

He relaxes and begins describing a wetlands survey he's proposing, and in an unguarded moment, Jane recovers a feeling about him that occurred to her the first time they met. Here is an attractive, interesting, intelligent man, who loves the outdoors as she has come to, who puts his words into action. Are we feeling something, she asks herself? Is his wanting her to be at the party more than a desire to preempt the awkwardness of being among an unfamiliar crowd? Why didn't he invite Raven to ride with him? Jane glances to Russ and Charlie's car ahead and sees Raven half-turned in the front passenger seat, tossing her hair, spiking out her hands, enthralling both men at once with some dramatic tale. It dawns on Jane that *A Christmas Carol* must be well into rehearsals, and does that mean Brandon is in town? Yet she hasn't seen or heard from him, and for her part, she didn't put his name on the invitation list. Now here is Tim inserted in her thoughts, and she doesn't automatically dismiss him.

"You know," she says, "if you'd like to bring a guest to the party, that would be fine."

"No, no, there's no one, just me. Oh...You mean you're bringing someone, your actor friend." He looks flustered again, and Jane smiles to herself.

"No, just me," she says. "Let's go check for harle-quins."

They regroup with the others and tramp along the beach, then over the rocks. While Hortense sets up her scope, Roy scans the slate-blue ocean through his binoculars. Temperatures are still seasonable, in the mid-forties, and the wind today is light, so he doesn't get chilled. He has checked the rare bird alerts on the Internet, but there's nothing out of the ordinary in southern New England. His eyes move from wave to wave, then lift and systematically travel the sky. What's missing? What can he possibly sight for his five hundredth bird? He could do it with a dovekie, the smallest member of the auk family. The size of a starling, dovekies are chubby black-and-white creatures with almost no neck or tail. They breed in Greenland and Iceland and winter offshore in the North Atlantic, but they can be blown in toward the coast by storms. If he did sight a dovekie today, he would have the honor of reporting it. A dovekie, a dovekie for number five hundred. Just one more bird.

Russ and Charlie have spotted a duck they can't identify, and Melanie is huddled with them over her bird book.

"It's an immature white-winged scoter," says Charlie, pointing to an illustration of a bland brown duck with two faint white patches on its face.

Russ shakes his head and points to another, almost identical picture below. "It's an immature surf scoter," he says.

"Look at the bill," Hortense cues, beckoning them back to the scope. She already knows it's a white-winged by the emerging basal knob on its bill; the distinctive wing patches won't be clearly visible until the bird flaps or flies. But, teacher to the core, she'll let them figure it out for themselves.

"White-winged," maintains Charlie.

"Surf," says Russ.

"Let me see." Raven adjusts the focus on the scope

and peers through it. "That's not a duck. It's an otter or a beaver or some swimmy animal."

In a flash, up goes every pair of binoculars. Not far from the scoter, a whiskered gray-brown head pokes out of the water, peering around like a submarine periscope.

"Seal!" the cry goes up.

"Well, I knew it was something like that," says Raven modestly.

The seal sticks around, giving them a good show, bobbing up for a while, then submerging and reappearing a dozen yards along. As they exclaim over its antics, they compare notes of previous seal sightings, relate adventures on whale watching tours off Cape Cod. Melanie wants to know how long a seal can hold its breath underwater, and since no one knows the answer, Hortense suggests she research it in the school library or on the Internet and report back next week.

"Everybody is happy," Jane remarks, standing a little to one side with Tim.

"We're an easy bunch to please," he agrees. "Did you see the eider out there?"

She searches through her binoculars and gives a confirming nod. "Are all the duck species that are going to come for the winter here now?"

"Pretty much. Any migratory birds that haven't yet made the journey south better hurry or they'll be spending the winter with their tail feathers frozen in the ice."

Jane stares out at the ocean, a cold, rocky blue. Say the word "duck" and most people automatically picture the half-tame mallards that paddle on the pond in any city park. She has already begun to learn differently, yet she's finding herself less than enamored of these new birds. Why? Floating complacently on the water, they're far easier to spot and identify than warblers hiding in the trees. There are enough species to make it challenging, enough intriguing habits and behaviors to merit interest. It might be that ducks don't sing in the melodious notes of the spring songbirds;

there's not much poetry in quacks and croaks. But more important, ducks don't fly like other birds do, especially not the hawks of October soaring. Though they cover long distances, the ducks' flight is straight and level, pedestrian. Otherwise, they sit on the water and swim; they are the seaplanes of the avian world. I want something to *fly*, Jane thinks, and it's only now that the hawks are mostly gone that she realizes how much she misses them. She keeps looking up, hoping to see a bold silhouette carving the wind far overhead. Without them, the air seems empty, the sky forlorn.

Bam! The sound jolts everyone, heads whirl to the right. On tiptoe and waving both hands at the seal to be sure he sees her, Melanie turns, too. Her face crinkles. What is this they're looking at?

Down the shoreline to the west, just visible beyond a rocky headland, a tent is floating on the water. It's small and brownish-gray with sloped sides and a slightly peaked roof. How can a tent float on the sea? Melanie camped in a tent once before her accident, but that was on land. It was a summer sleepover at a girlfriend's house, and the mother let the four girls spend the night in sleeping bags in the family's tent erected in the backyard. They giggled and ate potato chips, which crunched all night beneath their sleeping bags. But this tent floats on water. She's about to ask Hortense how when she realizes they're already explaining it to each other. The man Tim who is Jane's friend uses the word "camouflage" which means the men in the boat underneath the tent are hidden, and Tim says they have to have both a state hunting license and a federal Duck Stamp and actually the Duck Stamp is one environmental program that truly works, raising funds for habitat preservation and—

"No!"

Everyone turns at Melanie's wail. Their faces wear the remorseful expression adults get when they realize too late a child has been listening to grownup talk and too much reality has slipped in. Hortense reaches a hand toward her, but Melanie pulls back. Hunters are coming! That *bam!* was a gun! She has to warn the seal and save the ducks! Clumsily, she runs toward the rocks.

"Run, run!" she cries, flapping her arms. What she means is *Escape! Fly away!* but in her alarm she can't locate the right words. The ducks don't seem to hear her, until another voice joins in.

"Scram!" Raven yells at the top of her lungs. She grabs Melanie's hand so the child won't dash out onto the tide-slicked rocks, and now Raven and Melanie are holding hands, jumping up and down, using their free hands to wave wildly. The seal pops underwater. A few of the ducks nearest shore take flight, only to plop down again a short distance beyond, not sensing any real harm.

"Shoo, ducks, shoo!" Charlie calls, then Russ, both of them fluttering their fingers outward as if they're trying to scatter away a flock of chickens. Leave it to Raven to make this ridiculous, Jane is thinking, when Hortense, too, begins calling.

"Fly east, east!" She shoves her hands in the direction she wants them to go. Roy can't shout, his voice is too old and cracked to add much to the clamor, but he takes off his mittens and claps his hands, adding the smacking noise to the din.

Jane and Tim exchange glances. This is crazy. Then Tim grins.

"Beat it, ducks! They've got guns!" he yells, and with a shake of her head, Jane joins in. "Go, ducks, go!" They stand in a row on the rocks, shouting and whooping and jerking their arms. The ducks, obviously convinced that these lunatics present a clear and present danger, take to the air and miraculously head east. Everyone on shore raises a cheer. Away to the west, the hunters can't hear them and would only be amused if they could. The ducks will only come back again.

Everyone else knows that, too, but Melanie is radiant, clutching Raven's hand. She thinks she has saved the ducks forever, so it will be good to leave now and preserve that illusion. As they head to the cars, Jane sends a smile to Raven over the others' heads. Dramatic and crazy as Raven can be, there are situations where her spontaneous tactics work better than anything Jane could have planned. But instead of responding with a conspiratorial wink, Raven looks as elated as Melanie. She, too, wants to believe she has saved the ducks forever.

They pull up at the front gate of Deerfield, and before they disperse, Jane reviews their upcoming schedule. They will have two more regular Sunday walks, then the weekend before Christmas they'll do their all-day Christmas Bird Count to wrap up the season.

"Can I join you for that?" Tim asks.

"Glad to have you any time," Jane replies, both of them wondering why these preliminary conversations have to be so feeble. She wishes she could ask him in for a cup of coffee, but she's due at the house to decorate the tree for Charlotte and Bella. Besides, there's a matter she needs to clarify.

"Raven, got a minute?" she asks, detaining her as the others leave. "I need to know, is Brandon back? Wasn't he going to be in your play?"

"Brandon? No, he's permanently in New York from what I hear, the newest soap opera heartthrob. Dan and Amy are the lovely Cratchits." Raven's eyes narrow, and a grin puckers her lips. "So it's you and Tim, is it? I saw you two huddled back there. Pretty sexy guy for a biologist."

"Never mind. You can go now," Jane replies. "By the way, have you told Burt?" She directs a meaningful glance toward Raven's pregnancy, well concealed beneath her jacket. "Is everything okay?"

"Oh, we're fine." Raven flips up her hand and saunters off with a breezy wave.

Jane stops at the cottage to drop off her knapsack, and for a moment her eyes sweep the small, tidy space. She never got around to putting up pictures or picking out new curtains, but then she's never been one for interior decorating and knickknacks. The cottage, as is, is her, and the idea that someone else may be moving in next spring seems strange. What, regrets? she chides herself. Three more walks and then you're leaving, right? The long-shot engineering positions she applied for didn't pan out, but this past week she submitted her resume to a half dozen more likely companies. Having Brandon definitely out of the picture will make the job search easier; letting Tim enter the picture or succumbing to any sentimental notions about her cottage will only complicate things. Yet suddenly it does seem complicated. Is she going? Is she staying? She must make up her mind. She meant to give notice by the first of December. That's today.

She steps out of the cottage, closes the door behind her and gazes upward. If she were Raven, she would no doubt ask the goddess for a sign, but except for a lone crow flapping into a bare tree, the sky is empty. She recalls the day Raven started that philosophical discussion: If there were no birds, would humans ever have imagined they could fly? No. How could you fathom flying if the sky were perpetually empty, if there was nothing in it to make you conceive the possibility of reaching into this other realm? Without flight, the sky would be bereft of purpose. Just as there must be fish in the deep, there must be birds in the air. There must be something to wheel joyously through it, to skim the clouds and race the wind, to lift a feathered wing or tip an aileron and glide, dive, loop, spin, barrel roll, hammerhead. Somewhere deep inside her, the maneuvers begin to paint themselves in invisible brush strokes, but staring into the blue canvas overhead, Jane sees only an ordinary day. She walks on to the house, thinking it must be the untangling of Christmas lights and finding hooks for the ornaments that's resting ever so gently on her mind.

Chapter 30

The opening of Charlotte's "Retrospective in Retrospective" at the art association is not an unqualified success, although the fault lies not in the number or caliber of the attendees. People, all the right people, begin arriving promptly at four, and despite the open house nature of the event, there is very little dashing in and out, none of this "Just dropped by for a quick peek, darling," which implies that the speaker, if dressed up, is en route to some far more scintillating engagement or, if dressed down, finds this a necessary social obligation to dispose of before returning home to slouch in front of the TV. No, the turnout is exemplary, and most people are suitably attired, the men in jackets and ties, the women in cocktail dresses or long skirts or velvet pants with lamé tops, many in festive red or green to mark the holiday season. Still, there are a few of both sexes who do show up in jeans and tatty sweaters, as if to prove to one and all they're no slave to fashion. Why, they're so yawningly sophisticated they could show up in burlap and still project class. Well, they don't, and Charlotte doesn't hesitate to greet them with a frostily contemptuous look that runs disapprovingly up and down their choice of clothes. One of the offenders is among those invited to Deerfield for the second party, and to her Charlotte says solicitously, "Don't stay too long or you won't have time to go home and dress up for my soiree. You are coming, aren't you?" The woman slinks out by four-thirty.

The refreshments, too, are adequate, cut glass bowls of fruit punch and eggnog sprinkled with grated nutmeg, silver trays of cookies and cakes and lemon poppy seed bread. Years ago, they used to present quite a spread at the art association openings, gourmet cheese and fruit, a dessert table, an open wine bar. When they discovered how many people, feeling too lazy to cook, viewed the occasion as an opportunity to gobble up plates of crudités and brie, they cut back to cookies and cake. Today, Charlotte has eliminated the wine as well; she wants only true art lovers at her opening, not riffraff coming simply to swill Chablis. But no one complains. Most of them will be attending the second party at Deerfield afterward, and they're not about to overindulge on snickerdoodles when a lavish buffet lies ahead.

Charlotte's appearance is right, too. She wears a black satin gown with a modest scoop neck and full skirt, a red sash and a matching black bolero jacket. The red sash is what does the trick, a striking band of color that makes you look twice to appreciate the expensive fabric of the dress. Her gold-and-diamond necklace and earrings are heirloom pieces, not overly ornate but an effective reminder of the generations of Deerfield wealth. *I was rich, I am rich,* Charlotte's image says to the guests as she greets them in an informal reception line consisting of the art association director and several board members who have squeezed themselves into secondary positions. *My family founded this museum, and this is my show.*

The one matter that keeps the opening from being quite ideal is something Bella warned her about early on. People don't understand that to view her retrospective properly they must begin at the end of her life and work backward. Despite the clearly worded explanation on the cover of the program, despite the obviously clockwise flow of the gallery itself, the guests take one look at the five present-day portraits of an older Charlotte and switch direction to begin with the blind young lovers. Can they not read? Do they need the instructions tattooed on their fore-head? Footprints on the floor to direct their feet and tow their brains along? Throughout the painting of the portraits, she and Bella had argued and debated this issue like a scale tipping back and forth. People aren't idiots, they won't need captions beside the pictures or arrows on the wall. People are idiots, they will need captions, arrows and a shove in the proper direction. Now the scale is weighing down in favor of the lowest common denominator.

"No, no," Charlotte gently admonishes the mis-creants, posting herself at the door to reroute them the minute it's clear they are heading astray. Most accept the correction with polite good humor, but others, those blue-jeaned culture slobs, sigh wearily, as if to say they don't need to be told how to appreciate art. Melanie, arriving with her father, grasps the instruction immediately when her father reads it to her from the program as they wait to check their coats. Go backward? Melanie's brain can do that. It's forward her brain won't go. When she and her father arrive at the door where Charlotte is standing guard, Melanie blurts eagerly, "Which way is backward?"

"This way," says Charlotte, pleasantly surprised at the child's sagacity.

Melanie grabs her father's hand and moves from picture to picture, staring and studying and pursing her lips. This is Art, and Art is Important. Her brain doesn't recognize the un-aging portraits as the same person standing at the door because the five women in these pictures look prettier. The second series of the woman frozen into the jagged ice block puzzles her. How did she get in that ice? Did she go exploring at the North Pole? The harlequin picture is easy. That's Halloween. Then comes a three-piece painting with overlapping edges and swirling red colors and spatterings of blue dots. There's something sad about this, an emptiness, as if something got lost. Melanie can't explain how you can feel an emptiness, but sometimes she feels like this inside herself.

Then her mouth drops at a most disturbing picture,

lots of old-fashioned people punctured with bullet holes. Somebody got mad to do that! She asks her father who the dead people are, and he says funny names like Picasso and Van Gogh, pointing to but not actually touching the faces, because you're not supposed to touch art. Melanie doesn't know any of the dead people. Maybe they were outlaws, the kind you see on posters in cowboy TV shows that offer a reward under the headline *Wanted: Dead or Alive.*

The next two portraits make perfect sense because Melanie has seen them before. The first one, the picture of the widow in black holding the hands of two pale children, is in a book in her father's library. It's Mrs. President Kennedy whose husband was assassinated, and she had to stand on the curb with her children while the horses pulled the coffin past. The one of the bride asleep on the altar is from her illustrated fairy tales. It's Snow White lying on a golden sunbeam, waiting for Prince Charming to awaken her with true love's kiss.

In the very last picture, the painter was forgetful. These people, one pinkish, one olive-tan, don't have eyes or noses or mouths, only outlines of bodies and hair on their heads and between their legs. Melanie knows about the hair between legs because she's starting to get some herself, little tickly stuff which at first worried her, but Ms. Shaw said that's what happens when you grow up, and would Melanie like her to speak to Melanie's father so he could arrange for her to learn more about it? Melanie said yes, but so far her daddy hasn't said anything, and Ms. Shaw did say it was all right. Melanie studies the painting of the two naked people, and suddenly she gets it.

"Adam and Eve," she says, poking her father's arm, then pointing her finger toward the painting. He says, yes, sure, that's it, and seems relieved. He started out reading to her from the program as they stood before each portrait, but his expression quickly grew displeased. "Flagrant exhibition-ism," he muttered. "Just look at the pretty pictures, Melanie." He must be happy she got Adam and Eve right.

"I like going backward!" she exclaims to the lady at the door, her eyes bright.

Charlotte beams upon her. Such a sweet child, too bad she's so overweight, quite a lovely face really. "Would you like some punch and cookies?" she asks. "They're on a table in the next room."

"Thank you!" Melanie's hand flashes up in a wave. "Hortense! Roy! I'm here with my daddy!"

Only then does Charlotte recognize the girl. Why, it's that fat child who comes for the walks on Sunday mornings, the one Charlotte spied on with her binoculars before Bella took them away. And didn't Bella say the child was retarded or dim or something of that nature? Charlotte exhales a sigh. Of all people to understand what a "Retrospective in Retro-spective" really means.

Yet the paintings are well received. You can feel the change in the atmosphere of the room. People come antic-ipating one of Charlotte's usual superficial shows, then slow down as they begin circling the gallery. In the end it doesn't matter whether they go forward or back. It's different this time, not a string of pretty pictures to be dismissed at a glance, or contrived, derivative efforts that fall short of the mark. These paintings force the viewers to pause and grapple with them, and when they do, there's an unexpected resonance like a thrumming in the chest. They pull out threads of common experience, love, loss, loneliness, and they tie those threads together in the small room. People can feel it, and it makes them edgy that Charlotte has tapped into what they thought was their private experience. Whatever titillating details they have gained about her life story are unimportant. What matters is the insights they are at this moment confronting about themselves. As the paintings take hold, the viewers drift to Charlotte with genuine compliments and craving serious talk. They want to hear how she perceived and grasped this panorama of her life. They want to know at what moment the paintings came alive and refused to accept the brush strokes she meant to lay down and told her instead what they needed to be. They tell her what they've felt when they painted or loved or suffered a broken heart. Did she feel that burst in the chest, that painful implosion that collapses the self so the art can get out?

Yes, Charlotte did feel that as she painted, she knew it at last as never before. You cease to be and instead are taken possession of. You are chosen and enthralled. Art takes you as its lover, and you rouse each other to ecstasy. For precious moments, you are alive, alive, *alive!* Then it's done, and you're left spent, staring at the canvas and realizing there is a portion of your soul in it that you can never get back. But it's worth it, oh, it's worth the forfeit. These paintings have moved people, and by that achievement Charlotte is an artist at last.

Standing in the lobby, on the bottom step of the carved wood staircase that leads to the second floor, Bella and Jane remark the transformation on Charlotte's face. Bella, having watched the paintings in progress, arranged the exhibition, written the program and previewed the hanging of the show, feels no need to step into the gallery to peruse the pictures. Besides, she lived it. She knows. She knows.

Jane did go in once, but the room is crowded, and in spite of the sharp December air outside, it's growing stuffy in the gallery. She'll come back alone later this week and take her time over the show, though it's hard for her to comprehend why anyone would want to put their private life so brutally on display. She feels almost flayed. If this is art, the price is too high.

Of all the viewers, only Jane and Bella realize that one painting is missing from this canvas autobiography, a picture of a sixteen-year-old girl in terrified labor in a stone-walled basement, while in the upper corner a stunted figure is hurrying a small bundle away. Why didn't you paint that one? Jane is tempted to ask Charlotte. You can't have forgotten. Doesn't it weigh as heavily on your conscience as it has on Bella's all these years? Or was every way you tried to paint it too painful? She can't ask, of course, won't violate

Bella's confidence, but she can offer Bella, if she wants it, a chance to talk.

"I was thinking," she says casually. "Would you like to come by the cottage sometime this week? We could plan a little more about the review in January."

"That would be nice," says Bella, and to Jane's surprise, Bella presses her hand.

For a minute more they watch the mingling guests. The birders have dressed up for the evening, Roy, Russ and Charlie in handsome suits, Melanie in a purple dress. Hortense, big, tall hearty Hortense, is a revelation in rose-colored lace. "A fine figure of a woman," Roy complimented her in front of everyone as he helped her remove her coat, "and splendid as a butterfly!" and the words are surprisingly accurate as more than Roy's impression of the gown's loosely gathered sleeves and flowing skirt. Hortense *is* a butterfly, emerging from the rugged cocoon of her usual outdoor garb. Carried away by his poetry, Roy proceeded to extol Jane as a "forest nymph." She fingers the buttons on the bodice of her dark green dress and smiles, quite sure "nymph" isn't the word he intended, then she turns to Bella, intending to share the anecdote. But Bella, in the very best of her black dresses, suddenly looks distinctly unwell, and her hand is clutching the carved knob atop the staircase's newel post.

"Are you all right?" Jane asks. "Do you need to sit down?"

"I'm afraid I may be coming down with something, stomach flu, perhaps. Also, I am very tired." Bella makes a slight gesture at the hubbub around them.

"Yes, I'm sure," says Jane, not convinced. It's only five o'clock, but she and Bella were to leave early anyway and return to the house where the caterers are setting up. "Maybe we should go now?"

"Yes, I think so." With an effort Bella steps down from the staircase, just as Tim Hennessey makes his way toward them with two cups of punch.

"I thought you ladies might be thirsty," he says.

"Thanks, but we have to get back to the house and check in with the caterers," Jane replies.

"Then I'll come along and help." He sets the punch out of the way on a table and shrugs one shoulder self-consciously toward Charlotte's gallery. "Lots of people in there babbling about dynamic symmetry and graphic counter-points."

Jane laughs at the sheepishness of his gesture, a confession that he's crossed into foreign territory. "We'll spring you in exchange for your assistance folding napkins or polishing forks or whatever else needs doing," she offers.

"Fork and napkins I can handle," says Tim. "Art I leave to the artists."

An hour later at Deerfield, the evening becomes truly elegant. The great room is decked in garlands of fresh pine boughs pinned with red velveteen bows. The ten-foot tree glitters with Austrian crystal icicles, brightly colored Mercury glass, and heirloom ornaments from Christmases long ago. Jane had marveled at the decorations as she put up the tree. Unpacking each one from its tissue paper was like uncovering a treasure from the past, and Charlotte and Bella, infected by her pleasure, had grown merry themselves.

Tonight the whole crowd seems possessed of a festive spirit. The buffet is superb, and uniformed waiters offer trays of hors d'oeuvres and flutes of champagne. The husband-wife duo of harpist and flutist play Mozart and Bach. A fire blazes in the long-unused fireplace, real logs Jane has hauled in and heaped on, and the smell of mulled cider spices the air. Even the blue-jeaner chastened by Charlotte arrives properly re-dressed, and there's a feeling that nothing is out of place in this rarefied atmosphere. When Charlotte enters, a deliberate half hour late to her own party, no one begrudges her the grand entrance. On the contrary, they burst into applause as she sweeps, and she does sweep, into the room. Charlotte presses their hands and exchanges air kisses. Her triumph is complete.

"My, isn't it wonderful!" Eyes bright, Hortense clinks her champagne flute to Jane's, and Jane wonders, amused, if the flush on her cheeks is really from standing too close to the fire. Only Raven is absent, unable to take the night off from the theater, and Jane hopes the competition of Charlotte's soiree isn't having a deleterious effect on attendance at the playhouse. And Burt—Jane glances around, wondering why he hasn't appeared, until her friends' laughter draws her back into their circle.

"And to think when we see each other next Sunday for the Christmas Bird Count, we'll be in our hiking boots and bushwhacking clothes again," Russ laughs.

"About this bird count," says Melanie's father, inviting Jane aside. Melanie hovers anxiously near. He has been nice to everyone so far, worn his best tie like she asked him to, took her shopping yesterday and let her pick out the purple dress and her first pair of real two-inch high heels and even wear lip gloss. She hopes everyone has noticed the lip gloss. She has the tube in her purse if she needs to put on more. She pats the purse, a small beaded bag the saleslady in the store said was just right for an evening affair. "You tuck in your comb, lipstick and a tiny bottle of perfume. Do you need perfume, too?" Melanie nodded emphatically—she had to have perfume, how could she go to a party without it?—and her father smiled and told the saleslady that would be fine. Now here is Melanie all dressed up in a mansion like Cinderella at the prince's ball. Her brain picks up Jane's voice.

"No, we don't have a set itinerary or timetable. We'll start here in the morning, then go down to the beach for shorebirds and around the point for ducks. Roy and Hortense know a few other parks and ponds nearby, and we'll carpool to those. We'll take bathroom and lunch breaks, and Melanie can bring snacks and check in with you on her cell phone, if you'd like."

Her father hesitates, then allows himself to let go. "No, that won't be necessary. Melanie really enjoys coming here, and I've given her my permission for the whole day."

Melanie claps her hands together, and Jane and her father smile at her. Now it really is like Cinderella because she gets her magic wish to come true. Her father tells Jane he will ensure she's properly dressed for the weather, and he expects them to have her home before dark. His voice gets a little severe again, like it does when he's telling her teachers or the doctors what's right for her, and then, as if he can feel Melanie's chest tightening, he relaxes and says, "I only want her to be safe and have a good time." Jane assures him they will.

So the party is wonderful, they collect a pile of presents for needy children, and at the evening's close, as the caterers are wiping the kitchen counters and the valet parkers are darting into the cold to fetch the guests' cars, Charlotte stands at the door basking in the thank-yous and con-gratulations of the departing crowd. Melanie and her father walk to their car holding hands. Russ and Charlie hold hands, too. Roy escorts Hortense, her eyes sparkling, a high flush on her cheekbones, to his car. When they meet again next Sunday for the bird count, no mention of her slight slide into tipsiness will pass his lips. Jane and Tim start walking toward her cottage, dragging their feet a little, remarking on the brightness of the stars in the midnight black sky. Halfway there, his hand brushes hers as they walk, then palm slips into palm and they regard each other with slowly growing smiles. In the contentment and glow, no one notices that someone is missing from these farewells. No one notices that Bella is gone.

Chapter 31

Bella had meant to hang on longer, till the first week of January if possible. To die just before Christmas struck her as disruptive and rude. Here are all these people dashing about shopping, decorating, caroling and partying, alternating bursts of heartfelt goodwill with frayed tempers from the long lines at the stores and post office, the parking lot snarls. Who has the time or inclination in the midst of such merriment to attend a funeral for a crooked old woman of no importance? Bella knows people will fill the pews, but it will be more out of social propriety and to have their presence, as opposed to their absence, noted by Charlotte, than out of any true mourning for Bella. Whereas, if she could have waited until after New Year's, when the gaiety is over and three dreary months of winter lie ahead and people look at each other and beg in boredom, "What do we do now?", a funeral would at least perk up the social calendar.

But only an hour into Charlotte's soiree, Bella knows she won't make it. The cancer has been steadily consuming her since those vague stomach aches of spring. The pain ramps up, you medicate and adjust to it, then it ramps up again, a grinning torturer. There will be no reprieve. *Now,* the disease insists, as Bella takes a last long look at the happy assemblage in the great room at Deerfield. *This is it.* She can barely clump up the stairs in her high heels and reach her bedroom on her feet. She sets two sealed envelopes on the night table and gets into bed still attired in her best black wool dress, smoothes her hair to ensure no strands have escaped from her topknot. She meant to discuss all this with Jane, but Jane is smart, she'll figure it out. Then a glass of water and the pills, and the little poisoner proudly descended from a long line of Borgias has poisoned herself. As Bella's eyes close, there are many last questions or prayers she might put to God, to beg forgiveness for her sins against him, to forgive him for his sins against her. To request a vision of her mother, welcoming her open armed, be it to heaven or hell. No. Bella's last conscious plea is that no one at the party notice her absence. The last thing Charlotte's secretary wants is a shriek and a commotion while guests are in the house.

Bella gets her wish. The caterers leave the kitchen tidy and spotless. As they exit the back door, an overweight waitress bends with a grunt to pick up the final bit of debris, a soggy piece of green lettuce that got squashed under somebody's shoe. At the front door, Charlotte waves good-bye to the last guest. Then discovering herself alone amidst the echo of congratulations, she mounts the grand staircase to locate her missing secretary. "Bella?" she whispers at the bedroom door, peeking through the dark at the child-sized form beneath the covers. Well, let her sleep. She's worked hard lately and been troubled by some persistent bug that has kept her haggard and rundown. There will be plenty of time for the two of them to replay Charlotte's triumph tomorrow.

The shriek comes the following morning.

"Bella? Bella? Wake up, sleepy! Bella...? Bella! No, no, no, noooooo!"

Down in her cottage, Jane doesn't hear it, of course, yet when Charlotte's frantic phone call sends her racing to the house, she feels the shriek gathering around her, sweeping her through the front door and up the stairs, invading her eardrums, her heartbeats hammering as she runs to Bella's room and lurches to a halt three feet inside the door. There lies Bella, stiffly doll-like in her black dress, the bed covers torn back and rumpled where Charlotte tried to shake her awake. There huddles Charlotte, sobbing on the floor. A sense of incomprehensibility permeates the scene. Jane has seen corpses before, a few elderly relatives and friends lying embalmed in cushioned caskets at funeral parlors during calling hours. But here at home, in her own bed, Bella still retains an illusion of belonging in the world around her. As Jane walks cautiously forward, her own name suddenly stops her, hand lettered on a white business envelope on the bed-side table. In trepidation, she reaches for it. It contains one sheet, handwritten and neatly folded in thirds.

Miss Avery, Please take care of her. Bella.

Jane turns over the plain white paper, vainly search-ing for more. Take care of her how? And how are we to take care of you? She stares at Bella's oddly peaceful form, torn between a desire to embrace and squeeze life back into the body and a growing horror—she's dead, this is a corpse. Then she gathers herself, steps forward and gently takes Bella's hand.

"What should we do?" Charlotte cries, yet not surprisingly, predictably, Bella has seen to the next steps as well. The second envelope on the table, a manila packet, is addressed To Whom It May Concern, and glancing from that to the instruction Bella has left her, Jane thinks, *It does concern me now*. She helps Charlotte to a chair, brings a glass of water and tissue, makes the necessary phone calls. While they wait for the ambulance to arrive, Jane opens the manila envelope. On one sheet of paper is a straightforward request for a Catholic mass at St. Joseph's and private burial in the churchyard. There is also a sealed document, pre-sumably a will, addressed to Charlotte's lawyer. Finally, to satisfy the legalities and with a plea that there be no autopsy, Bella has spelled out the reason and method of her death. Ovarian cancer, the diagnosis of which can be confirmed with the doctor she visited in August. Suicide by overdose, one tablet left in an unlabeled plastic container as proof. Bella doesn't say where she obtained the pills, but it's amazing what you can get, and get cheaper, on the Internet.

Jane re-enfolds Bella's hand in hers, and the lifelessness of it, no blood rhythm, no warmth, no answering touch, sends a flood of wetness to her eyes. Charlotte, still in the dressing gown she donned when she awoke, cries brokenly behind her, slumped in the chair. In a flash, Jane understands how it has been all these years, how Bella's one crooked column of vertebrae kept two people erect, that Bella's purpose in life was to supply the backbone Charlotte lacked.

"I don't know what to do! Please help me!" Charlotte begs her.

"It's all right. Shh, it's all right," Jane soothes and goes to her.

Over the next few days Jane stays not in her cottage but in a spare bedroom in the main house. She talks to the medical examiner, to the people at the funeral home named by Bella in her instructions, to Father McCaffrey at St. Joseph's Church. She helps Charlotte compose the death notice for the newspaper. She answers the phone, the door. Bella specified there should be no wake or viewing of her body, but when Father McCaffrey solicitously inquires if the family would like to have a tea, prepared by the church ladies, in the church hall following the mass, Jane sends Charlotte's acceptance. The service takes place that Thursday morning, and afterward people approach Jane as well as Charlotte to express their condolences and reassure them it was a lovely, uplifting memorial. Personally, Jane thought the old priest dry and rather mournful, and she guesses Bella must have known this is how it would be. But overall, Bella has observed enough of the formalities to let everyone feel satisfied, including God himself.

Back at Deerfield after the burial, Charlotte begs her to stay a while in the house, and Jane reluctantly agrees. She doesn't want to make this a permanent arrangement, but she can understand Charlotte's unwillingness to be alone. The house has always seemed far too large and empty for two old women; with one gone, the place is cavernous. Yet huge as the house is, when Jane walks through it she feels increasingly trapped, as if every way she turns she'll bump into a wall. When Charlotte awakens from a fitful nap, Jane tells her firmly she must return to the cottage. She'll come again in the morning, and Charlotte can call her in the event of an emergency.

Gray-faced, Charlotte assents. Without Bella, she seems stripped not only of backbone but personality, and as Jane crosses the lawn and glances back at the house, she has a vision of Charlotte as she must have been when Bella first knew her, a moderately pretty, moderately talented, moderately rich girl. If she had possessed any one blessing in abundance, the beauty to be a great seductress, the clear gift of a great artist, enough wealth to be truly powerful, that one trait might have defined her. But Charlotte's portion in life, though more generous than most, was split three ways and diluted. Then along came Bella and attached herself to this malleable girl. Could it be that Bella was not only a backbone but a leech, as dependent on Charlotte as Charlotte was on her?

Jane shudders, both from the cold outside and at the harsh twist of her thoughts. As she enters the cottage, she gets a call from Hortense. With the exception of Melanie, the birders were at the mass that morning, but Jane hadn't much chance to speak with them or Tim, who attended with members of the land trust.

"I just wanted to ask if there's anything I can do to help out over there," says Hortense. "You looked a little tired at the church."

"I'm okay. Do you think it went all right, Hortense? I've never arranged a funeral before, not that it was much of one. But it's all Bella wanted."

"You did your job with composure and grace. Funerals are always difficult, no matter how well everyone holds up."

"Thanks. I don't think it's really sunk in yet. I don't know quite how to mourn for Bella, and in a way, I can't mourn, someone has to keep things running here, and

Charlotte is in no state to do it. Oh, that's another thing...
Hortense, I'm sorry, but I don't think it would be appropriate
for the birders to come here this Sunday for the Christmas
Bird Count."

"No, of course not, but...," Hortense's voice slows.
"Haven't you heard about the blizzard?"

"What blizzard?"

"The one they're predicting for this weekend, starting
Saturday afternoon. They're saying it could be worse than
the Blizzard of '78. Of course, they've been saying that about
every winter storm ever since it happened."

"What Blizzard of '78?" Jane shakes her head in puzzlement, having barely flipped on a TV or radio in the past
three days.

"Oh, I forgot," says Hortense. "This is your first
winter here, isn't it? You've never heard about our famous
storm. You better let me fill you in before you turn on the TV
or you'll be terrorized to death."

"Please do," says Jane, and Hortense launches into
her tale.

"Well, back in February of 1978, a raging blizzard
descended on New England. It was a whacker of a nor'easter,
and because it stayed stationery off the coast it just kept
dumping snow, snow and more snow. Most places got two
to four feet, more in drifts. I remember the cars on my street
frozen into mounds like white elephants. It shut down
virtually everything for a week, schools, offices, public
transport. Some people got stranded in their houses for days
waiting for the plows to make it through."

"That sounds serious," says Jane.

"Oh yes, it was quite serious. I don't mean to mini-
mize what nature can do. It was such an event that even now
one little snowflake will start people screaming, 'Blizzard of
'78! Blizzard of '78!' and rushing to the grocery store for
supplies in deadly fear they'll be snowbound. And it's always
bread and milk they grab off the shelves, don't ask me why.
Then the 'blizzard' turns out to be two inches of white stuff

that won't even stick together to make a snowman."

"Does this happen often?"

"At least once a winter, if the weather forecasters can whip up enough of a frenzy. It's almost a New England tradition. I expect we'd feel cheated without it." Hortense pauses for a chuckle. "Anyway, we're not canceling the bird count yet, but I'll stay in touch and let you know. If we do go, come with us, Jane, at least for a little while. You might be ready by then to get out of the house."

"Thanks, Hortense."

Jane hangs up, heats a can of chili, and flips on the six o'clock news, channel surfing to compare weather reports. It doesn't take long to discover there is indeed a strange phenomenon taking over the brains of an otherwise intelligent-seeming populace.

"We could be looking at eighteen to twenty-four inches," gloats one forecaster, as if announcing the arrival of manna from heaven.

"Turn to our website for hour by hour tracking of this potential super blizzard," urges another.

A third channel pledges their exclusive Doppler radar and team of veteran reporters will keep viewers abreast of everything they need to know, from road conditions to emergency shelters to keeping pets safe during the storm.

There are numerous references to the Blizzard of '78, although the current storm is still forty-eight hours away.

The next morning's weather reports are even more excited in tone, although Jane notes that the forecasters periodically temper their enthusiasm with a few judicious qualifiers. *Potential* is a popular adjective. *If* atmospheric conditions persist. At the same time, the radar images are beginning to look more ominous, and when she starts up to the house to check on Charlotte as promised, she's caught off guard by the frigid air that stings her cheeks, the glaze of white frost on the lawn like a crunchy carpet underfoot. Charlotte, in her dressing gown, is listless and puffy faced, and Jane finds herself in control by default. She brings in extra wood and stacks it beside the fireplace, locates matches in the kitchen, a flashlight in a utility closet. The stock of food in the cupboards and refrigerator seems adequate. Nevertheless, she makes a list of supplies, including another flashlight, batteries and bottled water. Whether the predicted storm turns out to be a doozy or a dud, it can't hurt to play it safe.

"I'll run into town and pick up what we need," she tells Charlotte, and driving in, she takes stock of Deerfield's location, the farthest residence from town along the shore road. A heavy snowfall could indeed keep them isolated for a day or two until plows arrive, and if they lose power...The vision of herself and Charlotte shivering in blankets before the fireplace in a freezing cold mansion gives Jane pause. Then common sense asserts itself. They can stay bundled by the fire, heat water if needed, they'll have plenty to eat. Just stay warm, be patient and read a good book. What did Isaac and Mehitable Mowry and the other colonial families do in the long bitter winters that were surely more severe than the current globally warmed ones? To their eyes, this fabricated panic about the storm would seem absurd.

It seems even more absurd when Jane reaches the grocery store. The shelves are wiped bare, the checkout counters are crowded ten deep. One woman has a month's supply of baby food jars and disposable diapers piled into her shopping cart. A pudgy man has a twenty-five-pound bag of cat kibble atop a case of toilet paper. Others have taken the Arctic expedition approach, heaping their carts with a mountain of canned goods. For some reason, halved peaches in syrup appear to be particularly essential to survival. Those at the head of the lines have bread and milk, sometimes as many as a dozen loaves and a half dozen gallons. Those at the end of the line grumble loudly about hoarding behavior; they got only one loaf and one gallon before the shelves went bare. All along the lines an unofficial competition is in progress to see who can top who with the most harrowing story of the Blizzard of '78.

Jane decides to forego the bottled water. Between the supplies at her cottage and the kitchen at Deerfield, she and Charlotte will be fine. She swings by the hardware store and purchases one of the few remaining flashlights and packages of batteries, then stops at the library. Burt is at the circulation desk as she hands over her selection of books.

"Hi, Burt. How's the Great American Novel going?"

"Okay." He flashes her card under the scanner to read the bar code, then the three books in quick succession.

"I thought an old-fashioned New England snowstorm would be the perfect opportunity to curl up with some novels and a cup of cocoa," she adds.

"Sure." He stamps the books with the due date and passes them to her. "January tenth. Next, please."

A mother with two children has come up behind her, and Jane steps aside to let them get their books processed. Why the cold shoulder? She hasn't seen Burt in months, but the last time she did they parted on good terms. He isn't any more friendly to the mother and the two little girls, pointedly ignoring their excitement about which storybook they're going to read first.

"I'm sorry I haven't seen you in a while," she says, stepping back to the counter when the family has gone. "I sent you an invitation to Miss Deerfield's party last week-end…You've probably heard about her secretary's death?"

"Yes." Burt relents a little. "I'm sorry, although I didn't know her. And I did get the invitation, but I couldn't make it."

"And Raven had the play that night, I know." Jane nods. "Listen, maybe the three of us could get together sometime for—"

"Raven and I split up."

The words chop down like a hatchet, and Burt presses his lips tight. Well, how would you feel if you're twenty-seven and some woman a decade older—yes, she's finally told him that—adds, Oh and by the way, I'm pregnant. She claims she didn't know early on. How can you not know you're pregnant? Now it's conveniently past the three-month mark, and that makes everything a little more difficult, though not impossible, to solve. Except she doesn't want to solve it, she's going to have the baby. He doesn't have to marry her. With or without him, she will raise the child. On her salary as a waitress? Right. Even if you toss in what he makes as a library clerk, their whole lives are about to go down the tubes, and she refuses to see it. He can forget the Great American Novel, and she can sure forget an acting career. Besides, if she lied to him about her age, how does he know she's not lying about this? Once, once they did it without protection. But there could have been other guys, he and Raven didn't live together, he wouldn't know if she was seeing anyone else. Now he's trapped, good and trapped, because even if it is his and she does absolve him of financial responsibility, do you think he wants that knowledge about himself hanging over his head the rest of his life?

Jane stares at Burt, stunned. His usually mild face is so flushed with anger he couldn't get a word out if he tried. A short line of patrons has accumulated at the checkout desk, and she backs away as Burt grabs and stamps books. He doesn't have to say anything. Jane can guess.

She drives home, reviewing the situation. The last time she saw Raven, almost three weeks ago on the Sunday walk, Raven gave no clue of this. Jane calls the playhouse and reserves two tickets for *A Christmas Carol* for tomorrow night. The storm isn't due to arrive until dinnertime, and there shouldn't be enough snowfall that evening to keep her truck from getting the few miles to the theater and back. She can see Raven and talk to her after the performance. She isn't quite sure who the second ticket is for, maybe Charlotte. She's still very listless and drained, relying on Jane to field phone calls and handle incoming mail. Hortense is right; a few hours out of the house might revive them both. Then Jane has a second thought: Tim. When he walked her to her cottage after the party, they stood kissing in the night, parting with plans to do the bird count together. In the sorrowful days following Bella's death, that plan dropped out of sight. She should call, find out where they stand. If a snowstorm is coming, wouldn't it make sense to invite him to Deerfield before the weather kicks in? Then her phone rings in her hand.

"I just called to see how you're doing," says Tim.

"I'm okay," she answers. "What is this blizzard mania that's gripped everyone?"

He laughs. "Just take it as an endearing New England quirk, although if you check *The Old Farmer's Almanac* you'll see the entry for December 20-22 does say 'severe blizzard conditions.'"

"Then there's definitely *not* going to be a blizzard," she replies, thumbing the pages of her copy, "because if you check the predictions for the first three weeks of December you'll see they also warned we'd have two snowstorms by now, neither of which has materialized."

"Nonetheless, have you got your bread and milk yet?"

"I couldn't, the store was bought out. Anyway," she continues, when they've finished laughing, "I was wondering, in view of this impending natural disaster, whether you'd like to come down here tomorrow? I have tickets for Raven's production of *A Christmas Carol*, and I know it would make her happy if we came to see it. Then I can put you up afterward. That way, if we do want to join the bird count, you wouldn't have to battle any weather to get here Sunday morning."

"I'd like that." There's no joking now, only a warmth, an anticipation between them. "I have some paperwork to clear away, but I could be there by five or a little after."

"That's fine. See you then," says Jane, and when they hang up, the prospect of being snowbound has suddenly become downright attractive.

Chapter 32

A classic New England nor'easter begins as an area of low pressure riding up the East Coast. As the low intensifies, it builds up gale force winds, pounding surf and flooding rain. Circling in counterclockwise direction, the winds smack down from the northeast, hence the storm's name. An unrelenting nor'easter can batter the Atlantic Coast for days, grinding off beaches and pulverizing shorefront architecture. In winter, as it pulls down air and snow from the frigid north, blizzard conditions can occur. Those that make the record books, like the Blizzard of '78, leave death and destruction from the Chesapeake to Maine.

Yet by five o'clock that Saturday afternoon at Deerfield, the wind is still hardly more than a stiff albeit icy breeze and not a snowflake has alighted. Jane has stopped tuning in the weather reports, which have become excessive and extremely repetitive. Several of the TV stations have turned to almost continual storm coverage, interspersed with old footage from the Blizzard of '78 and interviews with climatologists, emergency management experts, snowplow drivers and local police chiefs. One climatologist advises that to be rated a true blizzard, the coming storm must produce temperatures below twenty degrees Fahrenheit, sustained winds of at least thirty-five miles per hour, and sufficient falling and/or blowing snow to reduce visibility to one-quarter mile for at least three hours. With specific goals to root for, the media people become cheerleaders urging the storm on. Expect rapid intensification! Extreme severity! This could paralyze the region! The hyperbole and bad grammar reach new heights when a wide-eyed, baby-faced weatherman declares, "This killer storm is aimed right at us like we're staring into the ominous twin barrels of a fully loaded, half-cocked, double-barreled shotgun!"

What storm?

Jane glances out her kitchen window, though there's not much to see in the winter dark. Tim will be here shortly, and they're still on for the play. She has decided to cook dinner, which, given her lack of culinary skills and the mounting pile of vegetable peelings in the sink, should be quite a trick. What exactly is parboiling anyway? Up at the main house, only a couple of lights in the studio emit a feeble, disembodied glow, and Jane pauses, a half-skinned carrot in one hand. The picture of Charlotte alone in that stone fortress continues to disturb her. She's dressed and eating, Jane fixed them both a lunch of soup and sandwiches, and the housekeeping service has been around to do the weekly cleaning. But when she tried to help Charlotte sort out her banking and bill payments, little was achieved.

"Bella used to do this. Bella always handled that," Charlotte could only repeat when Jane questioned invoices or tried to verify amounts.

"Did she pay your accounts on-line, on the computer?"

"She did everything on the computer," Charlotte replied, and with permission, Jane accessed the financial files. Too quickly, it began to feel like an invasion of privacy. Better to contact the bank and the attorney and request they sit down with Charlotte for a meeting. If Charlotte intends to stay at Deerfield, she will need to hire a new secretary and some household staff as soon as possible. *Miss Avery, Please take care of her.* Jane shakes her head. She'll try to honor the request for the time being, but to step permanently into Bella's place is not in her plans.

"Jane! Jane, open up! It's me!"

A pounding accompanies the cheery call at the door, and she startles out of her reflections and half jumps to open it. Raven grins at her.

"Hi! I came to bring you back your tickets. Wow, cold, isn't it?" She laughs, teeth chattering, hugging herself. She's dressed in her usual inappropriate attire, a flouncy skirt and thin turtleneck sweater, laced black boots and a shaggy vest that might once have belonged to a Mongolian yak herder. The wind tosses her skirt and whips her hair, and Jane sees the first snowflakes materializing, feels the bite of tiny crystals hitting her cheeks.

"Come in," she says, beckoning.

"Thanks." Raven pulls a small envelope from her shoulder bag. "The thing is, I saw these tickets with your name on them at the box office for tonight, and I didn't want you making the trip for nothing. Because I knew you'd come, I knew you wouldn't let me down. We'll do a makeup performance next week if we can, so the tickets are still good, even for another performance next spring. March, maybe we'll do one in March, though not *A Christmas Carol*, of course." She rubs her palms. "Could we make some coffee? Decaf? I'm pregnant, remember."

"I'll put the kettle on. Are you all right?"

"Me, sure, fine. I should have grabbed a pair of gloves, that's all."

Jane eyes her doubtfully. Raven's cheeks are dark red with cold, and she inhales the warm air of the cottage in small gasps.

"Well, you didn't have to deliver my tickets. I was going to pick them up at the door tonight."

"No, but I told you. It's canceled, all the performances are canceled. Everything in town is closed, the stores, the restaurants, everything except a few bars, naturally." Raven snorts a laugh, rolls her eyes, rubs her arms. She can't seem to stay still. "Even last night, people were already staying home—can you imagine?—and I had two shows apiece booked for today and tomorrow, matinees and evenings, because I got bus tours. They called and canceled this morning, and it's not even snowing yet—can you imagine?" She flings her hands jerkily toward the windows.

"What do you mean people aren't coming?" Jane shakes her head in bewilderment. Has everyone gone crazy? It's a fifteen-minute drive at most to the theater from any point in town, and the last she heard, the snowfall won't begin to accumulate before midnight. What's wrong with these New Englanders?

"They're not coming," Raven repeats. "Okay, maybe it's not the best production ever. Bucky's gotten really jolly again about being Scrooge, and Amy got sidelined with laryngitis last night so I had to jump in as Mrs. Cratchit, not that I couldn't do it. But it's still *good*, Jane, and I couldn't have picked a better play, could I? I checked out theaters where they do *A Christmas Carol* every year, and they always get a packed house. People make it an annual holiday tradition. And the matinee, they could have come and been safely on their way home by now. They were on a *bus*. A bus can handle a little snow."

The teakettle reaches a shrill, and Jane half turns toward the sound. But Raven's face is crumbling, a gasp heaving up out of chest as her body doubles over and convulses on a sob.

"I spent all the money, Jane! Advertising, costumes, salaries, programs. I had to spend it up front to publicize, and now the bus tours want refunds. What am I going to do? I'll be sued for mismanagement and fraud!"

She drops onto the couch, head between her knees, sobbing, the teakettle shrieking like a banshee on the stove. Jane runs and shoves it off the burner, flips off the heat and runs back to her friend.

"Raven, Raven." She sits on the couch, and Raven engulfs her, sobbing. "Raven, listen, it's going to be all right. Raven, can you stop crying? Are you listening to me? Raven…"

The crying won't stop. It has a life of its own, like a

third entity on the couch between them. It wavers from giddy to nervous to a wracking pain, while Raven shudders and shakes in Jane's arms.

"It's okay," Jane repeats to no effect, beginning to feel afraid. "Raven, please." A rap sounds on the door, and with Raven clutching her, Jane can only shout over her shoulder. "Come in!"

"Hi," Tim begins, the smile dropping off his face like a rock at the sound and the sight before him. He sheds his snow-dusted jacket en route to the couch. "What's wrong?" He sits on Raven's other side, and Jane fills him in as best she can.

"Okay, Raven." He pries her arms from around Jane and squeezes one of her hands in each of his. "We're going to calm down now, okay? Listen to me, Raven. It's time to calm down."

Raven can't look at him. She bows her head, crying, while Tim keeps a firm grip, his thumbs massaging the backs of her hands, his voice maintaining a steady tone. He doesn't force her to look up or make eye contact, just keeps stroking. For several minutes more, the crying goes on. Then it stops abruptly, and Raven starts talking all over from the beginning, laryngitis, jolly Scrooge, bus tours, Tiny Tim's costume, advance ticket sales, child actors, wages, mismanagement, fired. Then suddenly there's more: Burt has turned on her, denying the baby is his. She didn't expect him to marry her, but she never imagined he'd accuse her of lying. How could he say that? How could anyone believe she would lie about her child? She isn't asking him for money. She's going to support the baby herself, she was going to make everyone proud. She had a real plan this time, to become a theater manager, a steady job with real benefits, build the playhouse into a year-round operation. And it was working, the budget was tight, yes, but they would at least have broken even. She couldn't foresee this storm and a whole weekend of lost revenues. How could anyone foresee a storm?

Jane and Tim exchange glances over Raven's head. Underneath her stream of anguish and woe is a yearning anyone can understand. To matter. To be someone. To count. To get life right. Raven blurts on, agonizing over mistakes, what-ifs, missed chances, as if she's riding a merry-go-round she can't get off, the bright music and colorful ponies blurring into one circle of grief. Finally, she exhausts herself, her voice hoarsened to a raspy whisper, her throat dry from crying, and falls silent. Jane sits on one side, Tim on the other, still stroking Raven's hands.

"I'll make us something to drink," says Jane, rising cautiously. "Chamomile tea, I think I have some."

She boils fresh water in the kettle, brews a pot and spoons honey into three mugs. Raven lifts her head to accept the drink, her face bruised and ravaged.

"I'm sorry," she whispers, her eyes pleading with Jane. "I'm sorry. It was like the whole world fell apart, everyone bailing out on me, and there in the box office was this envelope with your name."

"It's all right. I'm glad you came." Jane puts her arm around Raven's shoulder. "You want to take a nap? You look exhausted."

Raven nods. "I haven't slept much lately."

"Come on."

Jane guides her to the stairs, and Raven makes the best exit she can, wiping her cheeks and apologizing to Tim.

"It's okay," he murmurs. "Get some sleep. You're safe here."

Upstairs, Raven sits on the bed and fumbles to undo her boot laces. Jane helps her get her skirt and sweater off, finds her a sweatshirt for warmth and tucks her under the covers. In bed, Raven turns away, embarrassed, but when Jane reaches over to pat her arm, Raven catches her fingers. Jane sits on the bed until sleep loosens the contact, then wearily heads downstairs.

"Is she all right?" Tim whispers.

"Asleep," Jane confirms, keeping her voice low.

"She was pretty agitated, not that she doesn't have reason to be."

Jane reaches for her mug of tea and sips it, although it's gone cold. Once before, Raven came to her door in distress, when she first learned she was pregnant. Then she bounced back almost miraculously and charged ahead with renewed plans. It's an enviable talent, and Jane suspects that by morning, although her problems won't be any less real, Raven will be recovered and even upbeat. It's what that psychologist in California wanted her to do, break down and spill her anguish, purge herself of guilt over Jill's crash in one climactic catharsis. She couldn't, not because she's made of sterner stuff, but because that's just not how she is. Maybe someday there will be someone she wants to tell about her past, someone with whom she's planning to spend her future.

"Well, Raven obviously trusts you and was smart enough to come here," Tim continues. "But what about this guy Burt? Should we contact him?"

"No. He's not going to be any help, although he may come around in time." Jane sets down her mug. A paternity test after the baby is born should quickly settle the issue of fatherhood. Financial support can be coerced, if Raven opts to pursue it. She also grants the shock it must have caused Burt when Raven presented him with the news. Yet she can't help thinking, *What a weasel!* Burt, so noble about his literature, so ignoble when confronted with his own responsibility for life.

"Raven will probably feel better by morning," she says, "and thanks for the way you calmed her. Was that some special technique, rubbing her hands like that?"

"No, I just had a feeling we shouldn't let her ball up into herself, and maybe it helped to hear a different voice."

"Well, it worked." Jane glances toward the kitchen. "About dinner...I had this recipe, and it got as far as a pile of vegetables in the sink. Do you have any idea what parboiling is?"

"Not a clue, but I can scramble eggs."

"I can toss a salad."

"So we won't starve in the coming blizzard," says Tim, grinning.

As quietly as they can, they fix dinner. Taking their plates to the couch, they channel surf through "total storm coverage from your exclusive weather expert station," "the most up-to-date radar tracking," "the biggest network of on-call experts," and vows to be "tireless in presenting twenty-four-hour coverage of this impending catastrophe."

"It's going to be a blessing when the power does go out," says Tim, switching off. They don't need a weatherman to hear the cottage windows rattling in the increasing wind or to see the white flakes flying sideways past the panes in the blackness. Raven doesn't waken, even when the phone rings at nine o'clock.

"Oh dear, Jane," says Hortense, "I'm afraid we are going to have to cancel the Christmas Bird Count. Those blasted forecasters are right for once. Even if we don't get a full-scale blizzard, it's going to be a nasty storm. I've already talked to Roy, and he agrees."

"Can we reschedule it for after Christmas? Didn't you tell me the counting period runs until early January?'

"Yes, we'll do that. I'll contact Melanie and Russ and Charlie, although they've probably crossed it off anyway. What about that nice man from the land trust? You don't suppose he'll try to drive here tomorrow morning?"

"He's already here, Hortense."

"Oh." There's a moment of puzzlement at the other end of the line. Then, "Ohh," says Hortense. "Well, in that case I won't worry about you being alone."

She chuckles and hangs up before Jane can add that Raven is there as well, occupying the only bed. She turns to Tim. He's gotten the gist of the conversation, and he returns her rueful look with one of his own. It isn't exactly the evening they had planned.

"Look," he says, "go bunk with Raven. If you have a sleeping bag or a pillow and some blankets, I'll be fine on the couch."

"I'll see if I can get them without waking her." Jane tiptoes upstairs and down again with one blanket, her sleeping bag and a pillow. "It's all I have."

"That's fine." Tim shakes the blanket open. As it flaps past Jane, she catches the corner, and for a minute they stand holding opposite ends.

"The couch *is* a little wider if you pull the cushions off the back," she says.

"If we unzipped the sleeping bag...?"

"Spread it over the blanket...?"

"They do say that in extreme climatic conditions, you should share bodily warmth."

They step together, Tim draws the blanket around them, and their bodies close on a long, pleasurable exhalation that leaves nothing but a useless layer of clothes between them. The cottage gets steamy. Outside, the wind howls.

Chapter 33

At midnight the storm gets serious, and the snow begins to fall more thickly. From southern New Jersey through the mountains of New Hampshire it descends in blinding swirls, as if smothering the air in wet feathers. The sky is so dense with it, you can't step outside without breathing it up your nostrils, can't speak without flakes flying into your mouth. In the blackness and whirling white, all sense of direction is lost, and the wind lashes and snaps over the landscape like a whip. By dawn, what there is of gray light, eight inches cover the ground. Then the storm takes a respite, easing back to let the snow descend in constant, deceptive softness, flakes ghosting to earth, tree branches shawled in fresh white.

Melanie wakes up in the grayness, warm under her quilt, drowsing. Then her eyes blink open. This is it! The Christmas Bird Count! Her big day! She went to bed especially early to be ready for it, and Mrs. Egan made her a mug of hot cocoa with puffy marshmallows to sip before she fell asleep. She remembers waking up once very late in the dark and hearing her father's voice. He came home like he promised, and he's going to spend all the days right up till Christmas with her and after Christmas, too, maybe right till New Year's. He didn't let the storm stop him, not her daddy, and Mrs. Egan harrumphed it was all nonsense, people clearing the shelves of bread and milk when what you really wanted in a blizzard was a sturdy snow shovel and water-proof galoshes. Mrs. Egan doesn't think much of storms.

Melanie harrumphs at her mirror and gets herself dressed. Long underwear top and bottom, a turtleneck sweater, heavy corduroy pants, two pairs of socks, her hiking boots. Downstairs, no one else is awake. She pours a glass of orange juice and eats a bran muffin from the batch she and Mrs. Egan baked yesterday. Bran keeps you regular, Mrs. Egan always declares, although Melanie can't think what's not regular about Mrs. Egan, who chuffs and huffs about the house and cooks big dinners and says to people on the phone, "We do *not* take telemarketing calls, and I'll thank you to remove this number from your list!" As for Melanie, it's obvious what's not regular about her, and if bran muffins will help her brain damage get better, she'll happily eat them, besides which, they have raisins and taste good.

Still, she eats only one muffin this morning because Jane said they would take snack breaks, and Melanie loves snacks. Should she bring something to contribute? Yes, marshmallows, what a good idea! She gets the plastic bag from the cupboard. These are the big marshmallows, her favorites. The mini ones melt too fast and make a froth in your cocoa, whereas the big ones only get frothy on the outside and still have a nice squishy inside while they bob in the chocolate. Melanie puts on her scarf and jacket, stuffs the bag of marshmallows into one pocket, her bird book and cell phone in the other, slings her binoculars around her neck, dons her earmuffs and mittens, and sits waiting for Hortense and Roy to pick her up.

But they don't come, and Melanie starts to get hot. She'll wait for them on the front porch. Outside, it's like a winter wonderland, pristine and inviting, and she steps off the porch and makes a circle of footprints in the snow. Fun! She's the only one out on her street, a cul-de-sac that slopes down to the shore road, and she walks on to the corner. Won't her friends be surprised when they see her jumping and waving to greet them! But Hortense's green van doesn't appear, and only then does Melanie think to check her wristwatch. Twenty after eight? Oh no, how can that be? She twists her head left and right. Hortense and Roy wouldn't go without her! Didn't they hear her daddy say she could come this year? Or did they come early while she was asleep, and no one heard them knock or ring the bell? Oh no, oh no!

Melanie utters a cry and begins to run along the shore road. At the moment, the wind and snowflakes are light, and the eight inches on the ground are no obstacle to her pumping legs. The bird count! How could they leave her behind? They should have pounded on the door, pressed the doorbell until she awoke. She gulps air and runs harder. No storm is going to stop her! She knows the way, it's less than a mile, and when she reaches Deerfield, she's breathing so hard she's warm right down to her double-socked toes. She hurries by the front gate. No one is there waiting, or, a glance tells her, up the service drive by Jane's cottage, but if they follow their usual route, her friends will be at the pond, and she can catch up to them there. She'll take a shortcut, go a little farther down the shore road then cut diagonally across the big field toward the woods. Yes, that'll do it! She's halfway across the field when she sees a figure, and her heart and her feet stop.

The white deer.

Melanie draws in an awed breath, oblivious of the snowflakes blurring past her eyes. The white deer everybody got to see that special day in July when she wasn't there. Jane let her throw coins into the pond to make a wish to bring the deer back, and here it is. Melanie remembers the word they used, albino, and it's a doe like Bambi's mother because it doesn't have antlers. The white covers its face, neck, shoulders and back, as if it's wearing lace. She can make out the deer's brown legs like slender tree branches as the doe stands at the far edge of the field in the falling snow. They stare at each other through the white powder, the deer and the girl, as if they're figures in a snowglobe that encompasses all the visible world. The deer gracefully tilts her head, and Melanie tilts hers likewise. Then the deer raises her nose as if to feel the snowflakes hit her face, and Melanie does, too. The deer is talking to her. They've made friends. The doe knows Melanie won't hurt her.

The deer turns and slowly walks into the forest along the same path the birders always take. But Melanie has forgotten the birders, they've slipped out of her mind like last night's dream, and there's no bright red flash of a cardinal or the flapping of a blue jay or an invisible *chick-a-dee-dee-dee* to call her back to them. She follows Bambi's mother as she winds down to the pond, along its bank and across the footbridge into the second stretch of woods. As the deer moves, some of the whiteness falls off her shoulders, but when she brushes against a snowy branch, the white returns. Melanie wipes her dribbling nose on her mitten, although she doesn't yet feel cold. Deep in the trees, she isn't aware of the wind stealthily regaining force. She doesn't think how far she's come. Snow is soft, the deer is beautiful. They're going someplace magical.

"The wind's picking up again, listen," says Tim. He and Jane have been awake for a while, but they're in no hurry to get out of their makeshift sleepover on the couch. For one thing, the air on the other side of the sleeping bag is downright chilly, as they discovered several times during the night when either of them shifted in their sleep and the covers slipped, exposing a bare shoulder or thigh to goose bumps. Now that they're awake and snuggled into a nicely interlocked position on the cramped couch, neither wants to move an inch outside their toasty cocoon. The other reason they don't want to move is that this body contact just feels too good to be broken. Sharing the single pillow, lips within easy tasting distance, each with a hand free for roaming— why would anyone want to leave that? Their fingers slide and toy, their breath heats each other's neck. Again? he whispers in her ear. Again, she replies. They duck under the sleeping bag, muffling sound, grasping the increasingly askew coverings to shelter this or that body part. From above, the sleeping bag humps and twists as if two bears are trying to burrow into the same den.

"Well, well, good morning," says Raven's voice at the same instant a phone rings, and Jane, Tim and the sleeping bag fall off the couch. There's a moment of skirmishing for cover, then Jane clutches the blanket and oversteps the pile of clothes they shed last night to grab her phone. Tim, sleeping bag hastily pulled up to his waist, wriggles into his boxers under Raven's sardonic eye. She grins, a somewhat cracked grin that doesn't quite disguise her frayed face.

"How are you feeling this morning?" he asks, dropping the sleeping bag to finish his dressing.

"Fine," says Raven breezily. "Oh, I know I must have acted pretty fried last night. Well, I was fried, but it's okay now. Tomorrow is another day at Tara. Did I ever tell you about the time I played Scarlett O'Hara? It was a comedy skit, and Scarlett had narcolepsy, that thing where you fall asleep standing up, and so every time Rhett Butler thought he was going to score—"

They stop talking. Jane, wrapped in the blanket, phone crunched to her ear, is waving at them for quiet.

"No, no, she didn't, Hortense. We just woke up. Are you sure? What time did she leave? Can we do anything? Yes, let us know."

"What is it?" Tim pulls on his socks.

"Melanie. She's missing." Jane chews her lip. "Well, not missing exactly, but they can't seem to find her. They were wondering if she came here. Raven, were you awake earlier? Did you hear anyone at the door?"

Raven shakes her head. "I just came down. Are they sure she's missing? Maybe she's at a friend's or you know how sometimes they launch a huge search and then find the kid curled up fast asleep in a closet?"

"Her jacket is gone, and they found footprints outside her house, but there have been other kids playing in the street as well. Apparently, she did this once before, wandered out of her father's apartment in New York City in the winter and got lost in Central Park."

"We'd have heard her if she came here." Tim walks to the window seat and peers out. Snow is falling thick as eiderdown shaken from a skyful of ripped pillows. "Besides, everyone was notified the bird count was canceled."

"Not Melanie. She was already asleep when Hortense phoned and spoke with the housekeeper. When her father got in about midnight, the housekeeper told him, then they both went to bed. When they called Melanie for breakfast she was gone."

"Then she can't have gone far. It's only nine-thirty now." Raven perks up at the obviousness of it. "Maybe she just wanted to play in the snow. She's probably right in the neighborhood."

"I hope so." Still wearing the blanket, Jane slumps onto a stool. "Hortense said they're trying the neighbors, and her father is going to call the police."

"Why don't you get dressed?" Tim scoops up her clothes and hands them to her. "My truck has snow tires, and it's not that deep yet. We can probably get to Melanie's house and help search." He opens the door to test the validity of this statement, and a white gust blasts in.

"Shut the door! Shut the door!" Raven and Jane shout together, each hugging herself at the onslaught of cold.

"We can *try* to get to Melanie's house," Tim corrects.

"I'll come, too." Raven, still in her panties and Jane's sweatshirt, starts back upstairs for her clothes.

"No." Jane holds up a hand, recalling the flouncy skirt and Mongolian yak herder's vest in which Raven arrived yesterday. "Someone needs to stay here in case Melanie does get this far. Besides, Hortense said to sit tight. She's still at her house, awaiting word from Melanie's father."

For the next hour they take turns showering in Jane's small bathroom and eating breakfast at the dining table. Jane phones the house to check on Charlotte. She sounds lonely and listless, but as at the cottage, she has heat, utilities and food. Finally, Hortense calls again. There's no sign of Melanie. The police have begun an official search of her neighborhood.

"Let's go," says Tim.

The drive to Melanie's house is a crawl through a buffeting tunnel of wind and white cotton, visibility measured in yards. Every so often, they roll down the windows and shout into the snowstorm, "Melanie! Melanie!" in case she's somewhere along the shore road. The sound whips away, the wind blows in. When they reach the Babcock house, they find Hortense, Roy, Russ and Charlie already gathered but little to be done. The neighbors have been alerted and are combing the street. The police are traipsing the surrounding area, knocking on doors and checking toolsheds, garages and anywhere a child might hide. They share Raven's opinion that Melanie can't have gone far.

"Then why the hell can't you find her!" Peter Babcock explodes, throwing off Mrs. Egan's hands when she tries to calm him. The birders withdraw to a corner as the house erupts with distressed and strident voices. Where would she go? Why would she even go outside? To make a snowman? To rescue a stray cat or dog she saw from her bedroom window? Why doesn't she answer her phone? Everyone is so intent on making Melanie materialize that no one notices the obvious: Her binoculars and bird book are absent from the windowsill where she keeps them to look out at the birdfeeder. The police announce they'll expand the search and issue bulletins.

"Maybe we should try searching toward Deerfield," says Russ. "What if she did head that way?"

"I doubt we missed her en route," says Tim, "but we're no help here."

"I'm for it," says Roy, and the others nod. They're starting to feel in the way as Peter Babcock enters another irate exchange with a police officer. His squarish face and stocky body tense with frustration as the policeman repeats the assurance that they're doing everything in their power. Hortense advises Mrs. Egan where they're going, and the housekeeper's eyes well up in tears at the thought of Melanie lost in the woods. In Hortense's van and Tim's truck they journey back along the shore. The wind is in another lull, and the shore road is still passable, but there's no sight of the child. As they park in the service drive and trudge to Jane's cottage, the stone architecture of Deerfield emerges through a shifting white veil like a castle in a fairy tale gone wrong.

"Look!" shouts Roy. "Here!"

He has ventured a short way into the field to scan around, now he plunges forward, waving them to follow. Kitty-corner across the field marches a line of boot-sized holes punched into snow, the depressions already half filled in again. Melanie?

"But it's so far," Hortense murmurs, and yet it's not, a mere mile. Wrapped within the confines of the storm, their sense of distance blinded, they stare at each other to think they let their imaginations be so constricted. Melanie has hiked for hours with them, over rocky outcrops, up ridges, down valleys. She would go on for hours longer if only grownups didn't get so tired. As if to oblige them, the wind lifts the snowflakes in a sudden upward dance, like a can-can dancer tossing up her petticoats, and now it seems as plain as day, the trail of footsteps diminishing across the field, the same route they always take.

"Did you find her?" Raven shouts from the open door, clutching her yak vest across her chest.

"Maybe!" Jane calls.

They pile into the cottage, and Hortense phones Peter Babcock, but they can't wait for the police to arrive, not while Melanie is out there. Hortense, Russ and Charlie start off following the tracks. Roy drives Tim's truck down to the front gate to intercept the police and direct them to the cottage. Jane rings Charlotte to explain why there will be strangers tramping over her property.

"I'll get dressed and help," says Charlotte. "Please, let

me help. It's so lonely here."

"No, you need to stay at the house in case Melanie doubles back there. Go turn on all the lights in all the rooms. A friend and I will come check around the outside."

"Not you," Tim adds, catching Raven's arm as she heads with them toward the door. "You stay here so that when Roy comes with the police, you can fill them in on where everyone has gone."

Jane and Tim set out to plod through the snow around the house. Inside, the lights in the rooms come on one by one, as if Charlotte is searching for switches long in disuse. Most of the windows aren't large enough to send a strong illumination into the snowy grayness. Nevertheless, there's a chance Melanie will see them, and the task keeps Charlotte occupied. When Jane and Tim return to the cottage, Peter Babcock and the police are there, conferring over a map with Roy. Raven has been busy making sandwiches, coffee and a mess of the kitchen. Everyone wants to feel they're doing something.

"I can't believe we didn't see those footprints when we drove out this morning," says Jane, her stomach clenching.

"We didn't go that way. We weren't looking for them," says Tim.

"But maybe we should have been." She bites her lip as another thought hits. It's past one o'clock, and Melanie has been missing for over five hours now, five hours wasted. Peter Babcock doesn't lose any time reaching the same conclusion.

"I told you the first time I brought Melanie here that if anything happened to her I'd hold you personally responsible!" he yells, almost throwing himself at Jane. "You promote this place as safe and open to the public, you encourage people to hike on unmarked trails in all kinds of weather—"

Furious voices break out, Tim and Roy loudly defending Jane, the police chief ordering, "Mr. Babcock, if you can't cooperate, I'll have you driven home." The argument takes several minutes to quell, even after Tim and Roy drop out, leaving the chief to defuse Babcock's tirade.

"Don't worry," Tim whispers angrily, drawing her to him. "He's crazy. It wasn't your fault."

It wasn't your fault.

He can't have any idea how the words assault her, how the possibility of having another death on her hands stuns her mind. Her knees are starting to freeze right there in the cottage, her throat closing, her rib cage contracting on the thumping of her heart. In a minute she'll be paralyzed where she stands, just as she was every time she tried to walk toward her plane. She grabs the police chief's sleeve before the numbness can overwhelm her.

"Let's go, let's search!" she pleads, and the cop orders everyone out except Raven and Roy, who are to keep a lookout around the cottage in case Melanie returns on her own. Tim shoots Peter Babcock a glare and takes Jane's hand, never guessing how her legs are trembling, how grateful she is to him for physically pulling her toward the door. Her feet stumble over the sill, then correct and gain their balance as they hit the snow.

"You all right?" Tim asks.

"Yes," she says, feeling her body begin to work again as she steadies herself on his arm. "Yes, I'm fine, let's go."

"Well, I like that," huffs Raven to Roy as the door closes on everyone's exit. "How come we always have to stay behind?"

"Because you're wearing a dead sheep and I'm old," retorts Roy, disgruntled in turn. They clean up the kitchen from the sandwiches and coffee, then Roy zips on his jacket. "It doesn't need two of us to be here. You stay. I'm going to catch up with them."

"Well, I like that!" Raven shouts after him. "And it's not a dead sheep! It's llama wool or something!"

She sits alone on the couch, hugging her knees to her chest. Can't she do anything right? Can't she contribute anything? But how was she to know when she sought refuge here last night that she should have come dressed for a rescue mission?

"Okay," she says aloud, "at least I can turn on the TV and get an update for everyone on what this storm is doing." She presses the remote, and nothing happens. She tries the light switches and gets only a useless click. Great, now she's probably single-handedly caused a county-wide power outage. Then the cottage phone rings.

"Jane?" Charlotte's voice wavers. "Is that you?"

"No, it's Raven. Jane is out searching. In fact, everyone except me is out searching."

"Oh...I've lost power. I was supposed to keep the lights on for the little girl, but they've gone out. Is there any news of her?"

"No, Miss Deerfield. They're still looking."

There's a pause at the other end of the line.

"Please," says Charlotte, "I'm afraid. Can I come stay with you?"

Raven looks out at the falling snow. Though it's not far, she can't picture Charlotte trekking to the cottage, and what is she accomplishing here? She'll leave the door unlocked, tape up a big sign that says, MELANIE, COME IN! and write a message for the others to say where she's gone. Raven pats her shaggy vest, which, thank you very much, happens to be perfectly warm.

"Don't worry, Miss Deerfield. You stay put. I'll come take care of you."

As the afternoon wanes and the grayness deepens, the temperature drops to ten degrees, visibility hovers at a quarter mile, and the wind gusts to fifty miles per hour. The meteorologists are overjoyed; they have met the criteria and can now officially proclaim this storm a blizzard, or would if they could only get on the air. So far it doesn't rival in fierceness the Blizzard of '78, but there's still hope. The low that brought this nor'easter up the coast is holding stationery over New England. The winds might pick up further, and the snow keeps falling.

The searchers straggle back to the cottage in twos and threes, cheeks chapped, lips cracked, toes and fingers burning as they slowly return to life. Their voices are hoarse from shouting Melanie's name. In town, there has been no success either. The police, neighbors and other searchers have checked the school, library, park and anywhere else they can conceive a child might have gone. If Melanie did leave the house for a specific destination, she didn't arrive. She's either wandering aimlessly or huddled down somewhere and drifting into hypothermia. Exhausted and beaten, Peter Babcock becomes belligerent nonetheless when the police announce the search is over until tomorrow morning.

"That's it, Mr. Babcock," the chief repeats sternly. "It's time to get everyone home for the night."

"Wait a minute—"

Everyone turns to Hortense. As her eyes travel the group crowded into the cottage, her expression reconfigures from weariness to dismay to fear.

"Wait a minute," she begs them. "Where's Roy?"

Chapter 34

An hour after she began following the deer, Melanie is growing confused, although it's not the weather that disconcerts her. When the snowflakes started to nip her cheeks up on the ridge, she pulled up her jacket hood, snapped it under her chin, and tugged her scarf over her nose. As she descends into the valley, she's out of the brunt of the wind once more. What's confusing is the deer. Albino means white, but does it mean always white or does it mean an animal can change color, from white to brown and back again? Because that's what her deer seems to be doing. First the whiteness is on the doe's head and ears and back as she moves ahead of Melanie through the woods. Then the deer takes a little bound, a kick of her hind legs to jump over a log, and some of the whiteness shakes off. A few minutes later, the lacy pattern spreads over her again like a doily. Melanie wishes the deer would let her get closer. She loves those movies where the pretty girl feeds fawns or birds or even savage animals like lions, right out of her hand.

"Deer! Deer! I have marshmallows!" Melanie calls, although not too loudly because she doesn't want to startle Bambi's mother. The doe looks over her shoulder, her large brown eyes pondering Melanie, then ambles on, inviting the child to follow. It feels like magic unfolding.

Then the deer disappears. How did that happen? Melanie heard a noise behind her and turned to see if someone else was coming. It took her a minute to locate and identify the sound, a heavy limb creaking in the wind. When she turns back, the deer is gone, and all she sees is a welter of snowflakes falling in the forest, icing the bare trees, mounding on the sloping branches of the pines. The latter sight reminds her of Christmas trees, and she recalls her favorite ornaments, the blue velveteen bear dancing on a red ball, the little gray mouse clutching his wedge of Swiss cheese, a miniature copper teapot, the set of four carved wood birds Mrs. Egan gave her. There are a lot of others that Melanie always forgets she has, and when they emerge from their tissue paper wrapping in the big storage box, it's like getting new presents every year.

Now what was she thinking? Melanie waits for a new thought to enter her head. She's hungry, that's it. She takes off her mittens long enough to eat six marshmallows. They're good mittens, leather outside and thickly lined in curly fleece, and when she slips them back on, they make her hands warm again. She sets off after the deer, but there's no trace. At least now she can tell the others she has seen it, too.

It's then Melanie remembers she's supposed to be on the Christmas Bird Count, and it's strange she hasn't met up yet with Hortense, Roy or Jane. And where are the birds? She looks and listens, sees and hears nothing but trees, snow and wind. Maybe she should go back to the bridge and meet the others there? Yes, that's what she'll do. The problem is, Melanie is already lost and doesn't realize it and gradually getting tired. When she comes upon a big pine tree, she decides to rest. The pine's drooping branches come almost to the ground, and she crawls underneath them to the trunk. There is almost no snow in here, only a nice bed of pine needles, and Melanie is fat and she's warm. She curls up and falls asleep.

When she awakens, it's darker than she expected, even after she wriggles out from beneath the pine boughs. She's beginning to think she may be lost, but that's all right. She has her cell phone, and she'll give her daddy a call. Except the phone doesn't work. Uh-oh, did she forget to charge it again? But even that doesn't quite worry her because—smart girl!—she knows what to do when you're lost in the woods. Hortense and Roy have told her this many times. You hug a tree, and someone will come find you. But which tree should she hug? This one's trunk is too scratchy when she snuggles her cheek against it, and that one's too big to get her arms around. Melanie searches on. Once or twice, she imagines she hears her name far away like an echo. When the sound doesn't come again, she resumes her wandering. At last, she finds the perfect tree. It has smooth grayish bark, and it's halfway down a ledge in the lee of the wind. That's good because it's getting colder and dark, and Melanie has tramped through a lot of territory today. She brushes the snowfall off the tree's roots and wraps her arms around the trunk. She yawns.

It's not by any woodcraft or tracker's skills or even some intuition that Roy finds her an hour later. It's pure luck, because Roy is lost as well.

"Melanie!" he shouts, his reedy voice cracking in the wind, and a movement a dozen feet below him snags his eye. "Melanie!"

Melanie's head snaps up, and her mittened hand waves. She smiles. See? Hug a tree and someone will come find you. It worked. Smart girl!

"Stay there, Melanie! I'm coming to get you." Roy slides down the ledge, losing his footing and bruising his hip hard on a jutting rock. It's painful, but not nearly as painful as the cold that has already benumbed his nose, fingers and toes. When he tries to stop on the small shelf of rock where Melanie hugs her tree, his boots miss a step and he slithers halfway off the ledge. Melanie yelps a frightened cry, and Roy, grabbing a tree root, catches himself in time. Huffing for breath, he hauls himself up next to her.

"I'm all right," he bluffs, his ribs aching. "We're going to go home now."

They start up the ridge, but it's steeper than you would have thought going down. Both bundled in heavy clothes, Roy's hip grinding in pain, neither one of them is agile at climbing upward. Melanie takes off her mittens to get a better grip on the rocks with her bare hands, and with Roy boosting her from below, they make it to the top of the ridge. The full blast of the wind hits them again.

"Hurry, Melanie." Roy bundles her along in the growing twilight, squinting into the needling snow. He's feeling a little dizzy, too much exertion for a man his age, too much energy expended. He felt fine when he set out, walking vigorously, bellowing Melanie's name, propelled by a self-decree that no one was going to give up until they found the child. He was still steady on his feet when he crossed the footbridge, though his eyes were watering. He made his way to the first ridge mostly by feel. Then he thought he should strike northward, and heading into the wind he plodded step after step. It seemed to take hours, and when there was no sight of Melanie, he gave up and started south again.

Except, of all things, he came to a cemetery, an old cemetery by the look of it, although he wasn't about to stop and dig the headstones out of the snow to satisfy an idle curiosity. Instead he kept on. If he had lifted his head, he might have seen one of the PRIVATE PROPERTY–NO TRESPASSING signs Jane posted along the Deerfield boundary in October when she was worried about the hunting season, and he would have known he was going the wrong way, crossing westward into the state forest. But that's what Melanie did, too, and it's by that luck Roy found her. Now they both think they're still somewhere in Deerfield, and when they try to apply their knowledge of the paths and trees, the broken stumps and other landscape marks they've come to know over the summer, they only stray farther off course.

"Roy? Can we have a snack break? I brought marshmallows."

They find a cleft between two large rocks and huddle out of the wind to eat the marshmallows, soft and white like the snow. "Melanie," says Roy, "do you have your cell phone?" She digs it out of her pocket for him, dang-blasted gadgets, everyone always yammering on them, but he's glad she carries one now. Only it doesn't work—is he punching the right buttons? Everything is getting fuzzy, like they want to sleep, and Melanie yawns, patting her hand to her mouth.

"Where are your mittens?" Roy fusses, and it's funny about their voices. They can hear each other, but no one can hear them, so their words seem to echo away as if dispossessed of actual sound. Melanie can't imagine where her mittens are, so Roy takes off his gloves and fumbles them onto her reddened fingers. He stuffs his hands in his jacket pockets. Melanie asks if they should find another tree to hug. There's a big tall one over there, but Roy's legs are having trouble moving. He pushes Melanie deeper into the cleft and turns his back to the opening to shield her. As their thoughts drift into unconsciousness, Melanie yawns a story to Roy about a white deer.

Hours later, Roy wakes. The air is quieter, the wind and snow finally tapering. Maybe it's the quiet that brings him back almost to consciousness. He can hear himself think again. The sky is gray-black, still muffled in overcast, no glimpse of moon or stars. Mostly, what Roy feels is cold. His hands in his jacket pockets are frozen into half-curled claws. His boots lie like rocks at the end of stumps, no feeling in his legs from his shins down. He snuggles against Melanie, absorbing her bulk but no warmth. Forget moving his joints. They're welded shut with ice, and his vertebrae form one long, knobby icicle. His sparse eyebrows and eyelashes have gone brittle, and when he tries to run his tongue around the inside of his mouth, his teeth feel like a row of those miniature ice cubes they put in fancy cocktails. Hell, I'll be lucky to survive the night, he thinks, and the words sound in his head like he's heard them somewhere before. Did Jimmy Stewart say that in a movie?

Roy works a little spittle into his mouth and swallows it to make his throat feel less sore. Then he blinks a few times. There's something watching him in that tree Melanie wanted to hug, a big white bird. A snowy owl, yup, he's seen a few in these parts before. It's a cyclic thing. Most years they stay up north in the Arctic tundra, then you'll get one of those irruptions that bring them farther south. Usually, you see them during the day; unlike most of their nocturnal brethren, snowys are diurnal. Their preferred habitat is prairies, fields and beaches; they perch on haystacks, posts, dunes. Roy's mind scrolls effortlessly through the bird's ID, comforting to him as the psalms in the Bible might be to someone else in his situation. Except birder that he is, he can't help niggling over the habitat. You wouldn't normally see a snowy in a forest, they go for open spaces, although a storm like this could be a disruptive factor. The bird turns its head slightly, focusing a pair of sharp eyes on Roy. Wait a minute…That bird isn't wide or plump enough to be an owl, and that head's not owl-shaped either. What's the matter with him that he didn't spot that instantly? How embarrassing to jump to a wrong conclusion! That can be a bad habit with birders, getting hasty because everyone wants to be the first to claim a rare sighting. This isn't an owl at all. It's a big white hawk.

Roy grunts in satisfaction, and for a drowsy minute he and the bird contemplate each other. Wait a minute…a big white hawk?

Roy's mind leaps to attention, and his mouth opens in a gasp. It's the only part of his body still moving, and immediately his lips clamp shut at the intake of frigid air. Now only his mind keeps going, racing fast enough for all of him. A big white hawk, as large as a snowy, immaculate white head and breast, and unless it's a trick of the falling snow, he can glimpse black speckling in uniform rows on the wings and upperparts. Rapidly and systematically he eliminates bird after bird from the pages imprinted in his memory, accipiters, harriers, buteos—wrong size, wrong habitat, wrong coloration—eagles, osprey, skip right over the vultures, get to falcons. He knows what it is, oh, he knows what this bird is! But he forces himself through every possibility, male, female, adult, immature, dark phase, gray phase. He *knows*!

It's a gyrfalcon in white phase, a two-foot tall creature from the Arctic. To have one show up on the south coast of New England isn't unheard of, but none of the birders Roy knows has ever seen one here. They've had to go way north into Canada, north of the Maritimes. And this bird is magnificent, piercing black eyes, bayonet talons in yellow feet gripping the tree branch, pointed wings folded over a long, tapering tail. In medieval falconry, the gyrfalcon was the bird of kings, and some people attributed to it magical powers. Now it stares at Roy in regal impassivity, and Roy blinks back tears. The only possible fault, the only possible mistake in his identification, is that the habitat is still not quite right. Arctic barrens, his book would say, seacoasts, open mountains. But it's precisely when you have a storm like this that birds get blown off course and come to rest in a strange realm.

"Melanie." Roy nudges her with his chest because none of his limbs are moving, and his whisper breathes a frost on her jacket hood. "Melanie, wake up and look." She makes no answering movement, but this doesn't worry him. The bird isn't going anywhere. It's taking shelter just as they have done, and it will be there come morning. The gyrfalcon regards Roy in all its majesty, and he sees along its silhouette how the white feathers ruffle in the departing wind. He's certain, one hundred percent certain of his sighting, and that's the great thing about birding, isn't it? Keep watching long enough and anything can happen. Be patient and something extraordinary may alight before your eyes.

Chapter 35

There are some things no one will ever know.

They won't know that it wasn't an albino deer that led Melanie into the woods but an ordinary white-tailed doe, her brown coat powdered in clinging snow. They won't know there was a deer in the story at all, because when Melanie awakens from her hypothermic coma in the hospital, she can't remember anything of the twenty-four hours she was lost. Her mind is as blank as a sheet of paper, so other people fill it in for her.

They tell her she ate marshmallows to survive, they found the empty plastic bag in her jacket pocket, and Melanie willingly agrees because she does like marshmallows. They tell her that her bird book was in her other pocket, her binoculars around her neck, but her mittens were lost. Melanie is sorry about that. It's bad to lose things, but although she bites her lip in contrition, no scolding is forthcoming. Instead they hug her as they recount the frantic search, the endless night, and who is she, sweet pliant Melanie, to disagree? She listens carefully to their accounts and speculations of what she must have been thinking when she left her house, the route she took, the emotions she felt. You must have been cold, freezing, terrified, exhausted, worried, confused, lonely, scared. You were brave, coura-geous, smart, enduring, persevering, lucky, plucky. Melanie absorbs this fascinating information about herself, learns her adventure in their words. It's like a lesson at school where everyone else is smarter than you are, so the best course is to stick with the answers they give. In future, Melanie's memory of the event will be the story they have taught her.

No one will ever know that Roy saw his five hundredth bird, and what a bird it was! A gyrfalcon, oh Roy, how splendid! Hortense would exclaim if she knew, and Russ and Charlie would clap him on the back. They might head to the café for a celebration, tramp in in their snowy boots, warm their faces over steaming mugs of coffee, the others understandably a little envious but all the more eager to press on for that next miraculous sighting themselves. They won't know that Roy died happy, drifting off into a peaceful sleep while the gyrfalcon kept watch above. When the bird flies off in the calm light of dawn, it doesn't leave behind a telltale feather in the snow. This is nature, not a fairy tale.

It's a pair of deer hunters who find Melanie and Roy that next morning. Attired in fluorescent orange hats and vests, toting expensive guns, they contact the forest rangers on their phones and report their exact latitude and longitude on their hand-held GPS. Melanie's father thanks everyone for their effort, but his gratitude comes through gritted teeth. This whole rescue was botched from the beginning. The police should have been out in force the minute he called them, they should have had training in blizzard-type conditions, they should have exercised strict control over the various search parties both at Deerfield and in town. It's true the search was ill-coordinated, Hortense, Russ and Charlie plowing away across the estate before the police arrived, Roy impulsively taking off on his own and look what came of that. But what most appalls Peter Babcock is that in an unguarded moment in the middle of that long dark night, his daughter lost in the woods, he accepted that she might be dead. He *accepted*. It's the only thing that keeps him from suing everyone involved in this disaster, and to make up for it he'll ensure that once Melanie is safe at home, she will never be allowed out again.

Roy gets a hero's funeral. His son comes from

Oregon, his daughter from Florida. The old grandfather nobody could be bothered to visit is suddenly worth claiming as a relative, even by the self-centered teenaged grand-daughter whose scorn of Jimmy Stewart in *It's a Wonderful Life* prompted Roy to turn off his hearing aid. Hortense speaks the eulogy, forbidding herself to get weepy even when she describes Roy and Melanie together on their bird walks, ambling along at the end of the line, holding hands. Hortense naturally doesn't reveal the reason for this arrangement, namely Roy's persistent intestinal gas, and it doesn't diminish the deep affection between the old man and the forever-child girl. What everyone will remember is that it was Roy who found Melanie, who clearly gave up his gloves to keep her hands warm, who nudged her into the cleft between the rocks so his body could protect hers from the brunt of wind and snow. It never occurs to anyone that Roy himself was lost. No, he kept on until he found Melanie and was leading her to safety when night and the cold overtook them. Then he sacrificed himself to save her. The entire church is weeping by now, but Hortense, as always, bucks up and carries on. Jimmy Stewart would approve.

Another thing no one else will ever know: Why, after fighting, prevaricating, insinuating and delaying for years, would Charlotte Deerfield suddenly draw up a document stating her intent to create at her estate a nonprofit nature sanctuary to be administered by a board which she is to chair?

"I never authorized such a document!" Charlotte screeches at her lawyer, snatching it from him to peer at the line awaiting her signature. It's two days after Christmas, one day after Roy's funeral, and the attorney has requested a meeting at Deerfield to witness the signature and begin implementing the provisions of the trust. He asked Jane to attend also, because Jane, stunned to hear it, is named as the sanctuary's executive director.

"But this is what your secretary said you wanted," the lawyer protests. "She brought you the draft for your approval, then she and I met several times to revise it. I can give you the dates of our meetings." He pulls out a leather-bound planner and flips through the pages. "I was given to understand she was acting on your instructions while you were busy preparing for your retrospective at the art association."

"No! No!" Charlotte would pull at her hair if the gesture made any sense. She was just beginning to recover from Bella's death and feel she could go on when the little girl Melanie went missing on her property. After the power went out and Raven came to stay with her, they lit candles and by themselves got a decent blaze going in the fireplace in the great room. Raven stayed overnight, the two of them camping before the fire, eating sandwiches they made in the kitchen, and talking till late about the meaning of life. Raven told her everything, about her acting career, her pregnancy— what a fascinating, dangerous existence! The whole episode had inspired Charlotte to believe she could be independent and strong, until now.

"No, no," she says again to the lawyer, but the words are losing their force. What, after all, is she going to do with Bella gone? How will she maintain this echoing mansion and three hundred acres of land? Bring in a troop of servants, most of them lazy and dishonest, strangers in her home? Yet at the very least she will require a secretary and companion, a groundskeeper or handyman. Her glance falls pleadingly on Jane. *Help me, help me!* It's the same cry she uttered when, sixteen and pregnant, she ran to Bella, the cry that forever after shaped her life.

Jane, on the verge of becoming executive director of a newly created nature sanctuary, is trying to comprehend this incomprehensible turn of events. This is the sealed document Bella left in the manila envelope on her bedside table, and Jane had presumed it was her will. But think of it—what did Bella have to leave to anyone? She owned no house or land, no personal bank account or investment portfolio. She had no need of such; whatever final disposition Charlotte might eventually have made of her estate, it was always understood there would be a comfortable provision for Bella, should Charlotte predecease her. As for her personal belongings, there's her sewing machine and a few jeweled brooches and bracelets, gifts from Charlotte or one of the three husbands to acknowledge Bella's devoted service or a birthday here and there. Bella left no instructions regarding these items, apparently willing to let them revert to Charlotte. As for the rest, who needs some two dozen dark-colored dresses sewn for a stunted woman with a misshapen spine?

But why me? Jane thinks, staring at her name on the document. Because I'm here? The likely candidate? Or because I know what's in the cemetery? Is this a way to buy my silence by linking me inextricably to this place? She and Bella never got to have that talk in her cottage, nor did Jane ever hand in her notice on the first of December as planned. Meanwhile, this very morning she's had a call from one of the engineering firms to which she sent her resume. Can she come after New Year's for an interview? The salary is good, the situation promising. Yes, she told them, I'll come. It's not a bombshell she wants to drop on Charlotte today.

The attorney is already backpedaling. "Miss Deerfield, if there is any question that your secretary did not have your authorization to draw up this document, then of course we'll shred it and simply continue your existing arrangement with the town and the land trust concerning public access to your property."

"Jane and I will have to discuss it," says Charlotte, rising a bit unsteadily. Whatever else she has accused Bella of being in the past, her secretary was never frivolous. Bella did this on purpose to make her understand, and Charlotte does, and it makes her afraid. She never really thought she was going to die.

Over the next few days, as Charlotte frets and debates aloud the future of Deerfield, Jane offers comforting, neutral replies. Often, Charlotte asks her to come help with paperwork and correspondence, then to stay for lunch or dinner, which she expects Jane to prepare. Jane offers to teach her about Bella's computer, but Charlotte doesn't want to learn. She insists on raising Jane's salary to three hundred dollars a week to recompense her for the extra responsibilities, and Jane reluctantly accepts. She can guess what people in town are thinking, that this is a pretty cushy deal she's fallen into, walking into Deerfield a stranger last March and now she's Charlotte's private secretary and confidential adviser? Knew a good thing when she saw it, didn't she? Two old ladies living alone, no heirs, a valuable property ready to drop into someone's lap. Her suspicions are confirmed when the director of the art association telephones to lavishly assure Jane that naturally she, as well as Charlotte, is invited to the cocktail party the woman is holding on New Year's Eve.

Jane heads into town to the library and corners Burt.

"Listen, Burt, remember when we first met you told me you'd done some research on the Deerfield family, and you hinted there were secrets that had never come out?"

"That's right," says Burt defensively. Jane has caught him in the reference section where he's shelving books, and from her aggressive approach, he thought she might be coming to have a showdown with him about Raven. Burt is still stubbornly unready either to own up to any responsibility for the baby or to admit he's being a cad, yet guilty enough to feel paranoid that any friend of Raven's he meets might belt him for it. But it seems to be his novel that has provoked Jane's ire, and this he resents. He is determined to be a great writer, his opus is already over five hundred pages and practically halfway through the story, and he's not about to give away any surprise endings, although he hasn't a clear conception what the ending will be yet. Moreover, he's sticking by his claim that he doesn't betray people's lives, that everything he writes is pure unadulterated fiction. Burt won't truly become a writer, let alone a great writer, until he realizes the untruth of that. There is no such thing as fiction, only the universal experiences reshaped into new truths.

"You have to tell me what you know." Jane grabs his

sleeve, intent on an answer. As long as she's here, she would like to belt him on Raven's behalf, but the issues between Raven and Burt are something only they themselves can resolve. "I'm helping Miss Deerfield plan for the future of the estate, and if there's some unacknowledged heir, an illegitimate child, a mad sister in an insane asylum, anything, you have to tell me."

She practically shakes him, and offended both at her manner and her melodramatic plot twists, Burt scoffs. "Of course, it's not that. It's about opium."

"Opium?"

"The Deerfield family fortune was founded on the China Trade, and everybody thinks that means tea and porcelain and carved ivory. Sure, that's what they brought back, but what did they take over to barter? The Chinese were self-sufficient, they were the Celestial Empire, and they didn't need any knickknacks from the barbarians, which is what they considered all foreigners."

"Get to the opium, Burt."

"I am. What I'm saying is that the American traders had a few goods the Chinese wanted, namely furs, ginseng and sandalwood, but what the Chinese really fell for was opium. Most American merchants picked it up in Turkey and India en route to the Orient where they traded it to the Chinese. That's how the Deerfields really made their fortune. They were drug dealers."

Jane lets go her grip. "When was this?"

"From the early 1800s to the Opium War in the 1840s when China was finally opened to trade under modern conditions. I found proof of their involvement in some moldy sea journals in the historical society archives that nobody but me took the trouble to read."

"And that's it? That's the big secret?"

Burt looks miffed. "Would you like it known that your family fortune was founded on opium and that you helped spread addiction and misery throughout a population?"

"No, of course not," Jane agrees to placate him, although from what she recalls of American, and indeed, world history, most fortunes and empires are built by oppressing or exploiting someone, and to the best of her knowledge, no one is ostracizing the present-day Rockefellers and Vanderbilts because their ancestors were robber barons. "I just thought there might be something more recent, some family member I should get in touch with."

"Well, there may be distant cousins, and they always said Miss Deerfield's father was a playboy, so I suppose there could be illegitimate children. Why do you care? It's not as though she's on her deathbed, is she?"

He raises a suspicious eyebrow. Great, thinks Jane, should Charlotte die unexpectedly in the near future, people will probably assume I murdered her.

"No, she's fine. Okay, thanks, Burt. I'm going to the theater to see Raven. She told me she has some big plans." She lets the sentence be a quasi-question, inviting him to reply.

"I wouldn't know," says Burt stiffly. "I have to get back to work."

Raven is her old self again when Jane arrives at the theater restaurant. She's waiting tables and seeing her therapist, and although she won't be going back on the Prozac as long as she's pregnant, she hardly needs it she's so upbeat. Can you believe she was ready to do herself in that night the blizzard broke and she showed up at Jane's? Talk about overacting! Now that her head is back in the right place, everything will be fine.

"What about the canceled performances of *A Christmas Carol*?" Jane asks, sipping her coffee. It's early lunch, only a few customers to serve, so Raven has a minute to sit and talk.

"All straightened out. I mean, the books were a disaster, but no one could blame me for a blizzard, could they? The accountant is going to hocus-pocus it into a tax write-off or some such loophole for what I overspent in the budget.

Must be nice to have enough money to squirrel around like that. Of course, no one will ever hire me as a theater manager again, but now I know something important about myself, namely that I'm not cut out for an administrative job. It's just not me, and fortunately, my therapist helped me get to the bottom of that delusion." Raven rolls her eyes in self-exasperation.

"Then what's the new project you have coming up?"

"A cabaret to chase away the winter blues! Bucky and Eileen thought of it, and Eileen is going to direct. Music, dancing, comedy. You'd come out on a winter night to see that, wouldn't you? To have dinner and a few drinks and a lot of laughs? I play a vixen in one of the skits. Don't you think I'll be great at it?"

Raven parts her lips, and a come-hither look steals into her eyes. Her body posture elongates, her breasts tauten. The changes are so subtle you almost don't realize what's happening, and she's wearing a mustard-yellow waitress uniform and white apron beneath which is the growing bulge of a four-month pregnancy. Yet it's not a pose, it's a trans-formation, and Jane says admiringly, "You'll be terrific," remembering how Raven astounded her and everyone else with her portrayal of Maggie the Cat. If she can play Scarlett O'Hara with narcolepsy, she can play a pregnant vixen. Then the vixen vanishes, and she's Raven again, as if anyone, least of all Raven herself, understands who that really is.

"Meanwhile, I can still hit New York for auditions," she continues. "Brandon says I can crash with him anytime, and he'll help me however he can. You don't mind?" She reaches for Jane's hands and draws them to her so they're clasped halfway across the table. "I know you and Tim are sort of together now, but if you have any feelings left for Brandon, I promise I won't get involved with him. He's doing really well, they made his character on the soap opera a regular, did you know? And he asked about you when we talked on the phone."

Jane pauses a moment, although the situation doesn't require much contemplation. Brandon never actually said goodbye to her, but then he probably never considered their affair to be over. It just went on hiatus with an option for renewal at some future date.

"No, I don't have any feelings for Brandon, except to wish him success. You, too. I hope you get some great roles."

"I will. Wait and see."

At a nearby table, a couple pushes away their plates and looks around. The man signals Raven.

"Waitress, could we get our check?"

"Absolutely, sir." Raven pops up and gives Jane's hands a squeeze. "You're a really good friend, Jane."

She pops over to the customers' table, chatting vivaciously as she presents their bill and clears the plates. How she's going to get acting jobs in New York or get involved with another man when she's five months away from delivering a baby, Jane can't imagine. But that's Raven, and should this plan fall apart, it occurs to Jane that she knows someone with a big house and a lot of empty rooms where Raven could stay when the baby comes. Might Raven eventually take Bella's place?—not, Jane thinks, that anyone could ever fill Bella's high heels. But Charlotte and Raven have a lot in common, and for companionship's sake…Jane's tab is already by her coffee cup, and she leaves the payment and slips away, musing.

That night Tim phones. She hasn't told him or anyone else about the document moving Deerfield a step closer to becoming an official nature sanctuary. Charlotte could still tear it up, revise it, turn around and hand the property to the town or the art association. She's hinted at these options, almost as if begging Jane to push her into a decision. Then haughtily gathering herself up, she'll coldly remind Jane exactly whose property this is. Jane says nothing; it's not really her with whom Charlotte is arguing. It's the last tug of war between Charlotte and Bella, as if Bella is present in the room.

"Tomorrow is New Year's Eve," says Tim, "and I know with all that's happened, it hasn't exactly been a festive season for you, but is there any chance you feel like celebrating with me? It could be just a quiet night, if you want."

"Thanks, I can't." Jane hears his disappointment in the silence at the other end of the line. Tim came to Roy's funeral, called the day after to ask how she was feeling, accepted her answer that she needed a little time. Now she has to say it again. "I need a little time. I have to feel my way through some things that are still up in the air."

"Well, if you need a sounding board…"

"I have to be my own sounding board, Tim."

He backs off, and they talk about the possible acquisition by the land trust of a twenty-eight-acre parcel of wetland and a beetle species recently added to the state endangered list. After the night they spent together, he must be wondering why they're discussing insects at all. Jane musters a few artificial remarks, feeling the emptiness in her chest. She hasn't told him about the job interview either. It's in Washington, DC, far enough away to make a difference. Finally, she has to close the conversation.

"Tim, it's not you, it's me, and I don't mean that in the typical dating sense because I do very much want to see you again." She pauses for his reply.

"Okay," he says without pique. "If it's you, figure it out and get back to me."

He hangs up, and she misses his voice, the pleasure of connection to him even over the phone. It's dark outside the cottage, and Jane sits on the sofa alone.

Chapter 36

In the end, Bella wins that tug of war.

On the morning of New Year's Day, Charlotte peremptorily phones her lawyer and Jane and asks them to come witness her signature on the document Bella drafted outlining the establishment of a nature sanctuary at Deerfield. She reached the decision the evening before, after attending the cocktail party at the home of the director of the art association. Despite the holiday season being on the wane, she continues to receive an unprecedented number of invitations to luncheons, dinners, fundraisers and charity balls. Do people assume that since Bella's death she is lonely and in need of cheering up? Or do they assume that since Bella's death, she's likely to be thinking of her own mortality and therefore willing to hear about worthwhile causes that would welcome her esteemed patronage? In fact, both assumptions are true. Charlotte is terribly lonely, in bed at night, she cries herself to sleep missing Bella, and it scares her to contemplate her own eventual death and not know for sure what her final legacy will be. For both reasons, she accepts almost every invitation that comes her way.

"Besides, if I don't go to their parties, who will come to my funeral?" she asks the paintings ringed around the walls of her studio, as she waits for Jane and the lawyer to arrive. Who will come indeed? Had Charlotte died first, you can be sure Bella would have whipped every last breathing body in town into church and compelled a notable contingent of old friends and acquaintances from New York to put in an appearance as well. The pews would have been filled shoulder to shoulder, the volume of the hymns would have echoed off the vault. Anyone passing by would have stopped at the size of the crowd leaving the church and asked the driver of the hearse, "Did someone important die?" This would have made Charlotte happy.

Now, with the examples of Bella's and Roy's modest funerals fresh in her consciousness, she can't help but have premonitions about her own. She wants her passing to be a monumental loss, as Bella's is to her, and increasingly the feeling has crept over her that it will only be somebody else's gain. Maybe her only choice is to decide whose gain it will be. For a moment she's seized by a desire to bedevil them all and bequeath every square acre and every last cent to the Hare Krishna. Let the whole town have conniptions when they're overrun by chanting hippies in saffron robes! But when she turns to share the delicious joke with Bella, the studio is empty and the chortle dies in Charlotte's throat. Could Jane fill this empty place? She has proven herself highly capable at whatever she undertakes, and if she is going to be executive director of the sanctuary, why not Charlotte's personal secretary as well? That may even have been Bella's ulterior motive in creating the professional position for Jane. But Jane will never have Bella's sense of humor. There will be no more malicious cracks about the bad artists at the art association or attempts to sacrifice them to the heat and mosquitos on painting excursions to the pond. It will be efficient, but it won't be any fun.

Jane and the lawyer arrive, and Charlotte picks up the pen to sign. Last night at the cocktail party, the director of the art association praised her "Retrospective in Retrospective" just one too many times. Enough, she thought. I know it's good, not great, but very good. I'm proud of it, I've had my say. I have finally been a real artist. Now I can leave that wish behind for the third and final time. Thanks to Bella, she has a new role to fulfill as the founder of a nature sanctuary.

Not a bad ring to that, is there? Just as her grandmother is beloved in memory for her founding of the art association and her mother was beloved simply for her gentle soul, Charlotte will have a unique recognition of her own. Her establishment of the sanctuary will be written up in newspapers and conservation journals, and she'll become a role model for other rich people to emulate. As chair of the board, she'll oversee the sanctuary's development and accept the accolades for each milestone achieved. She will be invited to bigger, more important events than she is now; the governor is quite the environmentalist, she recalls. So little by little, what Bella envisaged will come to pass. Charlotte will be taken care of for the remainder of her lifetime, remembered and revered in perpetuity each time a visitor sets foot on the paths of Deerfield. Bella will eventually be forgotten by almost everyone, but she will be beloved by her god.

Now it's Jane who has decisions to make. She doesn't have to accept the position, and hefty salary, Bella has created for her.

"If you decline, it won't affect the formation of the sanctuary itself," the lawyer assures her. "We would do a national search to find an equally qualified candidate."

"Thank you." Jane doesn't reveal to the lawyer the irony of his statement. Hired precisely for her lack of qualifications, it will now require a national search to replace her. "I'll be able to give you an answer in a few days."

That afternoon, she hikes to the end of the ridge and looks south to the ocean. Over the past ten days most of the blizzard snow has melted, save for a few pockets in out-of-the-way places. The sky is a windless, pale blue, and the temperature, climbing steadily, is an unseasonably balmy fifty-one degrees. Jane sits down on the puddingstone rock, rests her chin on her knees and stares out at the horizon. She has been offered a rare opportunity. Why not embrace it? She would welcome the chance to make a contribution in a worthwhile field. She can go back to college part-time and pick up courses to earn a degree in environmental science or whatever is required to give her the stamp of credibility. She seems to have Charlotte's trust; more amazing, she earned Bella's. And despite what people in town might initially think about her hoodwinking a rich old woman, she can foresee that the key to overcoming that perception will lie in her own integrity. Moreover, she has dear friends here, Hortense and Melanie, Russ and Charlie, the ever-effervescent Raven, Jim and Lois when they return on their sailboat come spring. She has Tim Hennessey. She wants Tim Hennessey.

But there's also the job in Washington, DC. She's good at engineering, she excels at it, and maybe the fact that she once found it less than fulfilling wasn't the field itself but the lack of challenge in her particular job. Plus, her father lives there, and this firm also has wider possibilities, specializing in contract work for international agencies, foreign aid projects in developing countries. One current project is in New Guinea, and how far is that from Australia where her sister Susan lives with her businessman husband and two kids, about to be three any day? She hasn't seen Susan or her family in several years.

Jane fingers the moss on the rocks. It's still a vibrant lime green in January, and on her hike to the ridge she passed blue-green pines among the bare trees and patches of small fern-like plants on the forest floor. Not everything dies in winter, nor have all the birds disappeared. Blue jays, robins and towhees occupy the woods, a pair of mallards paddles on the pond. She remembers when she first learned how some robins winter over instead of migrating south, retreating deeper into the woods to gorge those red breasts on abundant berries until they're ready to burst out in spring. There's a joy in having witnessed it for herself. *I've seen it, I know.* It's the kind of knowledge you can fall in love with, yet if she does stay, it has to be for the right reasons. She has to be running to, not running from. She can't remain at Deerfield to forever bury a part of herself, as Charlotte and Bella did.

Do that and your safe haven will enclose you in walls of your own making. Stay long enough and the kindest sanctuary becomes a prison of the soul.

Jane lies back on the rock, fingers laced behind her head, staring at the beckoning sky. Last spring, that first sighting of a red-tailed hawk spiraling over Deerfield nearly caused her knees to buckle. When autumn came she forced herself to look upward at the hawk migration, convincing herself she could be content to marvel at their mastery of flight. Now the winter sky is empty, too empty. If it were up to her, she'd be in the air—

Then it happens, a ripping sensation as if she's being pulled out of her chest, and with a gasp, Jane's mind is above the earth as a bird would be, climbing into the silk-smooth sky. To the northeast she spots the stone towers and chimneys of Deerfield rising above the trees, and she envisions Charlotte painting in her studio, Bella at her computer or perhaps haranguing someone from the art association on the telephone. A coordinated turn to the west and she's winging over the state forest, a dense expanse of pine that marches and flattens towards the horizon in ranks of dark green. Then a touch of aileron to bank southward over the water, past the small beach and the deserted entrance booth where Elizabeth sat reading Chekhov all summer long, the rock ridges of the estate running like two knobby, pointing fingers toward the sea. Circling east, she overflies the field and glimpses her cottage, a tiny slate roof no sooner seen than gone. The shore road ribbons on northward to the harbor inlet and the waterfront of the town, but she curves back south and climbs. The altitude restriction over a designated wildlife refuge is two thousand feet minimum, and although Deerfield isn't yet an official refuge, she doesn't want the engine noise to stress the birds and animals below. From this height, there is no evidence of the trails she and the Sunday walkers have begun to wear in the woods, and she's glad of it. She banks steeply over the center of the estate, sighting down her wing to the pond. It's small from above, fringed by bare gray-brown branches, its surface a tarnished silver in the pale blue winter light. Jane pulls in tighter until she's circling the pond almost on wingtip, feeling its silent heartbeat. Then she releases the turn, descends, throttle out, flare, land.

Slowly, Jane sits up on the ridge. Walking, not running, she rises and follows the trail back through the woods, across the footbridge, along the bank of the pond. Through the trees to the field, then to her cottage and her truck. She sets off for the highway. You can't make a choice until you know for sure what all your choices are.

On the fence at the entrance road to the airport is that same rectangular metal sign, a silhouette of a white plane on a green background and the message LEARN TO FLY HERE! Jane parks beside the office and alights from her truck. It's growing late on New Year's Day, so she's a little unprepared to see someone inside. She pushes open the door, and a lanky, elderly man in an ancient leather flight jacket looks up from the desk in front of the plate glass windows that look onto the field. As Jane approaches, she sees a newspaper folded open to a half-filled crossword puzzle and a pencil with a worn-down eraser in the man's hand.

"Hello," she says, and words come out that she hasn't spoken freely in a long time. "I'm Jane Avery. I'm a pilot."

"Yeah?" says the old guy, not skeptically, because there are enough women fliers nowadays that it's no surprise to have one walk in. Rather, it's interest in his voice, recognition of a kindred spirit with whom he can spin a yarn. "What do you fly?"

"Well, that's just it. I'm not current, but I'd like to get back in the air."

"Oh, you should talk to Joe Reynolds. He owns that 172 there, rents it out for flight instruction. I help him with stuff here at the airport."

He points out the window to the blue-and-white Cessna, and Jane nods at the plane and the name, the same the mechanic gave her when she paid that disastrous visit almost nine months ago. She knows who the old guy is, too, because there's one of him at every little airport across the country. He used to fly, he might be a military veteran or maybe he fell in love with airplanes when he was a kid, and he hung out at the local field until somebody gave him a ride. Then he hitched another and another, until he picked up enough skills that he only needed a few actual lessons to earn his ticket. Now he's grounded, bad vision or a weak heart, but he can't stay away from the airport, he still loves to watch those planes take off and land, and he's always ready to hop in when there's an empty seat to fill. He's probably here today to escape a nagging missus, and his nickname is Buzz or Ace or Slim.

"Well, I just stopped by," says Jane. "Would it be okay to walk out on the field and take a look at the planes?"

"I guess." His forehead furrows a trifle. He takes his unofficial airport duties seriously. "You know, I hate to sound unfriendly, but just for security's sake, maybe you could show me your ticket?"

"Sure." She opens her wallet. Her pilot's license has been there all the time. "I'll have a quick walk around, and you can hold it till I come back," she says, taking it out and handing it to him.

"Okay, I won't look at your weight," he jokes.

Jane opens the door. Her hand doesn't shake, her legs don't freeze. The plane is a hundred feet away across the asphalt, and as her feet move toward it, her breath comes normally. It might be any of a thousand other days she's walked across a ramp to a plane and hopped inside. Later, maybe, she will retrace the long sequence of events and revelations and epiphanies that have finally broken the lock the accident put on her more than a year ago. Maybe she'll figure out why she had to walk so many miles over the trails at Deerfield just to traverse these last thirty feet toward a plane. The westering sunlight is glinting off the Cessna's windshield, and Jane's heart starts to beat a little faster than usual, but that's all right. That's the way it's supposed to feel when you're about to fly.

She covers the last steps and lays her hand on the wing.

Epilogue

Think of them as birds.

Zippy little experimental planes, feather light and fearless, are the high-energy kinglets. They live in almost constant movement, flitting about in the branches of trees, the sprites of the avian world.

Heavy twin turboprops muscle into the airspace around local airports, like self-important blue jays and noisy crows that force smaller birds to scatter.

The Harrier jet is named for the bird itself, a slim, low-flying hawk that glides and tilts buoyantly over the ground. It zeroes in on voles and vulnerable young cotton-tails, then drops on its prey, talons closing.

On an aircraft carrier rests a mixed flock of A-6s, F-14s, F-16s and more. Perched like seabirds on a gray rock offshore, waves lapping at the sheer cliff of iron hull, they fly reconnaissance missions and return to land on a perilously short runway in a stormy ocean.

Cargo planes, fully laden, are the lowly pigeons, reliable and plump.

Finally, watch the aerial acrobats, the air show and competition planes custom designed and built for the most daring, gravity-defying flights. Like hawks, they punctuate the blue, sweep in circles, loop, tumble, pivot on a wingtip. They play with the sunlight and float on the wind. They drop in a deadly spiral for the outrageous thrill of it, the earth spinning ever closer, running out of sky. Then at the last instant, they break free and level off in a heady rush.

Throttle out, flare, welcome back.

Author Bio

Photo by Dane Sponberg

Arliss Ryan is the author of three previous novels, *The Secret Confessions of Anne Shakespeare, How (Not) to Have a Perfect Wedding*, and *The Kingsley House*. She lives in St. Augustine, Florida, where she works as a writer and professional storyteller and leads bird walks at the state parks. She and her husband have two children. Visit her website at www.arlissryan.com

www.ingramcontent.com/pod-product-compliance
Lightning Source LLC
Chambersburg PA
CBHW050905250626
47155CB00001B/114